T0129213

A HEATED KISS

Aidan lifted her in the air and spun her around. "You did it."

Dana grabbed onto Aidan's shoulders, afraid he'd drop her, and quickly scanned the room for Carol, who seemed to have disappeared.

"I've got you, you know?" He continued to hold her as if she weighed nothing.

"Aidan, stop. I'm getting dizzy."

"Kiss me first."

"What? . . . Why?"

"Because I want you to." He'd stopped the spinning and slowly put her down on the ground, tipping her head back so he could go in for the kiss.

It started out slow at first, just his lips brushing her lips, soft and supple. When she twined her arms around his neck, he went in for more, melding his mouth to hers, working his way between her lips with his tongue. He tasted so good, like warm, sweet breath and yearning.

Cradling the back of her head in his hands, he hummed his pleasure as he took the kiss deeper . . .

Books by Stacy Finz

GOING HOME

FINDING HOPE

SECOND CHANCES

STARTING OVER

GETTING LUCKY

BORROWING TROUBLE

HEATING UP

Published by Kensington Publishing Corporation

Heating Up

Stacy Finz

LYRICAL SHINE
Kensington Publishing Corp.
www.kensingtonbooks.com

LYRICAL SHINE BOOKS are published by

Kensington Publishing Corp.
119 West 40th Street
New York, NY 10018

All Kensington titles, imprints, and distributed lines are available at special quantity discounts for bulk purchases for sales promotion, premiums, fund-raising, educational, or institutional use.

Special book excerpts or customized printings can also be created to fit specific needs. For details, write or phone the office of the Kensington Sales Manager: Kensington Publishing Corp., 119 West 40th Street, New York, NY 10018. Attn. Sales Department. Phone: 1-800-221-2647.

Lyrical Shine and Lyrical Press logo Reg. U.S. Pat. & TM Off.

First Electronic Edition: July 2016
eISBN-13: 978-1-60183-707-3
eISBN-10: 1-60183-707-0

First Print Edition: July 2016
ISBN-13: 978-1-60183-708-0
ISBN-10: 1-60183-708-9

Printed in the United States of America

ACKNOWLEDGMENTS

A special thanks to fire and arson experts Mark Johnson and John Darmanin for answering all my questions and for sharing their extensive knowledge of all things fire. Any mistakes, technical or otherwise, are mine.

Thanks to Miriam Morgan for being a beta reader. There's nothing like having professional editor pals.

As always thanks to my husband, Jaxon Van Derbeken.

And to everyone who made this book happen: my agent, Melissa Jeglinski of the Knight Agency; editor John Scognamiglio; production editor Rebecca Cremonese; director of social media and digital sales Alexandra Nicolajsen; and all the other folks at Kensington Publishing who worked tirelessly on the entire series. Thank you.

Chapter 1

The flames continued to lick at the structure as one of Aidan's fellow firefighters climbed onto the scorched top of the low-slung rancher to cut a hole in the roof for ventilation.

"It's spongy," the firefighter shouted over the roar of the fire.

"Then get down," the captain yelled.

He made it to the ladder just as the roof caved in.

Structurally, the entire home was toast—by tomorrow a heap of kindling. The best any of them could hope for was containing the blaze before it spread to the two neighboring houses. Unlike downtown Chicago, there was plenty of space here between homes, providing a good defensive zone. But it was drier than dust. Front yards consisted of nothing but brown patches of grass that had somehow survived the dry summer and strict watering rules.

If they worked methodically, though, he figured they could have this mother knocked down in another hour and could start a thorough overhaul. Already, a few guys had gone in with axes and hooks. Eventually, they'd rip out the ceiling, Sheetrock, windowsills, and door frames, checking for hot spots.

Aidan hadn't even officially started at Cal Fire when he'd gotten called out on the boomer. That's what they called a good working structure fire. He'd just completed his six-week training at the California Department of Forestry and Fire Protection's academy in Ione, a Gold Country town only slightly larger than his new home, Nugget. Although a seasoned firefighter and arson investigator back in Chicago, he didn't have experience fighting forest and wildland fires.

That was all about to change.

With California in its fourth year of record drought, wildfires burned at breakneck speed across the state. And Cal Fire was responsible for protecting thirty-six of California's fifty-eight counties, meaning millions and millions of acres.

Aidan gazed out over the scene. The owner of the house stood in her bare feet and a thin nightgown on the sidewalk, away from the crowd, helplessly watching as firefighters desecrated what was left of her home. Aidan grabbed a blanket from one of the engines and approached her. A paramedic had already checked her over for injuries. She'd apparently been awakened by the smoke alarm, had tried to open her bedroom door only to find it too hot to the touch and succeeded in crawling out the window.

"Here you go, ma'am." Aidan handed her the blanket.

She stared at the gray woolen department-issued throw, clearly wondering what to do with it. Even past midnight it was at least seventy degrees in Nugget and, with the heat from the fire, closer to a hundred near the flames. Aidan didn't want to point out that her nightgown was see-through. So much so that he could make out the smiley faces on her bikini underwear in the glow of the klieg lights.

"You might want to cover up," he said.

She immediately glanced down at herself and grimaced. "Oh God."

He helped wrap the blanket around her and said, "No worries," which, given her plight, was a pretty stupid thing to say. She'd just lost everything she owned. Everything but the car. It had been parked on the street instead of in her garage, which now resembled a stick pile.

"When will I be able to go back in?" She stared up at Aidan with golden eyes, and for a second he couldn't stop staring back.

It was the eyes, he supposed. They were unusual, like precious stones. Amber or tiger-eye, he couldn't remember the name. Anyway, they went nice with her brown hair. Truth be told, he liked the underwear too. A lot.

"Not tonight, that's for sure." They'd have to check what was left of the structure to guarantee its safety. "You have any idea what started the fire?"

Early on he'd smelled something like paint thinner or varnish. Arson investigators had extraordinary noses.

"I think I may have left a candle burning." She looked down at the ground, her face turning red, plainly mortified.

"In which room?" As soon as he got inside he'd likely be able to tell for sure.

"The dining room. I was trying to get the smell out."

"What smell?"

"From the stain. I was refinishing my table . . . I can't believe I did this."

At this point he had no reason to suspect her of anything nefarious. "You have a place to stay?"

"Dana!" A woman pushed her way through the gawking neighbors. "Are you all right? Cecilia called me. She heard about the fire from Jake. They're on their way over."

"I'm okay." She gazed over at the wreckage and her eyes welled up.

A Nugget police vehicle drove to the end of the cul-de-sac, parked, and Jake and Cecilia jumped out. Aidan knew them and a handful of other people through his sister, Sloane.

Jake joined Aidan at the curb while Cecilia fussed over the woman . . . Dana. "You know what caused it?"

"She thinks she left a candle burning." Aidan suspected the stain or paint she'd been using had probably been in close proximity to the candle. "I'll know better in a few hours."

Aidan glanced at Dana. It looked like Cecilia had brought her a pair of tennis shoes. "She have relatives or friends she can stay with?"

"Her family lives in Reno, but in this town they'll be no shortage of people who will take her in," Jake said. "We live just a block over and have a couple of spare bedrooms if she wants to stay in the neighborhood. My guess is the insurance guys will show up first thing in the morning."

"Yup. She should make sure she knows the extent of the damage and construction costs before she accepts a check." Aidan didn't want to see her get ripped off, and it had been known to happen. At least in Chicago.

"She's a real estate agent so I don't think that'll be a problem."

The captain waved him over and Aidan excused himself.

"Talk about your trial by fire, huh?" Captain Gregg Johnson reminded Aidan a little of his father. Barrel-chested, ruddy-faced and, according to word on the street, a leader who inspired unwavering loyalty. "Sorry to have pulled you in like this, but we're short staffed."

"Not a problem." Aidan was anxious to jump in, especially because he'd be wearing two hats: working for Johnson as a firefighter and reporting to the state fire marshal, who oversaw the agency's arson investigations. "She says she was staining some furniture and left one of those scented candles burning to deodorize the room."

"Yeah, seems consistent with the odor. Dana's no firebug."

That's what Aidan liked about this town. Everyone knew one another. "I'll go in and take a look around. Anything in there salvageable?"

"Not likely," Johnson said. "Can you come in tomorrow?"

"Yeah. I just have to sign the rental agreement on my new house. But it's only a couple of blocks from the firehouse."

"Tawny Wade's old place?"

Aidan laughed. Small towns were funny. "That would be the one. I don't think Sloane wants me to get too comfortable in her guest room."

"Nah, she and Brady love having you. The girl's been walking on sunshine ever since she knew you were taking the job. Us too."

It was nice to be wanted, Aidan thought as he made his way through the shambles of Dana's house. The guys had gone a little crazy with their axes. But with the property line being so close to the state forest, he knew they couldn't mess around. Those pines would ignite like dry kindling. He made his way to what was left of the dining room using a flashlight. The cracking patterns on the windows corroborated that the fire had started here. He could see remnants of burned rags. Dana had probably used them for her staining project.

"You the probie?"

Aidan looked up from a deeply charred table to see a guy in his turn outs, holding an ax, smiling. "That's me."

"Welcome. I'm Kurtis. Glad to have you on board."

"Thanks, Kurtis. Glad to be here."

Kurtis swept his flashlight around the wreckage. "Poor Dana."

"You know her?" Of course he did.

"She sold me and my wife our place in Graeagle. Nice lady and a straight shooter."

"Looks like she'll have to rebuild."

"Yep," Kurtis said and shook his head. "It's a shame."

At least she'd made it out. Plenty of times folks slept right through the fire and never woke up.

"Catch you later, probie." Kurtis continued through the house, looking for hot spots.

Aidan finished up in the dining room, satisfied with Dana's story. From what he could tell, one of the rags had caught fire from the candle. Add in the varnish and poof! Too bad. If the neighbor's places were anything to go by, it looked like it had been a nice house. Nothing fancy, not like his sister and Brady's palace, but comfortable. By the time he got outside, the crowd had dispersed. From the dark houses that dotted the tree-lined street, he figured they'd gone back to bed. Dana and her car were gone and Aidan wondered if she'd gone home with Jake and Cecilia.

"You done in there?" Captain Johnson asked.

"Yep. Unless you want me to help out with the overhaul."

"We're good. See anything suspicious?" Johnson tried to hide a grin.

"Looks like it went down the way she said it did. Where'd she go?"

"Maddy Shepard insisted she stay at the Lumber Baron tonight. Carol wanted Dana to stay at her place, but she's allergic to her cats."

"Who's Carol?" Aidan assumed that Maddy was married to Rhys Shepard, the police chief and Sloane's boss.

"She's Dana's real estate partner. The inn will be good—she'll be treated to some of that five-star service. Tomorrow"—he turned to the burned-out remnants of her house—"she'll have to deal with this."

Aidan got a ride back to the station with the captain and drove his own Expedition to Sloane and Brady's. They lived in Sierra Heights, Nugget's only planned community. He parked his truck in their driveway and punched in the key code at the front door. The place still blew him away. The McBride kids had grown up in a better-than-nice home in a safe suburb of Chicago, but this house was like something you'd see in *Architectural Digest*. A nearly four-thousand-square-foot log house with views that went on forever.

He went into the kitchen to see if there were any leftovers from dinner. Brady had grilled wild salmon that melted in Aidan's mouth and he was still thinking about those rosemary potatoes.

"You're eating at this hour?"

Aidan pulled his head out of the industrial-sized refrigerator. "Yeah, I'm starved."

"I don't know where you put it all." Sloane rubbed her eyes, tightened the belt around her robe, and grabbed a plate for him.

"Sorry I woke you up." Aidan had tried to be quiet.

"I was waiting up. Is it as bad as everyone says it is?"

"You mean the house?" He nodded. "It's a total loss."

"Ah, jeez. Poor Dana."

"You know her?"

"Just in passing, but still. All her stuff too?"

"Gone." He loaded the plate and heated it in the microwave.

"How did it happen?"

"She left a candle burning next to a couple of rags covered in furniture varnish."

"Seriously?" Sloane went slack-jawed.

When the microwave dinged she pulled out Aidan's plate and looked at it askance. "In a few hours it'll be time for breakfast."

"Can't wait." He chuckled, and she shook her head. "Hey, it's not my fault your boyfriend is a four-star chef. A guy can get spoiled living here."

"I can't figure out why you're not big as a house."

"Good metabolism." He shoveled a forkful of salmon into his mouth. "I probably won't have time for breakfast anyway. I've got to be out of here pretty early to sign the rental agreement for the house, then the captain wants me to come in."

"Wow. They're not giving you a lot of time to get settled."

"What's to settle? My furniture comes at the end of the week. I'll move it into the new house and get the cable connected. Done!"

"You like the house?" she asked.

"It's fine. More important, it's available, affordable, and a block away from the firehouse."

"You're lucky it's available. From what I hear, Tawny and Lucky's new house isn't even completely finished yet, but with the cowboy camp in full swing, Lucky needs to be on the property."

"Tell me the deal with these people again . . . the guy is a champion bull rider?"

"Mm-hmm. They own a big dude ranch on the other side of town where corporate types pay big bucks to pretend they're cowboys for a week. The rest of the time Lucky teams up with the Lumber Baron to hold destination weddings and events. Brady oversees the catering."

"And Tawny makes boots?"

"Beautiful boots. You see them in the garage when Tawny showed you the place?"

"Yeah. But I was too busy looking at the house to really check them out. Thanks for hooking me up with her, little sister. Although I've gotta say, I'm gonna miss Windsor Castle, here."

"You know you're welcome to stay as long as you like, even if you are eating us out of house and home."

The house was still new for Sloane and Brady, who'd just started living together. Aidan suspected the lovebirds wanted their alone time. Who wouldn't?

"Sue call?" he asked, trying to sound nonchalant.

"No. Wouldn't she call your cell?"

Yeah, that was the thing; she hadn't. It had been nearly seven weeks and not a peep.

"Aid, isn't that partly why you moved here? Because you knew it was over?"

"We just have stuff to settle, that's all." He felt responsible for her and wanted to make sure she was okay.

"Like what?" Sloane asked.

He slid his plate down the granite top of the center island. "You want some of this?"

"I'm going back to bed." She started to head out of the kitchen and stopped. "Did Dana have a place to stay?"

"The cap said she went to the Lumber Baron."

"Really?" His sister frowned.

"What? The place is plush."

"It's gorgeous. But she should be with people, not alone."

"Jake and Cecilia offered to take her home . . . her partner too. Apparently, the woman has cats and Dana's allergic to them. Maybe she wanted to grieve in private. Nothing wrong with that."

"Maybe," she said. " 'Night, Aid."

" 'Night, Sloane."

"Oh." She stopped in her tracks, "I forgot to tell you. Brady and I are getting married."

He pulled back in surprise. "When did this happen? Shit, am I interrupting your big proposal night?"

"Nah. I kind of feel like we're past that. Our big romantic thing was when he shocked me by buying this house . . . roses, champagne; it was awesome. We're just legalizing it is all."

"No wedding?"

"Hell yeah! Big party. We just have to figure out where and when. But don't worry, you're invited."

"Gee, thanks. Mom and Dad will be happy. They were starting to think of you as a tramp."

"That's because I am." She slid her arm up one of the pine pillars and feigned a little pole dance that made him want to wash his eyes out with bleach. "See you in a few hours."

Aidan put away the fish and potatoes and rinsed and loaded his plate into the dishwasher. Sniffing himself, he decided to jump into the shower. He stunk like smoke and char and sweat. Thank goodness Sloane had grown up with those smells or she would've kicked him out of her pristine kitchen.

She'd been the only one of his three siblings who'd failed to follow in their father's firefighting footsteps. Hell, their legacy in CFD went all the way back to both their maternal and paternal grandfathers. But his rebel sister had to become a cop.

After his shower, he checked his phone; an exercise in futility, but he couldn't help himself. It was four in the morning and he needed to get at least a couple of hours of sleep. Sloane had turned down the blanket on his bed; all that was missing was a little chocolate. Wow, she was getting married. The first of the McBride kids to take the plunge. Arron, the second oldest after Aidan, was always off-and-on with his girlfriend, and Shane, the youngest of the boys, was a manwhore. It had been Aidan who everyone had expected to settle down, not the baby of the family.

Good for Sloane, he thought as he slipped off to sleep. She'd snagged herself a good man. And they would take good care of each other.

Too soon, sunlight filtered into his room. "Christ, morning already?" he muttered to himself, covering his eyes with his arm.

"Aidan." Brady knocked on the door. "Sloane said you need to get out early. You want an omelet?"

He probably should make his own breakfast, or grab something in town, and not take advantage, but Brady seemed to like cooking for company and his food was out of this world. "If it's no trouble."

"No trouble at all."

"Okay, I'll be right out."

He took another quick shower just to wake up and dressed. By the time he made it to the kitchen, Brady had all kinds of things popping on that mammoth range of his. He poured himself a cup of coffee and took a seat at the island.

"You working today?" He watched as Brady fried up a pan of bacon.

"Yep. I've gotta streamline some things at Gold Mountain." He referred to the nearby resort that was part of the hotel group where Brady was executive chef. "At the end of the week I have to go to headquarters in San Francisco. Sloane's planning to take a few comp days and come with me."

"You miss cooking at the Lumber Baron?"

"I'm still in charge of the kitchen there," Brady said. "Occasionally, I'll fill in, test a few recipes. And of course orchestrate the food for the gigs we have with Lucky's cowboy camp."

"Hey, I hear congratulations are in order."

Brady grinned. "We're getting the ring in San Francisco. You wanna be best man?"

"Seriously?" Aidan reeled, a little stunned. It wasn't like Brady knew him that well, but Aidan supposed it was to make Sloane happy. Which put another check in Brady's box. "Of course. I'd be honored."

Brady grinned again and served Aidan an omelet big enough to feed two people. "Dig in before it gets cold. Sloane said Dana's house is a goner."

"Afraid so." Aidan glanced at the clock. He had to get a move on. Luckily, he ate fast.

"That's too bad. I think she's on her own here."

Aidan got that impression too, although she seemed to have people who cared about her. "I hope she has a good, honest contractor."

"To rebuild or for insurance purposes?"

"For both, depending on what she wants to do."

"I'm betting she wants to rebuild. An empty residential lot in Nugget isn't worth a whole lot, not like if it had a house on it."

Aidan shoved a few more bites into his mouth before taking his plate to the sink. "I'm supposed to be at Nugget Realty and Associates in fifteen minutes. You know where it is?"

"Main Street. Across from the Nugget Market. You better head out; it'll take fifteen minutes to get there."

It actually took twelve. This wasn't Chicago during rush hour. He locked up his truck—which he probably didn't need to do, but old habits died hard—and was halfway to the door when his cell phone vibrated in his pocket. He checked the screen and then the time. Apparently, Sue wanted to have their heart-to-heart two minutes before his appointment.

He'd waited seven weeks, she could wait an hour.

Chapter 2

The jeans were a little snugger than Dana was used to. She hoped that with a couple of hours of wear they'd stretch. But the yellow sleeveless blouse fit beautifully and was perfect for the heat.

At eight in the morning, the front desk had called, saying there were packages for her in the lobby and someone would bring them up. She'd opened the door to find a pile of shopping bags filled with clothes, shoes, boots, underwear, even a few silky scarves. Brand new, all from Nugget Farm Supply.

She barely knew the owners, Grace and Earl Miller, and had only been in the feedstore a handful of times. Yet, Grace—she presumed it was Grace—knew all her sizes. And her taste. Because the things she'd sent were adorable. After spreading out everything on the bed, she'd sat on the floor and cried. No one had ever been this thoughtful. No one. And she couldn't imagine how she would ever return their kindness.

Dana searched through the drawer of the writing desk, found a stash of hotel stationery, and made a list. When she got into the office, the first thing she intended to do was send the Millers a thank-you note. Then she planned to call Tawny Wade and rent her old house. Tawny had just listed the lease with Dana and Carol. They hadn't even put an ad in the *Nugget Tribune* yet.

The house was only two miles from Dana's old home, so she could easily keep tabs on the new construction. Plus, it was conveniently located near her office. Unlike most of the other rentals here—seasonal cabins tucked away in the surrounding Sierra mountains—it was winterized. And best of all: affordable. Dana had no idea how much her insurance would pay for rent. Although she had savings, as a real estate agent she worked on commission and never knew when her next sale would come. Right now the market was good, but it fluctuated like the New York Stock Exchange.

Griffin, bless his heart, had offered her any of the vacant homes in Sierra Heights. He'd heard about the fire, which by now had to be front-page news, and had tracked her down at the Lumber Baron. But living there and seeing him with Lina every day would be a special kind of torture. Plus, she couldn't afford one of those houses and wouldn't take charity, especially from a man she still had feelings for. She'd rather sell the vacant homes and make fat commissions than live in one of them.

She took one last look at herself in the full-length mirror, locked up the room, found her car in the small lot, and drove the four short blocks to Nugget Realty and Associates, thinking about all she had lost in the fire. Her grandmother's needlepoint that hung over the fireplace, the leather jacket she'd splurged on just last month for her thirtieth birthday, Aunt Roe's Franciscan Ware, and the old Calloway candy tins she'd collected from her family's factory. All gone. The pictures of Paul, too. At least those she could scan from her parents' albums. Like everything else of Paul's, they'd kept them in museum condition.

There was a Ford Expedition parked in the lot when Dana got there. For a minute she worried that she was late for an appointment. Without her phone—another casualty of the fire—she'd have to check the calendar on her work computer for her daily schedule. But she was pretty sure she didn't have anything today. Dana hoped Pat Donnelly and Colin Burke would be able to meet her later at the house and tell her what she was looking at money wise to rebuild. Before the insurance folks tried to lowball her.

She checked her face in the rearview mirror. Maddy had made sure there was a basket of necessities in her room, including mascara and lip gloss. The woman was a true angel. It was funny; Dana had always kept to herself in this town, not because she was a bitch or anything, but she was shy. Perhaps reserved was a better word for it. It was easy on the job; she just slipped into her agent persona, hiding behind the façade of an outgoing salesperson. Yet, when her house burned down, the townsfolk had rallied, treating her like she was deeply woven into their tight-knit community.

A blast of heat hit her the minute she stepped out of the car. Only June and the temperature already had climbed into the nineties, a sign that it would be a hot summer. And dry as cotton mouth if the drought persisted. As soon as she entered the office her skin prickled from the sudden change in climate. Carol had the AC cranked up cool enough to need a sweater.

"I didn't expect you in so early . . . or at all," Carol said, and Dana noticed a man sitting at her partner's desk. Must be the owner of the Expedition. "Don't you want to take the day to get situated?"

"That's partly why I'm here." She let out a sigh, remembered they had a client, and flashed her most professional smile at the man.

"This is Aidan McBride, Sloane's brother, the new firefighter," Carol said, and Aidan stood up.

"I was the guy with the blanket, remember?"

Now that she was paying attention, she felt her face flush. "I'm sorry. You look completely different without all that gear." Like Clive Owen in the *King Arthur* movie. He was . . . like . . . Just wow! After Dana got her tongue to work again she said, "Shopping for a home?"

"Just got one," he said.

"He signed the lease on Tawny's property." Carol beamed, ecstatic.

Dana silently cursed. They hadn't even listed the damn place yet. "Oh . . . wow . . . that's terrific." She tried to sound enthusiastic, but she was pretty sure her face had fallen to the floor.

Carol, not one to miss cues, saw her mistake instantly. "Tawny showed it to him and they worked out a deal. Oh boy, I screwed up, didn't I? The fire . . . you need a house." Carol looked at Aidan, obviously hoping he'd tear up the contract.

"It's fine," Dana quickly interjected. What kind of reputation would they get if they reneged on their clients' deals for personal gain? Finders keepers . . . "I have lots of options." *Liar, liar.*

"You sure?" Aidan asked.

"Of course. I'm a real estate agent, Mr. McBride."

"Okay." He appeared hesitant. "There doesn't seem to be too much for rent around here, though."

"I assure you, I have two other places I'm considering." Maybe she could live in one of Lucky Rodriguez's barns. "The house is perfect for you . . . right down the street from the firehouse."

"If you're positive, then yeah, it's perfect for me. My stuff's coming at the end of the week and I thought I'd start moving in today."

"Great," she said, and plastered on another fake smile. "Now, if you'll excuse me, I have a few phone calls to make." She needed to get Pat Donnelly and Colin Burke to rebuild her house . . . today, before she was homeless or spending her entire life's savings on a room at the Lumber Baron.

As she headed to her desk she heard Carol give Aidan the keys to the house and the packet they gave newcomers with numbers for local utilities, cable, and such. She pulled up her own contact list on the computer, focused on her to-do list, and wrote out a thank-you to the Millers. Later, she'd bring them flowers or some other token of her appreciation. Unfortunately, Nugget didn't have a florist or she'd have an arrangement delivered. She had so much to do she didn't know where to start and wanted to leave herself time to drive by her house to see if there was anything that could be saved.

She looked up to see Carol walking Aidan to the door. He sure was tall—had a good two to three inches on Griffin. And muscular, like he spent a lot time in the firehouse working out. Although he seemed nice enough, Dana suspected he thought pretty highly of himself. Guys who looked like him usually did.

"I am so, so sorry," Carol said as Aidan drove out of the parking lot. "It didn't even occur to me that you'd be interested in Tawny's place. Oh, Dana, we need to find you a house."

"I was thinking that maybe one of the units in the police chief's duplex might be available." It was up on Donner Road, a short drive to town. It had belonged to the chief's late father and his son now used it as rental property.

Carol shook her head. "Both units are taken. What about Griff? Perhaps he'd let you rent one of his houses until you figure out what you want to do. There's a chance your house isn't as bad as it looked last night and could be rehabbed in a few weeks."

That was Dana's greatest hope. "The market is red hot now. I'd hate to occupy one of those houses when we could be selling it." She and Carol had the listing on the entire planned community: fifty-five houses total, with an average asking price of eight hundred thousand dollars. Nothing to sneeze at commission wise.

Carol fixed her with a look, knowing how Dana felt about Griffin. "You're being ridiculous. This is an emergency."

"I'll figure out something, and if I don't, I'll cave and take one of Griffin's. Okay?"

"You know you're welcome to stay with us." Carol said. "You could get allergy shots for the cats."

Carol lived with her husband and three teenagers in a lovely Victorian on the other side of town. Between the kids' activities, Vance's home business—he ran a landscaping and snowplow service—and their menagerie of pets, their lives were chaotic enough without an extra person underfoot.

"Thanks, Carol. Let's see what Pat Donnelly says I'm looking at here."

Two hours later, she jetted over to her house to meet with the contractor and Colin Burke, a carpenter who worked with Pat and owned a furniture-making business. She'd already called the Lumber Baron and reserved her room for the rest of the week. Maddy had immediately called her back to say it was on the house, but Dana wouldn't hear of it. Summer was prime season for the inn. Reminded of how kind everyone was being, she pledged to be more outgoing in the future. She'd lived in Nugget for more than a year, and except for Carol and Griffin, she hardly knew anyone. Her fault, not the town's residents.

Harlee, Colin's wife and owner of the *Nugget Tribune*, and Darla, who ran the barbershop with her father, Owen, had repeatedly reached out to her to join their monthly bowling parties at the Ponderosa. She'd always made an excuse for why she couldn't go.

As she swung into her driveway, a couple of firefighters waved. She supposed they were back to make sure what was left of the structure was safe and sound to go inside. Seeing the house in daylight, the damage looked even worse than last night. The remainder of the wooden siding was charred so black it resembled pictures Dana had seen of war zones. There was an empty hull where the garage once stood—nothing but a concrete pad and splintered piles of wood. Her beautiful bay window had been taken down to the studs. And the roof: completely gone.

Dana took a deep breath, focused really hard on not crying, and got out of the car just as Pat and Colin pulled up. Time to face the music, which she presumed would be to the tune of a complete rebuild. At least she trusted Pat, who she'd recommended to a number of clients who'd bought acreage and wanted to build. In return, Pat had given her listings on a couple of his spec homes in the area, which she'd sold for a tidy profit. His reputation and workmanship were stellar. And everyone vouched for Colin Burke, whose carpentry was artistry.

Pat, a fatherly gray-haired man with a paunch, gave her a weak smile, gazed out over the burned-out shell of her house, and grimaced. "I didn't realize it was this bad."

Dana nodded, and for the second time tried to hold back tears. There was no time for crying. Colin walked up to where the front door used to be and was stopped by one of the firefighters from going any farther.

"You got a hard hat?"

Colin went back to Pat's truck and grabbed two from the bed, tossing one to the contractor before turning to Dana. "We don't have another one." Then he eyed her yellow blouse. "Pat has some coveralls back there. After we do a walk-through, you can suit up, use one of the hats, and one of us will take you through."

"Thanks, Colin. Take your time."

Captain Johnson waved her over. "The house is stable enough for your workers to go inside. But for safety purposes we'll need you to put up a fence, or at the very least post 'keep-out' signs until Pat either tears down the remaining structure or secures it." He gave her a gentle pat. "I'm sorry, Dana, but I'm afraid there's not much in there that's worth recovering."

She nodded because she couldn't speak; her throat was too constricted. Sitting on Pat's tailgate, she waited for them to finish going through the rubble. Sometime today she'd need to run to Reno, get a new cell phone, and check in with her parents. Then she'd have to figure out what to do about a permanent living situation.

She felt eyes on her and looked up to see Aidan McBride.

"Those your contractors?"

"Mm-hmm."

He sat next to her. "You gonna rebuild?"

"What choice do I have?"

"Sell, buy something else."

She let out a breath. "There's not much available in Nugget proper. Lots of ranches, farms, and land for sale on the outskirts, and there's Sierra Heights. But I was lucky to find a home in this neighborhood that I could afford. There are a few things for sale in your new neighborhood, but this part of town is a better investment."

Quite frankly, his side of town was shabby, a neighborhood developed in the 1920s for the town's heavy influx of railroad workers. And while vintage homes were extremely marketable, the bulk of them were small, rundown, and too close to the railroad tracks. As a result, she'd always had trouble selling over there.

Nugget, forty-five minutes from Reno and four hours from San Francisco, had always been a blue collar town, made up mostly of train employees, ranchers, and farmers. Her neighborhood, though, felt middle class. The yards were landscaped and the homes—mostly ranch style, built in the 1970s and '80s—freshly painted. *Pride of ownership* is what they called it in real estate lingo.

"Look," he said, "I know there isn't a lot around here for rent, and while your professionalism was commendable this morning, I could see in your eyes how disappointed you were to lose Tawny's place. It just so happened that timing wise it worked out perfectly for me. Otherwise, I'd be camping at my sister's place, which I could still do until I find something else. Or"—he hesitated—"you and I could share the house until yours is rebuilt. It's a two bedroom, and between my twenty-four-hour shifts at the firehouse and being called out on arson cases, I'll hardly be there. I'm still trying to sell a condo in Chicago, so it would help me with the rent. I've got enough furniture to fill the place. All you would need is a bed."

It was an extremely generous offer, Dana thought. And it would save her from having to live next door to Griffin and Lina. But she didn't know the man from Adam. He could be a serial killer. Unlikely, given that his sister was a cop with the Nugget Police Department, but you never knew.

"Think about it," he said, and tore a piece of paper off his clipboard, jotting down a telephone number. "You can reach me there. I'll be over at the house during the next couple of days getting it ready to move in."

"Tawny hired professional cleaners," Dana blurted, because she and Carol would never rent out a dirty house.

"The place is spotless," he assured her. "I got a new flat-screen in Reno and want to install the surround sound. I've also got a washer and dryer coming. No sense moving my old ones cross-country."

She supposed that was true. "I'll let you know by the end of the week. And thank you, Mr. McBride, the offer . . . it's above and beyond generous."

"Hey, if we're gonna be roomies, just call me Aidan." He got to his feet.

"Okay . . . Aidan." She watched him walk away, unable to help herself from staring at his butt. She wasn't usually that pervy, but a butt that good shouldn't go to waste.

About thirty minutes later, Pat returned. "You want the good news first or the bad?"

"The bad." Dana was definitely a bad-news-first kind of person.

"We're gonna have to do all new construction from the ground up."

She'd already figured that out. "What's the good news?"

"You can rebuild it the way you want it. Maybe add a second story with a big master suite. Expand the kitchen."

The house had been three small bedrooms and only one bathroom, which had been more than enough room for her. But having an en-suite bath and a contemporary kitchen would bring up the resale value of the house. Perhaps a big walk-in closet too.

"Won't that cost more money?"

"Not necessarily. Let's see what you get insurance wise and we'll work around it."

"Really?" Dana's mood picked up at the idea. This might just be a way to make lemonade out of lemons, and lordy, she'd been delivered a whole lot of sour. Her fault of course. How stupid of her to have left a candle burning? "How soon can you get started?"

"We could do the demo right away. But you'll need architectural plans approved by the city before we can start building. And we're still finishing Lucky and Tawny's house on the ranch. So it could be a while."

Not what Dana wanted to hear. "Once you get started, how long will it take?"

"That would depend on the plans, but, Dana, realistically, you won't be back in this house for a year."

That might as well be a lifetime, she thought. No way could she occupy one of Griff's houses for an entire year. And one of the seasonal cabins up in the hills was out of the question. She'd freeze to death in the winter. When she got back to the office she'd scan the *Trib* for rentals. Not everyone used a real estate agent, and maybe she'd find a hidden gem she didn't know about. A girl could dream.

"You'll guarantee me that my house will be your next project?" she asked Pat.

"Absolutely. And we'll try to get you in as quickly as possible."

"What do I do in the meantime?"

"You get those plans done. I'll get them through the city planning board, but we'll need blueprints pronto." He took off his hard hat and grabbed coveralls from his truck toolbox. "Put these on. Colin is waiting for you with a few ideas. He's got a good eye—as good as any architect."

By the time Dana got back to the office, her head swam with possibilities. Colin's vision for the rebuild included a great room off the kitchen, as well as a small office and powder room on the main floor. Upstairs, he had three bedrooms—one of them a huge master suite. The plan would use the same footprint as the old house but double the square footage by adding a second story. She really didn't need all that space, but if she could pull it off financially, the house would be worth a whole lot more and could wind up being her nest egg.

She immediately went online to search for rentals. There were exactly two: one she already knew about that had significant mold problems the owner refused to acknowledge, and a cottage on a nearby ranch. The rent was free in exchange for watering, feeding, and exercising the ranch's forty horses. Not only was it a full-time job but Dana didn't know the first thing about horses.

She was just about to check their competitor's website when Griffin came into the office. He had on shorts and a pair of flip-flops. Must be his day off—not that the man ever had to work a day in his life. He was independently wealthy because he was part Wigluk Indian and was entitled to a portion of the tribe's casino money, which was substantial.

"I've been looking all over for you," he said.

"Haven't had time to get a new phone. What's up?"

"I'm worried about you, that's what's up. Lina said you're staying the rest of the week at the Lumber Baron. Why, when I've got a planned community full of empty houses? Colin will lend you some of his furniture."

First off, the last person she wanted knowing her business was Lina Shepard. But given that Maddy was Lina's sister-in-law and she worked at the inn part time, Dana realized the impossibility of that. Secondly, didn't Griffin know how humiliating it would be for her to be reliant on him? Apparently, he didn't have a clue how much she'd cared for him . . . how much it had hurt her, knowing he'd been in love with Lina the whole time they dated? That's why Dana wasn't responsible for what she said next; the unrequited love gods made her do it.

"I'm renting Tawny Wade's place with Aidan McBride, Sloan's brother," she blurted.

Griffin's eyes grew large. Good, let him be taken aback. "How do you know Aidan?"

"Carol and I have been working with him on finding a place. It turns out we have a lot in common." Like they both didn't like living in their cars.

"Wow. That's great. Aidan's the real deal, man. And here I was worrying for nothing. You need money?"

"My house burned down, Griff, not my bank account." *Why did he have to be so damn nice?*

"Okay." He held his hands up. "Just trying to help."

"I know, and I really appreciate it. But I'm fine. How do you know Aidan?"

"Met him when he came to visit Sloane in February. He was a hotshot arson investigator in Chicago. The dude's like a total stud. Good guy to have as a roommate. This news will make a lot of people feel better about your situation."

Especially Lina, Dana thought.

He reached in to give her a friendly hug. "You let me know if there is anything you need, you hear?"

"Between Aidan's new flat-screen and the washer and dryer he recently bought, we should be fine." She smiled a little too brightly.

God, what had she gotten herself in to?

Chapter 3

"You hardly freakin' know this guy." Aidan sat on the stoop of his new house, hoping the neighbors wouldn't hear his telephone conversation. It was too hot to go inside.

"We've been seeing each other for the last six months and have worked together for more than a year, not that it's any of your business," Sue huffed.

Nope, it wasn't, but he didn't want to see her make a mistake. "Whatever you want, then."

She let out a mirthless laugh. "What I wanted was for you to get your shit together. Three years, Aidan. I wasted three years waiting for you to marry me. Anyhow, I just wanted you to hear it from me before you saw it on Facebook or Instagram. 'Bye, Aidan. Try to have a good life in California."

She clicked off and he wiped the sweat off his face with the back of his hand. Damn, it was hot.

He and Sue had been playing phone tag all day and now he wished he'd never called her back. She'd dumped him for Sebastian, a fellow schoolteacher, more than six months ago. It had been a wake-up call. Yet, instead of fighting for her, Aidan's solution had been to move to Nugget. Yeah, a shrink would have a heyday with that one. So what did he expect? Of course she'd moved on.

He blotted at his face again, noticing how many people were sitting out, trying to catch a breeze. It was the kind of neighborhood where folks didn't think twice about dragging their sofas, TVs, and a couple of forties onto the front porch. Not the classiest.

Still, you could see the mighty Sierra mountains in the distance, smell the pines, and hear the occasional train whistle, which sounded nothing like the "L." More like a beautiful riff on a blues harp. A dozen train songs came to mind. Just past the tracks was the Feather River. A few times he'd seen kids hiking down the street in swimsuits, carrying inner tubes. As soon as his stuff arrived, he'd get down there himself.

A brand new Outback pulled up, which seemed to be the car of choice around here. With its all-wheel drive, the car probably performed well in the backcountry, especially in the snow. Hard to believe Nugget got any on a day like this, when he could see steam coming off the blacktop.

Dana got out in those exceptionally nice jeans of hers and came down the walkway. He hadn't expected to hear from her until the end of the week—if at all. Even though he didn't really want a roommate, it had seemed selfish not to offer, given her situation. Hell, he'd seen her face cave the minute she'd learned he'd taken the place. Then she'd tried to pretend she had other prospects and he had tried to pretend he believed her.

But when he'd seen her later at her burned-down house, she'd looked so lost that he hadn't been able to help himself from making the offer. Playing the hero was sort of a problem of his. It went along with his profession, he supposed.

Now, looking at her, he wished he'd kept his mouth shut. She was hot and he'd been without sex for too long. He didn't need that kind of temptation lying in the bedroom next to his.

"Hey," she said, and sat on the stoop with him. "You waiting for a delivery or something?"

"Nope. It's boiling in there."

She nodded. "No air conditioning. If you're still okay with it, I'd like to take you up on your offer."

"Sure. You want to move in tonight?" He was staying at Sloane and Brady's until his furniture came. She could have the place to herself.

"I reserved my room at the inn for the rest of the week and it'll take a few days to get a bed delivered, so next week." She reached into her purse and handed him a check. "Here's half the deposit and the first month's rent."

"Thanks." He shoved it in his back pocket.

"Did you have a roommate in Chicago?"

"Until almost seven months ago I lived with my girlfriend. We broke up and she moved out. How about you?"

"No roommates since college. I guess we should make rules, right?"

He looked at her. They were both adults; what kind of rules? "Like I said, I have twenty-four-hour shifts at the firehouse and I suspect I'll be working a lot of overtime. You'll mostly live here alone."

"I just meant chores' wise. Like who'll be responsible for the yard work, cleaning out the refrigerator, that kind of thing?"

Great. He was living with a drill sergeant. "I'll do the yard. We'll split the indoor stuff."

"And groceries? Should we divvy up the shelves in the cupboards and fridge?"

Jesus, anal much? "However you want to do it, Dana."

"I'll take the bottom shelves in the fridge and pantry because I'm shorter." He nodded, trying to act like they'd resolved the next important thing to world peace. "I just need to measure my room. Which one is yours?"

"You can have whichever one you want."

"No, you should have first choice. It's only fair since it's your house."

"Then I'll take the one that isn't pink," he said, and she laughed.

"It was Katie's room. She's Tawny and Lucky's daughter."

She'd had leukemia but was in full remission. Aidan knew all about her. It didn't take long in this town to know everything about everybody. "You want me to paint it for you . . . unless you want to keep it pink?"

Dana was caught off guard by the offer. "I'll do it. I'm a good painter."

He got the impression she was type A enough to be good at everything.

"I'll go measure now and get going."

Aidan didn't know why, but he followed her into the house. She stopped in the living room and gazed at the walls.

"What do you think about painting in here too? Something cheery, like yellow."

"Whatever you want."

She gave him a long perusal. "You're awfully accommodating."

Yeah, until his girlfriend wanted marriage. Then, not so accommodating. "It's just paint."

For the second time he noticed her eyes. Golden, fringed with thick, dark lashes. She had a cleft in her chin and shiny brown hair that fell to her shoulders. It didn't look like she had much in the chest department, but it was hard to tell with the blouse she had on . . . and the fact that he was looking made this living-together thing an extraordinarily bad idea.

Clearly he needed to get laid. Six months was a long time to go without sex. Okay, there'd been that one time, four months after Sue had left him for Sebastian, when he'd gotten drunk and messed around with the bartender from Players. But it had never gone further than a few kisses and some over-the-clothes petting.

Someone knocked on the door and Aidan went to get it. Brady and his sister, who was holding a house plant, came in. They looked around the empty house and Sloane sighed loud enough for Aidan to hear. What did she expect? When his stuff got here, the place would look better.

"Happy housewarming." Sloane shoved the plant at him and did a double take when she saw Dana. "I didn't think you would be working today. We're so sorry about your house, Dana."

Brady tilted his head to meet Dana's eyes. "You doing okay?"

"I think I'm still in shock." Her cheeks pinked. Aidan assumed it was because she'd burned her house down and by now everyone knew about it. "I'll be fine."

"We were actually on our way to the Lumber Baron to leave something for you," Brady said, and Sloane pulled an envelope from her purse.

"It's a Williams-Sonoma gift card," Sloane said. "We figured you'd need kitchen stuff."

"I don't know what to say." Dana took the envelope and seemed a little bashful about it. "Thank you. Thank you so much." She turned to Aidan. "I'll just measure my room and let you all visit."

"Take your time." He watched her disappear inside the pink room and called, "You need help?"

"Nope. I do it all the time." Right, real estate agent.

Sloane fixed him with a WTF look. He shook his head as if to say *not now.*

"When's your stuff coming?" Brady asked. He clearly could take a hint better than Aidan's brainless sister.

"My moving truck, tomorrow. The washer and dryer came about two hours ago." Before Sue had called him back.

"What do you plan to do with the garage?" Brady asked.

It had been Tawny's studio and a makeshift shop, where she sold her sample boots and seconds. It had heat, drywall, and tons of shelving.

"Park my truck in it."

"All done." Dana came out of the bedroom and shoved the tape measure in her purse. "And again, thanks for the gift certificate. You really didn't have to do that."

"It's not much," Brady said. "If there is anything we can do, you let us know. You got a tough break there, Dana."

She nodded, and Aidan got the sense she was a little choked up.

"You have a key, or should I make you a copy?" he asked her.

"We keep a spare for all the rental properties in the office. I'll make a copy of that one." She headed to the door, cleared her throat like she wanted to say something but instead shyly slinked out.

As soon as they heard her car pull away, Sloane said, "She's living here . . . with you?"

"It's a long story." Aidan waved his sister off, not wanting to get into what a pushover he was.

"We've got nothing but time." To prove her point, she sat on the floor in the middle of the living room.

Aidan turned to Brady for support, but his soon-to-be brother-in-law motioned for him to fill them in. "She didn't know Tawny had shown it to me and had planned to rent it while her place is being rebuilt," Aidan said. "But I'd already signed the lease. Then I got to feeling guilty about it, so I offered to share. I didn't think she'd actually take me up on it."

Sloane smirked. "You two are a little old for doing the roommate thing. Seriously, Aidan, why do you always have to be so nice?"

"It seemed unfair for me to take the only decent rental in Nugget just so I could plant my ass here a few days a week."

"It was the right thing to do, bro." Brady backed him up. "And I think Dana is trying to impress you with them tight jeans."

They weren't any tighter than Sloane's; they just looked a hell of a lot better on Dana. "That's the way they wear 'em these days, Grandpa. If you don't believe me, ask your fiancée."

"Not Dana. Every time I've ever seen her, she's been in one of those dress-for-success suits with the little scarf deal tied around her neck."

Sloane glared at Brady. "I didn't realize you were paying so much attention to Dana Calloway."

He pulled her up from the floor and kissed her. "Nah, only you, sweetness."

"Maybe you two ought to get a room," Aidan said and rolled his eyes.

Sloane ignored him. "You think it'll be weird? You don't even know her."

"It's just temporary until she gets her place back." Or until one of them found a new living situation. "Why, is there something you're not telling me about her?"

"I don't know anything about Dana other than that she and Carol are the go-to real estate people around here. She doesn't seem to get involved with town stuff . . . keeps to herself, mostly."

"Griffin used to date her," Brady said. "I could ask him if you want."

Before coming to Nugget, Brady had had a brush with a stalker. Aidan knew that made him hypercareful.

"Nah, she seems fine to me." So she'd dated Griffin, Nugget's resident billionaire. Aidan found that interesting. "And like I said, I'll mostly be living at the firehouse. We'll rarely see each other."

"And when you need alone time, you can always come to us," Sloane said. "Oh, and by the way, Sue left a message for you. Something about how you guys keep missing each other and she thought she'd have better luck finding you at our house." She lifted her brows in question. The silent message: *What's so important?*

"We touched base," he said, hoping to leave it at that.

"And?"

"She's getting married next weekend." Aidan watched his sister's mouth drop open.

The house seemed darker than usual. "Mom, you home?"

"In here."

Dana followed the faint voice into the den. "Why do you have all the lights out?"

Her mother just shrugged and muted the sound on the television. The air smelled stale. Dana opened a few windows.

"The air conditioner is on." Betty got out of her wing chair, went to the thermostat, and switched off the cooler. Only fifty-eight years old, she'd gone completely gray, her once lithe frame stooped over like an old woman's.

"Dad still at the factory?" It was six; he should've been home by now.

"Fourth of July."

Dana had forgotten the holiday was just a week away. Calloway Confections was famous for its seasonal red, white, and blue chocolate stars. Cadbury might have the lock on chocolate Easter eggs, Hershey on Christmas Kisses, but only Calloway did the Independence Day stars. This time of year, her father worked overtime to make sure the stores were stocked.

Dana used to love going to the factory with her father, where she would spend hours in the observation room with her face pressed against the glass, watching hundreds of chocolate candies, toffees, and caramels roll from conveyor belts into the old-timey tins that had become Calloway's signature. Her great-grandfather had founded the company, and since her father had taken over the reins, Mars, Hershey, and Nestlé all had come calling. Next to them, Calloway was small potatoes with limited distribution—just the West and Southwest. But the name had become synonymous with quality, and Goliaths like Hershey wanted to add it to their list of luxury candy brands.

Dana had pleaded with her parents to sell, take the money and move away. Away from the river and the memories and this house, once the happiest of places, now a mausoleum.

"Aren't you going to ask about my meeting . . . where I'll live?"

Her mother had returned to the chair and unmuted the sound on the TV. "Of course, dear."

Dana grabbed the remote and turned the television off. "The contractors say it'll take a year to rebuild. But they also have some wonderful ideas of how I can add a second story and reconfigure the main floor to have a bigger kitchen and a great room. It'll really increase the resale value."

"That's certainly something positive." Betty gazed out the window into the distance.

"In the meantime, I'm sharing a house with a local firefighter," Dana said, but her mother was no longer listening. She'd slipped into Never-never Land.

Dana presumed that wherever that was, Paul was there too. Her father at least pretended to be present. She supposed he had to emerge from the grief that gripped both her parents like a fist long enough each day to run his company. He'd been the one she'd called the night of the fire, hoping he'd come get her from the Lumber Baron. But he'd simply told her to sleep tight and things would be better in the morning. Sometimes she wondered whether her parents would even have shown up to claim her body if she had died in the fire.

"I'm taking a swim," Dana said. It was ninety degrees in Reno.

She climbed the long staircase to her old bedroom and pawed through her chest of drawers, looking for a swimsuit, planning to take one back with her to Nugget, along with whatever clothing she found that still fit her. Most of it was stuff from high school that she'd left behind when she'd gone to USC. Like everything else in the nearly nine-thousand-square-foot brick behemoth, nothing had been touched since Paul's death. Her room looked exactly the same as when she'd left it. Thank God Sally still came every day or the place would be covered in dust and cobwebs, like Satis House in *Great Expectations*.

At the back of one of the drawers, she found a one-piece, stripped, and shimmied into it. It was snug, the bottom wedging up her butt, but no one would see her. Jogging back down the stairs, she went through the sunroom, threw the doors open, and closed the screens. The house needed light and fresh air. From the casita she grabbed a fluffy towel, threw it on a deck chair, and did a high dive from the board into the water, staying under for as long as she could hold her breath. It felt so cool that she wished she could stay beneath the surface forever.

After running around Reno most of the afternoon, buying a new phone, mattress, clothes, makeup, and other necessities she'd lost in the fire, she'd been ready to collapse from heat exhaustion. She would've stayed the night here, in her old bed, and headed back to Nugget first thing in the morning, but the oppressiveness squeezed her like a vice. Watching her mother, a woman once so alive, sit in front of the television, catatonic . . . it was too much.

She swam a few laps, got out, and toweled off. Instead of going in the house with her wet suit on, she took it off in the casita, hung it on a hook to dry, wrapped herself in the towel, and went back to her room to dress. She rummaged through her closet and found a couple of pairs of old pants and shirts she could at least use for painting and hanging around the house. In the drawers she found a few nightshirts and a silky robe she'd forgotten about. Now that she'd be living with Aidan, her sleepwear would need to be modest. It wasn't that she walked around in the buff, but nothing like the see-through nightgown she'd had on the previous night when he'd seen her underwear and God knew what else.

Her face flushed just thinking about it. It was ridiculous, but Dana felt twice as embarrassed because Aidan was so insanely good-looking. She wondered what his ex was like and why they'd broken up. Clearly it had been serious if they'd been living together.

Dana pulled down a duffel from the top of her closet, packed the clothes she planned to take, and carried it down the stairs.

"Are you leaving, Dana?" Her mother came into the hallway.

"Yes. I have a forty-five-minute drive and want to get to Nugget before it's dark."

"What do you have there?" Betty eyed the duffel bag.

"Just some old clothes I found to hold me over until I can replace everything I lost in the fire."

"Nothing of Paul's, right?"

"No, Mom, nothing of Paul's."

"Okay, dear, have a good trip home."

Dana didn't bother to remind her that she no longer had a home. "I love you, Mom. Tell Dad I'm sorry I missed seeing him."

But she had already drifted back into the den, probably to watch her programs.

Dana loaded the single piece of luggage into the back of her Outback and drove past the Riverwalk, where a smattering of people were taking advantage of the fading daylight on the beach. It was all so picturesque, with the old buildings in the foreground and the newer restaurants, boutiques, and gazebos that dotted the river's edge. She still remembered that day fifteen years ago as vividly as she saw it now. It hadn't had the glitzy businesses back then, but the beach was just as crowded. Paul hadn't died there—that had come later—but it was where it had all started.

She tried to shove the memories away, maneuvered a few city streets before hopping on the highway to Nugget. Moving to the small railroad town had been a fortuitous accident. After college she'd relocated to Lake Tahoe, close enough to her parents to check in on them yet far enough so she wouldn't be consumed by their dejection. She got her real estate license, started selling homes, and fell hard for a local developer, who later jilted her for the wife of his partner, a woman he'd secretly loved for more than a decade and had conveniently forgotten to tell Dana about.

As an antidote, she buried herself in work. One of her clients, frustrated by Tahoe's exorbitant prices, had seen an ad for Sierra Heights and wanted to know more about Nugget. The town was only a forty-minute drive from Tahoe and had its own lakes, rivers, and plenty of outdoor recreation. What it didn't have was high-end casinos, fancy shops, and trendy restaurants. The homes in Nugget, though, were half the price. She wound up selling the client a house in Sierra Heights, meeting Carol, and agreeing to become her partner at Nugget Realty and Associates. Carol, a broker, owned the agency but wanted to spend more time with her family. Dana needed a fresh start and saw Nugget as a burgeoning real-estate market with the perfect opportunity to make her mark—and her fortune.

And to prove it had been the right decision, Griffin had given her all the listings for the homes in Sierra Heights, a development he'd bought out of bankruptcy as an investment. They'd begun mixing business with pleasure, and this time she thought Griffin could be the real deal, only to find out he was obsessed with Lina. As far as breaking up with her, Griff had been a lot more of a gentleman than Tim, who'd unceremoniously dumped her as soon as the other woman had become available.

That was when Dana started examining her life and saw a disturbing pattern. Since her childhood, she'd always been second runner-up. To her parents, Paul had always come first. And after he'd died, she'd moved from second place in their eyes to nonexistent. The same had happened with Tim and Griffin as soon as they could be with the women they really wanted. Even in college, she'd been repeatedly passed over by men, by teachers, by employers, by opportunities that came her way and inevitably landed in someone else's lap.

She'd responded to the epiphany by applying herself even harder to her career—the one place where she could come in first. In Plumas County she ranked number one in sales as compared to the other agents, and if this year's numbers surpassed last year's, she'd continue to lead. She might not be rich, but she'd at least found an area of her life where she could finish on top.

By the time she pulled into the Lumber Baron parking lot, the sun had fallen behind the mountains and her stomach was growling. She probably should've grabbed something in Reno. She glanced across the square to the Ponderosa with reservations. The bottom line: She didn't like eating alone in restaurants. Intellectually, she knew it was silly. Lots of people—male and female, single and married—went to cafés, movies, even bars alone. Just not her.

But if she didn't want to go hungry she had no choice. The inn didn't have room service, only breakfast and wine and cheese in the afternoon, which she'd already missed. She decided to leave her things in the car and stroll over to the restaurant, which also had a bar and, of all things, a bowling alley. The dining room was quite nice and the food decent. She'd taken many a client there for lunch and dinner.

It wasn't until she was seated that she noticed Griffin and Lina in a booth toward the back and silently groaned. They waved to her and she wanted to disappear through the floorboards. To make matters worse, Griffin motioned for her to come join them. As if that was going to happen. Uh-uh, no way. She pretended to take a call on her new phone, hoping he'd think she was doing business or meeting someone. But no such luck. He got up and loitered next to her table until she finished her fake call.

Dana plastered on as pleasant a smile as she could muster. Griffin was still her most important client, after all. "Hi."

"Lina and I want you to come sit with us." He may as well have said, *Lina and I think you're pitiful.*

"Actually, I'm—"

"Hey," a deep voice rumbled behind her, and the next thing she knew, Aidan was pulling out the chair across from her.

If he hadn't just saved her from telling a mondo lie, she would have thought he was damned presumptuous for helping himself to her table. Correction: She still thought Aidan was damned presumptuous but was inordinately thankful that he'd gotten her out of a jam. The last thing she wanted to do was break bread with Lina Shepard.

"I didn't realize you had company." Griffin smiled like he thought she and Aidan were on a date. Fine, let him think what he wanted.

"Have you met Aidan?" She knew he had, but it made her feel less gawky to pretend he hadn't.

"Yeah, of course. How you doing, Aidan? How's the new job?"

"All good." Aidan got up and shook Griff's hand.

"I gotta get back." He nudged his head toward his table, and Dana watched Aidan follow Griff's direction and give Lina a long, appreciative look. *Great.*

After Griff left, Aidan buried his face in the menu. "What are you getting? Maybe we should share a few things."

She didn't know yet what she wanted to order. But for him, she highly recommended the humble pie.

Chapter 4

Crap. Maybe he'd interrupted something he shouldn't have. But by the time Aidan saw Griffin, it had been too late. He had already started toward Dana's table. When he'd come in, the restaurant had been crowded, and he hadn't wanted to sit at the bar. And there was Dana with a whole table to herself.

He gazed at her over the top of his menu. She really was very pretty. Different from Sue, with her compact body, dark hair, and amber eyes. Sue was tall and voluptuous with auburn hair—and great legs that went on forever.

"You finish your errands?"

"Mm-hmm." She had her eyes glued to the menu, like it held the secrets of life.

"In Reno?"

She put the menu down. "I got a phone at Costco and paint for the house at the hardware store."

Aidan eyed her new phone. "Give me your number." Pulling out his, he programmed in her digits. "Here's mine."

"Uh . . . okay . . . I guess it would be prudent in case of an emergency." She plugged in the numbers he gave her.

A waitress came to take their orders and both of them put their phones away. Dana got a salad and Aidan went for a steak with all the fixings, a side of onion rings, and a plate of nachos for the table.

Dana lifted her brows. "You must be hungry."

"I didn't eat much today. The nachos are for both of us to share," he said defensively. "Tell me about yourself."

"Like what? You already know I'm a real estate agent and that my house burned down."

"Like are you from here, what are your hobbies, your favorite TV shows? It's called a conversation."

"I'm from Reno and I don't have any hobbies or favorite TV shows. How about you?"

Who didn't have hobbies or favorite shows? Fine, he'd break the ice. "I'm from Chicago, where I was a firefighter and an arson investigator. I like football and baseball and just about any other sport you can think of."

"Why did you leave Chicago?"

Their drinks came and he took a swig of his beer. Some kind of microbrew from around here. Good stuff. "I came to visit my sister in February and fell in love with the place. All the wide-open spaces, the mountains, the fresh air. A job opened up with Cal Fire and my sister put in a good word for me. Here I am." It wasn't the whole truth but close enough.

"You must be tight with Sloane."

"I am with all my siblings."

"How many more do you have?" She sipped her iced tea. Nice lips, he noted.

"Two brothers. I'm the oldest, Sloane's the baby. My brothers and dad are also firefighters. How about you? Sisters? Brothers?"

"I had a younger brother . . . Paul. He died when I was fifteen."

"I'm sorry, Dana. That's tough. Was he sick?"

"No, he drowned . . . well, sort of."

He waited for her to finish.

"It's called 'secondary drowning.'" She paused, like she was trying to come up with the best way to explain it.

"I know what it is." He'd never actually had a case but had been warned about it in training. "How did it happen?"

"We were tubing in the Truckee River, near where we lived. Paul went out farther than he should have and his tube got caught up on a rock. He wiggled out of the tube to pry it loose and got caught up in the current, which dragged him under. Luckily, another tuber pulled him out and got him to shore, where he coughed up a lot of water. After a short rest he seemed fine, even went back in the river for a little while."

Aidan signaled for the waitress to refill Dana's iced tea. "Is that when it happened?"

"No, we made it home. Paul went upstairs, said he wanted to take a nap. We figured he was knocked out from spending the day in the sun. My mother checked on him a couple of hours later and he had white foam around his mouth and blue lips. She called 9-1-1, but Paul never made it to the hospital. He died en route."

"Did the medical examiner find water in his lungs?" Aidan knew that was typically the case.

She nodded. "They said he died from asphyxiation from drowning."

"Ah, jeez. How old was he?" Having seen many deaths in his line of work, Aidan knew it was the worst when the tragedy involved a child.

"Thirteen."

"That's rough." He reached out and grasped her hand. "I'm really sorry, Dana."

She gazed out over the restaurant, growing distant. "Thank you. It was a long time ago."

The server came with all their food at once and the conversation changed to the weather.

"Is it always this hot here?" Aidan pushed the nachos closer to her.

"Hot in the summer and cold in the winter. But even so, it's been unseasonably warm. And the drought hasn't helped things."

He nodded, stuffing his face with steak. The beef here was phenomenal. "What else did you do in Reno?"

"Got a bed." She turned red and quickly deflected by adding, "And some suits for work."

Clearly the attraction thing wasn't one-sided, he mused. Yet there would be no beds involved between them. Nope, that would be a colossally bad idea.

"I guess it'll take you a while to reacquire all the things you lost," he said. "Was any of it irreplaceable?"

"Tins from my family's candy company. I collect them. Some of the ones I lost were antiques." She shrugged and tried to put on a good face. "Hey, it could've been worse, right?"

He wished all fire survivors saw it that way. "What kind of candy company?"

"Calloway Confections." When she saw the name didn't register with him, she said, "You'd know it if you were from California or Nevada. Chocolates, caramels, toffee."

Aidan grinned. "You gonna bring home samples?"

And just like that Dana lit up. He'd seen her phony smiles in the real estate office this morning, but holy hell, a real Dana Calloway smile was something to behold. It was as if she shined from the inside out.

"You like candy?" she asked.

"I've been known to have a sweet tooth."

"Then I'll bring some home."

"So why didn't you work in the family business?" From the time he'd been a boy he'd known that, like his father, he'd be a firefighter. Same with his brothers. Sloane had been the only one to go in a different direction.

"I like real estate," she said, but something in her demeanor told him there was more to the story. But he'd leave his investigative skills to the job; she was entitled to her privacy.

"Yeah? Is it pretty good in Nugget?"

"It's getting there. Originally, I was in Tahoe. You can't touch anything there for under a million dollars and the competition among agents was fierce. Here, I feel a little like the prospectors who founded this town . . . like there's going to be a gold rush."

"I thought Nugget was founded first by loggers and then the railroad."

"Yep. But the Gold Rush helped feed this town. A lot of the first merchants made their fortunes from the miners."

"Pretty interesting stuff. So you came to make your fortune?"

"Carol offered me a good opportunity, and I like the idea that her agency isn't a national chain. Mom-and-pop, just like my family's business."

Tawny Wade and Lucky Rodriguez took the table next to theirs and Aidan waved. He only knew Tawny from the house and Lucky not at all, but the couple was pretty tight with his sister and Brady. They waved back and Tawny got up and came over.

"I heard from Carol that you two are sharing the house." Wow, news traveled fast here. "I'm so sorry about the fire, Dana. What a terrible thing. Do they know how it started?"

"I left a candle burning," she said, and looked down at her plate.

Aidan gave her credit for coming clean. "One of the most common causes of house fires," he added.

"Are you planning to rebuild? Because that's such a nice neighborhood." Tawny glanced over at Lucky, who appeared to be ordering.

"As soon as Pat and Colin are done with your new house, they'll start on mine."

"That's good. They're doing the finish work on ours now, hallelujah. We've been living in a construction zone these past few weeks. But we needed to be on the property for the cowboy camp . . . and for planning the wedding. I should get back, but I'm glad two good people are living in my old house."

When she left, Aidan asked, "You going to their wedding?"

"I don't know them very well and wasn't invited. I think Carol is going."

He'd gotten the sense from Brady, who was catering the reception, that everyone in town, including him, was invited. Provided that he didn't have to work, he planned to go because he'd never been to a wedding in a barn before. That was where they were holding it. It would've been nice to know someone there besides his sister and her fiancé.

They made random conversation while they ate, and when the bill came Aidan took it.

"What are you doing? Let's split it down the middle," Dana said.

"Nah, you only got a salad and I hijacked your table."

"I ate your nachos."

"They were for both of us. Don't worry about it. You'll get me next time. Plus, you're supplying us with candy." He put his credit card on the table and saw her glance over at Griffin and his girlfriend's booth.

Aidan wondered what that was about. Maybe she was still hung up on the guy. The girl he was with was gorgeous, but she looked young. He figured Dana was in her late twenties—also young.

"When are you moving in?" he asked her.

"I'll probably bring my toothbrush over tomorrow or during the weekend." She laughed, and he thought she had a good attitude. Most people would still be crying over all they'd lost in the fire.

"They delivering your bed soon?"

"Tomorrow," she said.

The waitress took the card. "Then I'll probably see you tomorrow. I'm not on until Monday."

After the bill got squared away, he walked her to the inn and helped her unload a few of her packages, then he went to Sloane and Brady's.

"You want some dinner? There are leftovers in the fridge," Sloane said. She was doing laundry to pack for her and Brady's trip to San Francisco in the morning.

"I ate at the Ponderosa."

She stopped what she was doing to look at him. "You dealing with this Sue thing?"

"What's to deal with? I'm not sending a gift, if that's what you mean."

"Aid, don't be such a guy. I know you; you're dying inside."

"I screwed up . . . not much I can do about it now." He'd tried—just not hard enough.

"Why did you screw up? That's the question. You think you're one of those guys who's afraid of marriage?"

"I don't know." He lifted his shoulder.

"Well, don't you think you should try to figure it out?"

"Yeah, I'll get right on that." The last thing he wanted to discuss with his sister was whether he had a commitment phobia. The sorry truth was he didn't know. His parents had been married for close to forty years and still made out in the kitchen. So it wasn't like he didn't have good role models. Family had always been important to him and kids, yeah, he wanted them. Yet, with Sue, every time she'd brought up marriage his blood had run cold and his muscles tightened. The question was moot anyway; Sue was getting married this weekend.

He went up into the loft and turned on the TV. As far as Aidan was concerned, it was the best room in the house. Giant flat-screen, wet bar, big leather sofas. The rest of the house, except for the kitchen, was filled with flowery, slipcover crap. Poor Brady had to check his dick at the door.

Tomorrow would probably be his last night here. He'd use the weekend to unpack his stuff and get settled in at the new place before reporting to work. It would be interesting living with Dana. She was wound tighter than he usually rolled. He got the impression from earlier that she was the type to tack chore charts and bathroom schedules to the refrigerator. Hey, he'd been the one to suggest being roommates, and now he had to stick to it. At least her half of the rent would come in handy until he sold his condo and no longer had a mortgage to pay.

The problem was he'd never lived with a woman he wasn't sleeping with, and Dana could become a temptation. In most cases, he wasn't against doing what felt good as long as everyone knew the ground rules. But Dana didn't strike him as the bootie-call roommate type. And he wasn't ready for another relationship. He was too busy trying to figure out where the last one went wrong.

The next morning, Dana crammed herself into another pair of tight jeans compliments of the Millers. Ordinarily, she didn't dress this casually to meet with clients, but today she was reshowing ranch property to a couple who'd recently sold their ten-acre spread in Sonoma County for a mint and were looking to relocate their sheep and alpaca farm to Plumas County.

She pulled on the new cowboy boots, thinking they would be perfect for walking through the thick brush during snake season. Last time she'd shown them the place, she'd worn high heels and felt like an idiot. Since then, she'd learned that looking professional meant dressing appropriately for the situation. You didn't wear sweats to show a four-million-dollar mansion or Givenchy to sell a hog farm. For the final touch, she threw a lightweight blazer, a Macy's purchase during her Reno foray, over a T-shirt. At least it was supposed to be cooler today.

Before leaving, she let her eyes roam around the lovely room. This would be her last night at the Lumber Baron. Tomorrow, she planned to move into the house. With Aidan. After last night's dinner she was even more conflicted about the living situation. Not because she didn't trust him—all concerns about him being a serial killer had vanished. But the man was too damned sure of himself. She could tell he thought he could get any woman he lay his eyes on. And the truth was he probably could. Although he wasn't as classically handsome as Griffin, who reminded her of a young Matthew McConaughey, Aidan had the whole tall, dark, and rough thing going for him. The swarthy skin, slightly crooked nose, deep-set blue eyes, and angular face—very piratical. And he was strapping. More than two hundred pounds if Dana had to guess. All of it muscle.

When she got to the office, the Griswolds were already there. They'd driven up early that morning.

"You ready?" she asked, knowing they were raring to go.

Although the couple's buyers—a neighboring grape grower who wanted to expand his vineyard—said they could rent back until the spring, they were anxious to be in a new place by fall to give their sheep and alpacas plenty of time to acclimate before the spring shearing. The Griswolds owned a wool and fleece business.

"We sure are," Walt said, grinning. Dana liked them a lot.

They took her car to the property, which was seven miles outside of town.

"Did you do the research on the well?" Walt asked.

She motioned to the binder she had in the backseat. "It's in there, along with the property survey. It looks like the seasonal creek is part of the parcel. And, Josephine, I talked to a local repairman about the Wedgewood stove. He's pretty sure he can get it working again."

"Oh, that's wonderful." Josephine handed the binder to her husband. "What about the roof?"

"The owner says he hasn't done anything for twelve years but that nothing leaks. My advice is that we add that to our list to get him to come down on the price. Maybe even get him to put on a new roof."

"The well looks good," Walt said. "According to this, it pumps one hundred and fifty gallons of water a minute."

"I think our biggest concern is whether we'll like it here." Josephine sighed. "We have all those fabulous restaurants in Healdsburg, and San Francisco is only ninety minutes away."

"Josephine, we can't afford to live there anymore," Walt chimed in.

Dana laughed. "That's the problem with an overinflated real estate market. Even when you make a fortune on what you sell, everything costs a fortune. This is the deal here: no gourmet restaurants, no fair-trade, wait-an-hour-for-your-drip coffee places, and no trendy shops. And the closest thing to culture is cowboy poetry at the grange. But it's real, it's beautiful, and it's affordable. And I think it's the up and coming place . . . but don't take that to the bank just yet."

"You're a good egg, Dana," Walt said.

"You guys should stay at the Lumber Baron tonight . . . my treat. Get the flavor of the town, eat at the Ponderosa, maybe check out the mill pond in Graeagle. I'll admit Nugget doesn't have the chichi factor Healdsburg does, but it has its own charm. And more important, it's retained its agricultural roots."

"That's for damn sure," Walt said. "Sonoma has turned into a playground for the rich and famous."

Two hours later, the Griswolds sat in Dana's conference room, writing up paperwork for an offer. Dana had gone to get them cold drinks from the refrigerator when her cell phone rang. Aidan.

"Hi," she said, surprised to hear from him. "What's up?"

"I got called out on a suspicious fire in Lassen County. Looks like I'm gonna be here a few days. My moving truck is coming and my sister and Brady are in San Francisco. Any chance you could unlock the door and let the movers in?"

"What time?"

"They gave me a window of between two and six. Maybe you could put a note on the door to call as soon as they get there; that way you don't have to wait for four hours."

"All right. But how will they know where to put everything?"

"I'll have to deal with it when I get home. Could you just make sure to lock up after everything's delivered?"

"Of course."

"Thanks, Dana. I'm sorry to stick you with this."

"It's not a problem." She wanted to get a start on painting anyway.

After they ended the call she smiled at the Griswolds. "Sorry about that."

"Don't be silly." Josephine waved her hand in the air. "Life happens."

Indeed it did. "I'll call the listing agent to let her know we have an offer and hopefully we'll hear something soon. Should I see about getting you a room at the Lumber Baron?"

"We've got animals that need feeding and it's a four-hour ride back," Walt said. "As much as we'd like to take you up on your offer, we've got to get home, Dana."

"All right. Keep your fingers crossed and your cell phone on. I'm thinking we should hear back fairly quickly. There will probably be some back and forth, though."

"That's what I figured," Walt said.

Dana got their signatures, made sure the documents were in order, and walked the Griswolds out to their car.

"Let us know as soon as you hear something," Josephine said.

"I will. It's a good offer. Maybe a little less than he's willing to take, but we've left you some wiggle room."

She watched them drive away, went inside to email the offer to Century 21 in Quincy, and called to make sure they'd received the email and that the listing agent had her cell number. Before going to meet Aidan's movers, Dana took a detour to Farm Supply with a gift for the Millers.

The store was the size of a warehouse and carried everything from tack and feed to clothes and kitchenware. Grace was at the counter, ringing up a customer, when Dana walked in. She browsed the aisles, waiting for Grace to finish.

"How you doing, Dana?" Grace called across the store.

"Good." With the customer gone, Dana carried the basket she'd made to the cash register. "I just wanted to thank you so much for all the clothes. You saved my life." She motioned at the jeans and the boots. "Did Carol tell you my sizes?"

"She sure did. My daughter and I had a wonderful time picking out everything. I'm glad it's working for you. We don't carry the suits and professional clothing you usually wear, but I figured you needed some starter pieces until you could get to a department store."

"Everything is beautiful, Grace. I brought this for your family. It's Calloway candy from my family's business, coffee, and assorted other goodies."

"Now, honey, you didn't have to do that. I'm guessing you've got enough going on. Pat was in this morning and said you're planning to rebuild, which I think is a wise decision. That's a lovely neighborhood, and it seems to me a house there is worth something. But you'd know that better than I would."

"I still have to see what I'll get insurance wise, but nice homes here are going for more than two hundred and thirty dollars a square foot."

"When are you talking to the insurance people?" Grace asked.

"Monday."

"That's good, and I hear you and Sloane's brother are sharing Tawny's old house." Grace let out a catcall whistle. "Now if I were thirty years younger . . . Watch out, Mr. Miller. That man is all brawn. I met him over at the inn; he stopped by to drop something off for Brady."

"It's strictly a roommate situation," Dana wanted her to know. It wouldn't do to have people gossiping about her.

"Well, maybe you could fix that, if you know what I mean." Grace arched her brows.

Dana never would've guessed that sweet, gray-haired Grace Miller, who ran the feedstore with her husband, was an oversexed cougar. She really needed to get to know the women of Nugget better.

"We're strictly platonic."

Grace made a face like *what a shame*, then launched into an entirely different topic. "Anything going on with the Rosser place?" Next to McCreedy Ranch, it was one of the largest cattle spreads in the county. The owner, Ray Rosser, had been charged with murder for shooting a man he claimed had stolen his cattle and needed to sell the ranch to pay his legal expenses. People here hadn't stopped talking about it.

"Nothing. I'd hoped a cattle company would be interested in it, but it's a huge investment. And with the drought, people are culling their herds, not looking to expand. At least we've managed to temporarily lease the property to a rancher from the valley who's trying to fatten up his cattle on whatever grazing land he can find."

Until moving here, Dana had never sold agricultural land. With no knowledge of farming or animal husbandry, she'd become a quick study. "Grace, if anyone comes through here who's interested, let 'em know Ray is motivated."

"I bet he is." Grace made a face. "According to Owen, he's pretty much signed over everything he owns to his legal team."

Dana thought it was probably true but wasn't at liberty to discuss it. "I have to run to the new house. But again, Grace, I can't tell you how much I appreciate the clothes. What you did for me . . ."

"Honey, we're all here for you. You remember that."

She felt warmed by the words and chided herself for not making more of an effort to get to know people. She just wasn't good at putting herself out there.

It was one thirty, leaving her just enough time to grab a burger at the Bun Boy, Nugget's only other eating option besides the Ponderosa, before heading to the house. She ordered at the drive-through speaker, drove to the window, and waited until a kid—probably a Nugget High student—handed her a white sack. On the short drive over, she ate half the fries and stayed in the car with the air conditioning on to finish her burger. Afterward, she tossed her wrappers in the trash and began unloading. Paint, the new bedding, and bags of supplies she'd bought in Reno. In her new bedroom she changed into painting clothes and a pair of old tennis shoes and went in search of a ladder, finding one in the garage.

Over the next hour, she taped off the moldings, covered the floor, and started priming the walls. She used a brush to cut into the tight spots between the wall and ceiling but made real progress with a big roller. In no time, the pink began to disappear. Before getting her license she'd worked in a real estate office that did a lot of its own house staging for clients. That was where Dana had learned to paint, as well as a handful of useful decorating tips.

By the time the room was primed, her bed came, and Dana had the delivery men set it up in the middle of the room so she could continue painting. In the heat, the primer would dry fast, and she might even be able to get on the first coat of color—a hydrangea green that would complement beautifully her new pink-and-green-striped bedding.

Not long after the bed guys left, Aidan's moving truck appeared. Like with her bed, she had them cluster the living room furniture in the middle of the room. She hoped to have it painted before Aidan returned. He actually had some pretty nice things, including a sectional sofa that looked like it came from a Pottery Barn–type store. The ex-girlfriend must've picked it out, she told herself, and again wondered what the story was there.

She wasn't sure if he wanted to paint his room—the color was nice and already went with his stuff—so she directed the movers to set the sleigh bed against the wall with the nightstands on each side. Okay, Dana was probably being sexist, but his bedroom furniture also had the mark of a woman. Not that the pieces weren't masculine enough, just a little too matchy-matchy. Aidan didn't strike her as the coordinated type.

Although he'd been pretty good about marking the boxes. Still, she would've used a black marker with a fine point. Less likely to bleed that way. All the cartons were starting to make the small house claustrophobic, so Dana went outside to get a breath of fresh air. That was when her phone rang.

Hoping that it was the listing agent on the Griswolds' property, she checked the display. New York.

"Dana Calloway," she answered.

"Hi, Ms. Calloway. I'm planning to visit next week for a few days and was wondering if you could show me some properties."

"Absolutely." Dana hadn't had any clients from New York yet. "Did you get my number from Carol at the office?"

"No. I tried the office and got a machine. Your number was on the ad in the *Nugget Tribune*."

Good, Dana thought. Advertising in the online newspaper was bringing them business. It amazed her how many people across the country subscribed for the real estate listings. Nugget might not be Tahoe or Palm Springs or the Napa Valley, but slowly it was starting to attract buyers looking for vacation and retirement homes at a good price.

"What specifically are you looking for? Houses, property, something in an upscale planned community with lots of amenities?"

"A place for horses with a house."

"Do you have a number of acres in mind?" The more information Dana got up front, the better she could narrow down the options.

"No, not really. I'll know it when I see it."

In Dana's experience, people who said things like that just wanted to play. But you never knew when a lookie loo might turn into a real buyer. "You want to go out next Friday? I could make arrangements for a few viewings. Once we see a couple of places, I'll get a better feel for what you have in mind."

"Wonderful," the woman said, then briefly paused. "I will need you to sign a confidentiality agreement, however. Will that be a problem?"

Confidentiality over what? Who was this woman? "Are you a celebrity?" Dana couldn't help but ask.

"Something like that." She laughed, but Dana thought it sounded harsh and bitter. "It's difficult on the phone . . . and I can't explain it unless you're willing to sign the NDA."

"I'll be perfectly frank with you: I've never been faced with this sort of thing before." The most famous person Dana had ever sold a house to in Tahoe was a Sacramento anchorwoman for one of the local network affiliates. In Nugget, none of her clients had been famous. "I'll have to talk to my agency's broker. I don't think it'll be a problem, but I'd like to check first."

"I appreciate that."

"In the meantime, I'll pull several listings to send you. Uh, you do realize that at the close of escrow anything you buy becomes public record?"

"Yes. I'll be buying as a corporation," she said. "Shall we talk tomorrow, then?"

While the call wouldn't have been peculiar in Los Angeles, here in Nugget it was downright strange, leaving Dana beyond intrigued. "Absolutely."

What her mysterious client didn't know was that Dana could sign all the nondisclosure forms in the world, but as soon as one of the townsfolk spied a famous person in Nugget, word would spread faster than a New York minute.

Chapter 5

When Aidan got home on Tuesday he went straight from the firehouse to his new home. He hadn't had a chance to call Dana to make sure everything had gone well with the movers. In fact, he'd barely had time to breathe. North of Susanville, two morons—brothers—had set their farmhouse on fire, hoping to collect the insurance money.

The old place had gone up like a bonfire. The flames spread, burning four hundred acres of forest and ranchland, destroying six structures, and injuring three firefighters. After an extensive investigation, the police hauled the brothers in and locked them up on arson charges. Dingbats, the both of them. They were just lucky no one had died.

The driveway was empty, so Aidan pulled his Expedition in and got out into the blazing heat. It had to be at least one hundred degrees today. The first thing he planned to do on his days off was get a portable air conditioner for the house. Unpacking could wait.

He unlocked the door, stepped into the living room, and staggered back. The whole room had been arranged, including his pictures. The walls had been painted a pale gray that matched the dark gray sectional and the blue zebra rug. She'd hung some kind of fabric shades that scrunched up over the windows. Sue had picked out the furniture, but he had to say Dana seemed to have a better knack for putting it all together. Before leaving for Chicago, he'd suggested that Sue take everything. She'd declined, saying she wanted to start from scratch with her new man—the one she was marrying this weekend.

He popped his head in the kitchen, which had been freshly painted, and someone had stenciled a rooster and the word "Bistro," on the wall next to the table, which had been set with colorful placemats—not his. The house had gone from plain Jane to stylish in four days. He'd give it to Dana; she got shit done. It looked like all his kitchen stuff had been unpacked.

His bedroom was also arranged, the bed made, and some of his clothes hung in the closet. Boxes filled with his winter clothes, underwear, and sports equipment had been stacked along the wall. He'd have them unpacked in no time.

In the bathroom, she'd hung a new shower curtain. Something neutral, not too girlie, which he appreciated. She'd made two stacks of towels. He knew which stack was his because she'd fastened little chalkboard signs to the shelf with their names. Just like grammar school.

He went back in the kitchen and stuck his head in the refrigerator. The bottom shelves were packed with food. His shelves were bare. Well, he couldn't expect her to shop for him too. Out of curiosity, he checked the pantry. Again, the bottom shelves were well stocked, and she'd filled the top shelves with Calloway candy. There had to be at least a dozen different kinds. He stuck the chocolates in the fridge and opened a tin of caramels, popping three in his mouth. Damn, they were good—and unexpectedly salty. He looked at the package. "Made with the finest sea salt," it said.

Hmm, good idea, he thought. It cut the sweetness. But he needed real food and decided to hit the Nugget Market as soon as he found an air conditioner. First, he needed a shower. On his way to the bathroom, he couldn't help himself from peeking inside Dana's room. Everything matched. The walls, the bedding, the window coverings. She must've worked around the clock.

Aidan shut her door, stripped down in the bathroom, and jumped in the shower. He'd left his toiletries at Sloane and Brady's, so he'd have to forgo shaving. After four days away, he'd gotten pretty scruffy. He used Dana's soap and shampoo and hoped she wouldn't mind. There'd be no way to hide it because he smelled like her. Peaches and vanilla.

He dried off, wrapped a towel around his waist, and headed to his bedroom when who should he meet coming down the hallway but Dana. She got one look at him and covered her eyes with her hands.

"Sorry, sorry. Oh God, I just knew this would happen."

"What?" he said. "It's not like I'm naked."

"Well, you may as well be."

"You've never seen a guy's chest before?"

"Of course I have."

He had a good mind to flash the rest of himself. Instead, he took his sweet-ass time walking to his room. "I know you're looking."

"No, I'm not."

He heard her door bang shut and smiled. The lady was a prude. Aidan shuffled through the boxes until he discovered the one he wanted, sifted through the contents, found underwear and cargo shorts, and tugged them both on. He shoved the rest of the stuff into his dresser drawers. In another carton, he found his T-shirts, pulled one over his head, and unpacked the rest. Two boxes down, ten more to go. They could wait till later.

He found a crate of tennis shoes stashed in the closet and put them on without socks. Too hot. In the kitchen, he found Dana making a sandwich.

"The house looks great, like a freaking model home. Thanks for doing all this." He looked around the kitchen, noting her little touches everywhere. Matching towels hanging from hooks near the sink. A big bowl of fruit on the counter. She'd even put a list of emergency numbers on the refrigerator. "To repay you, I'm gonna install us some sort of cooling system, even window fans if that's all I can find."

She lifted the hair off the back of her neck, and for some reason, he found it sexy as hell. "That's great because it's been so hot in here I can't sleep at night even with the windows open. This is pretty unusual for the Sierra. Typically, it cools down in the evening. Where do you plan to go?"

"I don't know. Is there a big hardware store around here?"

"Reno has the biggest ones. But you could try Mountain Hardware in Clio. We could call first." She grabbed a phone book out of a drawer. Yep, she was that organized.

He used his cell to call, and while he waited for someone to answer, asked Dana, "Slow work week?"

"Are you kidding? I sold two places. One, a farm on the outside of town to this really great couple who raise sheep and alpacas."

A man from the hardware store came on the phone and Aidan

paced around the small kitchen, telling him what he needed. He signed off and said, "They've got a couple different window units. I say we get one for every room."

She blinked up at him. "That'll cost a fortune."

"Nah." He shook his head, then noticed the back door had a screen and opened it. "We don't need one for the kitchen, just the living room and two bedrooms. I'm paying, anyway."

He watched her cut her sandwich in half and his stomach growled. "You want one?"

"If you wouldn't mind. I need to go to the grocery store and stock up." He was off for four days, unless he got called out again.

"Help yourself." She motioned at the bread, deli meat, and cheese. "There are sodas and waters in the fridge. Chips in the cupboard."

"Thanks. And thanks for the candy. The caramels rock. So you sold two places, huh? Is that a normal week?"

"There is no normal in real estate. But it's been good this summer so far. The second place I sold was in Sierra Heights. These people had been considering a place there since winter. I think the guy did well in the stock market and finally broke down. It's a good sale. How 'bout you? I heard about the fire on the news. Those brothers really thought they'd get away with torching a house? Who does that . . . I mean, besides accidentally?"

Aidan smiled. She'd probably never live down leaving that candle burning. "It's more common than you'd think." Professional arsonists were smart and good at covering their tracks. Luckily, the brothers were neither.

They sat down to eat, and Aidan noticed she was wearing a navy skirt, matching blazer, panty hose, and high heels, like Brady had described. "Aren't you hot in that?" He liked her better in jeans. They showed off her ass, and on a scale of one to ten, Dana's ass was off the charts. But he supposed this was more professional.

"I was thinking of going back to the office, but I'd rather come with you to the hardware store."

"Sure. What do you need?" Sue had always hated anything having to do with home repairs.

"Nothing I can think of right now, but I always find stuff when I'm there."

He grinned. "Yeah, me too."

"I'll just finish lunch and change."

They ate together at the table. For dessert he broke out some of the chocolates and Dana started doing the dishes.

"I'll get 'em," Aidan said. "You go change. I'd like to get this done while I still have a second wind because pretty soon I'm gonna need to crash."

"A lot of long hours?"

"Yeah. But now I get time to recoup."

"It'll only take me a few minutes to be ready," she said.

Aidan highly doubted it. He had a sister and had had plenty of girlfriends. He gave her thirty minutes minimum. But true to her word, she came out of her room in less than ten, wearing a little sundress that showed off a good deal of skin. And cleavage. Dana had more on top than he'd originally thought. Pretty legs too.

"That's better." It took him a second to realize he'd said it aloud.

"Pardon?"

"I just mean you'll be cooler now."

She looked a little self-conscious. "Grace Miller from Farm Supply gave it to me. I wouldn't ordinarily wear something like this, but I lost all my clothes in the fire."

If the clothes had even remotely resembled the suit she'd just been wearing, Aidan thought the fire did her a favor. "Why, you don't like the dress?"

"I do. I just don't think it's me."

"You want me to be one hundred percent honest? The dress is hot on you."

Her face flamed like a four-alarm fire. "Okay, let's not talk about it anymore."

"It's up to you, but most women like being told how hot they are."

"I'm not one of them," she said, and walked out of the house and climbed up into the passenger side of his SUV.

He followed her and cranked the AC as soon as he started the engine. "How do we get there?"

She gave him directions and they drove in silence until they reached the highway.

"Griffin must be happy about the house you sold. Jeez, the homes on both sides of my sister's place are vacant."

"I'm working on that," she said, seeming to perk up now that they were talking about real estate. Aidan couldn't help but notice that her nipples had also perked up from the air-conditioning. "Little by little we're getting more interest, especially since prices in Tahoe, Truckee, and Glory Junction have gone through the roof. So what's going on with your condo?"

"Unfortunately, not a damn thing."

"Maybe you're asking too much."

Aidan had already slashed the price twice. "According to my agent, we're good."

"Is it an undesirable neighborhood?"

"It's a great neighborhood. But the place is only one-bedroom."

"Ah," Dana said. "One-bedrooms can be a tough sell."

Yeah, that was what Sue had said when he'd bought the place. At the time, he'd been planning to live there alone. Upon deciding to go back to school to become a teacher, she'd asked to move in to save money.

"Someone will buy it eventually. If not, I'll rent it out," he said.

She told him which turn to take and a short time later they pulled up in front of the hardware store. It looked small from the outside, but inside the shop was crammed full of merchandise. Aidan thought it had as much stuff as a Home Depot. A clerk told them where to find the window air-conditioners.

"There's been a real run on 'em," he said, and Aidan hung back to talk to the old guy for a while. As long as he was new to the area, he wanted to get to know people.

Dana left them to their conversation, which started with the weather and took a quick detour to the best places in the region to fish. Aidan needed to get a license and thought about going to Lake Davis over the weekend. Brady had taken him there when he'd visited in February and he'd fallen in love with the lake in the woods.

Eventually, he broke away to explore the store. He found Dana in the storage aisle, eyeing a closet organizer. No shock there. In a short time, he'd figured out that she liked everything in its place. It was part of that anal retentive thing she had going.

"You getting that?"

"I was thinking about it. It seems like it would be pretty useful."

The thing, with its various shelves and hanger rods, seemed stupid to him, like it would wind up giving her less space than just leaving the closet the way it was. But he kept his mouth shut.

"I don't know what the measurements of the closet are, though."

She stood there chewing her bottom lip, reading the information on the box over and over again.

"It's a standard reach-in closet. Eight feet wide, thirty inches deep. It'll work . . . if you really want it."

"I definitely want it. Are you sure, though? I mean, how do you know the closet is standard?"

"I'm a firefighter. We know stuff like that."

She looked at him to see if he was joking. He wasn't; firefighters really did know stuff like that. They practically lived and breathed blueprints. It was not only crucial to know how a building was laid out for fighting a fire but paramount in a rescue situation.

"I'll get a cart," he said.

By the time he returned, she'd dragged the box off the shelf. He hefted it onto the flat cart and they headed to the air-conditioner aisle. They had a couple of different models.

"I suppose you know the size of our windows too?"

"Yep." He chose the ones that said they would cool up to a 250-square-foot room and loaded three onto the cart. "This should do us."

On the way to the cash register a big display of rafts and other water toys caught his eye. Aidan was pretty taken with the River Run, a fancy inner tube that had armrests, a headrest, and compartments to hold his beer. He grabbed one and threw it on the cart. Dana hitched her brows.

"What? You want one too? I'll get it for you." He reached for a second box, but Dana put her hand on his arm.

"No thanks."

Then he remembered about her brother and felt like an imbecile. "Ah, hell, Dana, I'm sorry."

"It's not that," she said. "I just prefer swimming in a pool to floating in the river."

"Okay. You ready to go, then?"

"I am. But I'm paying for my own air conditioner."

"Nah, I've got it covered. It's the least I can do after you did all the heavy lifting on the move."

She started to squabble with him, but he threw his credit card down. After she paid for her closet organizer, they headed to the door. That was when a little boy about three or four emerged from the paint aisle, sobbing his head off.

Aidan scooped him up and asked, "Hey, little guy, what's the matter?"

The kid, now eye level with Aidan, stopped crying and just peered at him. Aidan looked around for a parent but didn't see a soul.

"You lost, fellow?"

The boy didn't say anything, just continued to stare at Aidan like he was an alien. At least the kid didn't talk to strangers.

"I'll search the store," Dana said and started walking up and down the aisles.

A few minutes later, the clerk grunted something and nudged his head at the glass door.

"Ah, Jesus," Aidan muttered, and then quickly shut his mouth. "Is that your mom out there?" He brought the child closer to the window and pointed to a woman standing by a pickup on her cell phone, clearly engrossed in a conversation.

"Mama, Mama!" the boy shrieked.

"Hey, Dana, we found her," Aidan called.

"Where?" She trotted back and followed the direction of his eye roll.

With one hand, he wheeled the cart, and with the other he carried the boy outside. The woman looked up, held the phone to her ear with her shoulder, and waggled her hands to take the child into her arms without even breaking a sentence. As Aidan loaded their purchases into the back of his Expedition, he could still hear her complaining about her boss or whoever she was bitching about.

"Can you believe that?" Dana said as they drove away.

"I wonder if she even noticed he was missing?" He shook his head. His old man would've chewed the woman's head off, but what was the point? There was no changing a person that self-absorbed.

When they got home Aidan took the air-conditioning units into the house. "You see my tools?"

"I put them in the garage," Dana said. "You want me to get them?"

"I'll get 'em." He found the heavy metal box easily enough on one of Tawny's many shelves. Christ, Dana had even organized the garage.

He brought the whole thing into the house and got to work installing the first unit in the living room, securing the brackets to the window's metal frame. Within ten minutes he had the air conditioner up and running.

He stood in front of it, letting the cold air wash over him. "Ah."

Dana laughed. He liked the sound of it. Throaty and genuine. He didn't figure her for a giggler, which was good because he didn't much like gigglers.

"Next," he said, and grabbed the toolbox with one hand and the second box with the other, heading to Dana's room.

She opened the door for him, and again he noticed how neat and perfect everything was. He got the unit installed in no time flat and turned it on. Then he headed to his own room, Dana trailing behind him with the last unit. The truth was, he was fading fast and was gonna need to sleep soon. So of course to spite him, the air conditioner gave him all kinds of problems. After messing with it for what seemed like forever, he finally got the metal screws into the frame, adjusted the height of the unit just right, plugged in the sucker, and let it rip. The cooler blew out a steady stream of cold air. Yep, now he'd sleep well.

"Would you mind terribly carrying in my closet organizer and lending me your tools?" Dana asked.

"I'll do it for you in the morning, Dana, but I've got to sleep now."

"I can do it myself."

Having a sister who would shoot anyone who challenged her self-sufficiency, he knew better than to insist. "Okay. I'll bring it in for you."

He went out to the truck and lugged the large box into her room. Then went back to his room for the toolbox and returned. "There you go."

" 'Night, Aidan. Thanks for the air conditioner." She stood in front of it for a few seconds just like he had. The only difference was, it blew her dress up. He enjoyed watching her frantically pull it back down.

In his room, he quickly stripped and got under the covers. A few minutes later he realized he didn't have curtains, and the late afternoon sun was streaming through his windows. Shit. Tomorrow he'd have to get blackout shades. Given his schedule, he often slept during the daytime. In the meantime, he pulled the blanket over his head and shut his eyes. He slipped off to sleep only to be awakened by a loud crashing and a litany of curses that would've done a dock worker proud.

"Make it go away," he muttered, and prayed that if he stayed under the covers long enough, Dana would give up and stop making noise.

But ten minutes later it sounded like she'd driven an eighteen-wheeler into the wall. "No rest for the weary," he said out loud, threw the blanket off, and put his clothes back on.

When he entered her room, she sat in a pile of parts with her face in her hands. She had changed into yoga pants, and was putting the damn closet organizer in—backward.

"Here, give me that." He took the hammer from her. Apparently, she thought she could beat the organizer into submission. "Get all this stuff out of the way."

The mess was probably sending her into a tizzy. The bed was already piled with clothes, a couple of handbags, and shoes. For a woman who'd lost everything in a fire just days ago, she sure had a lot of crap.

"No, I can do it. You go back to bed."

He fixed her with a look that said *Who can sleep with all this racket?*

When he started dissembling the pieces, she shouted, "What are you doing?"

"You did it wrong."

"No, I didn't. I read the instructions."

"Well, that was your first mistake." He demonstrated how the shelves were on the wrong side.

"Oh," she said, like it was a giant revelation that shelves should face out, not in.

"First you put the tracks in, then you add the rest of this stuff." He looked down at the rods, racks, and shelves that were now strewn across the floor.

"That's not what it said in the directions."

He picked the instructions up, crumpled them into a ball, and tossed them into her white wicker waste basket. For a second he thought her head would explode.

Then he found his drill and deftly screwed the tracks into the wall. For the next hour he built her a closet organizer that rivaled the one on the box, using scraps of lumber he'd found in the garage.

"You want shoe racks down here?" He was trying to use every inch of space.

"That would be great." She sat cross-legged on the floor, handing him tools from time to time.

He trudged back out to the garage to see what he could find, returning with a couple of shelves that already had lips on them. Tawny must've used them for her boots. Aidan attached them to the back of the closet at an angle for easy access. In the process of scrounging, he'd also come across a few spare hooks and screwed them into the only wall space left. Dana could use them to hang belts, scarves, or whatever.

He gathered up his tools and sent Dana after a broom and a dustpan. She took over the cleaning and then he watched as she gleefully hung up her clothes, organizing each piece by color.

"This is even better than my old closet. Thank you, Aidan. Seriously, this is a dream."

He watched some more as she carefully selected which shoes should go where, deliberating over every choice. Honestly, he'd never seen a woman happier in his life. And for some bizarre reason he found it endearing. It must be sleep deprivation, he told himself.

"You think you could let me go to bed now?"

She turned to him and nodded. "I'm sorry. Yes, of course, go sleep. And thank you so much for doing this."

For a second he thought she was going to hug him. But he got the sense that Dana wasn't terribly demonstrative. Maybe if he was a file cabinet or a spice rack she'd really let her emotions flow.

Still, he fell asleep with the image of her lining up her handbags in perfect straight rows and a smile on his lips.

Chapter 6

When Dana woke up the next morning Aidan was still asleep. She crept around the house as quietly as she could, getting ready for a breakfast meeting at the Ponderosa with Pat and Colin. The insurance people were ready to write her a check and she wanted to make sure the money would cover the rebuild.

She knew what homes sold for in the neighborhood, but estimating construction costs was better left to the experts. Hopefully, she'd have enough to build the two-story house Pat and Colin envisioned. Wouldn't that be something?

Afterward, Dana planned to preview a few places for her new client, who she was itching to tell someone about but couldn't. Not after she'd signed the nondisclosure agreement. Dana had explained to the client that as soon as someone in Nugget recognized her, word would get out. She'd understood but didn't want Dana going to the tabloids with financial information and personal details. Clearly she'd already been burned.

And if the tabloids were to be believed, this particular celebrity had financial problems, which made Dana wonder why she was real estate shopping. When she'd asked about her price range, the client had been vague.

"Just show me proprieties that are between twenty and sixty acres with a home," she'd said.

That described more than half the listings in the county. Dana opened her closet and chose a scarf from the new hook Aidan had put in for her. Then she stepped back to admire the orderliness of it all. The neat rows of shelves, the adjustable hanging baskets, and the convenient shoe racks. Aidan had done a remarkable job.

Handy. Good-looking. Nice to small children. As far as she could tell, Aidan McBride was Mr. Perfect.

"What are you looking at?" Speak of the devil. Mr. Perfect stood in her bedroom doorway shirtless, his jeans only halfway buttoned and with a bad case of bedhead. Still, the disheveled look seemed to work for him.

"My closet. You sleep well?"

"Yeah. I would've slept longer but the sun woke me up. Where can I get shades for the windows?"

"Reno. Bed Bath and Beyond. You want directions?"

"I'll find it. Where you off to?" He eyed her suit.

"To meet my contractor and, after, work."

"You have any coffee?"

"It's on my top shelf, right-hand side, in front of the Quaker Oats. Help yourself."

"Thanks. I'll replace it as soon as I go to the store."

"Don't worry about it." She looked at her watch. "I've got to go."

"Have a nice day," he said and headed toward the bathroom. A few seconds later she heard the water running.

She went outside and the hot air hit like a furnace. Only nine and it was already a boiler. Shrugging out of her blazer, she hung it on a hanger in the backseat and cranked up the air conditioner. The one Aidan had installed in her room worked like a dream.

She drove the short distance to the square and found a parking space right in front of the Ponderosa. Pat and Colin were already holding a seat for her. Griffin was eating a big plate of waffles at the bar. She pretended not to see him and headed straight for her party's table. It was immature and horribly unprofessional, considering he was her most important client . . . but he'd dumped her for Lina Shepard. She was entitled.

Pat waved over a server to take her order, pulled out a chair, and graced her with a warm smile. He was a nice man.

"How you make out with the insurance folks?"

"Pretty well, I think." She gave him the figure they had given her and he nodded, pleased.

"We can bring it in for that. Look what Colin drew up for you."

Colin unrolled a set of blueprints on the table and when the server came, he made room for Dana's coffee. They ordered—she just got toast—and Colin proceeded to explain the elevations. She hadn't expected drawings so soon and a tingle of excitement went through her.

"We're hoping to save you the cost of an architect," Pat said. "After you and Colin hash out the plan, we'll get a structural engineer in to make sure it'll work."

"Sounds good," she said, studying Colin's sketches. They were very clear, making it easy for her to visualize the house. "I like them a lot. My only suggestion would be making the upstairs hallway smaller and giving some of that square footage to the second bedroom." It seemed tiny to Dana.

"I can do that," Colin said. "If we could get city approval, I could also give you a wood-burning fireplace in the master bedroom. If not, we could do gas."

"Really? It wouldn't send us over budget?"

Colin looked at Pat, who said, "Nah."

She continued to scan the plans when the food came and paid particular attention to the kitchen. New kitchens added 83 percent of their cost to a home's value. "Could we make the pantry bigger with those pull-out shelves?"

"Yeah, but it'll eat into your breakfast nook."

"Hmm, I see what you mean. Can I take these home and think about them for a few days?"

"Of course you can," Pat said. "But the sooner we get them through city planning, the sooner we can start."

"What's going on with Lucky and Tawny's house?"

"We'll be doing the punch-out in a few weeks." Pat put his napkin in his lap and started digging into his omelet.

"Wow. So I'm going to get a totally new home?"

"Yep." Colin grinned and, like Pat, began eating his breakfast.

For the next half hour they talked about finishes, flooring, and appliances. By the time Dana made her way across the restaurant to the door, her head was swirling with color schemes, flooring materials, and window treatments. That was when a hand reached out and tugged her over to the bar.

"Those the plans for your rebuild?" Griffin asked and sipped his cup of coffee.

"Oh, hey, Griffin, I didn't see you sitting there. They are."

"I saw you, Colin, and Pat looking at 'em. What do you think?"

"I love what I've seen so far. They think they can double the square footage of my old house."

"That's great." He sat there for a couple of minutes, looking as gorgeous as he always did. "You know I would make you a deal on any house you wanted in Sierra Heights, right?"

"It's very generous of you, but I like where I live," which was just far enough away from him to give her peace of mind.

"How's it working out with Aidan? Grace told me you two were in the hardware store yesterday."

Jeez, what was it, national news? "We needed some stuff for Tawny's house."

"So it's going okay?"

"Couldn't be better." *In fact, we have Tantric sex every night.*

"I'm glad. He's a good guy."

The gall, Dana thought. She could read Griffin like a book and he was actually hoping she and Aidan were in the beginning stages of a love connection, which they weren't. Not even close. Couldn't Griffin at least have the decency to show a modicum of jealousy? He couldn't because he wasn't. He had Lina.

"Yes, he is." She looked at her watch. "I've got an appointment."

"Yeah? A hot buyer for one of my houses?"

"Not this time, I'm afraid, but I really need to run."

"Hold up a sec." He pulled a few bills out of his wallet, laid them on the bar, and followed her outside. "Dana, are we okay?"

"Of course." She was probably smiling a little too brightly, but he'd caught her off guard. "Why wouldn't we be?" God, could she be any phonier?

"It just seems like you're avoiding me these days."

"No. I've just got a lot on my mind with the house and all."

"I get that, but even before the fire you seemed a little distant."

She blew out a breath. "Honestly, I get the impression Lina isn't too thrilled about me. I didn't want to do anything that made the situation uncomfortable for the two of you, especially given our work situation." Which was completely true. The other part was that it hurt too badly.

"You and I are friends, Dana. I hope good friends. No one, not even Lina, is going to change that."

It was a nice thought in theory, she supposed. "I hope so."

"It's the way it is." He stood there, more than likely hoping she would assure him how great it had been to be dumped for someone else. "I know, you've gotta run. But we're good, right?"

"We're fine." She tried for that bright smile again but somehow couldn't quite recapture it. Instead, she started to back up, and that was when she slammed into something hard.

Griffin bobbed his head in greeting to whoever was behind her and trotted off. Unfortunately, she knew who the hard body was even before she turned around.

"What was that about?" Aidan asked, close enough to her ear that it tickled.

"Nothing," she said and faced him. "What brings you to the Ponderosa?"

"Breakfast. You eat yet?"

"Yes. I was just leaving."

He wrapped an arm around her like a guy would do to steady his drunken buddy. "You okay? It appeared you two were having a difficult conversation."

"Never been better. Not difficult, just weird."

He studied her like he was trying to get a read on whether she was upset and settled for "Whaddya got there?"

She followed his eyes to the cardboard tube tucked at her side. "My blueprints. Colin drew them up. I'm planning to fine-tune them over the next couple of days."

Wearing a smug smile, he said, "I'll help you. I'm good with house plans. Wanna come sit with me while I eat?"

"I have to get to work," she said but had to admit she was tempted. He was a charmer and, for some inexplicable reason, made her feel good. She suspected he had that effect on the entire female population. He possessed an innate ability to zoom in on a person as if she were the only one in the room . . . or the world, for that matter. "Appointments."

He shrugged, as if to say *suit yourself.* "See you later."

In the office, Dana found Carol taping the new listings to the window and glanced at them to see if there was anything she'd missed. Nope, she knew them all.

"How did the meeting go?"

"Really good. Colin drew up plans."

"Already? That's amazing. You're in good hands with those guys. When you're ready, Vance will do your landscaping."

"Maybe if you-know-who buys something, and my commission is big enough, I could put in a pool."

Carol laughed. "You don't want a pool. Believe me, they're more trouble than they're worth."

But Dana sort of did and, while she was at it, a pool boy who looked like Aidan. Funny that she didn't want him to look like Griffin.

Through the plate-glass window she saw Harlee drive up. Uh-oh; Dana hoped the reporter hadn't caught wind of their secret client. The buyer wasn't even due in until tomorrow afternoon. Dana had gotten her a room at the Lumber Baron, where she planned to stay in disguise so no one could identify her. Dana thought it was crazy. What a way to live.

"Hi." Harlee breezed into the office in a cute cotton tank dress. Dana wished she had the nerve to wear the trendy kind of stuff Harlee looked so fashionable in. "I was in the neighborhood and thought I'd pick up next week's listings."

"Good timing," Carol said. "I just finished typing them up. Let me print them out."

"Perfect." Harlee walked over to Dana's desk. "How are you doing? I heard you met with my husband today about your rebuild."

Dana didn't know Harlee well, but she was married to Colin. Once or twice Dana and Griffin had socialized with the other couple, as well as Harlee's best friend Darla and her boyfriend, Wyatt, who was a Nugget police officer. They were all about the same age, early thirties—a rare species in Nugget. But Harlee, a reporter and the owner of the *Nugget Tribune*, was much more outgoing than Dana.

"We did," she said. "He drew up beautiful plans. How are you?"

"I'm good, but then again, a fire didn't burn down my house. Colin and Pat will take good care of you."

"They've been great throughout this entire process," she said. "I'm very appreciative."

If Dana had to pay an architect, it would eat up a big chunk of her construction money, and Colin had a fantastic eye. He'd designed his and Harlee's home and he made stunning furniture carried in stores throughout California.

"We look out for one another in this town." Harlee glanced at Dana's suit. "I know Grace put together a package for you, but if you need more clothes I have tons of outfits I never wear any more . . . things left over from my big-city reporting days. You're welcome to come over to raid my closet. I think we're about the same size."

Dana blinked. It was such a generous offer. "Thank you. I might just do that." She wouldn't but was really quite staggered that Harlee had made the gesture.

Carol joined them and handed Harlee the printouts. "There are a couple of brand-new listings in there."

"Great. More than half of my out-of-town readers subscribe for these." Harlee waved the stack of sheets in the air. "So keep them coming."

Carol laughed. "Hey, it's working great for us too. Sales have never been better."

"I'd better get going." Harlee headed for the door and called over her shoulder to Dana, "Call me when you want to come over."

"Will do." After Harlee left, Dana turned to Carol. "That was really nice of her."

"Harlee is a nice person and Darla is a doll. I always wondered why you weren't more friendly with those girls."

"I guess I'm more of a homebody." What she was, was shy.

After Paul died, she'd retreated into herself. It was easier than making up excuses to her friends about her zombie parents. In college, she'd put all her energy into her studies. Now, she supposed, she did it with real estate.

"I'm taking off to preview some properties before tomorrow." Dana grabbed her purse and a folder containing the information about the places she wanted to check out.

"Do you plan to bring Ms. Confidentiality to the office?"

"I'll have to play it by ear. But if she wants to make an offer"— Dana crossed her fingers—"we'll have to come back here."

"Good luck and call me if you need any help."

"I will," Dana said. "Thanks, Carol."

She got in her car and headed for the backroads, where most of the properties were. Some of the parcels had been for sale a long time, and Dana wanted to reacquaint herself with them. Others, especially the real remote ones, she'd never had reason to view before.

But Ms. Confidentiality had made it clear she wanted off the beaten track. Dana assumed she needed a refuge from being a celebrity and her recent scandal.

Just as she pulled up to the first place, her cell phone rang. It was the client, with a change of plans.

After breakfast Aidan went to Reno. Except for the airport, he hadn't seen much of the town but knew it was called the "Biggest Little City in the World." He could kind of see why. It had just about everything, and legal gambling to boot. At some point he'd like to come back to check out the nightlife. For now, though, he just wanted to get his blackout shades, hit Costco, and get back to Nugget.

He found the Bed Bath & Beyond easily enough. Dana seemed to think they would have what he was looking for. Not for the first time, he wondered about the little scene he had witnessed between Dana and Griffin that morning. "Scene" was probably too strong a word for it. But there was something going on there. He could tell from Dana's body language. She'd been upset, yet had tried to put on a brave face. Aidan noticed she did that sometimes. With the fire, when he'd gotten to Tawny's house first, and then this morning with Griffin.

She was an odd little duck, that was for sure. He'd never seen someone get so hung up on trivial details. *Who's going to take out the trash? How should we sort the recyclables? Toilet seat up or down?* He was still waiting for the bathroom schedule. Despite it, he found her highly entertaining and incredibly self-sufficient. And it certainly didn't hurt that she was easy on the eyes.

Inside the store, he found the drapery aisle, and sure enough, they had exactly what he was looking for. He loaded a few shades into a cart and paid at the cash register. An hour later, he hit the highway back to Nugget, his truck filled with groceries. The scenery changed every few miles or so, from high desert to green forest. From his first visit, he'd felt an affinity for the land, so different from his native Midwest. His family was convinced he'd come to lick his wounds after the debacle with Sue. But for a long time he'd been thinking about change, about uprooting himself from a life that had become too predictable and staid.

At home, he put everything away and installed his shades, pulling them up and down to make sure they worked right. Closed, they co-cooned the room in restful darkness. Yeah, he thought to himself, the place was definitely coming together.

After lunch he decided to get the remainder of his stuff from Sloane and Brady's, making the quick drive across town. His sister was home, sitting in the living room, reading a wedding magazine, when he got there.

"You all moved in?" She got up from the couch and began waving her hand in front of his face.

"What the hell is the matter with you?"

"Nothing." Again with the crazy hand movements.

"Don't you have to work?" he asked.

"I'm graveyard tonight. Should I wear this?" She stuck her knuckle under his nose, and that was when he saw it. The ring.

Aidan let out a low whistle. "How much that set Brady back?"

"A lot. But I'm worth it."

He grabbed her ring hand and dragged her to the French doors. "Let's see if it'll cut glass."

"Unhand me, you freak."

"Congratulations." He kissed her on the forehead. "I'm the best man, you know? Other than getting the rock, how was Frisco?"

"If people around here ever heard you calling it Frisco, they'd gut you." She plopped back down on the couch. "Frisco was fan-freaking-tastic. We stayed at the Theodore in the penthouse suite. Brady got his work done early so we could play. I loved it so much I was even considering having the wedding at the hotel. But now Brady and I are thinking we'll have it here, in Sierra Heights. Set up tables and a dance floor over the pool, string up twinkly lights, and open the rec room to the outside. What do you think?"

"Sounds good to me. You pick a date?"

"We're playing around with September. It's a good month in California . . . warm and clear. We just have to make sure it's okay with the other residents."

He mussed her hair like he used to do when she was just a pip-squeak. "Let me know and I'll get my tux out of storage."

"Hey, Aidan?" She tugged him to the couch and pulled him down. "Are you okay with this weekend . . . with Sue getting married?"

"There's not a whole lot I can do about it." She gave him a pointed look. "What?"

"It doesn't seem like you tried."

"Of course I tried," he said. "I asked her to come back, didn't I?"

"Did you go to her apartment and serenade her, get down on bended knee and beg? You didn't even fight for her, Aidan. You got in your truck and moved to California. And I have to wonder why."

"You ever think that maybe I wasn't the one for her? We were together three years. She dates this guy all of six months and they're walking down the aisle."

"Brady and I only knew each other for three months. Before us, he was like you, allergic to marriage. So maybe it's not marriage you're averse to; maybe she just wasn't the one for you, because I know you were the one for her. She loved you, Aidan. All she wanted was to be your wife and the mother of your children. But a woman can't wait forever."

He didn't want to talk about this anymore. "I've gotta go."

"Of course you do. You're the king of avoidance." Sloane shook her head. "Want to come over Saturday, use the pool and have dinner with us? We'll barbecue."

"Yeah, maybe. I'll let you know."

"If you don't want to talk about it, we won't talk about it. But don't be alone, Aidan."

He went inside the guest room, gathered up his stuff, and grabbed his toiletries from the bathroom.

"I'm taking off," he said and gave Sloane a hug. "Nice ring."

Dana came home to find seven kids in her driveway, eating Otter Pops, while Aidan blew up their inner tubes with an electric air pump.

"Hey." He bobbed his head at her.

"Going to the river?"

"Yep. Want to come?"

"No thanks." It had been a hell of a day and all she wanted to do was soak in the tub with a glass of wine. Besides, it seemed a little late for the river. In an hour it would be dark. "Be careful."

"I always am." He tossed one of the kids the last tube and they followed him like the Pied Piper down the street, sucking on their ices.

He'd only been here a couple of days and was already making friends with the neighborhood children. To satisfy her curiosity, she went inside, opened the freezer and, as suspected, it was filled with Otter Pops. She was living with a twelve-year-old. She found a bottle of chardonnay in the refrigerator, uncorked it, and poured a glass. Taking it into the bedroom, she quickly stripped and slipped into a robe. She wanted to get in the tub before Aidan got home. No more hallway nudity.

As the bath filled, Dana took a few sips of wine, tested the water, and got in, resting her glass on the edge of the tub for easy access. Ms. Confidentiality had surprised her by coming in a day early. Apparently, she needed to get out of New York before another sordid story broke about her. Dana wasn't clear on all the details, only that her client's boyfriend was wanted by the feds and she planned to hide out at the Lumber Baron.

She wanted to start touring properties first thing in the morning. Clearly she hoped to hole up here until the media unearthed a new scandal about someone else. It was a shame she'd been mired in her boyfriend's controversy because Dana found her show and books to be inspiring. Women all over the country did.

Dana soaked until her skin started to wrinkle, then got out and put on a pair of drawstring shorts and a cotton T-shirt. On her bed, she unrolled Colin's plans and took the time to study them, trying to visualize the floor plan. She heard the front door open and close and, a short time later, the shower go on. And as much as she tried to concentrate on the blueprints, she kept seeing Aidan's broad, naked chest from the other day. The towel wrapped around his narrow waist, barely concealing his butt. And those long, strong legs . . .

She got up and turned the air conditioner on. At the sound of the water stopping, she opened her door a crack, got her wineglass, and started for the kitchen just as Aidan came down the hall wearing nothing but that towel again. Little droplets of water glistened in his chest hair and Dana had to force her eyes up to keep from staring.

"You hungry?" he asked as they passed.

"I don't eat after six."

"Well, I'm making pasta if you want some." He disappeared inside his bedroom before she could respond.

Who ate pasta at eight at night? She poured herself another glass of wine and got the coffeemaker set up for the morning. She was scheduled to pick up her client at nine.

Aidan came in wearing a pair of low-slung cargo shorts and a T-shirt that stretched over his mile-wide chest. "You sell any houses?"

"Not today. But maybe tomorrow."

His brows winged up. "Yeah? In Sierra Heights?"

"No. This particular client wants horse property." The description seemed vague enough that Dana didn't think she was violating the confidentiality agreement.

"A lot of acreage?" He got a pot out, filled it with water, and put it on the stovetop to boil. "I need to get in there." Grasping her around the waist, he shifted her away from the pantry.

His hands were big and they seemed to linger. Although that could've been Dana's imagination, because she liked the way they felt on her. Strong and firm, but at the same time gentle.

"She hasn't been too good at communicating about what she wants; just that she'll know it when she sees it."

"That's gotta make your job more difficult," he said, and tore open a bag of spaghetti.

"A little bit. A lot of times people just don't know what they're looking for. I like the role of narrowing it down for them. We'll probably drive around to a number of different places until something clicks. Sometimes this job requires mind reading and a psychology background. What did you do today?"

"Got my shades, got groceries, went to my sister's house and got the rest of my stuff."

"How was the river?"

"Good. The kids said the water is usually deeper. I figure it's low on account of the drought." He poured half the contents of the spaghetti package into the boiling water.

She watched as he started the sauce in a second pan, dicing tomatoes and crushing fresh garlic. He seemed to know what he was doing. Good at multitasking, he began setting the table for two. She didn't stop him because everything smelled so good. It wouldn't kill her to have just a taste, Dana told herself.

"Where did you learn to cook?"

"Firehouse. Everyone has to take turns." He grabbed her bottle of wine and poured some into his sauce.

"Is there anything you're not good at? Cooking, building closets, putting out fires, blowing up kids' inner tubes . . ."

He laughed, then grew somber. "I've got some stuff I'm not good at."

"Like what?" She sat at the small kitchen table and continued to watch him cook.

"You go first." Aidan pulled a strand of pasta out of the pot to test it.

"Of things I'm not good at? It's a long list. The only thing I'm really good at is selling real estate."

"Nah," he said. "You're good at organization and at putting a house together." He pointed at the stenciled rooster on the wall to prove his point.

She shrugged. "I learned some staging tricks, is all. I'm certainly no interior designer."

"You've got a good eye for color. I like what you did with the paint in the living room."

Aidan strained the pasta, grabbed two plates out of the cupboard, dished up both servings, which he topped with the sauce, and told her to eat up. She twisted a few strands around her fork and took a bite.

"Mmm, it's good."

He nodded. "So what's the deal with you and Griffin?"

Dana nearly choked on her food. "There's no deal with us, other than he's my client."

"Brady said you two used to date. I certainly got that impression this morning."

She waved him off. "That was a while ago. He's with Lina now." Grabbing the chardonnay off the counter, she poured herself another glass. "You want some?"

He got up and pulled a goblet out of the cabinet so she could pour him the rest of the bottle.

"You're just friends now?"

"Yes, and like I said, we do business together." Dana took another bite of her spaghetti.

"Is that what you were talking about this morning? Because it seemed sort of intense, like he might've upset you."

"He just wanted to know if I was avoiding him." She didn't know why she was telling Aidan this. It wasn't like it was any of his business. But she didn't have anyone else to talk to.

"Are you?"

"A little." Okay, a lot. "It's been difficult ... with Lina. She doesn't like me."

"Jealous?"

"Yeah, as if she has anything to be jealous about. She's beautiful, tiny, and Griff's totally in love with her . . . and was the entire time we dated."

Aidan got up to get more spaghetti and sat back down. "Why do women always compare themselves to one another? Maybe she thinks those same things about you and feels threatened."

"She knows Griffin is crazy about her. He stopped dating me because he was hung up on her."

"But you're still stuck on him?"

"Nope," she said, and pushed her plate away, stuffed. "I'm off men for the foreseeable future."

Aidan raised his brows. "Sex too?"

She shook her head. "I can't believe I'm having this conversation with you. What about you? Why did you and your girlfriend break up?"

"She fell for her coworker. They're getting married Saturday."

That was a bit of a bombshell. "As in tomorrow?" What woman in her right mind would leave Aidan McBride for a coworker? Look at him: a perfect specimen of a man who not only cooked but made shoe racks.

"Yeah," he responded, and twisted the last of his spaghetti onto his fork.

"Ah, Aidan, I'm so sorry."

He hitched his shoulders. "Let's look at your blueprints after dinner."

Okay, she could take a hint. He wanted a subject change. Fine. "Sure."

Dana got up and took her plate to the sink, washed it, and put it in the drying rack. She started to clean up the kitchen and rummaged through the cabinet, where she found containers to put away the leftovers.

"I miss my Tupperware," she said, eyeing Aidan's generic stuff with trepidation.

"I bet you do. You probably had one in every size and color coded. Red for meat and green for vegetables."

"I did not." But she laughed.

"I'll finish here; go get the plans," he told her.

He spent an hour telling her all the places she should put smoke alarms and sprinklers.

"I've got to get to bed, Aidan." She yawned, rolled up the blueprints, and neatly tucked them back into the tube. "I'm meeting that client early." And she had to be sharp.

"Good luck with that."

"Thanks." She started for the bedroom and stopped. "You want to do something Saturday? You know, to keep your mind off the wedding."

"I'm going to my sister's for a barbecue."

"Oh . . . that's good."

"Wanna come?"

"Nah, it's a family thing."

"No it's not. It's dinner, and Brady's cooking. You should take advantage of that."

"Maybe," she said, knowing she wouldn't go. Dana hardly knew Sloane and Brady. "Let's see how it goes with my client."

"Your call," he said, and went back to cleaning up the kitchen.

Chapter 7

Gia couldn't sleep, got up to find the remote control, and flicked on the television. She'd promised herself she wouldn't do this. Wouldn't torture herself by watching the late-night entertainment shows, where she was the butt of every joke.

The financial self-help guru whose boyfriend had organized one of the largest Ponzi schemes in recent history was hilarious.

Schadenfreude, she supposed. The snark on social media had gotten so bad that the network was on the verge of shutting down her show. Gia couldn't blame television executives. How could she tell millions of women how to attain financial independence when she herself had been duped by a money swindler and a con artist? For that reason, her syndicated column had already gotten the boot and her latest book could only be found in the remainder bin.

She suddenly felt a tremendous affinity for Martha Stewart. At least insider trading had no bearing on whether Martha could bake a cake. But getting rooked by a third-rate investment banker—who happened to be the man she'd loved and trusted—didn't speak well for her financial acumen. Or her taste in men. Not only had he stolen her money, he'd stolen her livelihood.

Thank goodness she still had plenty of assets left, including her Fifth Avenue penthouse, which was worth a pretty penny. Unfortunately, not everyone could say the same. Evan Laughlin had left a lot of people in complete financial ruin. And while Gia was solvent—at least for the moment—she knew all too well what poverty felt like.

That was the whole reason for her plan . . . moving to Nugget. She still had the means to make it happen, but her reputation was in tatters. So she'd have to improvise . . . buy the house and land . . . bring her horse . . . lay low until the scandal blew over.

Even if she lost the seven-figure-a-year TV contract, the lucrative speaking engagements, and the hefty advances for her self-help books, she'd figure out a way to manage. Like before, she'd do it the old-fashioned way—making sound investments. And nothing could be sounder than California real estate. Given the drought and the economy, there were fire sales on agricultural land all over the state. "Buy low and sell high" wasn't just the mantra for trading stocks, Gia told herself.

Based on her drive from Reno to Nugget, she'd liked what she'd seen. Tremendous views of the Sierra Nevada and its endless bounty of rivers, lakes, forests, and desert. It was the way she remembered it from all those years ago. The last vacation before her Dad had suffered a massive heart attack and died. The town, which consisted primarily of a commercial district built around a verdant square, and the obligatory Main Street, wasn't as charming as other towns she'd seen in Northern California. Still, according to what she'd read, it attracted some degree of the state's booming tourism trade and was close enough to more popular destinations to get their spill-offs.

Yet, because of its general remoteness and its frigid winter temperatures, land here was cheaper than in the rest of the state. Gia didn't think that would last too much longer and she wanted to get in before prices spiked. All part of her long-term plan.

In the meantime, this inn was lovely and luxurious—something you would find in a big city—and a good place to take a few days to rest and regather her wits. She'd stayed sheltered in her room since she'd gotten here, fearful that even with a scarf wrapped around her head and sunglasses to cover her face, people would still recognize her. Even the little online paper here had carried Gia's column with her picture on it. For that reason, she hadn't been able to check out either one of the town's two restaurants or any of the shops. Tomorrow, she told herself. The fact was, she couldn't hide forever.

She got out her laptop to see how the Nikkei 225 Index had closed, tried to ignore her emails but couldn't. There were at least five from reporters who wanted to interview her, three from her agent, who probably wanted to let her know whether her show had been canceled, and two from her mother, who she hadn't had time to call back.

Just wanted to make sure you arrived safely, the message read.

The one thing Gia would truly miss was being on the same coast as her mom, who lived in a retirement community in Boca Raton. Gia had paid cash for her mother's house, taken care of the association fees, and funded whatever incidentals Iris couldn't afford. They'd been through hell and back together. And Gia had made sure her mother would never want for anything ever again. At least Evan, the son of a bitch, hadn't connived Iris into investing in his bogus scheme. Ironically, Gia's mother was almost childlike in her grasp of high finance, making her an easy mark. But she'd been smarter—perhaps less greedy was more accurate—than any of Evan's dupes, keeping her life's savings in low-risk government bonds.

Gia looked at the clock. If she didn't get to sleep soon, she'd be dead on her feet while Dana toured her around the town. Before crawling back under the covers, she shut down her computer and flicked off the television.

Tomorrow would be the first day of her new life, she told herself, and nearly gagged at the cliché sentiment. But there was something to be said for starting over. Gia had been stuck in overdrive for so long, she hadn't had any adventures. Her biggest challenge had been juggling too many commitments. Here, she could focus on what she really loved: her horse, the great outdoors, and helping women achieve financial liberation. Only in this case, that woman would now have to be her.

Gia had on a big floppy hat, a scarf, and oversized sunglasses when Dana picked her up at the Lumber Baron. Dana thought she looked ridiculous and, in a place like Nugget, was only calling more attention to herself. If Gia wanted to avoid being recognized, she'd put a big bulls-eye on her head. But Dana didn't have the heart to say anything.

"I printed out a list of the places I'll be showing you today." Dana handed Gia an accordion file. "In there you'll find information on each property, including prices. We're not looking at anything under twenty acres and nothing over eighty. But if you change your mind, I have a few smaller parcels we could get into today. And the homes in Sierra Heights, the planned community I told you about, are all on lockbox."

"No, I'm not interested in a development." Gia studied the list. "These have potential, though. I'm particularly excited about this sixty-acre hay farm."

"We'll go there first, then." It was on the way to three other properties Dana planned to show her. "Just remember, the houses on some of these parcels are little more than mobile homes."

Dana wanted her to be fully prepared. She got the impression Gia was expecting lush paddocks, fancy stables, and manor homes. Most of these places were strewn with farm equipment parts and outbuildings that had seen better days. The owners or foremen lived in modular or modest ranch houses.

She pulled off on Tank Farm Lane and maneuvered her Outback over the rutted dirt road. "In winter this'll be a nightmare in the snow. I would suggest paving it. But that could take a big chunk of change."

Gia took off her hat and glasses and tossed them into the backseat. Dana thought she was actually more attractive in real life than on television. Peaches and cream skin any woman would kill for, light blue eyes, and sandy blond hair.

"It's sure dusty," she said.

Dana turned on her sprayer and windshield wipers and continued up the road until she came to a white stucco house. As she pulled into the driveway, two dogs circled the car, barking. Jasper came out of the house, holding a cup of coffee and calling to the dogs.

"He said he would make himself scarce for the showing," Dana said, disappointed. Buyers in general didn't like looking with owners hovering. Gia, of course, had her own set of reasons. "Let me go talk to him, see if he's headed out."

"Morning, Jasper." She walked toward him.

"Sorry about the dogs, Dana. I'll lock 'em up in the garage. I gassed up the ATV if you want to take your client out to show her the property lines. You could also take the fire trail with your car, whatever is easier. The door's unlocked." He nudged his head at the house. "I'm going into town. Give me a ring if you need anything."

"Thanks, Jasper. I'll call you later if there's any news." The man desperately wanted to sell the place so he and his wife could retire near their daughter in Sacramento.

"I'd appreciate that." He tipped his hat, got in his truck, and drove away.

Dana went back to the car. "Coast is clear."

Gia got out. At least she'd worn jeans and tennis shoes.

"I thought we'd look at the house first and then I'd show you around the property."

Gia didn't say anything, just shielded her eyes from the sun and looked around. Together, they went inside the house.

"It's a three-bedroom, two-bath," Dana said. The place was tidy, but to someone of Gia Treadwell's stature, it probably looked like a box. "It's got central heating and there may be hardwood floors under the carpet."

Gia walked into the kitchen. "It's bright."

And dated, Dana thought. Unexpectedly, Gia didn't turn her nose up at it. She explored the bedrooms, peeking inside the closets, then took a look at the bathrooms.

"Let's look at the property," Gia said.

For the next forty minutes, Dana drove her around the land in the Outback. What they couldn't see from the car, they viewed by walking. When they left to go tour another property, Gia didn't say much. It was the same with the next two places. She took her time examining every nook and cranny but maintained a poker face throughout the morning. Dana could read Braille easier than she could read Gia.

"Look," Dana said, "I don't want to seem pushy, but it would help both of us if I knew what you liked and what you didn't like . . . and what's out of your price range."

Gia let out a sigh. "The truth: I didn't really like any of them, but I don't want you to think I'm a prima donna."

"I don't at all. Usually my clients don't like ninety-five percent of what they see. My job is to hone in on that five percent. But I can't do that if I don't know what you're thinking. So don't hesitate to tell me, 'Dana, this place won't work for me.' Buying a home takes time."

"That's the thing, Dana, I don't have time. I'm about to lose my show and the last thing I want to do is be in New York when it all crumbles."

Dana looked at her agog. "How do you know they'll cancel you? Don't these types of things run their course? Won't they just wait until there's another big scandal?"

Gia played with a loose thread on her shirt. "My boyfriend . . . now ex-boyfriend . . . bilked thousands of people out of their life's savings, college funds, and retirement money. . . . Some had to sell their homes just to scrape by so he could sit on a tropical beach somewhere, drinking Mai Tais with their hard-earned money. These poor victims want blood. Preferably his blood. But they'll take mine in a pinch."

"But the FBI cleared you," Dana said. "You were a victim too."

"Most people don't believe that, and even if they did, they don't want to see me recouping my losses by preaching financial gospel . . . telling people on national TV how to avoid predators and scammers. They don't want to see me living in a four-million-dollar Manhattan penthouse while they've been forced to file bankruptcy." Gia took a deep breath and gazed out onto the horizon.

"I'm sorry. This can't be easy."

Gia lifted her shoulders. "It is what is. What's next on the tour?"

"Ordinarily, at this point in the program, I would take you to lunch and we'd go over the pros and cons of what we'd already seen so I could get a better idea of what to show you next."

"I am hungry," Gia said. "But how likely is it that people won't recognize me?"

"I could drive us through the Bun Boy and get food to go. Not the most elegant lunch, but in the car people would be less likely to recognize you. You do realize, however, that it's just a matter of time?"

"I just don't want the tabloids to know I'm here to buy property. I can see the headlines now: 'Evan Laughlin's victims go bankrupt, Gia Treadwell goes shopping.'"

Dana had to admit it wouldn't look good. "As long as you don't mind eating takeout. We could find a nice spot to have a picnic."

"Sounds good to me."

They drove back to town, and Dana joined the line of cars waiting to give their order at the drive-through.

"Funny place," Gia said, glancing out the window at the lawn, where wooden tables and benches were jammed with diners. "It seems to do a great business."

"Even in winter," Dana said. "There's no seating inside, so people either take the food home or eat inside their cars."

When they finally got to the speaker, Dana asked for two cheeseburgers with sides of curly fries and vanilla shakes.

"I haven't been this decadent in years." Gia ducked down a little so no one at the window could make her out. "Pretty soon I won't have to worry about the camera adding ten pounds."

"Even if you gained ten pounds you'd still look thin," Dana said. Unexpectedly, she felt quite comfortable with Gia. Her client was turning out to be much more likable than she would've expected for a celebrity.

Dana glanced at her watch. "We have an hour before our next appointment. On the way, there's a good spot near the river where we can eat."

Nosing the car out of the square, she headed to the highway, knowing the area she had in mind would be quiet. Dana turned off on a paved road and instead of turning right to Lucky Rodriguez's cowboy camp, she made a sharp left and then a right. Ten minutes later, she parked in a dirt turnout.

"We just have to hike down a few feet to the river. If I remember correctly, there's a picnic table there."

Gia got out of the car, stretched her legs, and took in the view. Dana grabbed their lunches and motioned for Gia to follow her. Just as she'd remembered, there was a weathered old table and two benches perched on a knoll above the water. She grabbed a couple of napkins from the sacks of burgers and wiped it down.

"This work?"

"It's lovely. Is this the Feather River?"

"It is. Usually, there's more water from the snow runoff from the mountains. But we didn't have much snow this winter." Dana handed Gia her food, and both women started eating.

"My God, this is good," Gia said with a mouth full of burger.

"The Ponderosa's food is delicious too. When you're ready to come out in public, I'll take you there for dinner."

Gia nodded. "I'd like that. So is this a park or something?"

"No, this is Rosser Ranch. Ordinarily, Ray Rosser would shoot us for trespassing, but he's in jail."

Gia laughed. "You're kidding, right?"

"Nope. He killed a cattle rustler and is facing murder charges."

"You've got to be making this up."

"I swear on my real estate license. When we get back, you can read all about it in the *Nugget Tribune*."

"Did he kill the rustler here?"

Dana shook her head. "Did you see the ranch we passed, the one with the big sign that said, 'Lucky Rodriguez's Cowboy Camp'? It happened there. But it was an anomaly. Nugget is about as safe as you can get." Dana didn't want Gia thinking the town was a hotbed of crime.

Gia got up, walked down the trail to rinse her hands in the river, and stared out at the endless pastures and the mountains beyond. "It's a spectacular place. Are those his cattle?"

"Ray had to sell his herd to help pay for his defense. The land's leased to another rancher who runs his cattle here, at least until Ray sells the ranch."

"It's for sale?"

When Dana nodded, Gia asked, "Can we make an appointment to look at it . . . officially?"

"Yes, I'm the listing agent. But Gia, it's over a thousand acres, and the asking price is more than your four-million-dollar Manhattan penthouse."

Gia's eyes grew large. "How much more?"

"Close to eleven." Dana knew that number was negotiable. If Ray's defense lawyers didn't get paid soon, they'd turn his case over to the public defender or a court-appointed attorney and Ray wanted the dream team. But as the listing agent, it would be unethical for her to tell Gia how desperate the seller was. "It's one of the largest and oldest cattle ranches in Northern California. The only one in the county larger is Clay McCreedy's spread, which butts up to this property."

"Still," Gia said. "Eleven million seems rather exorbitant."

"If you saw what kind of prime real estate we're talking about here you'd understand why." That was the truth, not Dana doing a sales job.

"Okay, show me."

"Let's go. It'll give me an opportunity to finally see what you do and don't like." Dana laughed because there was nothing not to like about the Rosser Ranch. "Let's drive up to the house and then I'll take you through some of the stables."

"I'm good to go." Gia scrunched up her trash, packed it in one of the burger sacks, and carried it back to the car with her.

When they pulled through the cobblestone circular driveway in front of the house, Gia's mouth fell open.

"This is what I'm talking about," Dana said. "It's eight bedrooms, all with en-suite baths, a billiards room, a wine cellar, a solarium, and a gourmet kitchen. There are guest quarters over the five-car garage, bunkhouses for the staff near the stables."

Gia unbuckled her seat belt and was out of the car before Dana could say more. She liked this enthusiastic side of Gia much more than the poker-faced Gia. Punching in the code to the lockbox, a key dropped out and Dana opened the door. Mrs. Rosser was in Colorado with her daughter, Raylene, indefinitely, so the house was vacant.

"The furnishings are included in the price," Dana said. "Or you could negotiate to buy the place without them."

Gia wandered through the grand foyer into the great room. "A lot of animal heads. Not really my thing."

"Ray is a big-game hunter."

"Yeah, apparently human too," Gia said, and Dana quickly covered her mouth to keep from laughing. "Regardless of the heads, the place is stunning."

Over the next hour they went from room to room. The property was too big to see all of it by car, but Dana showed Gia the pool and cabana, the stables, the barns, the horse paddocks, and the lily pond. The more Gia saw, the more her eyes lit up.

"Is the land dividable?" she asked.

"It's a little complicated. Based on the trust written up by Ray's grandfather, no Rosser can subdivide the property. It was his way of keeping his heirs from developing the land or fighting over pieces of it after he died. However, it's zoned agricultural, with a forty-acre minimum."

"I don't get it."

"It means that if you bought the land, you could divide it. However, it would be difficult, if not impossible, to turn the land into a housing division or a shopping center."

"But I can use it for commercial use as long as the use is somehow agricultural?"

"For the most part. It doesn't necessarily mean you could put a processing plant on the property, or a slaughterhouse. But some of these ranches—Lucky's, for example—goes under the header of agritourism, which means any kind of tourism that promotes agriculture."

Gia nodded, taking it all in. "You said someone is leasing the land for his cattle. If I owned the property, could I still lease it out while I lived here, and how much does a lease like that go for?"

"You absolutely can do that. I'd have to check how much the current rancher is paying, but the price fluctuates based on demand and the beef market. Right now the demand for grazing land is high because of the drought. But the lease is only for the spring, summer, and early fall. When it starts getting cold, the cattle will be moved to warmer climates."

"Wow," Gia said. "You know your stuff, don't you?"

"I try."

"I want it." Gia gazed out over the land. "But not for eleven mil. That seems too high."

"You have nothing to lose by making an offer." That was all Dana could really say, adding, "I can give you comps as far as dollar per acre, but not all land is created equal. This has plenty of water, an amazing house, and you're right on the river."

"How motivated is the seller?"

"He's sitting in a jail cell right now, fighting a first-degree murder charge." Dana could at least say that since it was part of the public record. It was up to Gia to read between the lines. "But if Ray entertains offers that are much lower than the asking price, you'll have some competition. Both neighbors, Clay McCreedy and Lucky Rodriguez, have shown interest in the property."

"Just not at that price," Gia said.

Dana nodded. "As your agent, I want to give you the best advice I can. But I'm also the seller's agent, which ties my hands somewhat. I would completely understand if you want to make an offer through another agency."

Gia deliberated a few minutes. "Nope, I want to go through you. You're knowledgeable, and I get the sense you're ethical, which, given what I've been through, is a breath of fresh air. How tapped in are these neighbors to negotiations? You're not representing them too?"

"No. It's all been informal. Ray and Clay are friends, so they talk, even from jail. Ray hates Lucky, but in this town nothing remains secret."

Gia chuckled. "I've never been involved with something like this . . . cattle rustlers, jailhouse real estate deals. . . . It's a little crazy here, isn't it?"

"A little bit. But it's a good place. You want to go to the office, or we can do the paperwork in your hotel room?"

"The office would probably be easier, right?"

"We have a small conference room that's private." Dana couldn't believe this was happening; even if Ray cut his price, it would be the most expensive property she'd ever sold.

"That'll work."

They hiked back to the car and Dana started for town, giving Gia a sideways glance. "Do you have to sell your penthouse first?"

"That won't be a problem. Though depending on the price we settle on, I may need a little time to gather up extra funds. You think we could do a sixty-day escrow?"

"Ray would probably be okay with that."

For much of the afternoon, Gia examined the comps, and together they wrote up a clean offer. She explained to Gia that given Ray's living situation, all communication had to go through his lawyers, and that it could take a little time to get an answer.

"I'll need it to pull together my own funding," Gia said.

After all the Ts were crossed, the Is dotted, and the paperwork signed, Dana ran Gia back to the inn.

"You sure you don't want me to bring you up dinner?" Dana asked as Gia got out of the car, searching the square like she expected a reporter to jump out of the bushes.

"They have wine and afternoon snacks in the hotel. That'll do me."

"You have my cell if you need anything. And I'll call you as soon as I hear."

Gia crouched down in front of Dana's window. "Remember, you're bound by the nondisclosure contract. As far as anyone is to know, the offer is being made by the T Corporation."

"Your secret is safe with me."

Gia would just have to trust her. Unfortunately, people had been known to walk right through confidentiality agreements into the pages of the *National Enquirer*. But somehow Dana Calloway seemed too honorable for that. Not to mention that if this deal went through, she stood to make a good chunk of change, more than any tabloid would pay her.

Gia's larger concern was coming up with the cash. Even though she'd offered a mil under asking, the idea of her taking on something like this with her job in jeopardy was insane. Delusional, really. No way would a bank carry her without a job and no prospect of one.

While she did have the funds, liquidating them at a time like this . . . not prudent.

But standing at the river's edge, smelling the sage, staring out over the majestic mountains, she'd instantly fallen in love. She'd always invested with her head, never her heart. But the land had called to her, reminding her of that summer long ago when life had been filled with endless possibilities. Before everything had gone to shit.

But once she was here, out of the spotlight and away from her detractors, she'd put her plan into motion and build up her fortune again. And if that failed, she'd always have the land to fall back on.

Chapter 8

"Just looking at the phone won't make it ring," Aidan said.

Dana blew out a puff of air. "At this rate I won't hear anything until after the Fourth." The holiday fell smack in the middle of the week, which meant Ray's lawyers were probably taking a five-day weekend.

He smiled at her, and her stomach dipped like she was on a roller coaster. She supposed those pearly whites did that to a lot of women. But if she didn't want to be another second placer, it would be best to ignore that heart-stopping grin of his. All day he'd been moping around over his ex's wedding. Clearly he still pined for Sue—that was her name—even though it had been close to seven months.

"Must be one hell of a deal," he said.

She'd told him that her client had made an offer on a piece of land outside of town, but that was it. Aidan didn't know it was the Rosser Ranch, that it was a multimillion-dollar transaction, or that the buyer was Gia Treadwell.

"I don't like my clients getting nervous."

"You seem to be the one getting nervous," he said, and sat next to her on the couch. "Come with me to Sloane's. It'll get your mind off that call you're waiting for."

"Thanks, Aidan, but I just want to relax at home. Yesterday was a long day."

"Ah, come on. Be my date; otherwise I'll feel like a third wheel." The man was pulling out all the stops.

His date. *Righhhht.*

"Uh-uh," she said. "I have my heart set on a *Downton Abbey* marathon."

"You can do that any time. Brady's cooking."

"I don't have anything to wear." She reached for the remote control and he got up. "Where are you going?"

"To look through your color-coded clothes to find you something to wear."

She shot up and chased after him. "Don't you dare go in my closet!"

"Why not? I built the damn thing." He opened her bifold doors and started pulling out stuff and holding up hangers. "This looks good."

It was one of the sundresses in Grace's package. It showed off too much boob and thigh as far as Dana was concerned.

"Uh-uh," she repeated.

"Why not?"

"It's too slutty."

"Slutty's good; put it on. Let me have a look." He winked, and again her stomach did a series of acrobatics.

"Aidan, get out of my room." She tried to push him, but he wouldn't budge.

"If I leave, will you go with me?"

He sure was insistent, and the truth was, she was curious about his sister and Brady. She didn't know either of them very well and yet they'd given her that gift card. And everyone went on and on about Brady's cooking. Other than one breakfast at the Lumber Baron, she'd never been to any of the weddings or parties he'd catered.

"Fine. But I want to be home at a reasonable hour."

"Why, you turn into a pumpkin?" He tossed her the dress and started to leave. "I've got work tomorrow, so we can't be out too late."

After he shut the door, she considered the dress, stripped, changed her bra and panties, and slipped it over her head. For a long time, she stood in front of the full-length mirror on the back of her door, assessing herself. Yep, boob central.

Aidan banged on the door. "You dressed?"

"Yes, but I'm—"

He didn't let her finish, just barged in.

"For goodness' sake, Aidan."

"Whoa." He just stared at her, his eyes bugging out of his head, making her feel even more self-conscious. "That'll work. Let's go or we'll be late for dinner." Aidan started to drag her out of the room.

"Stop, I want to put something else on."

He gave her a wolfish grin and threw her over his shoulder in a fireman's hold as if she weighed nothing. "No time."

She struggled to hold her dress down. "Shouldn't we at least bring something?"

"Like what?"

"Wine, flowers, I don't know." She pounded on his back until he put her down and ran into the kitchen.

She searched the fridge for wine and remembered she'd polished off her last bottle of chardonnay the night before. That was when she saw the Calloway candy and swiped a few tins.

"Hey, those are mine. What are you doing?"

"I'll get you more," she told him, and they headed to Aidan's SUV. "Just a couple of hours; then you have to take me home."

He looked over at her. "You know, it wouldn't kill you to be more social."

"I'm plenty social."

"Not from what I can tell."

"And I guess you would know my whole life story after being my roommate for all of a week."

He laughed. "I know enough."

"Really? Like what?" she challenged.

"Like if you wore that dress more often your social life would vastly improve."

She hiked up the neck. "You ever think that maybe I'm happy with my social life just the way it is?"

"Nah, you're too pretty to sit home every night organizing your underwear drawer." He winked at her again and she rolled her eyes.

"Is that the best line you have? *You're too pretty to sit home every night*," she mimicked. "Lame, Aidan."

He turned off the highway into Sierra Heights and whizzed past the empty guard station. In Brady and Sloane's driveway he pulled behind a RAV4.

"You ever been here?"

"Of course. It used to be one of the models I showed to perspective buyers. It's gorgeous."

Aidan came around to her side to help her out. For a smartass, he was the consummate gentleman.

"You have anything to put this in, a basket or something?" She held up the candy. "It seems sort of tacky to just hand them random boxes of chocolates."

He touched his nose to hers, and while he was there, he looked down her dress. "You're funny, Dana."

"You getting your eyes full there?"

"At the risk of being fresh, I'd like to get my hands full."

She swatted at him to knock it off, but her girl parts were saying something entirely different, like: *Go ahead and feel me up right here in the front seat of your truck.* But she knew he was only flirting with her because the woman he loved was marrying someone else. Today. Probably at this very moment.

They walked together to the house, Dana carrying the candy. There was a note tacked on the door that said, "Meet us at the pool." They followed a path to the rec center and opened the gate to the pool area, where Brady had taken over the outdoor kitchen and pizza oven. Sitting at the big island was, shit, Griffin. Lina emerged from the pool in a bikini like a freaking beauty contestant.

Dana tensed and Aidan put his arm around her.

"Is it too late to leave?" she whispered.

"Hey," Sloane called from the pool, where she sat on the edge in a swimsuit, dangling her feet in the water. "We've been waiting for you."

"Yup," Aidan said, trying to be discreet. "Sloane didn't say anything to me about them coming, so maybe they're just swimming."

"What took you guys so long?" Sloane came over. "Brady's making pizza for appetizers. Harlee and Colin are on their way. What do you have there, Dana?"

She looked down at the boxes of candy and felt like an idiot. "It's my family's chocolates."

"Holy crap." Brady had also joined them. "I never put it together that you were that Calloway. I love Calloway chocolates. I think they're even better than See's, and See's are pretty damn good."

"Thanks." She handed them to him.

Next thing she knew Griffin was hugging her. "I didn't know you were coming." He looked at Aidan and back at her and his lips curved up.

Lina waved from one of the big lounge chairs.

"Come say hi to Lina," Griff said, and Dana didn't know why they had to go to her. Why couldn't she come to them?

Aidan tightened his arm around her and she wanted to kiss him in sheer gratitude. They walked over to Princess Lina, who was rubbing tanning lotion on her shoulders. Like Griff, Lina gave her a big hug, which knocked Dana for a loop.

"I'm so sorry about your house. If there's anything you need while Colin and Pat are rebuilding, let me know. I'm home for the summer."

"Thank you," Dana said, feeling incredibly uncomfortable but mostly like a bitch because she wished Lina wasn't being so nice. Especially in front of Aidan.

Griffin introduced Aidan to Lina. And Dana gave him props for not ogling her in her tiny bathing suit. Harlee and Colin came through the gate carrying a big cooler.

"Want to get some pizza?" Aidan asked and steered Dana toward the big stone oven. Once they were out of earshot, he said, "I didn't know they were coming, I swear."

"It's okay. Today is about you, not me."

"What are you talking about?"

She stopped and put her hands on her hips. "Uh . . . your ex . . . getting married."

Aidan stepped back and shook his head like he had cobwebs in it. "Well, I'll be damned."

"What?" she asked.

"Nothing." And then he kissed her.

It wasn't much of a kiss, just a peck, really. If Aidan had had his druthers, he would've gone all in. Tongue and everything. But they were in the middle of a gathering and people were watching. But damn if Dana didn't drive him to distraction. Case in point: He hadn't thought about Sue once this afternoon. His whole focus had been on getting Dana to come with him. And when she'd put on that dress he'd nearly lost his mind.

"Are you crazy?" Dana stood there, staring at him like he had a screw loose.

But she hadn't tried to stop him. In fact, she'd wound her arms around his neck and had gone up on her toes to reach him better. When he'd finished the kiss, she'd almost lost her balance.

"I thought we should put on a show . . . you know, to demonstrate that we're over them."

"Everyone is staring at us." She walked away, her face red as a pomegranate.

He went to join the party and get himself a slice of pizza. Dana had already wandered that way, and he noticed she was getting quite a few looks, especially from his sister. Colin had opened the cooler, which was loaded with soft drinks and beer. Aidan grabbed two brews, thinking Dana could use a little alcohol.

The whole setup—the pool, spa, outdoor kitchen—was an excellent place for a party. Impressive without being over the top. Another couple with a little girl joined the group. Aidan went over to introduce himself.

"You must be Sloane's brother. I'm Samantha, and this is my husband, Nate, and this is Lilly." The little girl held her arms up to Aidan, so he put down the drinks, lifted her, and held her against his hip.

"Nice to meet you. You're the hotel people." They owned a fleet of hotels, including the Lumber Baron, and were Brady's bosses.

"That would be us," Nate said. "How you liking Nugget and the fire department?"

"So far, so good." He glanced over at Dana and saw her sitting at an umbrella table alone. "Brady's making pizza. Come on over and grab a drink." Aidan led them over to the oven.

"Here, let me take her from you." Nate collected Lilly, who had attached herself to Aidan like a barnacle. "She likes you. Lilly's usually shy around people she doesn't know."

"Kids just love my brother." Sloane grabbed Aidan by the arm. "Can you help me with something over here?"

She dragged him to the other side of the pool. "What's with you and Dana?"

"Nothing."

"Nothing, my ass. Why are you kissing her in the middle of my dinner?"

"I didn't realize I had to get permission from you to kiss a pretty woman. Did you call to ask me whether you could kiss Brady?"

"Give me a break, Aid. You're going through a bad breakup and she's going through . . . a fire."

"Sue and I have been broken up for nearly seven months. And in case you forgot"—he looked at his watch—"she's married to someone else now."

"Don't do this to Dana. Don't use her to get back at Sue."

"Clearly you don't know Dana. And as far as getting back at Sue, she doesn't give a shit who I'm kissing." Oddly enough, it didn't bother him. He'd been too busy enjoying the kiss with Dana to even let Sue enter into the picture.

"I don't get you." Sloane threw her arms in the air and walked away.

He went to grab the beers he'd set down and join Dana, who was no longer sitting alone. The woman, Harlee, was with her, discussing something about clothes, but she got up to go when Aidan joined them.

"What was that about?" he asked Dana.

"She liked my dress and wants to give me stuff she doesn't wear anymore."

"That's nice. Hey, I'm sorry about Griffin and Lina. I never would've intentionally put you in this situation. But it seemed to go okay."

"It's not like we're enemies or anything. It's just delicate, but Lina was gracious about it."

"How long were you and Griffin together?"

"I wouldn't say we were ever together, just dated. Griffin was always too hung up on Lina. Before me, they'd been a couple, then broke up while she attended USF. After she transferred to the University of Nevada, Reno, they got back together."

Aidan nodded. "You still have feelings for him?"

"Nope," she said, but Aidan didn't much believe her.

It seemed to him that she tried a little too hard to avoid Griffin. Hey, not his concern, although he hated like hell that he'd put her in a difficult position. Then again, all social situations seemed to be painful for Dana. She interacted with people just fine, but he got the impression she felt like an outsider. He didn't know why; the townsfolk were pretty inclusive.

"I'll get us some pizza," he said.

"Good, I'm starved. And then, after we eat, we can go."

"Relax! We just got here."

Aidan grabbed two plates and piled them with individual pizzas. Brady gave him an inquisitive look, the question clear: *WTF is going on between you and Dana?* There was nothing going on, but people should mind their own business. For some crazy reason, his entire family believed that at the eleventh hour Sue would come running back. Aidan knew differently, and a part of him was relieved. It was done between them. Her choice, not his. He wasn't the bad guy. But now he could move on.

"Tri-tip and chicken should be up soon," Brady said and pointed to a table loaded with platters and serving bowls. "Salads, beans, chips, and guacamole are over there."

"You need any help?" he asked Brady.

"Nah, I'm good here." He moved a few pieces of chicken away from the flame.

"Nice ring you got my sister, by the way."

Brady gazed over at Sloane, his face splitting into a big grin. "I like that it's official. There was a time when the idea of commitment . . . marriage . . . it sent me running for the woods. Not with your sister, though. So maybe it's all about being with the right person."

"Yeah, maybe." Aidan lifted his plate. "I better get this to Dana before the pizza gets cold."

He grabbed a wad of napkins and some silverware and brought the pizza back to the table. Dana passed him his bottle of beer and methodically cut her pizza into six perfect slices. Aidan just ate his whole, using his hands.

Dana took a bite. "Wow, this is good. I think it's the best Margherita pizza I've ever had."

Aidan fanned the roof of his mouth. "Good but hot."

"What did Brady say to you?"

He shook his head. "Nothing."

"Bull. He and everyone else now thinks I'm your rebound woman."

"Because we kissed? Nah, we were just goofing around. No one thinks that." Except for Sloane, who definitely did.

She took another bite of pizza. "Of course they do. Obviously you've never lived in a small town before."

He flashed a flirtatious smile, enjoying working her up, then pulled her into his lap. "Should we give them something to talk about?"

She quickly scrambled away, dragging that round rear end of hers across his groin, leaving him stiff as a rod. To hide the evidence of his arousal, Aidan tucked his lap under the table.

"Knock it off, Aidan. I'm not your rebound girl, your consolation prize, or a good-time distraction."

"I never said you were. You're my friend."

She glared at him. "You always kiss and hold your friends in your lap?"

"Not my firefighter ones, that's for sure. They're hairy and don't smell as good as you."

The truth was, he didn't flirt with his female friends either, but he really hadn't meant anything by the kiss. Dana was just fun to antagonize. And he liked seeing her go from uptight, cookie-cutter suits to sexy, low-cut sundresses. He liked watching her convert from stick-up-her-ass real estate agent to out-of-her-shell hot chick. Most of all, he liked being the one to provoke the transformation.

"Looks like our main course is ready." Aidan watched Brady take the beef and chicken off the grill. "Let's fix ourselves a plate."

"I'm stuffed from the pizza, but I don't want to pass up a chance to taste Brady's cooking. I've only had it one time before. I was meeting a client at the Lumber Baron when he was the chef there. It was only breakfast, but it was fantastic."

"According to Sloane, he caters every wedding, party, and event around here. Haven't you been to any of those?"

"Nope. This is my first Brady Benson party."

He wondered why. This wasn't the kind of town to leave people out, yet she hadn't gotten an invite to Tawny and Lucky's wedding. She might not be outgoing, but there was nothing dislikable about Dana. If there was, and he didn't know about it, Sloane would've told him. It seemed to him that she'd intentionally turned herself into the town wallflower.

"Well, let's do it." He got to his feet and helped her to hers.

"I understand you're trying to forget Sue," she whispered and gazed across the pool to Griffin. "And frankly I don't mind people thinking that you and I . . . flirt, or whatever. But try to behave yourself."

"I'll try," he said, attempting to look contrite while pinching her ass.

She danced away and he got waylaid by Harlee, who introduced herself and told him that she owned the *Nugget Tribune*, a digital-only newspaper.

"I want to do a story on fire season, especially given how bad it is this year. I'm interviewing Captain Johnson for the piece. But I want to do a sidebar on fire safety tips. Would you be up for that?"

"Absolutely." He liked being in the paper, and despite Sue's admonitions that he was calling too much attention to himself, he used to be quoted all the time in the *Chicago Tribune*.

She took down his cell phone number and Aidan caught up with Dana at the buffet, where she deliberated over whether to go for the chicken or tri-tip.

"Just take a little of both," he told her.

"I don't want to seem like a pig."

"Oh, for Christ's sake." He grabbed one of the serving forks, speared her a couple of slices of beef and a chicken breast, then proceeded to fill his own plate. "There's enough food here to feed a small country. No one cares how much you eat."

"Where you going?" She clutched his arm. "Our table is over there."

"Yeah, we're joining the party now." He put one hand at the small of her back and maneuvered her over to Sloane's table. He felt her stiffen, but to her credit, she didn't complain.

They took the chairs next to Harlee and Colin. Griffin, Lina, Samantha, and Nate sat across from them. Lilly was more interested in playing under the table.

"Brady, come sit," Sloane called.

He brought a platter of grilled shrimp. "Tell me what you think. I'm testing a new seafood vendor for the hotels."

Brady didn't have to ask Aidan twice. Scooping up a large spoonful, he put some of the prawns on Dana's plate and took the rest for himself. Out of the corner of his eye, he could see Sloane watching. Griffin too.

"I heard a rumor that you and Brady want to hold your reception here," Harlee said to Sloane. All eyes turned to his sister.

Sloane in turn looked sheepishly at Griffin. "Don't worry; we planned to talk to you about it first."

"Seriously, you want to have it here, by the pool?"

"We were thinking of doing a tent over there." Brady pointed to the lawn overlooking the golf course. "Maybe do one of those dance floors over the pool. What do you think?"

"I think it would be awesome." Griff high-fived Brady, then put his arm around Lina. "We'll let the other residents know we're throwing a private party."

"Nah." Brady waved his hand in the air. "We'll invite everyone in the development. That way no one will be pissed about losing out on their amenities for a day."

"Another wedding to plan!" Samantha gave Sloane a hug. "I'm so excited for you guys. To think Lucky and Tawny's is just two weekends away."

"How is that coming along?" Sloane asked.

"Perfect," Sam said. Aidan knew she was Breyer Hotels' corporate event planner and, like Brady with the catering, pitched in on local parties. "Completely organized, and by the time they come back from their honeymoon their house should be finished, right, Colin?"

"Barring any unforeseeable setbacks we're good to go. Then we move on to Dana's house." Colin gave Dana a thumbs-up.

"Are you loving the plans?" Harlee asked her.

"I am." Dana swallowed a shrimp before continuing. "I can't believe how big it'll be."

Apparently, the news hadn't reached Sloane yet because she had a questioning look on her face.

"Dana's adding a second story with all the bells and whistles," Aidan supplied.

"You've seen the plans?" Sloane asked.

"Of course," Aidan smiled at Dana and caught Griffin watching.

What was it with him? Aidan wondered. He seemed to be paying a little too much attention to a woman he'd dumped for someone else. It irked Aidan. Maybe Griffin got off on pitting two women against each other. Made him feel like a big man. Aidan was just about to shoot him a dirty look when he felt something tugging at his knees. Under the table, he found Lilly pulling herself up, using him to keep balance.

He pulled her onto his lap to shrieks of delight and a big toothy grin.

"How old is she?"

"Eighteen months," Nate said.

Lilly gazed at Aidan with big, adoring brown eyes and he fell in love. He definitely wanted one of these.

"Who knew I had a big flirt on my hands?" Nate said, and everyone at the table laughed.

"Kids love the big oaf," Sloane said. "It's one of those unsolved mysteries."

The ring of Aidan's cell phone filled the air, and for a second he felt too paralyzed to pull it from his pocket. What if it was Sue?

"Aren't you planning to get that?" Brady asked.

"Yeah." He handed Lilly off to Dana, got up from the table, and walked a distance to check the phone's caller ID. He stared at it for a few seconds and took a deep breath. "Whaddya we got?"

"A suspicious brushfire near Upper Jamison Creek Campground in Plumas-Eureka State Park. About fifty acres so far. Looks like I have to call you in early."

"You've got it, Captain."

Chapter 9

The day before the Fourth of July, Ray Rosser's lawyer finally called Dana. The old man wanted the buyer to come up thirty thousand and they'd have themselves a deal.

Knowing Ray, he just wanted to taunt his lawyers, who were champing at the bit for their fees. And just to throw a monkey wrench into the situation, Clay McCreedy had caught wind of the offer, stomped into Nugget Realty and Associates, and was sitting in the conference room this very minute waiting to have a word with Dana.

Carol, unfortunately, was on her way to Santa Cruz with her family for the holiday, leaving Dana on her own to tangle with the intimidating cowboy. He owned one of the largest cattle ranches in California, was a war hero, and when he told the townsfolk to jump, they simply asked, "How high?"

He'd never said or done anything that would lead her to believe that he was anything less than a gentleman. Yet, he could still make her pee her pants with one snarl.

"Here's your coffee, Mr. McCreedy." Dana shut the door and took the seat across from him at the table. "As I told you when you first came in, there's not really a lot I'm allowed to say to you."

"Ray already told me what this secret client of yours is offering. And while it's a hell of a price for land like that, I can't match it." He sipped the coffee while his piercing blue eyes locked on her. "I just want to make sure this corporation knows that Rosser's property is agricultural land. Putting in another Sierra Heights, a strip mall, or even a resort ain't gonna fly. I'll fight it tooth and nail and, Dana, I'll win. You'd be remiss in not telling your client that."

"Mr. McCreedy, my client is well aware of what the land is zoned for."

"No need to be so formal. My father was Tip and I'm Clay. These people cattle ranchers?"

He knew damned well the buyer wasn't a cattle rancher. While beef was a big industry in the West, the list of players was short. Word of an acquisition on this level would've spread faster than an outbreak of E. coli. "Clay, I can't give you that information."

He let out a breath. "I've got to wonder what all the secrecy is about. Folks here know their neighbors. That land has been in the Rosser family for more than a century. It's always been used to run cattle. At the rate we're going, California's farmland will shrink so small that we'll have to get our food from a laboratory. These people know that?"

"I think they do."

He made an exasperated sound. "When will we know who these folks are?"

"If and when a deal closes escrow, the buyer's name becomes public record."

"I'm already aware of the name, Dana. The T Corporation." He let out a cynical laugh. "I can't find one shred of information on the company anywhere. It's bogus. When will I know who owns it?"

When you see Gia Treadwell walking through the Nugget Market or getting an order of curly fries at the Bun Boy. "I'm really not at liberty to say."

"Well, I hope the T Corporation knows what it's getting itself into. Because if it intends to use that land for anything other than farming or ranching, that bullshit company can expect a hell of a fight on its hands." Clay swiped his hat off the table and stalked across the room and out the door.

That went well.

She waited for Clay to drive out of the parking lot in his big Ford truck and turned off the air conditioner. On her way out, she gathered her purse and paperwork, flicked off the lights, and headed home for lunch. Since Aidan had been on shift, the house felt so organized. She'd stacked all their subscription magazines in alphabetical order, divided their mail and put it in special holders with their names, and rearranged the garage. It was quiet too. Frankly, too quiet. She missed having him around, disrupting her tranquility, which was weird because she liked life orderly and peaceful. He, on the other hand, let kids wander in off the street to eat his Otter Pops, slung his wet bathing suit wherever it was convenient, and watched sports at ear-piercing levels.

Just for a change of scenery, she swung by the firehouse on her way home, and lo and behold, Aidan stood in the driveway washing one of the fire engines. She wondered if male firefighters were man-dated to do that particular chore shirtless. It was certainly a brilliant PR strategy; any female fortunate enough to get an eye load of Aidan's sinewy chest, all tanned and rippled, was sure to give to the Fire-fighters Foundation.

She pulled over and rolled down her window. "Hey, you can do mine next."

He turned off the hose and strolled over, big smile stretched across his face. "What's going on?"

"I just had a meeting with Clay McCreedy, who is not happy. How long have you been back?"

"We got in last night. That brushfire was a bitch, kept changing direction on us. Why is Clay McCreedy unhappy? He's the cowboy, right?"

"Mm-hmm. He's afraid my client is going to turn the Rosser place into a factory outlet mall."

"Is she?"

"The land is zoned for agricultural use only."

"That didn't answer the question." He stuck his face in the win-dow. "Where you off to?"

"Home, to eat lunch."

"Come in the firehouse and have a sandwich with me."

"Are you allowed to do that?" she asked, skeptical.

He opened the driver's side door and grabbed her hand. "Sure."

She tried to resist but, in typical Aidan fashion, he wasn't taking no for an answer. The last thing she wanted was for him to throw her over his shoulder like he'd done the last time. So she followed him, curious to see what the inside of the station looked like. It was a lot cozier than she would've guessed, and quite clean.

The living quarters held a series of dormitories, a kitchen, a din-ing area, and a TV room. Nothing fancy, just utilitarian furniture that appeared to get a lot of wear and tear. But homey. Aidan showed her a small gym where a couple of guys were bench-pressing weights.

"This is Dana, everyone."

The men grunted in acknowledgment, and Aidan led her to the

kitchen, where he proceeded to pull out half the contents of the refrigerator.

"Sit." He nudged his head at a nearby table and chairs and started building two sandwiches.

He put them on plates, cut each one crosswise, and served them up with a pile of potato chips and two cold cans of soda. "Dig in," he told her, taking a bite of his own sandwich. "So did this Clay guy give you a hard time?"

"Not really. I think he was just frustrated by my answers because I had to be vague. We're still in negotiations. I can't give out details at this point." Or at any point, according to the nondisclosure document she'd signed.

"He's that worried about an outlet mall?" Aidan took a gulp of his soda. Dana liked the way his Adam's apple moved when he swallowed.

"That was hyperbole. Sierra Heights was before my time, but it caused a big brouhaha with the residents. People don't like change, they don't like seeing their rural town becoming homogenized with minimansions, and I can't blame Clay for being concerned that the nation's largest agricultural state is at risk of being developed into track homes and shopping centers. But I can't tell him anything about my client's reason for wanting the property, especially while we're still in discussions."

"You think it's gonna happen?"

Dana shrugged. "My client, a corporation, really wants it, but we're talking big bucks. Ray Rosser just countered for more money."

"You told me it was a woman and she just wanted a piece of horse property," he said.

"It's a corporation now," which was totally true. "And there are some horses involved." She noticed he had circles under his eyes. "You look tired."

"Knocking down fires is tiring work." One side of his mouth tipped up in a sly half smile, and she was pretty sure she'd just developed a heart murmur. "As long as we don't get called out again, I'll sleep tonight and be in my own bed by tomorrow. What are your plans?"

She wasn't sure what he meant. "For what?"

"The Fourth. What, all this real estate stuff make you forget it was a holiday?"

She usually just sat home and gorged on Calloway chocolate stars. "What's there to do? Fireworks have been canceled on account of the dry conditions and the fire danger." Of course he was aware of that already.

"I thought we'd grill and invite a few people over."

He said it like they were a couple. "Hey, it's half your house; you can do whatever you want."

"Good. Then we're having a party. Get a few of your friends to come."

The only person she had to invite was Carol, who was in Santa Cruz. "A little late notice, don't you think?"

"No. Not when free food and beer is involved. You can bet some of these guys will come." He motioned toward the TV room, where a few men were sacked out on couches and easy chairs.

"My friends have busy social calendars," she lied.

"That's okay. We'll make it a small gathering."

We'll. He kept saying *we'll* as if this barbecue he'd concocted would be a joint effort. She didn't have any friends to invite, didn't know any of his coworkers, and didn't know how to grill. So what exactly was she bringing to this party?

One of the guys from the TV room wandered into the kitchen in a pair of Hawaiian shorts and a T-shirt that read, "Feel safe at night, sleep with a firefighter," and gave her a slow perusal.

"I'm Hutch." He stuck his hand out for Dana to shake it. "You the probie's girlfriend?"

"This is Dana," Aidan said, and Dana noticed he didn't address Hutch's question. "We're having a barbecue tomorrow. Bring your girlfriend."

"Yeah? I'll bring beer . . . and fudge," Hutch said. Dana thought the combo was rather random. "You live around here, Dana?"

"She lives with me."

Not knowing whether to clarify that they were only roommates, Dana decided to stay quiet. Less complicated. "And you? Where do you live?"

"Glory Junction."

"It's so cute there." Occasionally, she got a listing in the ski resort town, which was thirty minutes away.

"Born and raised." Hutch tapped his chest. "My mother and aunt own Oh Fudge!"

"You're kidding." That explained the fudge offering. "I love that place. We have something in common . . . my family owns Calloway Confections."

"Get out!" he said. "Calloway Confections . . . whoa, that's on a whole different scale than my ma's little business."

"They both make candy. And both operations are family run. That's the way I look at it."

"Right on," he said, and before Dana realized it, they were fist bumping.

She glanced over at Aidan, who shot her a grin, gathered up the sandwich plates, and took them to the sink.

"I better let you get back to work."

"I'll walk you out," he told her.

As they headed for the door, she turned to Hutch, who had his head stuck in the refrigerator. "See you tomorrow."

"Looking forward to it," he called back.

Outside, the temperature had risen at least ten degrees, and Dana couldn't wait to get out of her navy blue pantsuit. In the heat, the pants were starting to stick to her.

"You want me to make a Reno run tonight to get some food for the party?"

Aidan absently tucked a strand of hair that had come loose from her bun behind her ear. "Nah, wait until tomorrow morning when I'm off. We'll go together."

She supposed the big supermarkets would be open. "Okay."

"Stay cool," he said as she got in her car.

"You too." She turned on the ignition to get the AC running and suddenly asked, "Did you and Sue used to entertain a lot?"

"In the beginning we did."

"Why not later?"

He hitched his shoulders. "We had different ideas of what a party should be."

Dana was dying to know more but didn't feel right about prying. If Aidan had wanted to elaborate he would've. Yet she couldn't help wondering if it was one of the reasons Sue had run off with someone else. Crazy woman. In Dana's mind, Aidan McBride was the epitome of perfect. No one had ever made her feel more at ease and so included. Odd that it had taken a newcomer like Aidan to make her feel like she belonged in Nugget, even though she'd been here first.

"Hasta la vista," she said and pulled away from the curb, smiling. They were having a party.

Aidan got a kick out of watching Dana decorate. Like with everything else she did, there were lists and charts and Excel spreadsheets. If the act of organization didn't make her so damned happy, Aidan would've found it tremendously annoying. Not that he was a psychologist or anything, but he got the impression that it helped her cope with situations that made her nervous.

Like the idiotic closet organizer was really a metaphor for putting order back into her life after the fire had destroyed it.

"It's just a casual barbecue," he reminded her.

"I know." She looked up at the red, white, and blue paper lanterns she'd hung from the trees and winced. "Oh God, I overdid it, didn't I?"

"Nah. I like 'em. Very patriotic and festive. Good choice."

She beamed. "What about the centerpieces?"

"Meh." He rocked his hand back and forth, then laughed to show he was kidding. "It's all good, Dana."

The first guests to arrive were Sloane and Brady. They each carried a big bowl.

"What have you got there?" Aidan asked.

"Potato salad and spicy slaw." Brady stuck his bowl under Aidan's nose.

Aidan raised his brows. "A busman's holiday?"

"No." Brady shared a look with Sloane. "We didn't want to starve."

"Who else is coming?" Sloane examined the yard, checked out the flag bunting Dana had tacked to the porch railing and seemed to approve.

"A couple of guys from the firehouse and you and Brady."

"That's it?"

"I'm new in town; what do you want, a Cubs crowd?

"Dana knows people."

Aidan searched the yard for her, and when he couldn't find her, figured she'd gone inside. "Because of the short notice her friends were all busy," he said. In all honesty, he didn't think she had any friends to invite.

The fact that she seemed content enough to plan a nice gathering for his new Cal Fire friends—and to be included—both saddened and touched him. Sue had always been more interested in impressing people she thought were worthy—their lawyer, accountant, and anesthesiologist neighbors. Firefighters were just a little too blue collar in her book, even though all the members of his family were civil servants. From what Aidan could tell, Dana didn't have a snobby bone in her body; she just wanted acceptance.

Given her smarts, beauty, success, and sense of humor, she should have a wide social circle. He certainly enjoyed being around her, and not just because he wanted to get inside her pants, which he did.

Brady checked the coals on the grill. "Those aren't hot enough."

Aidan was too distracted scanning the area for Dana to pay attention to barbecue temperatures. "You got this for a few minutes? I've got to go do something."

He went inside and found Dana sitting on the edge of her bed in her room. "What are you doing?"

"Uh . . . just waiting until people get here."

"People are here . . . my sister and Brady. We're outside."

"I just thought maybe you wanted some time alone with them."

"Why? She's my sister. Come on." He pulled her up, and she followed him outside.

By then, Hutch, and a woman Aidan presumed was his girlfriend, and Kurtis and his wife had arrived. They greeted everyone and made room in the cooler for the drinks they'd brought. Hutch treated Dana like they were long-lost friends.

"I brought fudge," he said and put a white bakery box on the dessert table.

Dana pointed at a red glass bowl. "Stars."

"Hot damn." Hutch grabbed a handful.

Brady watched the exchange and said, "Calloway stars?"

"You bet. And Hutch's family"—she nodded at the firefighter—"owns Oh Fudge! in Glory Junction. Have you tried it? They make amazing chocolate."

"Are you kidding?" Sloane said. "That stuff is like crack. Every time we're there we get a piece."

Hutch beamed, undoubtedly proud of his family's enterprise. It was generous of Dana to make such a big fuss over the small-town fudge shop—Aidan hadn't been to a tourist place yet that didn't have one—when it sounded like her family owned the Godiva of the West.

Brady took over the barbecue, flipping burgers and pouring beer over the dogs, getting a good steam going. When Aidan tried to take over, Brady brushed him away.

"It's best to leave it to the pro."

"I've got a news flash for you," Aidan said. "It's not that difficult."

Brady laughed, and they both stood around the grill making small talk. Aidan thought his sister's fiancé would make a fine addition to the McBride clan. The guy could hold his own in the smart-ass department against Aidan and his two brothers, and he loved Sloane. Like really loved her; it was written all over his face.

His family had loved Sue. She'd gone to Zumba, or whatever the hell you called it, with his mother every week, had taught his old man how to make the perfect Manhattan, and had generally classed up a house filled with roughnecks. His brothers all thought she was smoking hot, which had made Aidan feel like a stud. And Sloane, the toughest critic of the bunch, had embraced Sue like a sister. He didn't think she or his mother would ever get over losing her from the family.

About three years ago, he'd met her at a Coats for Kids fundraiser in which CFD were big sponsors. She'd gone with her mother, who never met a charity she didn't like, and he'd attended with a contingent of firefighters. One look at her in a strapless black gown and a mass of red corkscrew curls and he was a goner. Just dead.

The organizers made sure to put a firefighter at every table and Aidan made sure to sit at Sue's. They talked so much, they barely touched their four-hundred-dollar plates of food. Hey, it was for a good cause. Kids got coats and he got Sue. He left with her phone number in his phone and a tentative date to meet for coffee. Soon, coffee turned into drinks and dinners and parties. The first time they'd slept together, she blew his mind, dancing for him under the stars on his balcony before they made love.

Those early weeks were like a dream, spending entire days in bed, wrapped in each other's arms. Sometimes they'd go away, stay at a fancy hotel with a hot tub or camp in a tent under an awning of trees.

Eventually, real life intruded and the romance didn't seem quite as shiny or as perfect. Sue began to complain that his work hours were preventing them from having a normal social life. Like her mother, she enjoyed attending charity events, the symphony, and the opera. Her father had left her a comfortable inheritance when he died, and although she wasn't rich, she could afford to attend some of Chicago's glitzier affairs. He attempted to explain to her that his job would never have banker's hours. At first, she tried to be understanding, but his unpredictable schedule became a constant bone of contention between them. It got to the point where she threw crying fits when he had to leave for the fire station.

"What do you want me to do, Sue? This is my job."

"Why can't you do what Eddy did and become a consultant? It pays better and you'd have regular hours."

"Because I don't want to be a consultant. I love my job."

"More than having a family?"

He didn't see how they were mutually exclusive. His father had raised four kids while working for CFD. More than half the employees in the department had families.

"You're being selfish," she accused.

"How is doing what my family has done for three generations being selfish? Sue, you knew what I did when we started dating." That was the thing; she wanted to change him. Wanted him to wear a suit and a tie, make a six-figure salary, hang out with Biff and Buffy, which no way, no how, would ever be in the cards.

"At least we should get married," she said. "We're not getting any younger and when we start having kids, you'll want to have a nine-to-five job."

"And if I don't? You think that's a good way to test a marriage?"

By the third year, they'd decided to live together so Sue could go back to school and get her teaching credential. She'd been a technical writer but was bored brainless. Aidan was trying to get promoted in the Office of Fire Investigation Division. The hope was that living under the same roof would give them more time together as their careers grew more demanding. Aidan knew that cohabitation before marriage was a big compromise for Sue, who subscribed to the whole why-buy-the-cow adage, but he wasn't ready to take those vows. The honest truth was, he was having serious doubts about the relationship, which was effed up because Sue loved him and everyone loved Sue.

Anyway, he never got the chance to question those second thoughts because two months after moving in together, Sue's mom died from a stroke. Aidan, and by extension his parents and siblings, were her only family now. She needed him more than ever, and he didn't want to let her down, not when she deserved security. That was when she became obsessed with having a baby.

"As soon I move up in rank we'll get married, Sue, and have a baby." But at the back of his mind he knew he was lying.

Apparently, she knew too, because six months later she moved out and started seeing Sebastian at the school where she was finishing her teaching program.

"So if you don't mind me asking, what's going on with you and Dana?" Brady asked, pulling Aidan out of his thoughts.

"We're just friends." He cast an eye over the partygoers and found her standing by herself, reorganizing the salads. "Jeez. Hang on a sec, I'll be right back."

"Don't worry about me, I've got it covered," Brady called.

Aidan walked across the yard to Dana. "Are you not having fun?"

"I totally am," she said.

"Then why are you here alone?"

"I just wanted to neaten the table up a little."

He gently clasped her shoulders. "You don't like parties, do you?"

Dana let out a breath. "It's not that I don't like them, I'm just not good at mingling and making small talk. The truth is, I haven't had a lot of practice."

"Why not?" He cocked his head to the side. "It's not like you smell or anything."

She tossed him a flippant smile. "I wasn't that outgoing as a kid, and after my brother died my parents and I sort of became recluses. By the time I got to college, I kept to myself."

"But you're a friggin' real estate agent, a salesperson. Don't you have to be good with people for that?"

She shrugged. "It's a job and I'm good at my job."

"Hang with me, then." He draped an arm around her shoulder.

"You don't have to, Aidan. Go talk with your friends. I'll be fine. I actually like watching people."

They both heard a car door slam at the same time. A few minutes later, Harlee, Colin, a cop Sloane worked with, and a woman with red, white, and blue hair—no shit—strolled into the party. Harlee saw them huddled together and wandered over.

"I hope you don't mind that we're crashing your barbecue," she said. "Sloane invited us."

"The more the merrier." Aidan grinned and watched the cop and Colin add more drinks to the cooler.

"I would've invited you," Dana stammered. "We just decided to have something yesterday and I figured you were already busy."

"We planned to bowl, but the place is packed with senior citizens. The Nugget Mafia is monopolizing two lanes."

"The Nugget Mafia?" Aidan asked.

"They're a group of old-timers who think they run the town," Harlee said. "One of them is the mayor, Dink Caruthers. And Darla's dad"—she nodded in the direction of the chick with the flag hair—"he's Nugget's never-going-to-retire barber."

Aidan figured there was a story there. But before he could ask more, flag hair joined them.

"Hi. I'm Darla." She shook Aidan's hand and reached out to stroke Dana's hair. "You need a moisturizing treatment."

Dana combed her fingers through the spot on her head Darla had just touched. "I do?"

Aidan tightened his arm around Dana protectively. After being with Sue all those years, he knew how catty women could be.

"You've got gorgeous hair, but with the dry weather . . . come into the barber shop and I'll fix you up. Maybe a little trim too."

"She did mine yesterday," Harlee said.

"Okay," Dana agreed.

He gave her a quick squeeze, and it didn't go beyond his notice that the other two women exchanged glances.

"You should come in too," Darla said and ran her fingers through Aidan's hair. She was an oddball, that one. "Nice and thick. I could thin it a little. So how are you liking Nugget?"

"I like it." He backed away a foot or two. "You live here long?"

"My father did. But I grew up in Sacramento with my mom. I only moved here permanently two winters ago." She gazed around the yard at the lanterns. "Looks so festive, right?"

"Dana did that," Aidan said.

Sloane caught sight of them standing together and came over to greet Harlee and Darla. "You guys made it." Both women hugged Aidan's sister. He didn't realize she had so many friends here.

"Is that Hutch over there?" Darla said, squinting at the group assembled near the grill.

"Yeah, you know him?"

"I cut half the guys' hair at Cal Fire. Hutch comes in occasionally but mostly uses a place in Glory Junction and probably pays twice the price. Everything in that town is a rip-off."

"So, Dana, there's a rumor going around that a big corporation is buying the Rosser place," Harlee said. "I'd love to get something in the *Trib* about it. You know anything?"

"It's not even close to being a done deal," Dana said, and Harlee's eyes grew round with excitement.

"There's actually some truth to it? I assumed it was bogus, like most of the rumors in this town. How do you know about it? Are you representing the buyer?"

"I can't really talk about it. Sorry."

"Can you talk about it when it's a done deal?" Harlee asked.

"I don't think so. But you'll figure it out."

"Whoa, you make it sound big. Are the buyers planning to build a resort or something?"

Sloane and Darla seemed just as curious as Harlee and started peppering Dana with more questions. Evidently, this passed as big news in Nugget. He really needed to get back to the grill to relieve Brady, but he didn't want to leave Dana to fend for herself against the nosy vultures. But Dana surprised him by laughing at her interrogators.

"Guys, I can't tell you anything." She mimed locking her lips closed with a key. "If it goes through, you'll know soon enough."

"Do you make a lot of money selling real estate?" Darla asked, effectively changing the subject. Aidan wondered if the hairdresser wasn't as dizzy as she looked.

"I do all right," Dana replied. "The problem is, you can have long dry spells where you don't sell anything. Recently, the market has been pretty good, though."

"What's the most expensive place you've ever sold?" Harlee asked.

"When I worked in Tahoe, I once sold a house for two million dollars."

"Holy crap," Darla said. "How much did you get of that?"

Even to Aidan, who was an investigator, it was a pretty ballsy question. But Dana didn't appear to mind, telling them a standard agent's commission. He watched her tell a story about the ugliest house she'd ever sold, and by the time he slipped away to man the barbecue she positively glowed.

"What's going on over there?" Brady asked him.

"They're talking real estate and asking Dana how much money she makes."

Brady chuckled. "It's a weird little town. Want a burger?"

"I want a burger and a hot dog. Here, let me take over."

"I got it," Brady said. "This is what I do."

"Is the cop who's talking to Hutch and Kurtis with Darla?" They'd come together, but Aidan couldn't see them as a couple. The cop had a buzz cut that reminded Aidan of a marine. Despite the patriotic flag hair, Darla struck him as . . . out there.

"Yep." Brady flipped three burgers in a row and topped them with cheese slices more deftly than any short-order cook. "She's a character, Darla. But good people. Both of them."

Aidan called to the crowd that they should start lining up for burgers and dogs hot off the grill and proceeded to watch Dana with the group of women he'd left her with. She seemed to be holding her own and even looked like she was enjoying herself. She had on one of those sundresses he liked, her legs long and shapely—and ghostly white. The lady needed a tan. She must've sensed him observing her because she offered up a shy smile and waved. He waved back, and something indefinable but intimate passed between them, something that made his heart move in his chest.

Chapter 10

Harlee had more clothes than a department store. Every time Dana found a skirt or blazer she liked, Harlee threw another one on the bed just to confuse her.

"You can have them all if you want," Harlee said. "Don't worry about offending me if there's stuff you don't like. I don't know why I bought some of these pieces in the first place. I used to have a shopping problem. If I saw something I wanted, I had to get it in every color. Thank goodness Colin built this house with big closets. But I need to get rid of a lot of these clothes before they overtake the house."

At the barbecue Harlee had once again insisted that Dana come over to her house to look through her clothes. It would've been insulting to turn her down, and Dana had always wanted a friend to play dress up with.

Harlee went into the hallway and wheeled another rolling rack into the bedroom. "I have so much that I'm forced to keep clothes in the garage." She pulled a red shift dress from the stand. "This color goes good with your hair and skin tone. Try it on."

"I don't feel right about taking all this." Dana looked at her growing pile of pantsuits, dresses, skirts, blouses, and jackets. "Even if you're trying to get rid of stuff, you could sell these clothes."

"Used clothes don't exactly fetch a fortune. I'd rather give them away."

"What about Darla?" Dana knew the two women were best friends.

"She's already picked what she wants, which wasn't much. The two of us don't exactly have the same taste. I would say you and I are closer in style."

Dana was stunned. "Are you kidding me? You look like a fashion plate. I'm just happy to look professional."

"You have . . . had . . . some nice pieces before the fire. Quality and very classic. But . . . and don't take this the wrong way . . . you dress a little too conservatively, in my opinion. I think the clothes from Farm Supply suit you better."

"It was so kind of Grace." Dana went in Harlee's big master bathroom to try the shift dress on but kept the door open a crack so she could still carry on a conversation. "She saved me from having to go out in public in a see-through nightgown the day after the fire, and everything is so cute. But it's all a little more fitted than I usually wear."

"That's why it looks good on you. Hey, just saying. And Aidan certainly seems to appreciate it."

"Huh, what do you mean?" Dana popped her head out of the bathroom.

"He can't keep his eyes off of you. I seriously think he's into you."

Dana came out in the dress. "No, he's going through a bad breakup."

"Oh? Do tell."

Dana didn't think she was betraying any confidences. Other than to tell her that Sue was getting married, Aidan hadn't disclosed much about his past relationship. "His ex dumped him for someone else."

"When?" Harlee wanted to know.

"About seven months ago. But the ex just got married."

Harlee appeared sympathetic at first but then shrugged. "Well, if you ask me, he seems pretty over it."

"I'm sure it's just an act. Men are good at not wearing their emotions on their sleeves." Especially an alpha male like Aidan.

"Perhaps. But you're providing quite a distraction for him from what I saw at the barbecue yesterday. He watched you constantly, followed you around like a puppy dog, and smiled at everything you said."

Dana didn't want to be a distraction to a man who was just longing for someone else. She'd been that enough times to know it ended up with her feeling used and broken.

"Everyone says you're just sharing the house together, but I left the party wondering." Harlee winged up her brows in question.

"We're just roommates, that's all."

Sometimes Dana suspected Aidan showered her with attention because he felt sorry for her. She got the distinct impression that the man was a caretaker—probably the reason he became a firefighter—and worried that Dana lacked a social life. That was why he dragged her into his.

"You never know," Harlee said. "That could change."

Doubtful, Dana thought, but if she could keep her heart out of it she wouldn't mind having a brief affair with him. It wasn't every day that a single woman in the middle of nowhere had access to a single man like Aidan McBride. Just the thought of being with him gave her shivers. Her times with Griffin had been nice, but Aidan struck her as the kind of man who knew his way around a woman's body. Dana's problem was she'd never been able to separate her heart from sex.

"The dress is perfect." Harlee made Dana turn around so she could view it from the back. "Add it to the pile."

"You don't think it's too tight?"

"Are you crazy? I think it fits you like a glove. It'll go from day to night with a little suit jacket and then some chunky jewelry for painting the town."

As if Dana ever painted the town. But she did adore the dress and could wear Spanx to keep her stomach from pooching out too much, she thought as she examined herself in the full-length mirror.

"You sure you want to give this up? It's a really great dress."

"I have one in blue that I like better. Plus, for working at the *Trib* the dress is too much. I don't have clients like you do. Around here, I can get away with wearing jeans and boots for most of my interviews." Harlee grabbed a jumper and a couple of maxi dresses off the rack. "Here, try these on."

Dana went back inside the bathroom. "I don't know about this." The jumper was snug, too short, and cut her torso in an unflattering way.

"Let me see." Harlee let herself inside the bathroom. "No good. I don't know what I was thinking when I bought that. Maybe it would look cute on Lina. She's tiny enough to pull it—" Harlee stopped talking, and an uneasy silence ensued. Dana didn't know why, but she started laughing.

"Sorry," Harlee said and chewed on her bottom lip. "Was that insensitive of me? I never knew whether Lina was the reason you and Griff stopped seeing each other."

"It's all right. I'm happy for Griffin and Lina." Not exactly the truth, but Dana was getting there.

"Try on the dresses." Harlee sat on the toilet with the cover down.

Dana, who'd originally felt self-conscious about changing in front of her, slipped off the romper and put on the yellow maxi.

"I'm not loving the color on you. Try the green one," Harlee said, and Dana switched dresses. "Now, that one is adorable. Definitely a keeper."

Dana stood on her tiptoes and backed up so she could see herself in the bathroom mirror. "I can't believe you're giving me all these beautiful outfits."

She loved everything and, even more, loved having someone to tell her what looked good and what didn't. Ordinarily, most of these clothes would've been too daring for her. But Harlee, whose taste Dana trusted, gave her courage to experiment with a new wardrobe.

"Yoo-hoo, anyone home?"

"We're in here," Harlee called.

Darla entered the bathroom, holding a couple of Bun Boy bags and shaking them in the air. "Lunch." She turned her attention to Dana. "Ooh, so cute."

"Doesn't that dress fit her perfectly?"

Darla put the bags down on the sink counter and started playing with Dana's hair. "You have such a gorgeous neck. Wear your hair up when you wear the dress. Very sexy."

"Should we continue the fashion show after lunch?" Harlee asked. "I'm starved."

Dana changed into her jeans and T-shirt and the three of them ate in Harlee's gourmet kitchen.

"This is a really beautiful house," Dana said, glancing around at the custom cabinetry and stainless-steel appliances. She had clients who would kill for a home situated on a private mountainside like this. "Colin does amazing work."

Harlee beamed. The love she had for her husband was so obvious. "What's going on with your rebuild?"

"Colin is working on changes to my plans. As soon as that's done, we go to the city for permits."

"I wish Wyatt and I could rebuild, or at least remodel," Darla said. "His house is fugly. Cottage cheese ceilings, rust stains in the tub, and funky carpet in the living room. He actually thinks it's nice."

"I told you I'd come over and help you rip the carpet out while Wyatt's working," Harlee said.

"I can't decide what to replace it with."

"As far as for resale, definitely go with hardwood." As soon as the words came out of Dana's mouth she felt bad. What if the hair stylist and Wyatt didn't like hardwood?

"That's what I'm leaning toward. It's just so expensive."

"I told you Colin would help with it," Harlee said.

"Colin has enough to do. We'll get around to it eventually. In the meantime, I've got gossip."

"Do tell." Harlee bit into her fried chicken sandwich and washed it down with a vanilla shake.

Somehow, Darla had known to get Dana a cheeseburger with no tomatoes and sauce on the side, with a large order of curly fries. She must've asked someone at the Bun Boy. Ah, the beauty of small-town living. Folks even knew your food preferences.

"Ray Rosser is talking plea bargain," she said, and Dana nearly choked on her Coke.

"He's not planning to take the case to trial?" Harlee seemed just as surprised.

The old man wasn't one to quit without a good fight. Perhaps the stakes were too high. First-degree murder carried a penalty of twenty-five years to life in prison. Even if he managed to whittle that sentence down in exchange for a guilty plea, Ray Rosser would never see daylight from outside a prison yard.

"Not according to my dad, who heard about the plea deal from Earl Miller at Farm Supply," Darla said.

Dana's brain ran a million miles a minute, trying to analyze what this could mean for her client. Gia hadn't gotten back to Ray on the additional thirty thousand dollars. A plea bargain, though, would save Ray money on what was sure to be a lengthy trial.

"How does Earl know about it?" Harlee asked. "If it's true, I'd like to get the story in the *Trib* as soon as possible."

Harlee got up and returned a few minutes later with a laptop. At the table, she flipped up the lid and began typing. Dana watched as she searched for results on Ray Rosser.

"I don't see anything about a plea deal in the Quincy paper," she said and continued typing. "There's nothing about it anywhere as far as I can tell."

"It doesn't mean it's not true. I bet we're the first to know." Darla downed the rest of her shake.

"How can you find out for sure?" Dana asked Harlee.

"I can call Del Webber, Ray's attorney, or George Williamson, the prosecutor. They probably won't tell me anything, though. Not unless it's a done deal."

It was on the tip of Dana's tongue to tell her to call the lawyers anyway when her own phone rang. Gia.

Aidan was supposed to have Thursday off, but he got called out on a suspicious structure fire. A goat barn on a farm outside of Nugget. By the time he arrived, firefighters had knocked down most of the blaze before it could spread to any of the other outbuildings, giving him plenty of time to search the perimeter and the scene itself. And he didn't like what he saw. Luckily, someone had evacuated the goats before they'd become barbecue. But the critters had gotten loose from the pen they'd been corralled in and were roaming wild, getting into Cal Fire's equipment.

"Can someone get these out of here?" Aidan called.

The police chief, Rhys Shepard, who'd apparently been called out too, laughed and started shooing away the animals nibbling on hoses and turn-out gear. Shepard gave a commanding one-handed whistle and two dogs came running down a path. They rounded up the stragglers, got them back inside the pen, and stood guard.

Aidan watched in awe. "They just know how to do that?"

"Yep," Rhys said. "It's in their blood."

"The owner have kids?"

Rhys gazed out over the herd of goats and nudged his head at a few of the babies as they ran through the corral, taking occasional sideways leaps into the air.

"Not those kinds of kids." Aidan's lips curved up. He had to admit they were damned cute. "The two-legged ones."

"Sean and his little brother, Seth. Whaddya got?"

"Firework mortars."

Captain Johnson joined them, took his fire helmet off, and mopped his forehead with the back of his hand. "You show Rhys what you found?"

A firefighter Aidan didn't know approached. The first thing Aidan noticed was that he still had his mask and hood on—a little overkill, considering the fire was out. Johnson rolled his eyes.

"Go kick rocks, Duke." When Duke walked away, Johnson muttered something about him being a whacker. A whacker was a guy who spent his day on Twitter and Facebook, telling the world about all the fires he'd fought when, in fact, he hadn't done dick.

"McBride show you the shed?" Johnson asked Rhys.

"I was just about to." Aidan motioned for Rhys and Johnson to follow him to a ramshackle outbuilding filled with electrical equipment, mortar tubes, and a collection of pyrotechnic chemicals he'd discovered earlier. "I found the remnants of a few of these"—he held up the cardboard tubes—"in the barn and suspect someone was celebrating the Fourth of July on the fifth."

"You think Sean or Seth?"

"And maybe a few friends." Aidan guided Rhys and his captain back to the burned-out barn and showed them a youth's denim jacket that had been badly singed in the fire. But it hadn't been damaged enough to obscure the ranch logo over the breast.

Rhys muttered something under his breath, then said, "So this was a group effort?"

"For all I know, the jacket was just sitting here when the fire started. The owner is an electrician, right?"

"Yep. The goats are his and his wife's side business. I know for a fact that he was doing electrical up at Lucky's ranch when the 9-1-1 call came in. Mrs. Rigsby was at the Nugget Market, where she works part-time. Nope, this has the mark of kids with too much time on their hands. And that jacket you found belongs to a neighbor boy . . . my godson." Rhys didn't look too happy about that revelation. "Let me round them up for you." He got on his phone and wandered away.

"Looks like you've got this covered," the captain said. "Good job. I'm going back to the house. See you later."

Aidan watched Johnson walk back to the engine with Duke, who still hadn't bothered to remove his gear, trailing him like one of those baby goats.

Twenty minutes later, Aidan and Rhys sat in the Rigsbys' kitchen, staring down two teenagers who only wanted to look at the floor. The doorbell rang and Mr. Rigsby got up to get it, while Mrs.

Rigsby made a pot of coffee. The two had come rushing home when they'd heard news of the fire.

Two more teens and one pissed-off father joined their ranks.

Aidan introduced himself. "Justin and Cody McCreedy, right?"

"Yes, sir," the boys said in unison.

"I'm their father, Clay. We've met a few times, unofficially."

"Good to meet you." Aidan glanced over at the boys, who, like their comrades in crime, found the checkerboard linoleum enormously fascinating. Clay was the cowboy who'd given Dana a hard time, already a strike against him.

The boys, on the other hand, he felt sorry for. He still remembered the time he and his brothers had snuck out of the house one summer night and taken a joyride in his father's Ford Torino GT. None of them had had a license, and he, being the oldest, had driven, taking a wrong turn and getting them lost in the process. Hastily trying to find his way back, he'd run a red light, got T-boned by a minivan, and was arrested. Aidan had never seen his father angrier. To this day, he, Arron, and Shane swore that smoke had poured out of Marty's ears—just like in the cartoons—when he'd come to bail their sorry asses out of police custody. It had been the arresting officer who had diffused the situation.

"Although what you boys did showed terrible judgment . . . someone could have been seriously hurt, or worse, killed . . . I'm just thankful that all we have here are a few banged-up cars." For the next part of the speech he'd looked straight at Aidan's dad. "I don't have to tell you, Marty, how this could've turned out. Thank God everyone is walking away from this okay."

The truth was, the Torino GT was never the same after the accident. Still, when they left the station, Marty gathered all three of his boys in a giant hug.

"You guys ever do anything like this again and I'll kill you."

Aidan would never forget the sheen in his eyes.

He turned to the four teens, each one ready to piss his pants, and said, "Let's cut straight to the chase. You were messing around with fireworks, the barn caught on fire, you got scared and ran off."

"We got the goats out first," Justin said. "And I called 9-1-1."

Aidan looked at Rhys, who nodded. "That was good, Justin. Not good that you were playing with the fireworks. They're illegal in

Nugget. If that fire had gotten out of hand it could've burned the entire town down and then some. Not to mention that you four could've been hurt . . . or worse."

Out of the corner of his eye he saw Clay's mouth pinch tight.

"We didn't mean it to happen," Sean said.

Aidan took a deep breath and nodded. "This time you boys were lucky. But there can't be a next time."

"We know," Justin said. "It'll never happen again." He seemed so solemn that Aidan suppressed a smile.

"You can bet your ass it won't." John Rigsby stood up from the table and glowered at all four boys. He turned his attention to his own. "The two of you are gonna pay, that's for damn sure. All that money you were saving for dirt bikes will now go to rebuilding the barn."

The man had every right to be angry, but something about his attitude didn't sit right with Aidan. It was almost as if John was putting on a show to demonstrate what a hard-ass he was in front Aidan and Rhys.

Aidan turned to the police chief. "I think we're done here. Rhys?"

"Yup." The chief nodded.

No one seemed more stunned than the kids themselves.

"You're not going to arrest us?" Cody asked.

"Nah," Aidan said. "But I am going to confiscate the fireworks. You guys know how lucky you were that this didn't turn out to be a full-fledged catastrophe . . . that no one wound up in the burn unit? I want you all to think about that." He made sure he included the parents in that last statement. What was Rigsby thinking, keeping all those fireworks in his shed where anyone could get to them?

"My boys would like to volunteer to come down to the fire station and wash latrines," Clay McCreedy said and eyed both his kids as if daring them to contradict his offer. "It's the least they can do after putting Cal Fire to so much trouble and expense when you folks have your hands full."

"What about my barn?" Rigsby asked and glared at Clay. Aidan got the distinct impression there was no love lost between the two men.

"I'm sure you've got insurance, John, but my boys will do their part."

Rhys stood up. "I think we're good here. Deputy Fire Marshal McBride and I need to know if there are any other fireworks, pyrotechnic chemicals, or mortar tubes besides what we found in the shed near the barn."

"Uh, that's my private property," John said, folding his arms over his chest. Aidan viewed the gesture for what it was: a sign of aggression.

"Not anymore." The chief moved toward the door. "Do we need to tear this place apart?"

"Not without a warrant," John spat, and got in Rhys's face.

Aidan moved between the two, not because the chief couldn't handle himself but because he wanted to neutralize the situation in front of the kids. "We just got done saying we're not charging anyone with a crime here. We don't need a warrant because these are exigent circumstances. I found enough illegal pyrotechnics to burn down half of Plumas County. We're taking them, and if you don't want us adding more chaos to what has already been a trying day"—he made a point of looking at the boys—"I'd step up here."

He was practically bumping chests with the guy, who looked like he spent a lot of time bench-pressing. Of course the onesie Rigsby tried to pass off as a shirt probably gave the illusion that he was more pumped than he really was.

"I know you were some hotshot arson investigator in Chicago, but here you're just a firefighter, not even a captain," John said. "So don't threaten me."

There was some truth to what Rigsby said. In California, Aidan was starting almost from scratch. He would have to work his way up to make captain, and most arson investigators here held that rank. Still, the state fire marshal's office wasn't about to overlook Aidan's expertise and experience, especially when the department was strapped for resources in rural locales like Nugget. He'd been designated a peace officer, despite the lack of rank, and was expected to investigate suspicious fires in the wilds of the Sierra Nevada.

"This isn't a threat," Aidan said and turned to Rhys. "Let's call in a team to go over this farm with a fine-tooth comb."

"I'm on it." Rhys grabbed his radio, but John, who'd been receiving death glares from his wife, stopped him.

"Fine." He puffed out an impatient breath, like he was doing them a favor. "I have more in the basement." It was always the ones who came on strong that folded the fastest.

Aidan would rather think John Rigsby was trying to teach his kids right from wrong. More than likely, though, he knew he and the chief were well within their rights to rip the place apart.

Rigsby led them downstairs to a semifinished room with a pool table, opened a huge storage closet, and pulled out shitloads of the stuff. Rockets, missiles, aerial repeaters, firecrackers, and Roman candles.

"What were you planning to do with all this?" Rhys asked.

"Sell it. I was working for a guy, rewiring his house, and he had all this stuff from a stand he used to operate every year around the Fourth of July in Nevada. He gave me a good deal."

Not such a good deal because it was all getting removed—and never returned. "You can't bring fireworks into the state without the California State Fire Marshal seal on it." Aidan turned over the packages to demonstrate there was no such seal. Another reason to confiscate it.

The three of them made several trips carrying up boxes.

"This is it?" Rhys asked.

John nodded. "Just this and what's in the shed."

Clay and his sons had left, but he figured McCreedy had been serious about sending the kids over to the firehouse for cleaning duty. In Aidan's opinion, that was the right way to bring up children. And knowing Captain Johnson, he'd have them washing the engines. The boys would probably get a kick out of it too. Aidan, Arron, Shane, and Sloane used to wash engines at his dad's station before Marty had become a battalion chief. Hanging out with their father and the other firefighters had been one of the highlights of being a kid. Water fights. Watching the Bears. Eating spaghetti dinners. The guys at the station were the McBride kids' extended family.

He and Rhys returned to the shed and loaded up the rest of the pyrotechnics in their two vehicles. Rhys agreed to store the cache at the police department until they figured out what to do with it.

"Nice job in there," Rhys said. "Don't take what John said personally. Even back in high school he was a dickhead . . . always thought the world owed him . . . always resented anyone he perceived as having more than he did. His wife's good people, though. Believe it or not, she's softened his edges. He never would've given in to us if she hadn't been standing there. The kid, Sean, is a holy terror. I was kind of hoping John would've volunteered Sean and Seth for work at the firehouse like Clay did . . . keep that kid out of my hair for a while. Clay's boys are good kids, though, even if I am biased."

"Hey, fireworks are pretty seductive to boys that age, hell to men my age." Aidan laughed. "They at least got the goats out and called 9-1-1. And Rigsby probably has insurance on the barn."

"Yeah," Rhys said and flashed a sardonic grin. "But let's hope it's a bitch of a deductible." With that, he drove away, leaving Aidan thinking that he and his sister's boss were going to get along just fine.

Aidan followed him to the highway and headed back to the fire station, needing to write up a report on the incident. Then he'd take the rest of his day off and see what Dana was up to. Maybe they'd go to dinner in Reno. She'd grown up there, so she was bound to know where the good restaurants were.

When he got home later, he found her at the kitchen table, eating one of his Otter Pops.

"Hope you don't mind that I stole one?" she said.

"Have as many as you'd like." Jeez, watching her eat the pop . . . yeah, not gonna go there. "What's going on?" He eyed the maxi dress she had on. Not her usual style, but he liked it. A lot.

"My client countered today on the Rosser Ranch. A few days ago, I don't think old man Rosser would've accepted her counter, considering it's not the full thirty thousand more he wanted. But due to new circumstances, we may have a done deal." She crossed her fingers.

"Yeah?" He couldn't help pulling her out of the chair and getting his arms around her. She felt even better than he'd imagined, soft and round in all the right places. "That's great. We've got to celebrate."

She tugged free of him—he might've been crushing her—and her face glowed with a combination of delight and surprise. "Really?"

"Hell yeah. This is a huge deal, right?" What, didn't she ever celebrate things like this?

"It's the biggest sale I've ever had . . . will probably ever have. But I don't want to jinx it."

"Okay." Aidan understood being superstitious. "Then we'll just go out to dinner. We'll do the celebration thing when everyone's signed on the dotted line."

"All right."

This, Aidan could tell, pleased her. He couldn't say why, but he liked pleasing her. She was no pushover but seemed inordinately appreciative of any overtures of friendship. Last night, at the party, he didn't think she even realized how charming she'd been. Once people got her talking, she'd been open, friendly, and nonjudgmental. It sounded like her family's candy business dwarfed Hutch's, yet she acted like they were in the same league. Sue always compartmentalized people. They were either in her strata or not worth her time.

"Where do you want to go?" Dana asked.

"What about Reno? I haven't really checked out the place."

"We can go there. You in the mood for Italian? I know a good place."

"Absolutely. Do we need a reservation?"

"I'll make one on the way." She held up her phone, then looked at the time. "But let's go now; I'm starved."

"Okay. Let me change first." Aidan was in shorts and a T-shirt he'd put on at the fire station. "This place have a dress code?"

She laughed. "You're in the West now. A nice pair of jeans will get you in just about anywhere."

He decided on a pressed pair of khakis and an Oxford shirt anyway. If it had been Sue's outing, she would've insisted he wear a tie. Instead, he splashed on a little cologne and called it a day. When he came out of his room Dana looked twice.

"Should I get dressed up too?"

"You are," he said and pointed to her dress. "That new?"

"Harlee gave it to me, and a whole bunch of other stuff." She stood up and smoothed out the wrinkles. "Do you think it looks okay? It's not something I'd ordinarily wear, but she and Darla made such a fuss that I . . . well, what do you think?"

"It looks great." He particularly liked the tube-top part. If he had to guess, she wasn't wearing a bra. She might even be going commando under the skirt; he didn't see any panty lines.

Aidan wrapped his arm around her waist. "Let's hit the road."

They made good time to Reno. Dana spent much of the ride making their reservation and returning calls to clients.

"I've been so caught up with the Rosser deal that I've been neglecting my other folks," she told him as she directed him to the parking lot of a strip mall.

"This it?" It didn't look like much, just a storefront with lace curtains in the windows and a worn sign that said "Gaetano's."

There were a million trendy restaurants in Chicago, and Sue had insisted they go to every one. None of them looked like this.

"Don't worry; it may not look like much, but the food's good," she said and stepped down from his truck before he could help her out.

True to her word, the place was packed. Even though they'd gotten a reservation, they had to wait for a table. Aidan ordered them drinks at the bar: Prosecco for Dana and a scotch for him. A stool became available and he grabbed it for her, leaning his front against her back as they shared a small swath of bar.

"You smell good," she said.

"Thanks. So do you." He sniffed her neck and, in the process, got a quick glimpse of cleavage as she bent closer to the bar to get her drink. He'd been wrong about the bra. She had some kind of lacy band around her breasts.

The hostess came, showed them to their table, and lit the candle. Dana buried her face in the menu and Aidan asked for refills on their drinks.

"Tell me about the fire." She put her menu down. "I heard you leave early this morning, and Harlee said something about it when I was at her house today."

"It was at the Rigsby farm. You know the family?"

"Not by name. Was anyone hurt?"

"Nah. The Rigsby kids got a hold of some of the father's fireworks and were shooting off mortar rockets. The barn caught fire and one of the McCreedy kids—they were involved too—called 9-1-1. They got the goats out in time, but the barn's a wreck."

"Did you help fight the fire?"

"It was pretty much knocked down by the time I got turned out. I was there in an investigative capacity because the captain suspected right off the bat that something wasn't right."

"The fireworks?"

"Yep."

The server came with their refills and took their orders. The place was old-school Italian, none of those tiny plates with food Aidan couldn't describe. He got the veal parm and Dana got the osso buco. He ordered them an antipasto plate and fried calamari to start.

"Was it dangerous going through the fire, looking for clues?" she asked when the waiter left.

"Nope. The dangerous part is putting out the fire. But get this: Rigsby got belligerent when we told him we were confiscating the fireworks."

Her eyes grew wide. "Like how?"

"Acting like an asshat by throwing his weight around. Eventually he gave in. It wasn't like he had a choice."

"Could you arrest him?"

"Technically. But I'm not into that. I just wanted to get the pyrotechnics out of there. That's all."

She leaned across the table. "Be careful. People out in the country sometimes get weird about authority figures. They don't like being told what to do, and a lot of these guys have guns."

"Yeah, I get that impression."

He enjoyed talking to her about his work. Sue had been attracted to the idea of his job because a lot of women were hot for firefighters. As far as the details of his day-to-day work, she couldn't have cared less. It bored her, which Aidan had never been able to understand. How could arson, the act of intentionally setting something on fire, be boring?

"Are the kids in trouble?" Dana asked.

"I gave them a pass because it was an accident. A boneheaded accident, but an accident just the same. McCreedy is punishing his boys by making them clean the firehouse. I didn't have the heart to tell him the kids are gonna love it."

"You certainly do." She laughed. "Are your brothers as passionate about being firefighters as you are?"

"Yep. We're all crazy in the head." He smiled at her. "So what are the new circumstances that make you think Rosser will take less money?"

The waiter brought their appetizers. Aidan took a bite of the calamari and it was freaking fantastic. Dana served him a crostino.

"The rumor is that Ray Rosser plans to take a plea bargain, which means he doesn't need to pay his lawyers for a lengthy trial." She passed him the antipasto platter and speared a calamari with her fork.

"Where did you hear that?"

"From Darla, who heard it from her dad and told Harlee and me."

She dipped the calamari in the bowl of lemon aioli and popped it in her mouth. "Harlee tried to pin it down for a story in the *Nugget Tribune*, but no one would talk. You think it's true?"

"I would have no way of knowing," he said. "What are they knocking the charge down to, do you know?"

"No. But he's facing first-degree murder if he takes it to trial."

"Is that why you think he'll accept your client's counter?"

"Not exactly," she said and served him some of the cured meats. "Try these, they're delicious. His lawyer seemed optimistic, like they just wanted to be done with the negotiations and get the place into escrow. Of course it's up to Ray. At least I think it's up to Ray. There are some rumors that he's already signed the property over to the lawyers . . . that they're the ones pulling the strings."

The server returned with their entrees.

"I'm already stuffed," Dana said.

Not him. He could probably eat both their meals. "Take a stab at it."

He cut into his veal and took a bite. Dana had been right; the food here was amazing.

She stuck a forkful of her osso buco in his face. "Try this. I'm serious."

He dutifully complied, and hell yeah, it was good. It made him wonder how many places like this he had missed in Chicago, eating at Sue's food museums.

"How'd you find this place?" He suspected she'd come here with Griffin, which made the food feel heavy in his stomach.

"It's been here a long time. When Paul was alive this was my family's favorite restaurant."

"Your parents don't come anymore?"

She gave a mirthless laugh. "No. Honestly, I can't remember the last time I was here. But the quality is still good, right?"

"Absolutely. The food is fantastic." He reached across the table and took her hand. "Is it difficult . . . does it remind you of your brother?"

"In a good way," she said. "It was our happy place, the place we came to celebrate things."

He lowered his voice. "Is that why you wanted to come?"

At first she didn't answer; then she said, "I guess subconsciously, yeah."

"Thank you for sharing it with me," he said. "I'll tell you what: When you close the deal we'll come back."

"Can I ask you question?" She didn't wait for an answer. "How is it possible Sue could've ever let someone like you go?"

He didn't get a chance to answer because his phone rang. His captain. Someone had tried to burn down the sporting goods store.

Chapter 11

The fire was all anyone could talk about the next day. Everywhere Dana went, someone spouted a theory. At the Gas and Go she ran into Owen while filling her tank. The barber, who'd never said so much as boo to her before, walked over to her pump and began spewing all kinds of crazy speculation on how it started.

"It was probably those Rigsby boys, trying to get even for having their fireworks confiscated. That Sean has always been trouble ... a regular juvenile delinquent."

Dana didn't know how burning down the sporting goods store would help them "get even" because the owner, Carl Rudd, had nothing to do with what had happened at the Rigsby farm. But she supposed it was as good a theory as any. At least the blaze had been confined to the back of the store, afterhours. No one had gotten hurt and the damage had been minimal. She figured she'd get the skinny from Aidan when he got home.

She hadn't seen him since they'd hightailed it out of the restaurant and back to Nugget. He'd gone straight to the fire and had come home sometime in the wee hours of the morning when she'd been fast asleep. This morning she'd left the house to go to the office before he'd awoken.

After getting gas, she headed to the Bun Boy to get a cup of coffee. Donna Thurston, the drive-through's owner, was absolutely certain Carl had accidentally set the fire himself and didn't want to 'fess up to save face.

"Everyone knows he's smoking again and throws his butts behind the store so his wife won't catch him. The idiot man apparently didn't get the memo about the drought and this year's fire danger. What does Aidan think?"

"I haven't seen him since he went to investigate."

Dana finally realized why she'd suddenly become so popular with the townsfolk. Aidan. It should've bothered her; instead, it gave her a zing of delight because maybe, just maybe, she was starting to belong.

The Bun Boy's owner leaned out of the take-out window. "What's going on with the Rosser property? I hear you have a live one."

Dana laughed. "We're still in negotiations. You think the rumor about Ray making a plea bargain is true?" She'd never stopped to gossip with the residents. But why not, as long as it was harmless?

"My take on that is even though there's no bigger SOB on the planet, Ray wants to do right by his family . . . set them up financially. He can't do that if he pisses away all the proceeds of the ranch on his lawyers, fighting an uphill battle. Let's face it, the man's guilty as sin. Gus may have been stealing his cattle, but Ray shot him in cold blood."

Dana thought it was an interesting notion, one she hadn't considered only because Ray seemed too selfish to think about anyone else but himself. But Donna had known him her whole life and was probably privy to a different side of him. Dana just wanted him to accept Gia's counter to his counter. Whatever he decided to do about his case was between him and his lawyers.

"You could be right," Dana said, putting the lid on her travel mug. "I'd better get to the office."

"You tell that young man of yours that we're waiting on him to do a restaurant inspection before we can get our open-flame permit. We're installing some of those Santa Maria–style barbecues."

He wasn't her man, but Dana had to admit she liked the sound of it. "I'll let my roommate know," she said, got in her car, and drove to Nugget Realty.

"Hey." Carol popped her head up from the computer when Dana walked in.

"I wasn't expecting you back from Santa Cruz until Monday. How was the beach?"

"It was great, but Vance was itchy to get back to work. You hear about the sporting goods store?"

"Aidan and I were having dinner when he got called away. You really think it was arson?" Dana couldn't imagine why anyone would want to set fire to Carl's store. Bad things like that just didn't happen in Nugget.

"I don't know what to think," Carol said. "But forget the fire. You were having dinner with Aidan?" She lifted her brows, waiting to hear the whole story.

"It was just a spur-of-the-moment thing . . . two people who live in the same house who didn't want to cook. We went to an Italian place in Reno I used to go to. Nothing romantic."

Though Dana wondered. Aidan seemed more than friendly, but she didn't want to read into things between them and be disappointed that it was all in her head. Besides, she'd caught him a few times looking at Sue's Facebook page on his laptop. She supposed it was normal to be curious. God knew she looked at Tim's all the time, even though they were completely over. But she suspected Aidan hadn't stopped loving Sue. And she wasn't going to be second place ever again.

"That's too bad," Carol said. "He seems like a good catch. Anything new on your client's counteroffer?"

Dana had been texting Carol in Santa Cruz with details. "Nope, still waiting to hear back from Ray's lawyer. I promised myself that I would block it out of my head and try to get some work done. The Arnolds are still interested in Sierra Heights but want to see a few homes outside a planned community before making a decision. I wanted to send them listings . . . try to get them to come up this weekend to look. What are you working on?"

"A couple from Walnut Creek is looking to buy a cabin up here. They want something near the river."

"Don't forget about that place on Feather Vista. It needs work, but the views are spectacular."

The phone rang and Carol answered. A minute later, she signaled to Dana that it was for her. "Del."

Showtime!

"Hello, Mr. Webber. How are you?" Dana wanted to cut to the chase but didn't want to appear overanxious. People around here got to the heart of the matter in their own sweet time.

"How you doing, Dana?"

"I'm fine. You have a chance to run the counteroffer by Ray?"

"I have," he said, and Dana could hear him shuffling papers in the background. "He's willing to go for it, including leaving the furniture."

Dana had to keep from gasping. Holy Toledo; she was about to close the biggest deal of her career.

"Ray, however, is adamant that Flynn Barlow maintain grazing rights for his cattle for the next two years. The Rossers and Barlows have been longtime associates in the cattle industry. Ray wants to keep his word to them."

"But payments for the two-year lease will go to my buyer." Gia had shown interest in the income because Dana doubted she would use the land to run her own cattle.

"Nope, Rosser wants that money."

Ray wants to keep his word, Dana's ass. He wanted to continue profiting off land that no longer belonged to him from behind prison bars. Nice scam. But Dana was Ray's agent too, so she held her tongue. "I'll run it by the buyer. If she's good with it, you think we could get this signed before the weekend?"

"That's the plan," Del said. "Between you and me, Ray's gonna plead guilty tomorrow. As soon as that's done, they'll move him to San Quentin to be processed. So let's get this done before he's transferred."

"The word's already out. Harlee Roberts, the local reporter, found out from one of her sources," Dana said. "Is it okay if I confirm it for her?"

"Sure. The cat will be out of the bag in twenty-four hours."

"What's he pleading guilty to?" Dana asked, curious herself.

"Second-degree murder with a gun enhancement . . . fifteen to life and ten for the gun."

Whoa, that was a lot of time. "I'll talk to the buyer and get back to you right away. Thanks, Del."

"Let's get it done," he said.

As soon as she got off the phone with Del, Carol hovered. "Well?"

"Ray went for it. Fifteen thousand more instead of thirty thousand." Dana explained the caveat about Ray continuing to collect the income from the cattle lease.

"It can't be that much money," Carol said.

"I think Gia will go for it."

"Woohoo!" Carol called out, and both she and Dana danced around the office like crazy women.

As soon as they calmed down, Dana called Gia.

"They've accepted!" she said, not bothering with a formal greeting. "But there's a catch. Ray wants to continue collecting on the grazing lease for the life of the contract . . . two years."

Dana heard Gia take a deep breath. "I was counting on that money. And now the land will be tied up, preventing me from doing anything to monetize it."

"Not necessarily," Dana said. "Not unless you want to run livestock too."

"Or plant."

The idea of Gia becoming a farmer seemed far-fetched to Dana, but she wasn't going to argue with a client. "I can tell them no, but the truth is, there have been changes in Ray's situation that will make it difficult for us to continue negotiating."

"Like what?"

"Tomorrow he's planning to take a plea bargain. I'm not clear on all the details, but according to his lawyer, he'll be moved from the county jail to San Quentin."

"Ah, jeez. What should I do, Dana?"

"It's up to you. But in a multimillion-dollar deal like this, it seems silly to walk away for twenty-five-thousand-dollars in land revenue."

"It's not the money," Gia said. "It's not having use of the land for two years. But I'm going to take the deal anyway."

"You sure? Maybe you ought to sleep on it?"

"I've slept on it long enough," Gia said. "When do I sign?"

Dana's heartbeat kicked up. "I'll email the papers to you right now. Print and sign what I've highlighted and I'll send you our FedEx number to overnight them back to me. Congratulations, Gia."

As soon as she finished up with Gia, she called Harlee at the *Trib*.

"Hi, Harlee, it's Dana. I've got information."

"About the fire at the sporting goods store?" Apparently, Ray Rosser was yesterday's news.

"Nope. It's about Ray Rosser."

"Seriously? Should I come over in person?"

"That would be good," Dana said.

Harlee had given her all those clothes and now Dana wanted to do something nice for her. She worked so hard running the paper and Dana respected everything she had built for herself. Darla too. Businesswomen had to stick together.

"What are you up to?" Carol smiled.

"Ray's going to plead guilty to second-degree murder. Del gave me permission to tell Harlee, who heard about it through the Nugget rumor mill but couldn't get it confirmed."

"That's nice of you to help her."

Dana stood up and pointed to her new outfit. "From Harlee."

"I thought it looked new. But since the fire, everything is new. It's a different style for you . . . a good style that shows off your lovely figure."

"Thanks, Carol," she said and wondered if Aidan would like it.

A little while later, Harlee's Pathfinder rolled into the parking lot and, armed with a reporter's notebook, she rushed into the office, out of breath. "I've been immersed in the fire and have been looking all over town for Aidan. You wouldn't happen to know where he is? He's not answering his phone."

"I don't," Dana said.

"That's okay. It sounds like you have a bigger scoop for me. So it's true about Ray Rosser?"

"Yep. He's pleading guilty to second-degree murder tomorrow." She told Harlee everything she'd learned from Del Webber.

"Oh my God, this is awesome, Dana." She stopped scribbling in her notebook long enough to give Dana the once-over. "The skirt and top are fantastic on you. I've got to run and get this Rosser story up as soon as possible. If you see Aidan, could you tell him to call me? I just need a quick quote from him for the fire story."

"He's right here," Dana said as Aidan came strolling into the office, looking tired but unbelievably hot in a pair of well-worn Levi's and a Cal Fire T-shirt that accentuated his muscles.

"I've been looking everywhere for you," Harlee said.

"You've got me now. What's up?"

"The fire . . . was it arson?" Harlee flipped through her notebook until she found a clean page.

Aidan leaned his hip against Dana's desk. "We don't think it was an accident and are asking for help from the public. Anyone who has information should call us." He rattled off a hotline number.

"Why do you think the fire was intentional?" Harlee asked.

"I didn't say that." Aidan smiled. "I said it wasn't an accident."

"Now you're just playing with semantics," Harlee said.

He grinned, evidently enjoying the wordplay. "I can't get into details, but let's just say there are some telltale signs."

"Like what?" Harlee insisted.

"Like signs I can't talk about. Not yet, anyway. But good try."

"All right, I'll check back with you later. I've got to get going. Now I've got two big stories. Thanks, Dana. You rock, girlfriend."

When Harlee left, Aidan asked, "What was that about?"

"I got it confirmed that Ray Rosser has accepted a plea bargain. And . . . Ray accepted my buyer's offer. It looks like the deal is going through."

Aidan lifted her in the air and spun her around. "You did it."

Dana grabbed onto Aidan's shoulders, afraid he'd drop her, and quickly scanned the room for Carol, who seemed to have disappeared.

"I've got you, you know?" He continued to hold her as if she weighed nothing.

"Aidan, stop. I'm getting dizzy."

"Kiss me first."

"What? . . . Why?"

"Because I want you to." He'd stopped the spinning and slowly put her down on the floor, tipping her head back so he could go in for the kiss.

It started out slow at first, just his lips brushing her lips, soft and supple. When she twined her arms around his neck, he went in for more, melding his mouth to hers, working his way between her lips with his tongue. He tasted so good, like warm, sweet breath and yearning. Cradling the back of her head in his big hands, he hummed his pleasure as he took the kiss deeper. She could feel further evidence of his desire hard against her belly and pushed herself into him as close as she could get without crawling inside of him. He felt so good. Strong, solid, and safe.

And that was when the little voice in her head reminded her that Aidan was on the rebound. He was strong, solid, and safe for the woman he'd lost and still loved. Not for her. For her, he was heartbreak waiting to happen. So little by little, as difficult as it was, she inched away from the kiss, trying to find her equilibrium.

Aidan reached out to steady her, running his thumb over her swollen lips. "You okay?"

"Yes. But we shouldn't do that in my office." Or anywhere.

"Then let's go home and do it." He tossed her a cheeky grin. The rogue.

"I have work," she said but couldn't help wondering what it would be like to go home with Aidan McBride as his lover instead of his roommate. If his kiss was any indication, he'd be good. Probably the best she'd ever had, which wasn't saying all that much.

"What about celebrating?"

"Still don't want to jinx it. No celebrating until the place closes escrow."

"I get that, but we've gotta do something." He scrubbed the scruff on his face as if he was thinking about where they could go.

"We already went out to dinner last night," she said.

"So, why can't we do it again, or something else fun? Let's go bowling."

"Don't you have an arsonist to find?" she asked.

"Sweetheart, it's not like the movies, where I spend my days and nights buried in the case. At this point we're in a holding pattern. But I'm a very patient man." He winked at her like that last statement had a double meaning.

Maybe Sue had left him because he was a big flirt and a lady's man. Otherwise, she'd been crazy. Who would willingly give up a man like Aidan McBride, firefighter hero, builder of closet organizers, and kisser extraordinaire? And someone who seemed to truly know what it meant to be a friend.

"I'll go bowling," she said, although she'd only gone once in her life, as Griffin's date at one of Harlee and Darla's bowling parties. It had been humiliating. Everyone at the party knew Griffin was in love with Lina and that Dana had been a mere placeholder.

"I'll pick you up at six. We'll start our date with dinner."

"It's not a date, Aidan. Just two friends and roommates hanging out."

"You call it what you want," he said. "I'm calling it a date, which is my First Amendment right."

He gave her a quick peck on the cheek and strolled out of the office. It wasn't until he was gone that Dana realized she didn't know why he'd come to her office in the first place.

Chapter 12

The kiss had left him short of breath, not to mention that the erection he was still sporting was killing him. As he sat in his truck, grasping the steering wheel in the real estate office's parking lot, he couldn't figure out why the kiss had thrown him off-kilter like it had.

It was an amazing kiss, no doubt about it. But he'd had other amazing kisses. He'd like to chalk up these unidentifiable feelings he had for Dana to the fact that after seven months he was sex starved and he found her extremely attractive. But that didn't explain why when he woke up this morning he'd had an urgent need to see her. So much so that he'd immediately showered, dressed, and drove to her office with absolutely no excuse for showing up. Thank goodness she hadn't asked because his only answer would've been, "Hell if I know. I just needed to see you."

Really, he should still be mourning the loss of Sue and figuring out why their relationship had gone bad. If it were up to Sloane, he'd be at a Dr. Phil retreat right now, exploring his feelings. The thought made him shudder. The strange part about Sue was that he didn't even miss her. Sometimes he missed the idea of her. But when he tried to visualize what exactly that was, it wasn't Sue's face he saw. Rather it was the security he'd felt in knowing he was in a partnership with a woman who his family admired and adored. A woman more polished than a fireman's dress shoes. A woman who knew what she wanted and how to get it. Except him. She hadn't been able to get him.

Even worse, he'd recently realized that having her happily married to someone else was actually a relief.

He drove the short distance to the Ponderosa. He needed coffee and breakfast, even though it was coming up on lunchtime. Steak and eggs would bridge the two, he told himself. His entire family teased him about his bottomless stomach.

Inside, the jukebox played country-western music. Oddly enough, songs about tractors and truck stops were starting to grow on him. From the moment he'd shown up in Nugget to visit his sister, the mountain town had gotten inside his head and wouldn't let go. He loved the countryside, the rugged mountains, and the towering trees. And he found that the people here suited him. Welcoming, close-knit, and always ready for a celebration of some sort. It appealed to his social side. Aidan loved people and they usually loved him back. There was nothing better than going to the Ponderosa or the Bun Boy and seeing a bunch of people he knew and striking up conversations with all of them.

It also worked as an investigative tool, which was partially the reason he'd wanted a table in the restaurant instead of a place at the bar. Being out in the open would give him better access to diners. On the way, one of the owners was leaving with a sweet bundle in her arms.

"My girl Lilly." Aidan reached over and bussed the top of the baby's head with a kiss as she reached her chubby arms out to him, shrieking in delight.

The owner—Aidan had seen her around the restaurant but had forgotten her name—said, "How do you know my daughter?"

"I thought she was Nate's daughter."

The woman laughed. "She is. She's also Mariah and my daughter. I'm Sophie."

"Pleased to officially meet you, Sophie, although I feel like I've known you for weeks, ever since I started eating at the Ponderosa. Now, Lilly and I go way back."

"I can see that." Sophie let him lift Lilly out of her arms. "She doesn't typically let people hold her. Anything new on the sporting goods fire?"

"Not yet. But if you or any of your employees saw anything out of the ordinary . . . anything that looking back on it now seems odd . . . I'd like to hear about it."

"Give me an example," she said, watching Lilly play with the sunglasses around Aidan's neck.

"A stranger lurking around the store. Someone familiar who seemed particularly nervous the day of the fire. Even if it didn't seem suspicious at the time, it might mean something now."

"Okay, I'll spread the word. So you definitely think it was intentional?"

"Unfortunately, yeah."

"Who would want to do something like that?" she asked, tugging Aidan's shades and neck cord away from Lilly. "Your glasses look expensive."

They were, but he didn't care. "Sometimes it's someone with a vendetta . . . a person who was fired or thought he or she was ill treated by the business. Sometimes it's someone who gets excited by lighting fires, and other times it's a person who likes to watch the spectacle. People running from the building. Emergency crews responding with their sirens blaring. That sort of thing. Then there are those who have something financial to gain by it. Sadly, there are all kinds of reasons."

"Poor Carl. I hope you don't think it's him." Sophie took Lilly from him when she wouldn't stop playing with his glasses.

He usually didn't talk about who was or wasn't a suspect. But as far as he could tell, Carl had no motive to burn his shop down. He didn't even own the building, and his deductible was so high, he wouldn't make much from the insurance money on the few store items he'd lost. "That's not the direction we're looking."

"Thank goodness. I'm glad to hear that. I've got to get going, but help yourself to any table in the place."

He chose one right smack in the middle of the restaurant. And within five minutes the barber helped himself to the seat across from Aidan.

"You looking at those Rigsby kids?"

Ever since Harlee had mentioned the Nugget Mafia, Aidan had been hoping to rub elbows with one of the town's "power brokers." "Excuse me?"

"For your fire. The Rigsby boys are looking real good for it as far as I'm concerned."

"Yeah?" Aidan responded. "You think I should focus on them, huh? What's your evidence?"

A waitress came, and he ordered them each a coffee.

Owen pounded on his chest. "Right here. I've got a feeling."

"Unfortunately, I need more than a feeling. You see anything suspicious?" The barbershop was kitty-corner to the sporting goods store.

"Nah. But I tell you, those kids are trouble. Their father ain't no saint either, and you know what they say: the apple doesn't fall far from the tree."

"I'll tell you a good way you could be very helpful to this investigation," Aidan said, and he could see Owen's ears perk up. "From your vantage point, you see the entire square. I need a spy."

"I could do that." Owen sat a little taller in his chair.

From what Aidan had heard, the man was better than the CIA and a twenty-four-hour security camera put together. "Great. That would be very helpful." Aidan wrote his cell phone number on the back of his business card and slid it across the table. "Call me if you see anything odd."

Owen pocketed the card. "That might be difficult. Ninety-nine percent of the people who live here are odd. You meet Portia Cane, the woman who owns the tour-guide company? Crazy as a loon."

Aidan stifled a grin; the guy was a real character. "Just keep your eye out for someone who strikes you as up to no good. I've got a feeling you'll be good at this."

Owen fixed Aidan with a look that said *don't patronize me, boy.* "So you're blondie's brother, huh?"

"Sloane?" Aidan laughed. "Yep."

The server came with their coffees, Aidan gave her his order and she rushed off to get it to the kitchen.

"I hear she and Brady are getting hitched."

"You hear correctly. They're thinking of having it at Sierra Heights."

"That's what Griffin tells me. So you're dating that little real estate agent who used to go with Griff?"

"We're not dating . . . still dancing around it. What happened between Griffin and Dana?"

"He's always been hot for Lina Shepard. But the girl's jailbait. She just turned twenty. They had a big shindig for her at the Lumber Baron. The boy practically proposed to her."

Aidan was pretty sure that was in February, the first time he'd come to Nugget to visit Sloane. She and Brady had been all dressed up, returning home from the party with enough firepower to take down

SEAL Team Six. They'd been running from some trouble back then. Thank God it was over now.

"Dana isn't into him anymore." He didn't know why he felt compelled to say that. Besides the fact that it made him sound like a high school girl, he didn't even know if it was true.

"From what I hear, you two are making cow eyes at each other."

Aidan laughed. "Where did you hear that?"

"I've got my sources." He got up and grabbed his mug. "I'll keep my eyes open and give you a full report."

"Sounds good," Aidan said and watched Owen walk through the entrance to the bowling alley.

The server returned with his steak and eggs and a side of pancakes. He'd just started digging in when Rhys pulled up a chair.

"Any leads?"

"I've got nothing," Aidan said. "How about you?"

"Nothing." Rhys eyed his mountain of food.

"You want some?" It seemed rude not to offer.

"I'm good." Rhys lowered his voice. "No way to know where the gas came from, huh?"

Whoever lit up the sporting goods store had used gas as an accelerant. Usually the sign of a beginner. A truly experienced "torch" would've used solid fuels found at the scene to make the fire look accidental. Stuff like garbage ignited with a little bit of flammable liquid that would have dissipated in the fire.

"Nah, that's like finding a needle in a haystack. Everyone here gets gas for their vehicles, farm equipment, you name it. What we need is someone who saw an individual carrying a gas can to the scene. I have a footprint I found at the origin of the fire, but nothing to match it to. Too bad there aren't any security cameras in the square."

"This ain't Rodeo Drive or whatever equivalent you had in Chicago."

"Nope," Aidan agreed. "But I enlisted Owen."

Rhys chuckled. "You and your sister are quick studies. No one knows the doings of this town like the barber. Any other McBrides want to work in Nugget?"

"You're stuck with just us for now." Aidan leaned over the table closer to Rhys. "My gut says this person will strike again."

"Yep, mine too."

"Owens seems to think it's the Rigsby boys. You have any thoughts on that?"

"I'd sooner put my money on the father. I don't see a motive, though. As far as I know, he doesn't have any kind of quarrel with Carl Rudd."

"To make me look stupid," Aidan said. Revenge was a top motive for arson. "He clearly has issues with my authority. What better way to make me seem incompetent to my supervisors than to set fires I can't solve?"

"I don't know, seems like a longshot. But I've been wrong before. A footprint isn't enough for a warrant." Rhys shook his head. "No witnesses, no nothing. Broad freaking daylight."

"And you don't think Rudd has anything to gain from the fire, financially or otherwise?"

"Nope. And setting things on fire doesn't strike me as Carl's style."

"What about the owner of the property?" Aidan checked the notes he'd made on his phone. "Trevor Thurston. You know the guy?"

"Yep. He owns most of the square, including the Bun Boy, which he runs with his wife. Solid citizens who'd give you the shirts off their backs. You look into his financials?"

"Nothing glaring. But gambling debts . . . a drug problem . . . they don't tend to show up on bank records, you know?"

"He's a pretty smart guy. Seems to me if he wanted to burn the place down and collect the insurance money he would've gotten it done."

The fire had been anemic at best. A lot of smoke with little damage. Firefighters had it out in less than thirty minutes.

"Could've just been bored kids, I suppose."

"Could've been," Rhys agreed. "We'll just have to wait and see. You ought to join us for basketball one of these days. We play at lunchtime. A few of the Cal Fire guys come, but they suck. Maybe you'll be better."

Aidan laughed. His sister had told him about the pick-up games and about the friendly competition between the Nugget police and fire departments.

"You bet," he said.

Rhys got up. "Sorry I interrupted your breakfast. Catch you later."

After he left, Aidan continued eating. He'd finished the pancakes and was making good work on the steak and eggs when a middle-aged blond woman slid into the empty chair at his table.

"Did Dana tell you about my kitchen?"

"Uh . . . I don't think so."

"You don't even know who I am, do you?" She didn't wait for him to answer. "I'm Donna Thurston, owner of the Bun Boy, and until you sign off on my open-flame permit I can't install the Santa Maria barbecues I just paid a buttload for."

"Okay . . . I can do that. But can I finish eating first?"

"Of course you can. In the meantime, let me tell you my theory on the sporting goods fire." She didn't even take a breath, just launched in to, "It was Carl."

Aidan sat up.

"He's been sneaking around his wife's back, smoking again. She'd kill him if she knew. He goes outside to the back of the store where he thinks no one is looking, then throws his cigarette butts on the ground when he's done. I told Trevor it was just a matter of time, especially in this drought, before Carl burned the whole town down."

Aidan let out a disappointed sigh. "Cigarettes, huh?"

"Yep. Case closed. You're welcome."

He wished it were that easy. "I'll look into it. Thanks for the tip. Why don't I meet you over at the Bun Boy in twenty minutes?" He didn't bother to tell her that today was supposed to be his day off. It was mostly shot anyway.

But tonight he and Dana were going bowling. And he planned to kiss her again.

Chapter 13

Dana couldn't decide between jeans or a sundress. She lay them on her bed, vacillating between the two. She knew Aidan liked the dress but feared her butt would hang out when she bent over to roll the bowling ball down the lane. The jeans, on the other hand, were tight and might just split up the seam.

In the end, denim seemed more appropriate for the Ponderosa, so she dropped her towel, slipped on a lacy pair of undies, and shimmied into the jeans. She paired the pants with the yellow sleeveless blouse Grace had given her from Farm Supply. It was too hot for the boots, so she put on a pair of strappy high-heeled sandals that had been part of her Harlee booty. They were too stylish for a bowling alley, but they were sexy. And for the first time in a long time, Dana felt like sexing it up. She even wore a push-up bra she'd ordered online.

From her bedroom she could hear the front door open and close and knew Aidan was home. He'd probably want to shower. Good thing she'd already done her hair and makeup.

There was a rap on her door. "You decent?"

"Not yet." She didn't want him to see the other clothes on the bed and know she'd agonized all afternoon over what to wear.

"I just have to take a quick shower," he said, and she smiled at how she'd called it right.

"Okay. I'm almost ready."

"You mind if we go somewhere other than the Ponderosa for dinner? I ate breakfast there."

"I don't care. You want to go to the Bun Boy?"

He groaned.

She opened her door a crack. He tried to get a look at her, but she wouldn't let him. "What's the problem?"

"I spent an hour at the Bun Boy doing an inspection so Donna can get an open-flame permit for some barbecues she wants to install. The woman talked my ear off and is a little bonkers."

"Oh, shoot." Dana held her hand to her mouth. "I was supposed to tell you about that and I forgot."

"Don't worry about it. I just don't want to go there for dinner and get cornered by her again."

Dana laughed. "She's not that bad, but we can go anyplace you want. We can even eat home."

"No, this is your night . . . even though we're not celebrating. Yet. What else is around here?"

"Not much, unless we go to a neighboring town. But by the time we eat it may be too late to bowl." The lanes closed at nine.

"We've got three hours." He looked at his watch. "I'll be ready in fifteen minutes."

True to his word, he found her in the living room thumbing through her mail, all set to go. His hair was still damp, curling around his neck, and he smelled like aftershave and something so good she wanted to burrow her face in his throat.

"Ready?" He tugged her off the couch and they headed for the door. "Where to?"

"There's an Italian place in Blairsden and an Indian place in Glory Junction. We had Italian last night, so I say we head for Glory Junction."

Aidan pulled a face. "I don't like Indian food. I'm being a pain in the ass, aren't I?"

"You shouldn't have to eat something you don't like. We can go back to Reno; plenty of choices there. But we probably won't make it back in time to go bowling. We can go another time; I'd rather have a good meal. Unless you have your heart set on it."

"No. Maybe we could catch a movie in Reno after dinner."

"That would be fun." She couldn't remember the last time she'd been to a movie. It had probably been with Griffin because she didn't like to go alone.

They got in Aidan's Expedition while Dana ticked off a few restaurants they could go to. By the time they crossed the Nevada state line they'd decided on a Thai restaurant Dana knew.

"You like Thai but not Indian?" she asked, watching him steer with one hand, his long fingers draped over the wheel.

"For some reason Indian food gives me heartburn. Not spicy Asian or even Mexican. Go figure. How about you? What kind of food don't you like?"

"I don't like gamy food like lamb or venison. And I don't like melon."

"Not even watermelon?"

"Nope. Can't stand it."

"Wow, that's a new one. My little brother doesn't like cantaloupe, but everyone in my family likes watermelon. I don't really love tomatoes."

"I can see that. It's probably a texture thing."

He slid her a smile. "Could be. You make any more sales today?"

"No, I just worked on the Rosser deal."

"You gonna retire when that goes through?"

"My commission won't be enough for me to retire, but I'll be able to upgrade a few things in my new house, maybe get some really nice furniture and a pool."

"You better invite me over to swim." He put his hand on her leg and she sat perfectly still, afraid he'd move it.

"Of course I will." At this rate, she'd invite him to move in with her.

She'd never known a man who made her feel as comfortable as Aidan. Despite how hot he was, how ripped, how charming, he was easy. He didn't judge her for being antisocial or shy or awkward. He was interested in her work, in her life . . . hell, he was interested in whether she liked watermelon. Even though she knew she wasn't, he had a way of making her feel like she was important to him.

"Besides Donna's inspection, what else did you do today?"

"Tried to gather intel on the fire. I'd hoped by now that someone would've come forward with information."

"Like who did it?"

"That would be optimal, but at this point even small clues would be helpful. Like someone finding a matchbook with a fingerprint or distinctive logo."

"Tell me how you know for sure that someone intentionally set the fire."

"No can do, sweetheart."

"Seriously?"

"Seriously. If details get out, the firebug will have an advantage by knowing what we know."

"I never thought of it that way," Dana said. "You have such an interesting job. I bet you never get bored."

"I don't. I love it. You like your job, don't you?"

"I do, but it's not exciting like yours. It's not like people are cornering me at cocktail parties, wanting to talk about real estate."

"They were at the Fourth of July party. *What's the ugliest house you ever sold? What was the most expensive?* It's all anyone wanted to talk about."

Dana hadn't thought about it, but Aidan was right. "Perhaps people were just trying to be nice."

"Or maybe they were legitimately interested in what you do."

She shrugged, finding it hard to believe. "Let's put it this way: They don't make TV shows about real estate agents. But they do about firefighters."

"At least a real estate agent's job doesn't wreak havoc on family life. We work crazy hours."

"You're doing important work, saving lives. Besides, you get extended days off, whereas my busiest days are weekends."

"So being with a guy who had to live half the week at the firehouse wouldn't bother you?"

"We're talking hypothetically, right?" *Of course they were.* "Nope. Not if he loved the work and it made him happy . . . of course he'd have to pull his weight at home. Not sit around on his days off, watching *Ellen*."

Aidan was quiet for a while, then asked, "Where is this Thai place?"

"Make a right up here." She directed him to the restaurant, which matched Gaetano's in its understatement. Just a stucco box with a faded sign off the main thoroughfare.

He parked and got to her door before she could get out, helping her down. "You look beautiful tonight, by the way."

She rolled her eyes.

"Dana, can't you ever take a compliment? Jesus, woman, spend some time looking in a mirror, would you?"

She knew she wasn't as beautiful as Sue. Of course she'd snooped on Facebook and in some of the photo albums on his shelves that he was always looking at. His ex had those classic good looks that turned heads. Auburn hair and a curvaceous figure, like Geena Davis in *Thelma and Louise*. At best, Dana could be called cute. Back before Paul had died, her father used to call her bug. Like cute as a bug in a rug. Now he didn't call her much of anything.

Aidan put his hand at the small of her back and opened the restaurant door. It wasn't as crowded as Gaetano's but most of the tables were full. A young woman took them to a booth in the corner.

"Don't worry," Dana said. "What the place lacks in atmosphere it makes up for in food."

It was even blander than Dana remembered. White walls with strategically placed flat-screen TVs and unappetizing pictures of the restaurant's signature dishes on the wall. She hoped Aidan wasn't getting the willies.

But when she gazed across the table at him, he seemed totally relaxed. Maybe he went to a lot of hole-in-the-wall divy-looking places in Chicago. A server came and took their drink orders, suggesting they get Thai mojitos.

"Sounds good," Aidan said and nudged his head at Dana.

"Sure. Why not?"

They gave the waitress their food orders before she dashed off to another table.

"Cool place." Aidan gazed around the dining room and she wondered if he was being facetious. "You come here with your family too?"

"No, they've never been." They didn't eat out anymore. "But it's near where they live. Sometimes I eat here when I visit them." She got takeout.

"What are you doing this weekend?" he asked.

"Working. I have a couple who's interested in Sierra Heights but wants to see a few homes outside the planned community before they make a final decision. And someone wants to interview me about selling his cabin. Apparently, the owner is talking to a couple of other agents."

"What will he ask you in this interview?"

"Most of the time, sellers want to know what price I'd list it for. Usually the agent who gives them the highest price wins. But in the long run it's stupid because you can't sell an overpriced piece of property."

"So you'll tell him the truth?" Aidan asked.

"I'll just tell him what the comps are and let him decide for himself. It's a sweet place, though. I'd like to have the listing."

"What's so great about it?"

"It's on a beautiful piece of property, overlooking the river. The main level is an open floor plan. Upstairs, there's a big loft. The kitchen was completely redone two years ago. The guy is pretty handy, so he did a lot of the work himself."

"How much do you think he can get for it?"

"I'd say somewhere close to three hundred thousand dollars. It's only about seventeen hundred square feet."

He smiled at her.

"What?"

"I'm allowed to smile at you if I want. But the truth is, you light up when you talk about real estate."

Most people would probably find it boring, but she loved finding the right house for the right person. Whether it was a starter home or a multimillion-dollar property, she played a role in helping people find their dreams.

Burning with curiosity, Dana couldn't help herself. "If you don't mind my asking, what does Sue do?"

"She's a middle-school teacher."

Their drinks and appetizers came. Aidan served her a few spring rolls, grabbed one for himself, and stuffed it in his mouth.

"Does she like it . . . being a teacher?"

"I think she does. We didn't talk about work much."

That seemed incongruent with the Aidan she knew. Perhaps they were too busy having sex. "What did you guys talk about, then?"

"She was social . . . had a lot of friends. She liked to tell me about their outings together, about parties, the theater. She gossiped a lot."

"You didn't go with her . . . to parties and the theater?"

"When I could, but I was gone a lot. Kind of the nature of the work I do."

She bit into one of the spring rolls. "Do you think that's why she left you?"

"I think it was part of the reason, yeah." Understandably, he didn't want to talk about it and she didn't want to pry. "What about you? Anyone serious, besides Griffin?"

"There was a developer in Tahoe. We met through real estate, obviously. But it didn't work out."

"How come?"

"It turned out he was in love with his partner's wife. When she dumped her husband, he dumped me. Sort of the story of my life." She didn't know why she'd told him that. It made her sound pathetic.

"How old are you?"

"Thirty." She started in on the other spring roll and realized she'd broken her self-imposed rule of not eating after six two nights in a row.

"You've got plenty of life left; make a new story." He winked.

"How old are you?" She'd wondered for a while.

"Thirty-seven."

The rest of their order came. They'd decided to go family style; that way they could sample a little bit of everything. The waitress put the food on a lazy Susan in the middle of the table, the kind found in Chinese restaurants. When Aidan didn't think she was looking he held the tray so that it wouldn't rotate when she tried to turn it. He thought it was hysterical.

They talked so much she didn't realize two hours had gone by. She also felt tipsy from the Thai mojitos, which seemed to keep coming.

"What movie do you want to see?" he asked.

"I don't know. What's playing?" She wasn't up on her movie releases because she never went to the theater anymore. Especially now that Aidan had ordered Netflix.

He got out his phone and searched the film listings in Reno, ticking off a few. They'd already missed the first evening showings of the ones that sounded interesting. The next viewings didn't start until close to ten. That was a lot of time to kill.

"We could go to my parents' house." The words were out of her mouth before she could take them back.

What a colossally bad idea. But she hadn't visited them—or heard from them for that matter—since right after the fire, and they were due for a welfare check. It was a big house, she told herself. She and Aidan could sit in the casita, maybe take a dip in the pool.

"Sure," he said, and flagged their waitress down, motioning for the bill.

"Let me pay for my half." Dana reached inside her purse.

"Don't even think about it."

"Then I get to pick up the check next time."

He squared up, left a tip, and they went outside into the hot summer night. Pinks and blues streaked the rose-colored sky. Soon it would be replaced by neon greens, reds, and golds from the surrounding casinos.

Inside Aidan's truck, he turned on the engine and got the air conditioner going. She told him how to get to her parents' house, taking him through a warren of city streets. As they entered Old Southwest Reno, driving on the leafy tree-lined streets, she saw Aidan begin to take notice of the large historic homes.

"This is where you grew up, huh?"

"Mm-hmm. Take a right there and an immediate right onto the private lane."

He followed her directions and proceeded up the long and winding road. "Pretty genteel."

She supposed it could be called that. When they got to her parents' circular driveway, Aidan did a double take and let out a low hum.

"This is like freaking Beverly Hills. Where should I park?"

"Just pull up in front of the house, near the fountain." Usually she parked under the porte cochère, but they wouldn't be here that long. And it wasn't as if her parents would notice anyway.

Aidan turned off the ignition and continued to stare at the house, which would probably look imposing to anyone. Built in 1906, the Mediterranean mansion had belonged to Dana's grandfather. When he had gotten ill, her family had moved in to help take care of him. He'd left the house to them when he'd died.

"We going inside?" he asked.

"Of course."

Again, he came to her side of the truck to help her out, and she unlocked and escorted him through the huge oak entry door, into the marble-floored foyer and through the massive formal living room. She couldn't remember the last time anyone had sat on the damask couches or velvet settees. For as long as she could remember, her family had gathered in the den.

She led Aidan in that direction. "Mom, Dad." Her voice echoed off the walls.

The television blared in the next room. The house was spotless as usual, but the rooms felt airless. Dana would bet Betty hadn't cranked open a window since the last time she'd visited.

"Mom? Dad?" No one answered, her voice probably muffled by whatever program they were watching.

She wanted to find a spot for Aidan so she could check on her parents and then leave them to their show. Funny, with all the rooms in the house, she couldn't think of one single solitary place to deposit him that didn't feel alien. This had been a mistake. She started to make a detour for the kitchen—the back door—when she heard a weedy cry for help coming from the den.

Aidan didn't wait and rushed in with Dana close behind. Sprawled on the floor was her mother.

"Mrs. Calloway?"

Startled, Betty stared up at Aidan from the Aubusson rug as he loomed over her.

"Are you all right?" Dana bent down, took her mother's arm, and started to lift her until Aidan stopped her.

"You feel any pain, Mrs. Calloway? We don't want to move you if you're hurt."

Betty looked at Dana, who replied, "This is Aidan. He's a friend of mine. He's also a firefighter." What she was trying to say was that he had emergency training. But it didn't seem to compute with Betty, who continued to stare at him like he was an intruder. "What happened?"

"I must have fallen asleep and somehow rolled out of the chair."

Aidan cast an eye over the chair and the side table. He was probably looking for booze, but Dana's parents didn't drink.

"I'm fine," Betty said and scrambled to get up.

Aidan lent her an arm. "Not too fast."

Once on her feet, Aidan checked her pulse and asked her a few questions. The day, her first and last name, and how many fingers he was holding up. She supposed he was checking for a concussion. Dana didn't see any cuts, bruises, sprains, or breaks, at least not to the naked eye.

"Where's Dad?" she asked.

"He went up to bed."

Dana glanced at the grandfather clock. It wasn't even nine.

"I think I'll go up too," Betty said.

"All right. Why don't I walk you?"

"That's not necessary, dear." She grabbed her reading glasses off the coffee table and started to walk away.

Dana couldn't help herself. "Wouldn't you like to know how my new house plans are coming along?" Or the fact that she was about to close the biggest deal of her career?

"You can tell me all about it in the morning," Betty said. "Good night, dear."

She didn't even thank Aidan or say goodbye, nice to meet you, or any of the other pleasantries normal parents say to their daughter's friends. Dana could feel her face heat in embarrassment.

That's when a strong arm wrapped around her waist. "Don't sweat it," he whispered in her ear. "Show me the house."

"It's just that . . . she didn't used to be that way . . . she's broken."

"I know." He tucked a strand of hair behind her ear. "It's sad, but tragedy does that to some people. How are the plans for your new house coming?"

A tear leaked from her eye and rolled down her cheek. "They blame me . . . for Paul. I was there. I should've known."

He pulled her down on the sofa. "No one could've known. It was a fluke, Dana. Trained emergency response teams have missed it, even doctors. You were fifteen."

She wiped her nose with the back of her hand, then got up to find tissues. When she came back, Aidan was standing in the hallway looking at the family pictures on the wall.

"That you?" He pointed at a picture of a thirteen-year-old Dana getting ready to go to their club's annual father-daughter dance.

"I was channeling my inner Tiffani Amber Thiessen." When Aidan's face registered a blank, she said, "Of *Beverly Hills, 90210.*"

"Oh." He chuckled. "You were beautiful then and you're beautiful now."

She wondered how much of the compliment stemmed from him feeling sorry for her. "How about the nickel tour so we don't wake them up?" Dana nudged her head at the second story.

"Sounds good. It's a beautiful place."

"Thank you. It was my grandfather's and, before Paul died, a real home." She took him through the main level, going room to room. "We spent all our time in the den and even put our Christmas tree there."

In the sunroom, she opened the row of French doors and flicked on a switch. The whole backyard lit up, illuminating the pool, the casita, and an oasis of palm and yucca trees.

"Whoa." Aidan stepped outside. "You've got a whole world out here."

"You want to go for a swim?"

"I don't have a suit." He lifted his brows and gazed up at the second story.

It would be just Dana's luck that one of her parents would come out on the balcony to find their daughter and her very male friend skinny-dipping. A long shot, but Dana wasn't taking any chances.

"I'll find you one," she said and beckoned him to follow her into the casita.

Inside, she grabbed the one-piece she'd worn last time and rummaged through a basket where her mother had always kept spares for guests. She went through a pile, separating out the kids' suits. Granted, some of the patterns were dated, but for the most part, men's swim trunks hadn't changed much over the years.

"How about these?" She held up a pair of Speedo briefs and suppressed a laugh. God only knew where those had come from.

"Not on your life," he said, checking out the Spanish-style pool house.

"Michael Phelps wears them."

He shook his head. "Not gonna happen."

Too bad. If any man could pull off a Speedo it was Aidan.

"This is nice. You ever stay the night in here?"

There was a small bedroom off the living room with a queen-size bed, canopied in mosquito netting. Despite the dearth of bugs, once upon a time her mother had thought the netting was a romantic touch.

"Once or twice at slumber parties with the neighbor girl. We'd always get scared, though, and go running back to the main house." She found a pair of striped trunks and held them out to him. "What do you think?"

"Those will work. You handled?"

"Yep. You can use the bedroom to change. I'll use a dressing room outside."

He disappeared behind the door. She stripped in one of the three fitting areas near the outdoor shower. Aidan had a towel around his waist when he came out. She wouldn't have taken him for modest and definitely not for shy.

"They're a little small," he said.

"How small?" She pulled the towel away . . . and oh my! Aidan was very well endowed; the shorts left nothing to the imagination. "Will you bust out of them?"

"I wouldn't talk if I were you." He stared pointedly at her backside. "A little wedgie action going on there?" And then, for good measure, he stared a little more.

"Stop."

"Only if you stop." He nudged her chin up with his finger to keep her eyes off his crotch.

"Do you want me to find you something else?"

"These will be fine. Let's just get in the water." He walked out to the edge of the pool and cannonballed in. She motioned for him to keep the noise down.

"Sorry," he said and shook the water out of his hair. "I forgot."

She waded in slowly, even though the water was warm. Aidan vanished under the surface and appeared a few seconds later, tugging her toward the deep end. Fed up with how slow she moved, he wrapped her legs around his waist and swam backward with her.

He felt so good, the hard muscles of his chest pressed against her breasts and his hands flat against her wet back. Her own clutched his powerful shoulders as they floated under the starlit sky, a symphony of crickets serenading them.

Dana closed her eyes, feeling his erection surge against her and reveling in the intimacy of it. "What are we doing, Aidan?"

That's when he leaned in and kissed her, his lips tasting like chlorine and mojito. She cupped the back of his head, pulling him closer, devouring his mouth as he explored hers with his tongue.

"I'm tasting you." His hands slipped down and inched up the bottom of her suit until he held her bare butt in his hands. Squeezing both cheeks, he slid those clever hands between her legs. It felt so good and erotic that she readjusted her thighs to give him better access, never breaking free of his mouth.

Aidan glided one hand out, pulled the straps and the top of her bathing suit down, exposing her breasts, and fondled each one at a time.

He stopped kissing her long enough to look, his eyes darkening at the sight of her. "Oh, Dana. Beautiful, beautiful Dana."

"We're moving kind of fast here, don't you think?" Even to her own ears the words sounded perfunctory. She wanted this with him. She always had.

"Should I stop?" Laving her breasts with his mouth, he floated them to the edge of the pool where he boxed her in against the side. "It's entirely up to you."

She didn't answer, just untied the drawstring on his trunks, released the Velcro tab, and reached inside.

"Ah, Jesus." He tugged her hand out of his shorts. "You first. Put your legs down, baby, so I can get this off." With one hand he tugged her one-piece down and she kicked it away until it floated to the surface.

She stood before him completely naked. He kissed her some more, working his lips down her body while he continued to play with her breasts.

"Oh God."

"You like this?" He licked her nipples, taking each one into his mouth, while he went to work with his fingers between her legs.

"Aidan?"

"Hmm?"

"I want you . . . please."

He began spreading kisses over her belly. "We'll get to that, but first this. Put your legs over me." Aidan crouched down in the water and hooked her thighs over his shoulders until she floated on her back and reached under her butt to lift her up.

Before she knew it, he had his mouth down there, licking and sucking until she thought she'd die from how wonderful it was.

"Come for me," he said against her.

And she did, shuddering her release while calling his name. "Aidan. Aidan."

He pulled her up and hugged her close, shushing her with more kisses. Nearby, he snatched her floating swimsuit from the water, lifted her out of the pool, carried her to the casita in all her naked glory, and lay her down on the mosquito-netted bed. His pants lay folded on a chair and he began going through the pockets.

"What are you doing?" she asked.

He held up a small foil square, lost the swim trunks, and plopped onto the bed next to her. With his teeth, he ripped open the package, rolled the condom on, and began touching and kissing her all over again until she begged for him.

"God, I want you," he said, entering her a little at a time. "Has it been a while?"

"Mm-hmm. How about for you?"

"Seven months."

Not since Sue, she thought as he began to move inside her. Not since the love of his life left him.

Chapter 14

Aidan framed Dana's face with his hands and concentrated on his strokes. He wanted this to be good for her. The best it had ever been. For both of them.

"You okay?" he asked in a throaty whisper.

"I'm good . . . so good."

He was beyond good but wanted to go deeper and positioned her legs wider, pumping harder. Her breath caught and she let out a soft gasp.

"Don't stop," she pleaded, keeping rhythm with his thrusts, her hands clutching his back.

"Not on your life. You feel so good."

The truth was, he didn't know how much longer he could hold on sheathed in her tight heat. He was about to lose his mind.

Burying his mouth in her neck, he kissed her over and over again, while he squeezed her breasts. Two perfect, round globes with pebbled pink nipples. They were high and firm and delectable.

"Hang on a sec." He rolled her over so she was on top. "Sit up so I can look at you."

She hesitated. But when he flicked his thumb over her center, rubbing circles in her wetness, she moaned and slowly came up, arching her back to ride him.

"Oh, oh, this is . . ." She shut her eyes and quickened the pace.

"You've never done it like this before?"

"I didn't think I would like being so . . . well, you know." she said, bouncing up and down, losing all inhibitions.

"Jesus, Dana, with your body, you could own me like this." He clutched her hips, driving her faster, and sucked her breasts, making her moan and shout out.

She grabbed his shoulders, quivering as her body rocked from orgasm, calling his name over and over again.

He latched onto her lips with his to hush her. But he liked the noises she made, the way she said "Aidan." Hell, he reveled in them. They made something expand in his chest. And when he saw her eyes darken with heat, and maybe something else, it brought him impossible pleasure.

Aidan flipped Dana onto her back, propping himself above her so he could look his fill, and entered her again in one long, hard thrust. Surprised that he'd managed to last this long, he tried to take his time. But Dana wasn't having it, bucking under him, imploring him to come closer, to go faster.

He aimed to please and thrusted harder, pounding into her until he felt her breath hitch and her body spasm. That was when he let himself go, throwing his head back and rocking with her. The tremor that ripped through him felt euphoric, like he was having an out-of-body experience. Never before could he remember it being like this. He'd had good sex, even great sex, but nothing this intense.

"Dana?" He rolled off her and gathered her close in his arms. "What just happened here?"

"I don't know," she whispered. "Will it be weird . . . us living together?"

"It doesn't have to be," he said, rubbing circles on her back and kissing the sensitive spot behind her ear.

"We should probably make some rules, a list of dos and don'ts, so we don't turn this into an issue."

There she went with her rules and lists; she'd probably hang them on the refrigerator. "Could we catch an hour's sleep first?" He palmed her sweet ass and tucked her head into his shoulder. "I thought women liked to cuddle afterward."

"I do . . . but don't you think we should—"

" 'Night, baby." And with her nestled against him, he fell asleep.

By the time he woke, there was sunshine streaming through the shutters. Shit! He wondered if her parents were awake and if they'd noticed the lights on by the pool and his truck parked in their circular drive. Although from what he'd seen of Dana's mom, she didn't notice much. It was one thing to mourn a dead child years after he'd died—Aidan could sympathize—but it was a mortal sin in his book to treat her living one like she was dead too. Frankly, it had taken all his willpower not to call the woman on it. Couldn't she see what she was doing to Dana?

"Hey." He nuzzled her cheek. "It's morning."

"Huh." She came awake gradually. Disoriented, but so, so beautiful she made Aidan's chest ache.

She blinked at the clock on the side table, and Aidan watched as she slowly put the pieces together. "Uh-oh."

"Is this gonna be a problem?"

She looked at him like he was out of focus and she was trying to clear her vision. "You mean with my parents?"

"Yeah."

Letting out a humorless laugh, she said, "No. They won't even have realized we stayed the night. But I have a ten o'clock appointment."

"I can get you there in time."

She slid her legs over the side of the bed, holding the blanket against her chest, scanning the room. "I can't remember where I left my clothes."

"In one of those changing rooms outside. I'll get them for you." He reached across the bed for her. "Hey, come here for a second."

She suddenly seemed shy and guardedly leaned closer. Aidan kissed her.

"I have morning breath," she said and got up, pulling the blanket around her, and went to the bathroom.

Aidan grabbed his clothes off the chair and started to dress. He'd shower at home. Before Dana came out, he went in search of her clothes, came back in, and handed them to her through the bathroom door.

"Thanks." She emerged a little while later fully dressed and ready to go. "I just have to leave a note for the housekeeper about changing the bedding."

"Okay. You want to meet me in the truck?"

"That would be good."

Aidan figured she'd probably go inside the main house to check on her parents. "Come get me if you need anything." Like rescuing.

She flashed a wry smile and he left, finding his way back to the front of the house to his Expedition. For a house in the city, it had a lot of grounds. Everywhere he looked were expansive gardens, lawns, and terraces. The Calloways must have a hell of a landscaping team. Funny, he'd never figured Dana for a rich girl. He knew her family owned the candy company but had no idea that it was this profitable. Besides, she worked harder than most people he knew and seemed to be conscientious about money, not like a woman who'd been born with a silver spoon in her mouth.

From the looks of the house, the furnishings, and the manicured grounds, he'd say it was a pretty safe bet that she came from more money than Sue, whose family had been quite comfortable. Yet Dana acted more like someone from his family's background—good middle-class stock. Sue wouldn't even have considered a home in Nugget. Too rustic, too rural, too blue collar.

He took a few seconds to check out the front of the house. Last night he'd been too bowled over to take a really good look. In the light of day, it was very impressive. The place had to be a hundred years old but meticulously maintained right down to the water in the giant fountain. Strange that Dana's parents hadn't just let it go, like they seemed to have done with everything else, most notably their daughter. He'd seen the hurt in Dana's eyes when her mother had ignored her last night. If one of the McBrides' houses had burned down, his parents would've been involved in every aspect of the aftermath. As far as he knew, Dana hadn't even gotten a chance to tell her mother about the big real estate transaction on which she was about to close.

He got in his truck and checked his phone for messages. Nothing but a few emails from his folks and brothers. He'd hoped to get a few tips on the sporting goods fire but nada. It was already getting hot, and Aidan questioned the wisdom of turning on the AC. Running the engine might draw more attention than necessary.

But a few seconds later Dana opened the door and scooted into the front seat, throwing a bag at him.

"What's this?"

"Calloway candy. I used up your stash at our barbecue."

His lips curved up into a smile and he started the engine. "Thanks. Crack one open."

"Now?" She made a face.

"Yeah. Breakfast of champions."

He found his way back to the main road as she fed him chocolate. "Did you talk to your parents?"

"They weren't up yet." She fiddled with the vents until they blew maximum cool air. "Are we going to talk about it?"

He knew she'd eventually get back to her rules and regulations. "Why can't we just enjoy it? Without a doubt, our night together was the best thing that's happened to me in the last seven months." Maybe ever.

"We're roommates, Aidan. Last night could make things really strained."

"Why? You planning to bring men home?"

"Of course not. Are you planning to bring home women?"

He slid her a sideways glance. "Not the way I roll."

"So we're just planning to play house?"

He tilted his head against his backrest in frustration. Why couldn't women just live in the moment? "We should just see how it goes, don't overthink it. Can you at least try to do that?"

She sat quiet for a few minutes and finally said, "Fine, but don't say I didn't tell you so when it blows up in our faces."

"You're one of those I-told-you-so chicks, aren't you?" he teased.

"I'm just very practical."

No, she was scared shitless. He got that because he was too. In fact, he should be running in the opposite direction. But for some crazy-ass reason, he wanted to stick around to see what would happen.

"Are you going to work?" she asked him.

"Technically I'm off, but with the sporting goods case I thought I'd put in a few hours." Though he had nothing to go on.

"Is there a possibility the fire could've been an accident?"

"Not likely."

"That kind of stuff just doesn't happen in a place like Nugget. Although we had the cattle thefts and a big drug bust. Then there was the dead guy who washed up . . ."

Aidan knew that had been Sloane's case. Sad story. "It might've just been kids, but it was intentional."

"You'll solve it," she said.

"How do you know that?"

"Because you're good at your job."

He wondered if this was postsex flattery because she had no way of knowing whether he was a good arson investigator. Aidan was fairly sure he was the only arson investigator she'd ever met. However, it just so happened he was the best.

"Thanks for the confidence. You have time for coffee? We could drive through the Bun Boy."

"I'll just make a pot at home. As it is, I'm cutting it close because I still have to shower and blow-dry my hair."

He'd like to shower with her, but he had a feeling if he did, she'd really be late. But they should think about it in the future . . . for the sake of the drought.

"I'll make the coffee, you get ready," he said.

Her brows went up, and he got the impression the gesture alluded to them playing house again. She should know he wasn't very good at it. All she had to do was ask Sue.

The cabin was even more darling than Dana remembered. Immaculate and furnished tastefully, without too many personal touches.

What most sellers failed to understand was that their family pictures—no matter how sweet—eclectic art collections, and porcelain figurines actually distracted perspective buyers. Or worse: they creeped them out. People wanted to see themselves in a house, not the former occupant. That was why most model homes were decorated as generically as possible. No signs of a person's religion, political party, or what kind of clubs she belonged to. Unless it was the yacht club. For some reason, nautical themes—except fishnet strung on the walls like at Long John Silver's—were completely acceptable, even to people who didn't spend time on the water. Dana supposed it represented a lifestyle of leisure and glamour.

"So what do you think the house is worth?" Mr. Castro followed her around the cabin as she took notes.

"It's worth what someone will pay for it. The question is how shall we price it? For that I brought along a list of comparatives in the area. I thought we could sit down and look them over together." She really wanted the listing but knew Mr. Castro would be disappointed with her suggested asking price.

He'd gotten it in his head that the house should be priced at half a million dollars. If she had to guess, that was what one of her competitors had told him in order to get the listing. Well, she wasn't about to lie.

"Sounds good."

They sat at the dining room table, and Dana passed him a folder showing all the sales in Nugget over the last three months. It had been a good period as far as the number of sales but still paled in comparison to an urban community of this size.

"I don't see anything that compares to my property." He continued to scan the paperwork.

"Not exactly, but other than Sierra Heights, this area is pretty varied. Everything from large ranches and farms to one-room cabins." She pulled out another sheet from the folder. "These are homes that are currently on the market; your competition, so to speak. I've been in all of them. While none is as turnkey as yours, this one"—she pointed to a custom home two miles away—"is a thousand square feet larger and has a pad for a boat or motor home."

"It doesn't have a river view."

"Nope. And that's certainly worth some money. But this one"—she showed him another listing fresh on the market—"does."

"I've seen that house. It's a dump."

"It definitely needs work. But it's on ten usable acres."

"So what you're saying is half a mil is unrealistic."

"We could certainly list it for that and see what happens," she said. "But unless we find a buyer who falls so in love with this place that he or she doesn't care what other homes in the area are selling for, yeah, it's unrealistic."

He let out a sigh and waved the folder at her. "You make a good case. Why do you think Daniel from Heavenly Homes thinks I can do better?"

"You have a beautiful place, Mr. Castro. Anyone can see you've put a lot of love into it, and sometimes that blurs what's really happening in the market. We could list at that price, but I think you would wind up being disappointed."

"What do you think is realistic?"

"Priced to sell? Three hundred and fifty thousand if we go by the comps."

She figured that would put the kibosh on her getting the listing. No question Mr. Castro wanted more. But what he wanted and what he could get were two different things.

"How would you market it?"

"I'd advertise the listing on the *Nugget Tribune*'s site with a virtual tour. I have a videographer who does beautiful work, and your home is ideal for something like that. A lot of out-of-town buyers subscribe to the *Trib* for the real estate ads. Of course it would go on our website as well, in our newsletter, and to a number of other publications. And, depending on how you feel about it, an open house or two. Of course we'd hold an open house for local brokers as well. You live in Sacramento so it shouldn't be too inconvenient."

"How soon could all this happen?"

"I could get it on the MLS today. Get the videographer out here next week and do the broker's tour Thursday." Man oh man, did she want the listing.

"How fast can you sell it?"

She smiled. "Mr. Castro, I would be lying to you if I gave you a time frame. There is no way to predict something like that. But I'll do my very best."

"That other fellow said two months."

She merely shrugged. "Again, you have a beautiful home. I think potential buyers will be impressed. But I'm not going to tell you two months; that's just not my style."

"I like your honesty and I like your integrity," Mr. Castro said. "Let's do business together."

"Nothing would make me happier." Inside, she was jumping up and down. Dana pulled a set of documents from her briefcase. "This is our standard contract. Together, we'll fill in a price and all the other pertinent details, then I'll need you to sign everything."

Two hours later, she headed to the office, over the moon. She might even add the cabin to her list of places to show the couple interested in Sierra Heights. They were coming up today, staying the night and looking tomorrow. The cabin was smaller than what they were looking for, but you never knew. Ideally, she hoped they'd settle on Sierra Heights. Despite telling themselves they wanted more privacy, Dana could see the planned community was better suited to their needs and lifestyle. They had kids, were extremely sociable, and the husband was an avid golfer. In Sierra Heights he'd have a golf course as his backyard. She worried that a house in the woods would be too secluded for them. But she would let them come to that conclusion on their own.

Right now, she just wanted to set up a time for the videographer to shoot pictures of her new listing, go home, and take a nap. Last night with Aidan . . . she'd never done anything like it. Had never experienced that kind of passion. Not with Tim, not with Griffin, not in her wildest fantasies. She'd had a sneaking suspicion Aidan would be good, but not that good. If she didn't know better, she'd think it had meant something to him.

It wasn't that she thought he was a player or a user, or even the type to hook up with any convenient woman he could find. Aidan had too much integrity for that. But she'd been the first woman since Sue and understood the implications of that. She wouldn't be his last.

Carol's car sat under a shady tree in the parking lot. Typically, she didn't work weekends. That was where Dana came in. The day had turned sweltering, and just from the short walk from her car to the office she could feel perspiration drip between the valley of her breasts. That made her think of her parents' pool, which made her think of Aidan.

A gust of cool air hit Dana as soon as she walked into the office. "Hi," she greeted Carol, who was doing paperwork at her desk. "I wasn't expecting you today."

"A couple up for the weekend mentioned to Maddy that they were looking for a second home. She told them about Sierra Heights. They took a drive through, called the office, left a message, and because you were already out . . ."

"Are they serious?"

"As a heart attack. They're grabbing a bite at the Ponderosa to talk it over and should be back"—Carol looked at her watch—"in forty-five minutes."

"That's fantastic. Which model?"

"That's what they needed to talk about. She wants the Sierra and he says they can only afford the Pine Cone. How 'bout you? How did you fare with Mr. Castro?"

"I got the listing." Dana high-fived Carol. "Sounds like both of us had productive days."

"The market is hopping. Anything new with the Rosser place?"

Dana quickly sorted through her mail and waved a FedEx envelope in the air. "The papers! I just have to send them off to Del Webber and the ranch officially goes into escrow."

"Wow! That's by far the biggest sale this office has ever had." Carol came over to where Dana was sitting, pulled her up out of the chair, and hugged her. "You rock, girl."

"So do you, Carol."

Carol gave her another squeeze. "I'm running over to the Bun Boy. Want anything?"

"No thanks. I'm hoping to finish up a few bookkeeping items and take off. Tomorrow I've got that couple from the Bay Area."

"All right. If I don't see you when I get back, have a good rest of the day and good luck tomorrow."

"Right back at ya. I hope your folks get the Sierra." Dana crossed her fingers.

After Carol left, Dana tore open Gia's envelope to make sure the documents were in order. Everything looked perfect. She quickly jotted off an email to Gia to confirm that she'd gotten the paperwork and got her videographer on the phone. He agreed to do the photos of the cabin on Monday so Dana could have the virtual tour done in time for the broker's tour.

Dana tidied up her desk and was just about to leave when the door jingled. Griffin came in.

"Jesus, it's hot."

"Not in here. Shut the door before you let all the cool air out. You looking for Carol?"

"No. I was over at the Nugget Market getting charcoal and saw your car outside. Just thought I'd say hi."

For the first time since he'd gotten back with Lina she didn't feel like he was being patronizing. Just friendly. Maybe it had always been that way and she'd been too bitter to notice.

"It sounds like Carol may have a buyer for one of your houses. The couple is having a late lunch, mulling over which model."

"That's great," Griffin said. "Seems like business has picked up. What's going on with you?"

I had sex last night with Aidan McBride in my parents' swimming pool. "Not much. How about you?"

"The gas station has been crazy busy." Besides Sierra Heights, Griff owned the Gas and Go, where he also built and sold custom motorcycles. "Other than that, not a whole lot. It seems like you and Aidan are getting pretty tight."

"We're good friends." The fact was, she didn't really know what they were.

His lips curved up in a knowing smile. "Seems like more than that to me. I even heard you hosted a party together."

She was about to argue that they'd only thrown the barbecue as roommates; then it dawned on her that perhaps he was offended they hadn't invited him and Lina. "It was just a last-minute thing. Very small. We would've called you . . . I figured you had plans."

"We went to Clay and Emily's. They had a cookout at the ranch. But Harlee and Darla said yours was nice, that you went all out on the decorations."

"Like I said, totally impromptu." She racked her brain for a subject change, but he beat her to the punch.

"I heard Aidan's investigating the fire at the sporting goods store. He have any leads?"

"I don't think so, but he's professional and won't talk about it, even with me." She didn't know why she'd said that last part—like she was somehow privy to special information.

"I hope it turns out to have been an accident," he said.

According to Aidan, not likely, but she held her tongue. "Owen thinks it's the Rigsby boys."

"Sean? No way. That kid couldn't find his ass with a magnifying glass, let alone matches."

Dana let out a laugh. "I don't know him."

"I've caught him a few times at the Gas and Go trying to lift candy. He couldn't even pull that off, and we don't pay all that much attention."

"You should tell his parents," Dana said.

"You ever meet Sean's dad? He's a serious d-bag who would deny it. The mom's okay, though. How're the house plans coming along?"

"Good. They did the demo already and we're working on the permits. I'm excited about all the square footage that's getting added. I'm thinking about putting in a pool."

"A pool?" He scrunched his nose like it wasn't such a hot idea. "They cost a fortune and the upkeep's a nightmare. You and Aidan should just use the one over at Sierra Heights. Man, it's been hella hot. So much so that I booked Lina and me a trip to Hawaii after Tawny and Lucky's wedding. She's never been."

Dana felt a pang of jealousy. Not so much because she wanted to go to Hawaii with Griffin. That ship had sailed. But she longed to be part of a couple that took vacations together.

"That sounds lovely," she said and tried to mean it.

"I'm looking forward to it." He eyed the bag slung over her shoulder. "Looks like you're trying to get out of here. I didn't mean to keep you."

"I'll walk you out," she said. "It would be better if you weren't here when the clients come back."

He saw Dana to her car, got in his own, and drove away. A few seconds later, she followed Griff out of the parking lot and headed the few blocks home.

In the living room, she found Aidan asleep on the couch with the television on and the air conditioner cranked up. He looked sexy there, stretched out like a big pirate, his face shadowed in dark whiskers. She felt the urge to crawl in next to him and cuddle up but thought it would be presumptuous. One night of hot sex did not equal snuggling rights whenever she wanted.

She tiptoed into her bedroom so as not to wake up Aidan, changed into a pair of shorts and a T-shirt, and flopped onto the bed. Scooting close to the window, she turned on the air conditioner and lay there, letting the cool air roll over her like a beach breeze. She'd allow herself ten minutes of relaxation; then she'd get up and do a few chores. But her eyelids grew heavy and she'd started to drift off to sleep when the bed dipped from the weight of another person. Aidan. He reached for her, snugged her back against his chest until they were spooning. His hands covered her breasts, and a short while later she heard his heavy breathing. Asleep. And soon, she was too.

Chapter 15

Gia sat across from her agent in a midtown Manhattan restaurant, watching out the window as a cab driver and a motorist jockeyed for the same narrow lane. The cabbie honked his horn as the other driver tried to cut him off. Even from inside, over the chef's insipid playlist, she could hear the screeching of metal scraping metal.

"They're going to kill each other," Gia said, unable to take her eyes off the scene of the two men yelling, smashing into each other like bumper cars in Coney Island. "Seriously, they're willing to die to shave a fraction of a second off their commute. It's crazy."

"It's New York City in rush hour." Marci tapped her acrylic nail on the menu. "You know what you want?"

Yeah, Gia thought, to get out of this hell hole. To pack up her car and drive west, where the roads were safe and people didn't move at warp speed. Where she could breathe.

The waiter came and Marci turned to Gia. "I suggest you get a drink. Make it a double."

"That bad, huh?"

Marci let out a sigh. "It depends on how you look at it."

The waiter, who spoke with an accent Gia didn't recognize, tapped his toe impatiently.

"I'll have a Lemon Drop," she said, and Marci got a Negroni. When the server left, Gia asked, "Where do you think he's from? I couldn't place the accent."

"The Island of Pretensia." Marci always had a snappy comeback, probably why she was one of the most coveted agents in the country.

Gia laughed. "What did they say?"

"That they'll buy you out of your contract."

It was more than Gia had expected. She figured the network

would use something in the fine print, like, say, violating a morals clause by having a thief for a boyfriend. Then they could've pulled out without having to pay her.

"That works," she told Marci.

"They want to retain the rights to the name of the show."

"It's my name, for God's sake." *The Treadwell Hour: Financial Advice that will set you free.* "Why would anyone want a show with someone else's name? It's ridiculous."

"They don't want to use it," Marci said. "They just don't want *you* to use it."

"But it's my brand, albeit not a very good brand because no one wants to touch it with a ten-foot pole. But it's mine!"

"That's the thing; when your brand has weathered the storm, which it will, they don't want you taking your show on the road."

"In other words, they want to own me."

Their drinks came and Marci took a fortifying sip. Clearly she was not enjoying this. To the waiter from the Island of Pretensia, who by now knew exactly who Gia was and was lingering to eavesdrop, Marci said, "We could use some nibbles."

He propped his hip against the table. "Allow me to make a few suggestions."

"Just bring us out some of those dumplings . . . the ones with the pork . . . the quail eggs, and the house-made potato chips." Marci stared daggers at him, her message transparent: FO, pretty boy.

When he disappeared to the other side of the restaurant, Marci said, "Yeah, they want to own you."

"I don't want to give them my name."

"We could try to play hardball, but then they may just keep you, put your show on at midnight, and make you tape at four in the morning. There really isn't any way to stop them." She paused and let out another sigh. "They want you to announce that you're resigning."

"But I'm not. They're firing me. A resignation is the same as an admission that I did something wrong. The only thing I'm guilty of is dating an asshole." An asshole who bilked people out of their life savings.

"We'll leak it to the press that the network fired you. The American public isn't stupid, Gia; they'll know what's really going on here."

No, it would make her look weak and feed more fuel to the tabloids. The headlines had already been damning: "Grand Jury Convened to Look at Treadwell's Complicity in Ponzi Scheme." "Treadwell on the Treadmill to Prison." All lies.

How had her life gone from perfect to crap in the blink of an eye? At moments like this, she tried to focus on the future. She wasn't quite sure what that would look like, but it involved a small railroad town, verdant fields that stretched beyond the Feather River, and mountains and trees for as far as the eye could see. Peace and quiet and asshole free.

Their appetizers came, and this time their waiter didn't loiter. Even at five foot tall, Marci could be a fire-spitting dragon.

"I'll give them the name," Gia said, "but not the resignation announcement. They want to fire me, they can make their own damn announcement. Just let them know that if they libel me in any way . . . my attorney is on speed dial."

"Let me see what I can do," Marci said.

Gia wouldn't let the network push her around, but she wanted out of her contract and out of New York as fast as a bullet train.

"You asleep?" Aidan nuzzled Dana's neck.

"I was," she said in a drowsy voice.

"Sorry; go back to sleep."

She rolled over on her side, blinking at him a few times with those mesmerizing golden eyes he liked so much. "What time is it?"

"Five." He kissed her nose.

"Five? I feel like I just shut my eyes. I never sleep during the day like this."

"We had a long night." His lips tipped up in a salacious smile. "How was work?"

"I got the listing for the cabin. And Carol may have sold a home in Sierra Heights."

"The cabin you like so much?" He brushed a strand of hair away from her face. He liked touching her.

"The very one. I never in a million years thought I'd get it."

"You're on a roll, baby." His hands snaked up her T-shirt; she didn't have on a bra, giving him unfettered access to her breasts. "Want to fool around?"

Her eyes heated and she started to say something, stopped herself, and finally blurted, "I don't know what we're doing, Aidan."

"Working up to foreplay."

"You know what I mean."

Yeah, he knew what she meant. "I don't know what we're doing either. But I do know that I like you . . . that I think about you all the time. Do we have to analyze it?"

"Am I just convenient because we live together and there aren't a lot of single women in Nugget?"

"What?" he growled, because the question was patently absurd. "Dana, I was attracted to you from the first night I saw you . . . when you stood on the curb in a see-through nightgown with your smiley-face panties showing."

"You were?"

"It wasn't exactly a good time, considering your house was burning down, but under normal circumstances I would've asked you for your number."

"You would not have."

"Yeah, I would've. I liked the color of your eyes." Among other things. "You had this grace-under-fire thing going that I admired."

"No, that was shock you saw." She propped up on one elbow. "Is that why you offered to share the house? Because you were attracted to me?"

"The truth? I didn't want a roommate, but I felt bad for you. I also told myself that if we lived together, I couldn't put the moves on you . . . and I wanted to."

"What changed . . . about putting the moves on me?"

"That night at our party, it hit me that I wasn't going to make it." He ran his hand down her arm. "I know it complicates things."

She kissed him. "A little bit."

"Dana?"

"Hmm?"

"Off with the clothes, okay?"

She unsnapped her shorts, pulled them down, and wiggled out of them, leaving on just a pair of see-through panties. He put his hand there and found the lace wet. Dana pulled up his shirt and tugged it over his head, touching his chest and his abdomen until he hissed in a breath. Once her T-shirt came off, he couldn't get enough of her, touching and licking and sucking until her body bowed.

"Pants," she said in a breathy voice that made Aidan wild.

"You want them off?"

She answered by grabbing for his belt, trying desperately to unclasp the buckle. He shooed her hand away and undid it himself, sliding jeans and shorts down his legs. With one foot he kicked them off.

"Shit . . . condom." He rolled off the bed, sprinted to his bedroom, and returned as quickly as he'd left. "We're good."

Aidan looked down at her lying on the bed and almost lost his mind. He'd never seen a woman look at him like he was everything, the sun and the moon and the stars. Not Sue. Not anyone. And it humbled him, made him afraid that he'd disappoint her. Not in bed. He knew he had that covered, but in everything else.

She reached for him. And he came down on top of her, using his hands to balance his weight, and kissed her. Slender arms came around his neck, and he had the crazy sensation that this was what home felt like.

With one hand, and his teeth, he managed to open one of the foil packets and rolled the condom on. She arched her back in a wordless plea to take her, which he did. Thoroughly.

"I could grill us some burgers," he said, lying next to her in a postcoital haze.

"There are salad fixings in the fridge and a bag of chips left from the party. You do realize I keep breaking my no-eating-after-six rule with you?"

He chuckled. "I never met a woman who had more rules than you."

She nestled her head next to his shoulder. "Without them life would be chaos."

"I like chaos." He swung his feet over the bed, walked to her dresser, and opened the first drawer.

"What are you doing?"

"Checking something." He turned around, dangling a pair of her underwear. "Just as I suspected; you organized them by color."

"And type," she said, completely serious. "The thongs are next to the bikinis, which are next to the hipsters, and the boy shorts are at the far end. That way I don't have to search for what I need." Her eyes moved over him. "You're the best-looking naked man I've ever seen."

"Yeah?" Aidan cocked a brow. "How many have you seen?"

"Enough." She winked at him. Dana Calloway had a flirtatious streak.

"Want to share a shower . . . you know, for the drought?"

"How civic-minded of you." She laughed, letting her eyes linger on his erection. "Impressive. I'll meet you in there."

Aidan grabbed his clothes off the floor and started for the door. "Don't make me wait too long. We wouldn't want to waste water."

After their shower, they sat on the back porch and ate. The temperature had cooled and Aidan got lost in the blues, pinks, and reds that streaked the sky.

"You have any luck on your case today?"

"Nah," Aidan said. "Between you and me, I don't have a damn thing."

"Griffin doesn't think it's one of the Rigsby boys. He says Sean's too, uh, mentally challenged to have pulled it off."

The majority of arsonists had IQs below normal—typically between seventy and ninety. So Griffin didn't know what the hell he was talking about.

"When did you talk to Griffin?" He didn't know why, but it bothered him. The guy always seemed to be coming around.

"He walked over to the office from the Nugget Market today to say hello and asked about the case."

If the whole damn town wasn't obsessed with the fire, Aidan might've suspected Griffin because offenders liked to relive the crime by talking about it. For some of these guys it was like sex.

"You didn't tell him anything, right?"

"Aidan, I don't know anything."

He never used to talk about his cases with Sue, mostly because she hadn't been interested. But Dana always asked about his work, and more likely than not, he'd eventually tell her something he shouldn't. It was normal—at least it should be—to tell the woman you're living with about your day.

"Sometimes I might slip and give details about a case that I shouldn't. I know this town likes to gossip, but can you promise to keep quiet?"

"Of course; I would never tell anyone something you told me in confidence."

"Good, because I like being able to tell you stuff."

"You do?" She beamed.

"You're a good listener. What else did Griffin have to say?"

"He and Lina are going to Hawaii. She's never been. And that any time we want we can use the pool at Sierra Heights."

"How did the pool come up?" The idea that Dana might've said something about their sexcapade in her parents' pool niggled at him.

"God . . . you don't think . . . seriously, Aidan. He asked about the plans for my new house and I told him I was thinking of putting in a pool."

"From a firefighter's point of view, I love the idea. From a practical point of view, it seems crazy, given how cold everyone tells me the winters are up here. Besides, we've got a river right outside our door."

He realized his mistake when she suddenly clammed up. "Dana"—he tilted his head to look at her—"are you afraid to swim in the river because of what happened to your brother?"

"No. It's not even the same river. It just brings back that day."

And what she had lost, which Aidan now knew was more than Paul. She'd lost her whole damn family.

"I'm sorry, baby." He draped his arm over her shoulders, not knowing what else to say.

"It's okay. It's been a long time. Wanna watch a movie?"

"Is it gonna be a chick flick?"

"Probably." She stood up and he watched her wipe the dust off her butt.

"I'm in."

Dana made a bowl of popcorn and Aidan got through *Bridesmaids* thanks to Melissa McCarthy. They must've fallen asleep on the couch because he was awakened at two in the morning by the ring of his cell phone.

"Hello?"

"Get dressed; we've got another one," Captain Johnson said.

"Suspicious?" Aidan felt Dana stirring in his arms.

"Oh yeah."

"What?" she asked as he clicked off the call.

"Another suspicious fire. I've got to go." Out of habit, he was primed for an argument.

"Okay," she said. "You'll be careful, right?"

"I always am." He kissed her. "Sorry to wake you; go back to sleep."

In the time it took Aidan to get to the Bun Boy, firefighters had completely contained the blaze. He was startled to see an ambulance on site. He nudged his chin at the captain in question.

"The damned fire nearly took out one of our guys. The needle fairies say Duke's okay, but they're taking him to Plumas District Hospital for observation."

"Jesus." Aidan scrubbed a hand through his hair as he watched a paramedic shut the back doors of the bus on Duke and zoom off with their lights flashing.

"The idiot doesn't know what he's doing half the time, but this wasn't his fault. That fire burned fast and hot as hell."

"Accelerant?"

"That would be my guess, but you'll know better than me. It looks like it started in the supply closet."

Aidan went to check it out, bumping into Rhys on the way. "Sounds like we have ourselves another one."

"Yep," Rhys said, "and I sure as hell don't like it. This is the last thing we need in a dry, hot summer."

"Roger that."

Rhys and Aidan started for the building as a car came screeching into the parking lot. Donna jumped out even before the vehicle came to a complete halt. A man Aidan presumed was Trevor Thurston, Donna's husband, grabbed her arm.

"What the hell happened to my drive-through?" she bellowed.

"Welcome to crazy town." Rhys shook his head.

Aidan suppressed a grin and changed direction, hoping to head Donna off at the pass. He needed to keep the scene clear.

Trevor stuck out his hand to Aidan. "You know what happened yet?"

"Too soon." He watched Trevor closely. "Anything you know?"

"When I left at closing time, the place didn't look like that." Donna pointed at the charred remains of a storage room attached to the side of the building. "I need to get in there to assess the rest of the damage."

"Not yet," Aidan said. "Let me have a look and I'll get you in there as soon as possible. That room"—he motioned at the burned-out shed—"was it accessible from the outside?"

"Yes. It had a door on the outside and we kept a padlock on it," Donna responded.

"What did you keep in there?"

"Cleaning supplies, mops, buckets, rags, nothing too exciting."

"Okay, let me check it out. Wait here."

He walked across the parking lot to the Bun Boy building, where the police department had set up klieg lights. Sloane was probably here somewhere. The closer he got, the stronger the scent of disinfectant became. Pine oil, which was highly combustible, had a flashpoint at or above 140 degrees Fahrenheit.

As a couple of firefighters checked for hot spots, Rhys circled the wreckage and sidled up to Aidan. "It feels different than the last one."

"This one was more organized." Aidan crouched down and shone his flashlight on the ground. "He came through here and went straight to the storage shed."

Rhys examined the dirt. "I don't see any footprints."

"He dragged them clean." Aidan directed Rhys's attention toward a big tree branch on the ground. No burn marks.

He put on a pair of latex gloves, collected the branch, and used it to sweep the ground near the spot where he'd been hunkered down. "See?" The marks were identical. Aidan walked a few feet away. "But here we have tread marks that look similar to the footprints we got at the sporting goods store."

With Rhys's help, they photographed the impressions next to a ruler and marked the area so Aidan could make casts of the prints. Afterward, he made his way to the burned-out hull of the unit.

"He knew pine oil was in here and used it as his accelerant," Aidan told Rhys.

"You keep saying *he*. How do you know our suspect isn't a woman?"

"Arson is predominantly committed by males," Aidan said, searching through the debris for the lock Donna had told him about.

Eureka. He found the metal padlock lying in a pile of ash and rubble. "Can someone move that light closer?"

Rhys went and did it himself while Aidan studied the lock under a flashlight. It had been slit open, probably with bolt cutters.

"Whoever did this came prepared," Rhys said, clearly coming to the same conclusion as Aidan.

"Is it common knowledge what the Thurstons store in this space?" he asked Rhys.

"I don't know about common knowledge, but all it would take is someone to be standing around when an employee opened it. At one time or another half the young adult population in Nugget has worked here."

"And you definitely don't like Trevor for this?" To Aidan, he was the only one with a financial motive because he owned both buildings.

"Stranger things have happened, but I don't see it. This is his wife's pride and joy."

Except the equipment was old and in many instances outdated. Aidan had noticed that right off when he'd done his inspection. With enough insurance money she could go state-of-the-art. Aidan walked around the rest of the building, Rhys following. Other than the storage-unit side of the restaurant, there didn't appear to be much damage.

"Who made the 9-1-1 call?" Other than the inn, which was across the green, and the apartment above the Ponderosa, the square was dead after eleven o'clock.

"Anonymous." Rhys sighed. "We're trying to trace it."

Aidan would bet money their firebug made the call on a burner and tossed it.

"Hey." Sloane came trotting up. "Come see what I found in the Dumpster."

Aidan hadn't seen his sister since the Fourth of July and wanted to give her a hug. Probably not a good idea because they were working the case together. They followed her, and all three of them climbed up on the trash bin and flashed their lights inside. On top sat a work shirt that looked vaguely familiar.

Rhys hopped down, found a branch, and fished the shirt out of the garbage, careful not to touch it without gloves. Aidan, who still wore his latex, took it off Rhys's hands. A patch across the front pocket read "Rigsby Electrical."

Chapter 16

Dana had already showered and dressed and was in the kitchen making coffee when Aidan slipped into the house. He'd been gone all night and much of the morning. She heard him come through the door and greeted him in the living room.

"How did it go?" His eyes were bloodshot, he smelled like smoke, and he was so delectable she couldn't believe she'd been in his arms just a short while ago.

"Not too good. Duke, one of our guys, suffered smoke inhalation and had to be taken to the hospital."

"I saw that in Harlee's story. Will he be okay?"

"Yeah. But it could've been bad."

"It could've been you," she said, the thought making her queasy.

"Nah." He pulled her into his arms. "Duke's not the sharpest tool in the shed, and he's a show-off. I'm not saying it doesn't happen to the best firefighters, but in this situation it could've been avoided."

He stopped talking and stared at her with a goofy smile on his lips.

"What?"

"It's just nice of you to be concerned. Don't take this the wrong way, but it sort of reminded me of my mother and father. He'd come home after a big fire and she'd get on his case about the dangers of his job and then they'd wind up kissing."

He lowered his mouth to hers and gave her a big smooch while her heart expanded as big as the moon. She and Aidan were just so easy. Everything about him, about them being together, felt natural, like they fit.

"You off to work?" he asked, his hands playing casually at her hips.

"Don't change the subject. Do you know who set this one?"

He let out a breath. "I smell coffee."

She nodded. He definitely looked as if he could use a cup . . . or two. "It should be ready."

They went in the kitchen together, and Dana motioned for him to sit. She poured them each a mug, set them on the table, and got the cream out of the fridge.

"You know, don't you?"

Aidan left his coffee black and took a long sip. "Maybe, but something about it is off."

"Like what?"

"Like we found some damning evidence at the scene." He squinted his eyes and shook his head. "Too easy, if you ask me."

"What did you find? Harlee didn't have anything about evidence in her story. Only that the Bun Boy would be up and running in a few days, according to the Thurstons."

"That's because Harlee doesn't know about the evidence." He gave Dana a pointed look.

"Your secret is safe with me. I love this stuff . . . not that someone got hurt; I hate that. Or that the Bun Boy was damaged . . . but it's like *CSI*."

Aidan rolled his eyes. "I've got to take a shower." He sniffed himself and let out a low whistle.

"You're not planning to tell me?"

"Nope." He drained the coffee and got to his feet.

"Come on." She pouted, but he was unmovable.

"What are we doing tonight?"

And there went her heart again. No games, no waiting by the phone, no second guessing, just easy. This was what it was supposed to be like.

"The other day Harlee and Darla asked me to have drinks with them at the Ponderosa. But that's early . . . around five. After that you and I could go bowling. Or you could meet us for drinks."

"No drinks until we catch whoever is setting these fires," he said, and she guessed he was permanently on call. "But bowling sounds good. We could have dinner first."

"Perfect," she said, her belly quivering. They were like a real couple. A good couple. "So you're still not going to tell me, are you?"

"Come here." He crooked his finger at her and she got out of her chair. In her ear he hesitated for a second and then whispered, "You look hot in that dress."

She swatted his arm playfully. "You're bad."

"Nah, I'm good." He grabbed her in a fireman's hold and started to carry her into the bedroom while she pounded on his back.

"Aidan, I have a meeting in fifteen minutes. Put me down."

"You sure you can't be late?"

"I've never been late in my life."

He snorted and placed her on her feet. "Organized and punctual. Call me from the Ponderosa when you're ready for dinner."

"I will." She straightened out her dress, one of Harlee's hand-me-downs. Uh-oh. "What if Harlee asks about the case?"

"Tell her what you know." He laughed and took off for the shower.

Dana washed out her cup, sighed when she saw Aidan's in the sink, and washed that one too. On her way out the door, she grabbed her briefcase and took a few seconds to air out her car. Not even ten a.m. and it was stifling. Unable to help herself, she swung by the square to check out the Bun Boy.

The damage didn't look too bad. It was worse than the sporting goods store, though. A few people had gathered on the sidewalk to gawk, but there weren't many people out at this time on a Sunday. She noticed Owen milling around and unrolled her window.

"What do you know?" she asked him, feeling a little more outgoing than her usual self.

"You're the one with the inside track. What does your hot-shot fire investigator tell you?"

"Nada. He's by the books."

"Well, ever since he showed up, we've been having a lot of fires, starting with yours, missy. Seems like quite a coincidence, if you ask me."

"Aidan didn't set those fires," she said.

"How do you know?"

Because she'd burned her own house down, and as for the others . . . "I was with him when he got the calls."

"Convenient alibi, don't you think?" He tracked her with a gimlet eye.

The man was nuts. When he spied Dink, the mayor, walking into the barbershop, he headed after him.

She backed out of her parking spot, giving the Bun Boy one last, longing look. A week without curly fries was like a week without sunshine.

Her clients were waiting in their car when she got to the office. She unlocked the door, immediately switched on the AC, and waved to them to come in. The Arnolds were a nice-looking couple, probably in their early forties. Mr. Arnold was a pediatric cardiothoracic surgeon and his wife a social worker. They had three teenagers, and if anyone needed a vacation home, it was them.

"How was your night at the Lumber Baron?" Dana asked.

"It's such a pretty place . . . usually so tranquil," Mrs. Arnold said. They'd stayed there a few times. "But we had some excitement last night."

"The fire," Dana said, and thought, *terrific!* Nothing said charming country town like arson.

"Do you know how it started?" Mr. Arnold asked.

"No idea. But I know they're investigating."

"According to the *Nugget Tribune*, it was the second fire in a week," he said.

"It's very unusual for this town. It's probably kids . . . summer vacation . . . boredom. I have lots to show you today, including a turnkey cabin on the river that we just listed."

That caught Mrs. Arnold's attention. "That sounds nice. Are we seeing that one first?"

"We can if you like." Dana handed the couple a file. "The places we're seeing are all in there. I'd like us to swing by Sierra Heights afterward, just so you can make comparisons. Anyone need to use the bathroom before we go?"

Three hours later, she was ready to pull her hair out of her head. The Arnolds were truly lovely people, but they suffered from paralysis by analysis. Instead of leading with their hearts, they broke everything down into pros and cons. Would this house appreciate more than that house? They loved having views of the river, but they worried about flooding. What if they eventually wanted a pool; where would they put it? And the list went on.

She looked at her watch. They wanted to be on the road by two. Dana thought they had just enough time to swing by Sierra Heights, wanting it to be their last impression of the day. She cruised through the security kiosk, which, as usual, had no security. The Arnolds didn't comment on it, which, given how much they'd scrutinized every-thing else, gave Dana hope.

"It really is lovely." Mrs. Arnold sat in the backseat, gazing out the window.

"I was at a party here the other night. The host is a chef and he made pizzas in the outdoor oven, poolside."

"How does it work with the golf course again? Residents have priority?" Mr. Arnold asked.

"Mm-hmm." It's not like it was difficult to get a tee time. This was Nugget. "Would you like to see a few of the models again?"

"Perhaps that would be a good idea," he said.

An hour and fifteen minutes later, Dana and the Arnolds sat in her office drawing up an offer. Aidan was right; she really was on a roll.

"You have anything to eat around here?" Sloane stuck her head in Aidan's refrigerator.

He maneuvered her away and reached in for a package of bacon. "I'll make you a BLT."

"Really? Okay."

"It'll be generic compared to Brady's. But beggars can't be choosers."

She dropped into one of the kitchen chairs and glanced around the room. "Dana's a neat freak, isn't she?"

"What makes you think I'm not the clean one?"

"Uh . . . like I've known you my whole life. You're a slob. So what's her deal? She's kind of glommed on to you like a puppy."

"We like each other. What's wrong with that?"

"Nothing. I think it's great that you have someone to pass the time with until you figure out your shit. But don't go breaking her heart. She's not as resilient as Sue."

He thought Dana was pretty resilient, but she definitely wasn't Sue. "What shit am I supposed to be figuring out?"

"Why you let someone like Sue get away."

"Maybe it was all part of the grand scheme." He pulled a frying pan out of the cupboard, put it over a medium flame, and filled it with strips of bacon.

"So you could meet Dana?" She let out a snort of laughter.

"What's funny about that, Sloane?"

"She's so not your type. A: She's got a stick up her ass. B: She's lived here longer than I have and doesn't have any friends. And C: She's an introvert and you're the life of the party. Now, Sue was your type. Fun, social, outgoing. We loved Sue."

"So I've heard." Aidan turned the bacon. "Do me a favor, stay out of my love life."

Sloane held up her hands in surrender. "I was just trying to help and save a woman from getting hurt. Everyone can see she's enthralled with you. After Griffin dumped her for—"

"That's enough. You don't know the first thing about it."

"What are you saying?"

Aidan reached up for a cutting board to slice the tomato. "What I'm saying is, maybe I'm crazy about her."

Sloane narrowed her eyes at him like he was delusional. "Not more crazy about her than you were about Sue."

No, the rest of you *were crazy about Sue.* "Leave it alone, Sloane. It's my business; worry about your own love life. What's going on with the wedding?"

"Brady still wants to do it in September. I think it's crazy. There's no way we can pull something like that off in two months, and I want a dream wedding with all the frills and flounces. I know it's girlie, but it's what I want."

"Then wait," he said, spreading mayo on a couple of slices of bread and filling them with bacon, lettuce, and tomato.

"Then we'd have to wait a full year. Any later than September it starts getting cold around here."

Aidan lifted his shoulder. What did he know about weddings?

"Let's talk about the case," she said.

He cut her sandwich on a diagonal—the way she used to eat it as a kid—grabbed a bag of chips, a couple of sodas, and sat down to eat. "Not much to talk about until we hear back on the shirt from forensics. I'm betting that shirt was nowhere near a fire . . . that it was tossed in that Dumpster before the Bun Boy was lit up."

"You don't like Rigsby for this?"

"Of everyone we're looking at, he fits the profile best. He was pissed off about me taking his fireworks. According to Rhys, he's got anger issues . . . again, consistent with an arsonist. And he's not the kind of guy who likes to answer to the man, if you know what I mean."

"I do." Sloane bit into her sandwich and washed it down with a swig of cola. "It's hot in here."

Aidan got up and opened the kitchen door, leaving the screen closed. "Better?"

"Yeah, you have a nice breeze. So it sounds like Rigsby could easily be our guy. Why are you skeptical?"

"Because even a half-wit doesn't leave his shirt at the scene, and believe me, I've seen it all. People who've left fingerprints, dropped matchbooks, even business cards. But this is too . . . pat."

"Okay, then who would want to set him up?"

Aidan leaned over the table and ruffled Sloane's hair. It was fun doing this with his little sister. The family hadn't been too pleased when she'd run off to Los Angeles to become a cop. The McBrides were firefighters. But despite the trouble she'd had there—and it had been considerable—she was top-notch at her job. Tough as nails, his girlie sister.

"I got the impression Clay McCreedy hates Rigsby's guts. You know why?"

Sloane grabbed the bag of chips away from Aidan. "You're a hog. According to town gossip, Rigsby spread stories about Clay's first wife cheating on him with the developer of Sierra Heights."

"Griffin?"

"No." She shook her head, as if the idea of Archangel Griffin being involved in something sordid was beyond comprehension. "Griff bought the place out of bankruptcy. The original owner was up to his ass in debt and was apparently being investigated by the feds for cooking the books. Way before my time. But it turns out Clay's wife was doing the guy in a big way, and they wound up getting into a car accident together. She died."

"Ah, man."

"I tell you, sometimes this place is a soap opera. Anyway, Rigsby's son, Sean, heard enough from dear old dad to taunt the hell out of poor Justin over his mother's affair. Clay is protective of those boys. But if you're thinking he's setting fires in an attempt to frame Rigsby . . . no way. Forget about it. The guy's a pillar of the community, a war hero, and personal friends with the Thurstons and Carl Rudd. Absolutely no way in hell he'd torch their places of business, or any, for that matter."

"Okay. What about Trevor Thurston?"

"You mean for profit . . . the insurance money?"

Aidan nodded. The majority of arsons were for financial gain, usually carried out by professionals. And usually they got the job done. The sporting goods store and Bun Boy fires were pretty half-assed—thank God.

"I haven't found anything that shows he's in need of money. Bank records all look good," Aidan said. "What do you hear rumor wise?"

"Nothing like he has a five-hundred-buck-a-night hooker problem. Are you kidding? Donna would kill him."

From the little Aidan knew about the Bun Boy matron, Sloane was probably right. "I guess that brings us back to Rigsby. When are the results on the shirt due back?"

Sloane shrugged. "Hard to say. We're not in Chicago anymore, Toto. Plumas County can move slowly."

"Rhys and I want to wait before we go over to the Rigsby place, guns blazing. Could Rhys reach out to the evidence guys?"

"He can and he probably has. How's your guy . . . what's his name?"

"Duke. He's okay. Been tweeting about it like he nearly lost his life pulling victims out of a burning skyscraper." Aidan rolled his eyes heavenward. The guy was the epitome of a whacker. Still, it sucked that he'd gotten hurt.

"You on Tuesday?"

"Yeah. But I'll be off in time for Tawny's wedding. In a barn, huh?" Aidan couldn't get over it, although he'd known a couple of guys who'd tied the knot in a firehouse. Different strokes . . .

"It's beyond cool. Wait until you see it. And there should be lots of pretty cowgirls to chase after."

"I'm bringing Dana." He hadn't told her yet, but that was his plan.

Sloane chewed on her lip. Aidan presumed it was to keep from responding with a snotty reply.

"Why don't you like her? As far as I can tell, she's been nothing but nice to you and Brady."

Sloane folded the top of the chip bag. "Take these away from me. I don't have anything against her. I barely know her. She's just not for you."

He thought Sloane might be wrong about that. It was still early, but the more he got to know Dana, the more he became convinced she was just the thing for him.

Sloane gazed at the kitchen clock. "Duty calls, I've got to go." She brought her plate to the sink and helped put everything away. "Thanks for lunch."

"Any time. If you hear anything, let me know."

"You got it."

He heard Sloane's police rig pull out of the driveway and tidied up. Dana liked the place clean and he often left a mess. Her bedroom door stood open and he peeked inside. He found everything in its place: bed neatly made, pillows perfectly arranged, drapes symmetrically drawn. On a lark, he opened the closet. That too had stayed as organized as the day he'd built it. Only now, thanks to Harlee, there was a lot more clothing in it.

Everything smelled like her too, a soft, powdery fragrance that reminded him of flowers and sunshine. Hard to believe her house had burned down a few weeks ago. Sloane had been wrong; Dana was one of the strongest women he'd ever known.

His phone rang and he checked the caller ID. It was a Chicago area code, but he didn't recognize the number.

"Hello?" he answered. Nothing but air and the faint sound of someone breathing. "Hello? Anyone there?"

"Aidan?"

"Sue? You okay?"

"Yes, yes, of course. I was . . . uh . . . just calling about the condo. Have you sold it yet?"

He'd told her that he would give her half the proceeds from the sale even though he'd bought the place himself. But like the furniture, she'd declined. Perhaps she needed the money after all.

"Not yet," he said.

"I know someone who may be interested."

"Oh?" Why hadn't she called the listing agent?

"She's a friend of Sebastian's and she likes the neighborhood. I just thought . . . uh . . . that it might be helpful if I passed her name along."

"Yeah, okay, sure. Let me get a pen." Although what was he supposed to do with the information? Again: Wouldn't it have made more sense for Sebastian's friend to call Aidan's real estate agent?

He went back in the kitchen and rifled through the designated junk drawer, where he found both a pen and a pad of paper. "I'm back."

She gave Aidan the woman's name and number.

"Thanks. I'll pass it on to my agent." There was a long silence. Finally, he said, "How was the wedding?"

"It was good. How's California?"

"Good. It's nice living near Sloane and it's really beautiful here."

"You think you'll come back to Chicago?"

"To visit my folks and my brothers, yeah of course."

"I meant to live."

Weird question, considering the reason for her call was about him selling his condo. "Uh, no, I like it here. I like the job."

"Are you seeing someone?"

"Sue," he said, "what's going on here?"

"Nothing. I just don't like the way we ended. It's been bothering me. We were together a long time. I care about you. I care about your happiness."

"I care about you too, Sue. You know that, right? I want you to be happy. I've always wanted you to be happy. And to answer your question, yeah, I'm seeing someone."

More silence. "Sue, you there?"

"I'm here." Her voice quivered. "Are you in love with her?"

"I just met her." He could hear her crying on the other end of the phone.

"I miss you, Aidan."

The call was veering into inappropriate territory. Time to go. "You're married to Sebastian now, so you probably shouldn't be telling me these things. Look, Sue, I'm gonna hang up now. Thanks for passing your friend along."

He pressed the End button on his phone, dumbfounded. What the hell was that about?

Chapter 17

Aidan waved from the other side of the Ponderosa's dining room and Dana's stomach did a flip. He looked so hot in his faded jeans and polo shirt, better than any other man in the restaurant.

"Remember, you promised not to pepper him with questions about the fires," Dana told Harlee.

"But I can casually ask if there's anything new, right?"

"Yes. But if it's obvious he doesn't want to talk about it, you have to stop."

Harlee's lips quirked up. "You're cute."

"I think it's nice she wants to protect Aidan from the likes of you," Darla said.

"Hey," Harlee called out, "whose side are you on?"

Harlee's best friend shook her head, her big plastic peace-sign earrings swinging. Today she had on a purple pageboy wig. Her unconventional look was starting to grow on Dana. Hey, let your freak flag fly, right?

"Firefighters are so hot," Darla said. Apparently, Aidan was having the same effect on her as he was on Dana.

All three of them watched him walk their way.

He hadn't even had time to sit down when Harlee said, "You better have news for me."

Dana glared at Harlee and Aidan laughed.

"I've got nothing," he said, and Harlee pierced him with an I-don't-believe-you glower. "Seriously, if I had something, I'd tell you. I like the press." He winked at Dana. "Is that alcohol free?"

She poured him a glass of Arnold Palmer from the pitcher. "It's iced tea and lemonade."

"How are you ladies?" He turned to Dana. "How did it go with your clients?"

"Got an offer on a Sierra Heights house." She put up her hand for a high five. Instead, Aidan leaned across the table and kissed her.

Darla started fanning herself. "You guys are so cute."

Dana felt her face turn a dozen shades of red. Not only wasn't she used to being the center of attention, she didn't like it.

"You joining us for dinner?" Aidan asked Harlee and Darla.

"I've got to get home. Colin's making linguini tonight. When do you think you'll have something for me?"

Boy, Dana thought, Harlee never quit. Must be why she was such a good reporter. But when she found out Dana had been holding out on the news of Gia Treadwell moving to town . . .

"I've got to go too," Darla said. "Wyatt and I are going to the Indian place in Glory Junction."

"Does that restaurant have an actual name?" Aidan chuckled. "Ever since I moved here I've only heard it referred to as the 'Indian place.'"

"You know," she responded, "I have no clue what its real name is, but it's so good, right?"

Dana squeezed Aidan's leg under the table, knowing that he didn't like Indian food. He winked at her, and it struck her that they already had their own inside jokes. In a short time, they'd learned each other's idiosyncrasies.

Harlee and Darla said their good-byes, leaving Aidan and Dana alone at the table.

"Another sale, huh? You're tearing it up."

"I'm definitely having a good summer." Not just the sales, she thought.

He reached across the table and kissed her again. "Yeah, me too."

"Did you work on the case today?"

"Sloane came over and we threw some theories around, but nothing official. For the most part, I hung out, did some laundry, and tidied up. I know how you like everything just so," he teased. "Tuesday I'm back on for twenty-four hours, so you'll have the place to yourself."

"I don't mind sharing it with you." The fact was, he was a good roommate. Considerate, enjoyable, and not nearly as sloppy as he thought he was. "Tomorrow I'm meeting with Pat and Colin about my new house. They're ready to start and have already submitted my plans to the city."

"You feeling good about it?" He waved over a server to take their orders. They'd reserved a lane for seven.

"I am but nervous. I've never built a house before. There are a lot of choices to make."

"You tell Colin what I said about the sprinklers?" When she nodded, he added, "And no candles."

She frowned at him. "That was pretty stupid of me. To this day, I can't believe I left it burning . . . and next to rags soaked in varnish."

"If it makes you feel better, it's one of the top causes of house fires."

It didn't. Leaving that candle lit had been the dumbest thing she'd ever done, barring Paul's drowning. That had been unforgivable. Before she could respond, Sophie bustled over to the table to take their order.

"Hello. Sorry you had to wait."

"Not a problem," Aidan said. "How's Lilly?"

"She's good." Sophie gazed around the crowded dining room. "But if I don't get help soon, she'll have to move in here with Mariah and me. I'm not complaining, but it seems like every day the crowds grow larger. Part of it's summer of course. A lot of tourists. What can I get you?"

They both ordered, Sophie wrote it down, and said, "You're probably sick of everyone asking, but anything new on the fires?"

"Nothing that I can talk about."

"Can you say whether you think they're connected?"

Aidan appeared to be considering the question. "Different methods, which I can't go into, but too coincidental to make me think otherwise. The reason why I'm telling you this is so you can be extra vigilant."

Sophie's eyes rounded. "Do you think we're next?"

"I'm not saying that. But I'd like you and your employees to pay more attention than usual. You own the building, right?"

Dana dealt strictly in residential real estate, but she knew Trevor Thurston owned a few of the buildings on the square.

"Mariah and I do, yes," Sophie said.

"Who lives in the apartment upstairs?"

"Our cook, Tater."

"Not when you're busy like this, but at some point I'd like to talk to him."

"Okay," Sophie said. "I'll let him know. In the meantime, I'll get these orders in to him."

When she walked away, Aidan asked, "So clue me in on her and the situation with Lilly. Are she and Mariah . . . lesbians?"

"Uh-huh. According to Carol, who is way more tapped in around here than I am, when Sophie and Mariah wanted to have a baby, Nate Breyer volunteered his . . . uh—"

"Sperm," Aidan supplied. "Okay. Now it makes sense. I wasn't sure how it all worked. I know this is California, but no one here gives them any problems?"

"Why, do you have a problem with it?" she asked, and she could hear her own indignation.

"Nope. Don't give a damn as long as people are happy and aren't hurting anyone. But clearly not everyone feels that way, and maybe I'm generalizing here, but I would think small towns can be small-minded."

"As far as I know, there hasn't been any trouble. From what I can tell, everyone likes Sophie and Mariah." She waved a hand at the crowded restaurant. "It's not like their business isn't flourishing. The Nugget Mafia regularly eats here and practically has a bowling lane named in their honor. And the Baker's Dozen can't get enough of that baby."

"The Baker's what?"

Dana laughed. "A local cooking club. All women, except for Brady. Some might argue that they have as much clout in this town as the Mafia."

Aidan shook his head as if to clear it. "I'm still trying to wrap my head around the fact that my brother-in-law-to-be is a member of an all-women's cooking club."

"I guess you'll have to reevaluate small towns not being progressive."

"Weird little place, isn't it?"

"Yep, but in a good way," she said.

"Definitely in a good way because you're in it, which reminds me: I want you to be my date to Tawny and Lucky's wedding next weekend."

"Uh . . . I don't think so, Aidan. I wasn't invited and I'd feel like I was crashing."

"You'd be coming as my date. I was invited with a guest."

"This is different," she argued. "It's awkward when you sort of know the people and they didn't invite you." Especially when they'd invited Carol and just about everyone else in town. Dana couldn't blame them. It wasn't like she was close to the couple, although Carol wasn't either. Dana figured it was because Carol had lived in Nugget her whole life. Besides, weddings were expensive to throw; the bride and groom had to draw the line somewhere.

"That's ridiculous. I get to bring a guest and I want to go with you."

Dana looked around the dining room. They were sitting right next to the Millers, and she didn't want them hearing her and Aidan's conversation. "Can we talk about this at home?"

"Nothing to talk about. You and I are going to a wedding in a barn. We're gonna dance the night away to a country-western band and eat barbecue."

She shook her head. Aidan McBride was certainly on the domineering side.

Their food came and she let the topic of Tawny and Lucky's wedding drop. When they finished eating, Aidan announced that it was time to bowl. Dana tried to pay, but Aidan wasn't having it.

"Come on, you said I could pay next time."

"No, I didn't, or if I did, I was lying." He put his credit card in the bill holder.

"I'm selling properties left and right. I should treat."

"Sorry, I know I'm an outdated species, but not in my DNA. When you and I go out together, I pay! But you can provide the candy. Those little chocolate, pecan, caramel things. God, I love those."

Dana smiled. "They're called Pecan Petes, after my late great-uncle, Pete Calloway. According to my father, he came up with the recipe for his second wife, who grew up on a pecan orchard in Georgia. Originally, the candies were named for her. But after she divorced him and tried to sue for a portion of the business on the grounds that we were profiting off her name, my father changed the candies to Pecan Petes.

"That's a great story," Aidan said.

"I thought they should've named the candies Pecan Betties after my mom. She loves them too." Or rather, used to love them. When Paul died she gave up sweets just like everything else she'd ever loved.

Someone other than Sophie took Aidan's credit card and returned a few minutes later for his signature. Afterward, they crossed over into the bowling alley. Unlike the restaurant, decorated like an old saloon with lots of Victorian millwork and dark wood, the bowling alley was modern, bright, and noisy. Balls crashing, people cheering, and bells sounding from the arcade. As far as indoor entertainment in Nugget went, this was it. So the local kids, especially in summer, swarmed the place.

"Hi, Deputy McBride." The McCreedy boys came running up.

Dana mouthed, *Deputy?*

"Deputy fire marshal. It's my official title," he told her. "But you can just call me Aidan . . . or lover boy."

"Hey, fellows." He ruffled Cody's hair. "You know Dana Calloway?"

They stuck out their hands like teenage gentlemen and greeted her. The older one, Justin, looked just like his dad and had to be at least sixteen.

"When are you boys starting at the firehouse?" Aidan asked.

"Tomorrow," Cody said. "Justin can only come for a few hours because he has Junior Rodeo practice. Will you be there?"

"Not until Tuesday, but maybe I'll drop by. See how you're doing. Sean and his brother, Seth, coming too?"

"No, sir," Justin said and left it at that.

"You two bowling?" Dana asked.

Cody pointed a few lanes away, where Clay and his wife, Emily, sat, eating a plate of nachos. They waved and Dana waved back.

When the boys rushed back to their game, Aidan asked, "Who's the woman?"

"Clay's wife."

"I thought she was dead."

"That was the first wife. She died in a car accident with her lover." Carol had told Dana the whole sordid story. "The second wife's child was kidnapped close to five years ago, when she was with her first husband, living in the Bay Area. They never found her."

"Whoa, seriously? That's horrible," Aidan said.

"God-awful. I don't know her, but people say that she and Clay are very much in love. It's good they have each other, don't you think?"

"Sure. It can't hurt."

Spoken like a true guy, Dana thought. They found their lane, traded their shoes for ugly rubber ones, and tried to figure out the scoring system.

"Haven't you ever done this before?" Dana asked because she didn't know the first thing about bowling but had always wanted to try. Never having excelled at sports, she wondered how hard rolling a ball down a wooden lane could be.

With Tim, she'd told herself the same thing about golf. It had looked ridiculously easy hitting the ball into a hole, until she'd tried it.

"I haven't been bowling since I was a kid," Aidan said. "It wasn't the kind of thing Sue was in to."

"How come?" To Dana, it looked fun. Not serious or competitive, like tennis. Or strenuous, like mountain biking. And it didn't involve short white skirts or spandex.

He let out a humorless laugh. "Too working class. The closest we ever came was a game of bocce ball at a winery on a vacation in Napa."

"Was that a problem for you?" She shouldn't have asked. Soon, he'd be crying in their pitcher of lemonade about how much he missed Sue. Griffin had had a few of those moments. Instead of running for the hills, Dana had given him her shoulder. That had certainly worked out well.

"The vacation in Napa? I'm not much of a wine drinker, and that's about all there is to do there. She liked it, though. The working-class thing? No...yes...I don't know. We were different. But different can be good...exciting...sexy. My folks loved her." He scrubbed his hands through his hair. "I don't know why I just told you that. Let's practice for a while. Hopefully the scoring will come back to me."

She didn't know why he'd told her that either. It would've crushed her if not for the fact that Aidan remained completely attentive. He laughed when her ball bounced down the lane and headed straight for the gutter. Lifted her into the air and kissed her when she got a strike. And danced with her when he got one. They'd become quite a spectacle, and although she didn't like being the center of everyone's attention, she liked being the center of his.

They played two frames before they realized the scoring was automatic, which was pretty stupid because it flashed up on an overhead screen. Dana supposed they'd been too distracted by each other to notice.

The McCreedy boys stopped at their lane on their way to the snack bar and talked to Aidan some more. They wanted to know about being a firefighter. Were the fire engines hard to drive? Were there really poles to slide down at the firehouse? And had Aidan ever saved anyone?

He answered all their questions and asked them what grades they were in, and asked Justin about Junior Rodeo.

"How do you rope a steer?"

"I can show you," Justin said. "Just come over to the ranch."

"I'd enjoy that." They came up with a date and the boys ran off.

"Kids love you, don't they?" Dana pulled a ball out of the return machine. "At first I thought you just bribed them with Otter Pops. But they genuinely like you."

"Of course they do. Everyone likes me." He said it teasingly, but it was true.

She wondered why a popular guy like him would like a wallflower like her. "I don't think kids like me that much."

"All you have to do is make an effort and they'll like you. Kids are pretty easy that way."

She flung the ball down the lane, watching it bounce, swerve right, and take down two pins. "Why do you like me?"

Aidan sat next to her on the bench. "Isn't it obvious?"

"No. I'm not generally insecure." On second thought, maybe she was when it came to relationships. But as far as her professional life, she was damned proud of her accomplishments. She was smart, enterprising, and self-sufficient. A lot of women—and men—couldn't say the same. "You're just so outgoing and I'm a loner."

"I don't think you're a loner," he said. "I think you're shy. You're also clever, interesting, beautiful, sexy, and a tremendous businesswoman. All part of the reasons I like you, but not the biggest reason."

"What's the biggest reason?"

"You make me feel like I light you up from the inside out."

She sat there for a while, taking that in. That's how he made her feel, like she was perfect the way she was, regardless of their differences. Not second but first.

He nuzzled her ear. "Let's go home."

They changed back into their real shoes, brought the pitcher back to the snack bar, and walked to Aidan's truck, holding hands in the balmy night air.

"If I had a pool, we could go for a swim." She tossed him a salacious grin. That night at her parents' had been the most erotic of her life.

"We could sneak into the pool at Sierra Heights. Naked." Aidan sounded serious.

"I didn't realize you were an exhibitionist. Sorry, bucko, I like privacy."

"Do you now? Then we'll go straight home." He kissed her, letting his hands wander over her body before she climbed into his Expedition. Inside the cab, he continued his exploration over her clothes, making her nipples pebble against the soft cotton of her blouse. "I don't know if I'll make it."

"You'll make it." She laughed.

He took her hand and guided it over the giant bulge in his pants. "I don't think so."

"What are you suggesting?" She let her hand linger on his crotch.

"That we do it right here. It's dark; no one will see us."

"You're crazy." But his eagerness turned her on. No one had ever made her feel this hot or this sexual. She reached over and started to undo his belt, hearing him suck in a breath. Then she got down on her knees on the floor in front of the seat.

And his phone rang.

Chapter 18

Talk about bad timing. Aidan looked at the caller ID and muttered a curse.

"McBride here."

"Dangburnit! We've got another one," Captain Johnson said, and Aidan pivoted his head so he could take in the whole square. No flames, no smoke.

"Where is it?"

Johnson told him, and Aidan looked over at Dana. "Shit."

"How quick can you get here?"

"I just have to drop my date home. No more than ten minutes."

"Bust a move, then."

He put his phone away and Dana asked, "Another fire?"

"Yep." He got on the road, headed for home. "Don't freak out, but this one's at your real estate office."

"Oh God." She fumbled inside her purse for her phone. "I've got to call Carol. Wait, where are you going?"

"To drop you off so I can go."

"Take me with you."

"Honey, it's a fire, quite possibly a crime scene. There's no way in hell I'm letting you get near that."

"Fine, as soon as you drop me home, I'll get in my car and drive there myself."

"Jesus, Dana, not now. At least wait until they have the fire contained."

"It's my office, Aidan...my papers, records, computer...do you really expect me to sit home? I can assure you that as soon as I call Carol, she'll jump in her car."

He huffed out a breath. "You promise to stay back, not get underfoot, and for God's sake not do anything that'll put you in danger? I'm not fooling around here, Dana."

"I promise. How bad is it?"

"I don't know." But when they drove up, it looked bad.

The back half of the building was enveloped in flames. Aidan saw Kurtis and Hutch take their hoses to the throat of the dragon. A lot of guys working this one. In Chicago they called it an all-hands fire. Aidan didn't have his turn outs, but he figured Johnson had called him in to investigate.

Dana covered her mouth. "Oh boy."

"Stay here." Aidan started to get out of the truck as Dana grabbed for his arm.

"Be careful. And, um, Aidan, close your pants."

Shit, he'd forgotten about that. "Don't get out of the truck, you hear me?"

She nodded and he left, joining the captain and Rhys, who were huddled next to one of the engines.

"It's a worker," Johnson called.

"I can see that."

"They'll get it knocked down fairly quickly." Johnson got distracted and swiveled toward a couple of the guys. "Duke, what the hell are you doing?"

Aidan watched as Duke fussed with his hose nozzle, clearly oblivious that he had his back to the flames.

"Jesus Christ, the guy's junk. He's gotta have a high-up relative in Cal Fire somewhere."

Aidan wanted to sniff around the perimeter before the fire was extinguished. He borrowed gear from one of the engines and hurriedly dressed, sticking a helmet over his head. Staying out of the way, he made his way around the building, smelling and trying to discover the fire's origin, not an easy job in the chaos. But timing was everything. When he could get closer, he'd use a portable hydrocarbon sniffer, a handheld device that would help him determine if and where ignitable liquid residues could be found.

"Anything?" Rhys came up behind him.

"I smell gasoline." He pointed to an area near the building's back door. "I think the fire started outside, right about there. See how the bottom of the door has the most charring?"

"It's hard to see anything with everyone running around." Firefighters were now cutting into an exterior wall with their axes. They'd already opened the roof for ventilation. "I guess you've got a trained eye."

Aidan let out a breath. "Too soon to say for sure, but this doesn't look like an accident." From shreds of burned debris on the ground, it looked like someone had used a pile of garbage to ignite the building.

"Why suddenly on this side of town?"

Aidan hitched his shoulders. "Dunno."

It concerned him that it was Dana's place of business. If this was a vengeance thing directed at him by Rigsby, it would make sense that he'd go for something personal. It was no secret that he and Dana lived together. He didn't know how the sporting goods store and the Bun Boy fit in, unless they were just for practice.

"It seems to be escalating," Aidan said. "The first one was nothing. The second a little bigger. This one . . . ."

"It's pissing me off," Rhys said. "What the hell is in it for this guy?"

Aidan couldn't rule out money, which was the usual motive for arson. "Who owns this building?"

"Carol Spartan, not Thurston. There goes your theory on Trevor."

"He could be trying to throw us off." But it seemed far-fetched. "You get anything back on Rigsby's shirt?"

"Not yet. The sheriff's department promises it'll be this week."

A car pulled into the lot, the driver ignoring the yellow tape. Dana jumped out of Aidan's truck and he gritted his teeth. Why couldn't she do what he'd asked her to and stay put?

"Carol," Rhys said, obviously recognizing the car.

A few minutes later, both Dana and Carol approached. "When can I get inside?" Carol asked.

For the most part the flames had been extinguished. Aidan watched Hutch and Kurtis check for hot spots.

"Not for a couple of hours," he said, wanting time to comb the site for clues and take samples near the origin that would later be analyzed by a chemist for the presence of an accelerant. "It looks like it was mostly the back of the building." From what Aidan remembered of the office, the back housed the bathroom, a small kitchen area, and a conference room.

"I'm worried about files," Carol said. "Not everything was on the computer."

"Where did you keep 'em?"

"Toward the back, behind my desk."

"I'll be going in soon," he said. "I'll try to text Dana with a damage update, but I have to focus on my investigation."

"I understand," Carol said, her face ashen. "Whatever you could tell us we'd appreciate." Dana nodded.

"I'll do my best." Most of his focus, however, would be on the outside of the building. From what he'd seen so far, the arsonist hadn't broken in, just set the fire at the back door. "How did you get word of the fire?"

"Dana called me," Carol answered, and Dana gave him an odd look, as if to say, *You know I called her.*

"Where were you when you got the call?"

Carol pulled back, clearly offended by the question. "You think I set my own building on fire?"

"I have to ask," he said. "I know where Dana was."

"If you must know, I was at Sierra Heights. The couple who made an offer on a home there yesterday is still in town and wanted to take some measurements. Griffin can vouch for me, and of course I could put you in touch with the couple."

Aidan held up his hands. "Not necessary." There was no reason to suspect Carol. No one burned down their office when business was booming. "I just have to be thorough."

With that, she appeared to lose some of her pique. "You must think the fire was intentional."

Oh yeah, he thought. "Jury is still out."

Dana caught his eye and held his gaze, dubious. He hadn't fooled her.

"Can I talk to you for a minute?" He hooked his arm in hers and walked her to his truck. "I thought I asked you to wait in the Expedition."

"The fire is out," she huffed.

"The only reason you've been allowed to stay inside the yellow tape is because you came with me. I don't want you in harm's way, you understand?"

"Carol gets to stay."

"Carol owns the property. I can't focus on my job and worry about you at the same time. In fact, why don't you take the truck and go home? I'll text you when it's safe to come back."

"I thought you said you'd let us know how bad it is when you go inside."

"Will you promise to go home?"

She took some time to consider and finally nodded. He swiped the helmet off his head and kissed her.

"I'll let you know," he said. "I left the keys in the ignition."

"Okay. You'll be careful, right?"

"I'll be careful."

As soon as she drove away he called his sister, who he knew was off duty. "You hear about the fire at Nugget Realty?"

"Yep. I volunteered to come in, but Rhys said he had it under control. Is this related to the other two?"

"I think so, but I'm not sure yet. Do me a giant solid, would you? Dana just went home. I don't want her there alone."

"Sure. But why?" Sloane asked. "Are you being abundantly cautious because it was her office?"

"Yes. I don't have time to go into it now. I'll talk to you later." He clicked off before she could pelt him with a million questions. More than likely he was overreacting, but when it came to Dana he wasn't taking any chances.

"Hey," Rhys called to him from the back door of the realty office. "Take a look at this."

Aidan trotted over. On the ground was a melted blob of bright orange plastic, possibly a lighter. Next to it was a large boot print similar to the one he'd seen at the sporting goods store. He hunkered down to examine both. There were words on the plastic—Aidan suspected a company name and address—which, for the most part, had been obliterated by heat. The font, still decipherable, rang a bell, though. He scrutinized them until his eyes went blurry.

"I know where this came from," he said.

Dana and Carol spent much of the next day cleaning up the mess. Although they hadn't lost their files—they'd remained protected in metal cabinets that had turned out to be fireproof—their kitchen, bathroom, and conference room had been destroyed. And they now had a sunroof where the firefighters had opened up the ceiling for ventilation.

Carol glanced up. "I hope it doesn't rain."

"Pat's sending a crew over to at least cover the roof." First her house, now this, Dana thought to herself. At least they could salvage much of the front of the office, which had suffered significant water damage and was covered in ash and filth. "We'll have to replace the carpet and some of the furniture up here."

"I always wanted to do hardwood anyway," Carol said. "Vance is on his way to Reno to buy the new computers. Thank God we backed everything up. What the heck is taking the cleaning team so long?"

A representative from the insurance company had met them first thing in the morning and cut them a check for the repairs. Unlike with Dana's house, they needed to get the place up and running ASAP. Carol and Dana didn't want any disruptions to their business. In the Sierra Nevada, spring and summer were their best seasons for selling real estate. Typically, in winter, when snow covered the pass, sales slumped to nothing.

"These desks are probably savable," Dana said. "Let's carry them outside so they can dry and air out."

They each lifted a side and started to carry out the first desk when a pair of strong hands took the bulk of the load.

"What are you doing here?" Dana asked Aidan, pleasantly surprised. When she'd left the house that morning, he'd said he was going to spend the day working the case.

"I have some time on my hands." He bussed her lips right in front of Carol. "Where do you want this?"

She beamed at him, her insides contracting like they always did when he was around. "Outside in the sun."

He carried the desk himself and came back for the other one. Finishing the chore, he took time to look around, walking to the back and assessing the damage. In the light of day, it looked even worse than it had the previous night. "Jeez. You'll have to rebuild most of this."

"It shouldn't be too time intensive," Carol said. "The plumbing is still there. It needed updating anyway."

Dana marveled at what a good attitude her partner had. Frankly, the construction would be a colossal inconvenience. Workers constantly underfoot, noise, and dirt. Then they'd have to pick out appliances, fixtures, and a new conference table and chairs. The one true silver lining was that no one got hurt. Real estate agents, slaves to the convenience of their clients, worked odd hours. It was a miracle that neither one of them had been in the office at the time of the fire. It made her wonder if the person who set it had been scoping out the place to make sure the building was empty. At least there was that.

"You have any leads on who might've done this?" Carol asked.

"We've got a few things working," Aidan responded, keeping it vague. But Dana had gotten the sense last night that Aidan and the police were on to something.

Of course she was dying to know, yet she wanted to give Aidan space to do his job. She found the intricacies of his investigations fascinating and was so impressed with what he did. No doubt fire-fighters were heroes, but to her, he was doubly so. Then again, she was probably a wee bit biased.

Out the window, Dana saw a couple of trucks pull up. "Looks like the construction crew is here for the roof." A van drove up behind them. "The cleaning team is bringing up the rear."

Perfect timing, Dana thought; the cleaners could work around the roofers.

"You ladies interested in lunch? Seems like now might be a good time to take a break. Let these folks do their jobs."

"I've got to dash home to check on the kids," Carol said. "You two go."

"I'll be back in an hour," Dana said.

"Perfect." Carol let the cleaners in the front door while the roofers started carrying ladders and equipment to the building. "I'll just get the workers started and see you back here later."

Dana walked with Aidan to his truck. "Where are we going?"

"The Bun Boy reopened today."

"Really? That seems fast."

"Their damage amounted to a storage shed," Aidan said. "It's nothing like yours."

"Each one is getting worse." She got inside the passenger seat and belted herself in. "Why do you think that is?"

Aidan got in as well, turned on the ignition, and started the AC. "He's either getting braver or he didn't get enough attention with the first two. There's no telling. The Bun Boy?"

"I could definitely go for a burger." She reached over and kissed him. "Do you still have to do your twenty-four-hour shift?"

She could feel him tense. "Of course I do. Why wouldn't I?" he asked, his voice edged with annoyance.

"I just thought you've been working like crazy. I'm not a firefighter; how would I know how it works? Why are you being so defensive?"

He appeared to relax. "Sue used to give me a hard time about my hours. I guess I'm still sensitive about it." He'd alluded before to the fact that it had been a problem between them.

"I get it," she said. "I work all the time myself because I'm at the mercy of the client's schedule. I was just curious as to how it works."

"I wouldn't be on call as much if the fires weren't right here in Nugget. It would be ridiculous for the fire marshal to send someone else."

She nodded. "That makes sense."

"I'll be off in time for the wedding, though."

"You really don't think it'll be weird for me to go with you?" Admittedly, she was curious about Lucky's cowboy camp, having never been there. And the idea of being Aidan's date thrilled her.

"Nope," he said and squeezed her knee.

Cars crowded the Bun Boy parking lot. Apparently, it only took a few days of closure to get folks jonesing for their fried food fixes.

"Is there a table available?" Aidan gazed out the window at the picnic tables on the lawn. "There's one. You go get it and I'll order our food at the window. What do you want?"

She told him a burger, curly fries, and lemonade and headed out to grab the table. The temperature was cooler than it had been in days. Still nice to have shade under a large redwood tree. Aidan joined her with their drinks. She imagined they'd have to wait a while for their food order to be called.

"A lot of people ahead of us?"

"It would appear so," he said. "They looked backed up in the kitchen."

"I wonder when Donna plans to put in the barbecues."

"Before the fire, she seemed to be in a big rush. Maybe she put it on hold for a while until the crowds get back to normal."

Griffin pulled up on his motorcycle, saw the line, and started to leave. As soon as he spotted Dana and Aidan, he made a beeline for their table.

"I thought he was going to Hawaii," Aidan said, sounding put out. Dana blamed his grouchiness on the fact that he was working too hard.

"Not until after Tawny and Lucky's wedding."

"Great."

Dana could've sworn she'd seen him roll his eyes. Lowering her voice, she asked, "What's wrong with you?"

"I don't like how he's always coming around you."

Griff was too close for her to respond, but the idea that Aidan might be jealous . . . well, that had never happened to her before, and as childish as it was, she liked that he felt proprietary toward her.

"Howdy." Griff shielded his eyes from the sun. "The place is a zoo."

"It's like a grand opening." Dana laughed.

"I heard about your office." He shook his head and turned to Aidan. "What the hell is going on?"

Aidan lifted his shoulders. "We're working on it."

"I have security cameras at the Gas and Go." The station was on the same street as Nugget Realty.

"You do?" Suddenly Aidan showed a bit more interest in Griffin's company. "Would you mind if I came over and took a look?"

"Sure, but you can't see Dana's office from the Gas and Go."

"What can you see?"

"A little bit of Main Street, but mostly the pumps, the inside of the convenience store, and a small section of the mechanic bays."

"I'd like to check them out just the same. How many hours do your cameras record?"

"A few days," Griffin said. "Then it starts recording over itself. You should have yesterday on it, though."

"What about the day before?"

"Yep. Come over and check it out if you think it'll help."

"I'll do that, thanks." Someone called out their order and Aidan excused himself to get the food.

"You eating?" Dana asked Griff.

"I was thinking about it until I saw the line. There are hot dogs back at the gas station. You and Aidan going to the wedding?" He didn't need to say which wedding. In Nugget, it was just "the wedding."

"Mm-hmm," Dana said and gazed at her tennis shoes.

"If it's not assigned tables, save Lina and me seats next to you guys."

Somehow Dana didn't think that was gonna happen. "Okay. You taking off?"

"Yeah, I'm not dealing with that." He pointed at the growing group of people snaking around the building. "Tell Aidan to come in to the store anytime. I'm sorry about your office, Dana. These fires really suck. But I'm glad no one has gotten hurt. If you and Carol need any help cleaning up . . . or anything . . . let me know."

"Thanks, Griffin."

Griffin sauntered off, looking as drool worthy as he always had in faded jeans, motorcycle boots, and a T-shirt with the Gas and Go logo stretched across his wide chest. But for the first time he did nothing for Dana. Not so much as an imperceptible sigh. That was because she only had eyes for the gorgeous, tall, ripped man coming toward her.

"I got us soft serve too, because there was no way I planned to wait in that line again." Aidan put the tray down on the table and handed Dana a wad of napkins. "You might want to eat it first before it melts."

Ice cream before the main meal; that was Aidan McBride. "Okay." She reluctantly took a few licks of her vanilla cone, even though a month ago it would've been sacrilege.

He smiled at her, undoubtedly reading her mind. "What's the difference between this and having a shake with your meal?"

"That's why I don't have shakes with my meals . . . it's mixing dessert with the main course."

"Nothing wrong with that." Unlike her, he dug into his cone without hesitation.

"Why do you want to look at Griff's security cameras?"

"It's the only one on Main Street. I'd be remiss if I didn't look at them."

She put her cone down and started in on her burger. "But he said it only filmed the gas station and a little bit of the street."

He shrugged his shoulders. "It doesn't hurt to look."

She got the impression there was more to it than that, especially from the way his eyes lit up when Griffin mentioned having cameras. "You've got a reason."

She expected him to deny it; instead, he laughed. "You're too smart for your own good." He leaned over and kissed her. "Yeah, I've got a reason, but I'm not planning to tell you. Not since you and Harlee are best buds now."

"I would never betray your confidences," she argued.

"I was just teasing. I know you wouldn't. But I really can't talk about an ongoing investigation, not even with you, as much as I would like to."

"You would?" That amazed her. She didn't know a thing about firefighting or arson. Hell, she'd burned her own house down.

"I like how interested you are in it."

Dana did find his job fascinating. She leaned over and laid her lips on him. "I'm interested in everything about you," she said against his mouth, as he ardently returned the kiss.

They stopped when Aidan's phone rang. With the fires, every call had them on edge. He fished the phone out of his pocket, looked at the display, frowned, and put it away.

"You don't need to get that?"

"Nah," he said, and then hesitantly added, "It was Sue."

Dana's stomach dropped. "Why do you think she's calling you?"

"I don't know," he said, but she got the impression he did. "She called the other day about a friend of her husband's being interested in my condo."

"Did you talk to her then?"

"Yeah, for a little bit." He didn't elaborate, and she would've liked him to.

"Do you think this has something to do with that?" Evidently not, or he would've answered.

"I don't know. But you and I are in the middle of lunch and you only have an hour. This is our time. I'll call her later. It can't be that important."

That made her feel better about the situation. Still, his reaction to the call sent warning signals up her spine. She tried to tell herself this wasn't like the way it had been with Tim and Griffin. Aidan cared about her. But did he care about her more than he did Sue, or was this history repeating itself?

Chapter 19

Aidan's phone rang again. Afraid that it was an unrelenting Sue, he hesitantly checked the ID. Not Sue, Rhys.

"I have to take this one," he told Dana, got up from the picnic table, and found a private spot next to a nearby tree. "What's up?"

"We got the results back on both the shirt and the lighter. The shirt's got traces of accelerant on it. And you were right about the logo on the lighter: Rigsby Electrical. The problem is, he hands them out to clients like candy, so not exactly a smoking gun. Still, between the shirt and the lighter . . . You ready to take a ride over to the Rigsby farm?"

"I'm over at the Bun Boy and have to take Dana back to work. You want to meet there?"

"No, let's go together. Come over to the station when you're ready."

He walked back to the table, where a family of five was loitering, making it obvious they wanted Dana and him to leave soon so they could have their seats.

"We've got to go," he told her.

"Has there been another fire?" She immediately started collecting their trash and putting it in a neat pile on the tray.

"Not a fire." He grabbed the tray from her hands and dumped their wrappers in a nearby garbage can. "Rhys and I have a lead to check out."

"Oh?" She waited to hear what it was.

"I'll tell you later, but it could be promising." Although he didn't think so. His gut told him it was a red herring.

"It's not dangerous, right?"

"Not in the least." He reached for her hand and held it while they returned the tray to the takeout window and walked across the parking lot to his SUV.

Halfway there his phone rang again. Thinking it was Rhys with a new plan, he started to answer. Then he saw the caller was Sue and muttered a curse under his breath. Why was she suddenly calling him all the time? Like the first one, he let it go to voice mail. He'd handle it later.

"Who was that?" Dana asked.

"A friend from Chicago. I'll call him back after work." He hated to lie to her. But he could tell that Sue's previous call had bothered her and he didn't want her upset. There was no reason for her to be. "I'm sorry I can't help you more at the office."

"Carol and I are fine. We've also got two crews there. It's more important that you catch this jerk."

When they got to her office it looked like the construction team had begun its work in earnest on the roof, and the cleaning crew had filled an industrial Dumpster with debris from the fire.

"You want me to carry those desks back in?" By now they should've dried.

"No, you go do what you need to do. We'll take care of the desks. Besides, a little more air will help get the smoky smell out them." She kissed him. "Be careful and I'll hopefully see you tonight."

He lingered, wanting to tell her how important she'd become to him, but he didn't want to do it and have to rush off. Instead, he watched her walk from his truck to the building, admiring the sway of her backside. He'd never felt so relaxed in a relationship. No pressure to impress her or be more than he was.

A memory of his second date with Sue flashed in his head. She'd been upset with the way he'd dressed—a pair of dress pants and a white button-down shirt—and had canceled their dinner reservations. The restaurant had been her idea and he'd happily booked it, despite menu prices that cost as much as a week's salary. But when he'd picked her up, she'd looked at his clothes warily.

"I thought you knew a place like this calls for a jacket and a tie," she'd said. "It's not a big deal, I'll cancel."

He'd insisted the restaurant would lend him a jacket if it had a dress code, but she wouldn't hear of it.

"It's fine. Really, I don't mind if we don't go there."

Unfortunately, he'd been so blinded by her beauty that he hadn't seen a major red flag. Now he knew if you looked up "passive aggressive" in the dictionary, a picture of Sue would appear. Her favorite mantra was "I'm not angry," but she always was. She was angry that he didn't do enough for her, that he didn't spend "quality" time with her, and that he didn't care about making a good impression, which was code for not being materialistic enough.

The idea that she'd fallen for a schoolteacher was laughable. Aidan would guess Sebastian made even less money than he did. Maybe, like Sue, he had a trust fund. Who knew?

On his way back to the square he played Sue's messages on Bluetooth. The first one was a hang up. In the second message she hesitated. "Aidan? . . . Uh, it's me, Sue." And in a small voice, she'd continued, "I think I made a horrible mistake. I need to talk to you."

Why the hell was she doing this? With no time to think about it anymore, he pulled into a parking space in front of the police station, got out, and went inside.

Sloane and Jake had their heads together.

"What are you two up to?"

"Checking to see if Rigsby has a sheet," Sloane answered. Jake nodded in greeting.

"You want some coffee? I just made a fresh pot," Connie said. Aidan had only met her once or twice but knew she was the police dispatcher. Cal Fire went through county dispatch, but occasionally residents would call in fire type emergencies to the police department, in which case Connie handled them. "The chief's on a call."

"Sure." He turned back to Sloane. "Does he have one?"

"I couldn't find anything. Jake's double-checking."

It didn't seem like there would be too many jurisdictions to check; from what Aidan understood, Rigsby had grown up in Nugget.

Connie came back with a mug that said, "Homicide: Our day starts when yours ends."

"I thought I told you to get rid of that cup." Rhys had come out of his office and was walking toward them. "Seriously, it makes us look insensitive."

Connie shrugged. "It's a perfectly good mug. Besides, it's the truth, so man up, Chief."

Rhys shook his head. "I work with a bunch of goddamn lunatics. Come on back to my office."

Aidan followed him into a glass room. There were blinds to make the office private from the rest of the station, but Rhys didn't bother to close them, just cleared a bunch of crap off a chair and motioned for him to take a seat.

"We have enough to arrest Rigsby but probably not enough for the DA to charge him." Rhys took the chair behind his desk. "We could sit on him, do some surveillance, and strike when we catch him in the act. Or we could bring him in and see if he'll cop to it."

Aidan didn't like any of those options. Like Rhys said, arresting him was a waste of time if they couldn't pin anything on him in court. It was too dangerous to hope they'd catch him before he did real damage. And the idea that he'd simply give a full confession just by them asking pretty please was a pipe dream. Yet they couldn't do nothing.

"Which way are you leaning?" Aidan asked.

"Haul him in, scare the shit out of him with the shirt, and hope he spills."

"I didn't get a good feeling off Rigsby. I've met plenty of dudes like him, pumped-up gym rats who are resentful of the world. But my gut tells me he's not good for this."

"Why's that?"

"Because no one is stupid enough to leave his shirt in a Dumpster at the scene. Not even lugheads who like to play with matches."

"You'd be surprised," Rhys said. "But I hear you. What do you think we should do?"

"First, I think we should check the security tapes at the Gas and Go. See if we spot Rigsby filling a gas can with fuel, because it was used as an accelerant in two out of our three fires."

"What if we don't?"

"Then we question Rigsby and see where it gets us."

Rhys stood up and grabbed a set of keys on a hook behind his head. "Let's go."

Aidan followed him to his police SUV, and five minutes later they parked on the street in front of the Gas and Go, walking into the convenience store. The shop, which reminded Aidan of a small 7-Eleven, was empty. One of the mechanics saw them through a window from the garage and came over.

"Hey, Skeeter. Griffin around?" Rhys asked.

"He's upstairs. I'll get him."

Aidan peeked inside the garage, curious what they were doing with a vintage Ford pickup. It was mint green and, if he had to guess, built in the 1950s. Not ordinarily a car buff, he was impressed. The Ford seemed to be in perfect condition and held a little slice of history.

The guy—Skeeter—came back in. "He'll be right down."

"What are you doing with the Ford?" Aidan pointed through the window.

"Checking the brakes. The owner is taking it to a car show this weekend." He cued up a picture on his phone and showed it to Aidan. "That's what it used to look like until we restored it."

Aidan let out a murmur of appreciation. The photo showed a rusted, dented piece of junk. "Nice job. Must be worth a fortune now."

"Nah, but it's good-looking. The former owner primarily used it on his ranch to haul hay but kept it outside, where the elements took their toll. The new owner, a collector, only uses it for car shows, parades, that sort of thing, and keeps it in a garage."

"Beautiful job." Aidan turned when he heard Griff come into the store.

He nodded his head in greeting. "You come to view the security footage?"

"Yeah," Rhys said. "How far back can we go?"

"Friday. But the pictures will be grainy. Come on up to my office."

They went outside and climbed a staircase to a second-story apartment someone had converted into work space, leaving a small kitchen and a bathroom with a tub intact. Griffin had a television where they could look at the surveillance recordings. Pulling up a couple of chairs, he rewound the footage to midnight on Friday.

"This is the best angle I have of Main Street," he said.

"Actually, could we focus on the gas pumps?" Aidan asked.

Griff shot him a questioning look and changed the frame. "What's so interesting about the pumps?"

"Our arsonist used gasoline in two of the fires," Rhys said. "We're looking to see if anyone filled a gas can. But we'd like you to keep that information under your hat for the sake of the investigation."

"No problem, but a lot of people use gas cans, especially this time of year . . . for their boats, ATVs, Jet Skis, you name it."

"We're aware of that," Rhys said.

"Then why . . . ah, you're looking for someone in particular?"

"I didn't say that," Rhys said in a Texas drawl that Aidan noticed came and went with his mood. According to Sloane, the police chief had worked for Houston PD for more than a decade before coming back to head up his hometown department.

"Whatever." Griffin chuckled. "This'll take some time; you want something to drink?"

"I'll take a Coke if you've got one," Rhys said, and Aidan asked for one too.

Griffin handed Aidan the remote control and wandered into the kitchen to grab the drinks. They made small talk while Aidan fast-forwarded the recording until he caught a human in the frame. If he or she was just filling a car tank, Aidan moved on.

"Stop it for a second," Rhys said. "Isn't that Cal Addison?" It was a fuzzy picture of a man pumping gas into a red, five-gallon gas can.

"Don't know him," Aidan replied.

Griff came over and hunkered over Rhys's shoulder, scrutinizing the frame. "Yep, that's him."

Rhys laughed. "What? Did the bear T-shirt give it away?" He explained to Aidan that Addison and his wife owned the Beary Quaint, a motor lodge up the road. Aidan had driven past it a few times. A fire waiting to happen with all those chainsaw bears in the yard.

"He's got a fishing boat," Griffin said. "Takes it out on Lake Davis."

Rhys nudged his head at the screen, indicating that Aidan should continue fast-forwarding. They went through the footage over the next couple of hours. Aidan thought it was a little like watching paint dry, except for the occasional play-by-play on the various residents shown in the pictures.

"You hear he's getting a divorce?" or "You see that new Ram he just bought? That had to set him back at least fifty thousand bucks."

But by the time they finished, they still had nada. No signs that Rigsby had gotten his accelerant at the Gas and Go. So far, the only thing they had on the guy was the stinkin' shirt. They went back to Rhys's vehicle so they could talk without Griffin overhearing them.

"Should we yank him in?" Rhys asked.

"What other option do we have?"

Rhys checked his watch. "Hopefully, he'll be home by now. Let's ride over there, feel him out a little."

They took city streets to the highway, made the short trek outside of town, and turned up the Rigsbys' driveway. It looked like John had already started work on the fire-damaged barn. Aidan spotted a pile of debris that had been cleared away from the site and a fresh load of lumber. He gazed across the property, searching for the goats, and found them penned in a corral not far from the barn.

Rhys pulled up to the driveway and Mrs. Rigsby came through the door.

"Hello, Chief. Can I help you?" She tilted her head at the passenger's side window, catching a glimpse of Aidan.

Rhys got out of the vehicle. "Your husband home?"

"He's inside taking a nap. What's this about?"

Aidan stepped out and tipped his head in greeting to Mrs. Rigsby.

"We found something of his at one of the fires we've had in town," Rhys said. "We'd like to talk to him about it."

Looking from Rhys to Aidan, Mrs. Rigsby went a little pale. "I'll get him. Come in." She held the screen door open and led them into the living room. "Make yourself comfortable."

There was an upright piano in the corner and Aidan wondered who played. Though lived in, the room was cheery enough, with lots of family pictures, a lamp made out of horseshoes, and a colorful afghan thrown over the couch. He scanned the room, hoping to find clues. Often, arsonists got a cheap thrill from saving newspaper clippings or photographs of their fires. But nothing stood out to Aidan. Just a typical working-class home.

Rigsby came into the room a short while later in shorts and a T-shirt. Aidan couldn't tell whether he'd been sleeping or not, but he wasn't friendly. Hostile would be a better word for it.

"What can I do for you fellows?" He didn't sit, just stood there, glaring.

"Why don't you sit down, John? Or if you'd prefer, we could go down to the station," Rhys said.

"Letty says it's about those fires you've been having in town. What does that have to do with me?"

"We were hoping you'd tell us." Rhys was smooth, Aidan noted, no bumbling, hicksville cop.

"There's nothing for me to tell you. I don't know a damn thing about them, except for what I read in the *Nugget Tribune*," Rigsby said, choosing the recliner across from Aidan and Rhys.

"They weren't accidents." Aidan stretched his legs.

"That's what the *Trib* said. You think because of the fireworks I was somehow involved?" He smirked like he thought they were idiots.

"Nope," Rhys said and leaned back, resting his arm on the back of the couch. "It's because we found your shirt, covered in the same traces of accelerant used to start the fire, at one of the scenes. And one of your lighters at another."

Rigsby wasn't smirking anymore. If Aidan wasn't mistaken, the electrician blanched. "How do you know they're mine?"

"Both say 'Rigsby Electrical' on them."

Rigsby jumped out of his chair. "Those lighters I pass out like business cards . . . that could've been anyone. I didn't have anything to do with those fires and this conversation is over. I'm calling a lawyer!"

It was what Aidan had expected all along. People knew their rights. Rigsby would be a fool to cooperate without consulting with an attorney first.

"Now, I'd like you to leave." To emphasize that, Rigsby walked to the front door and held it open.

They could've arrested and held him on what they had. But to make it stick, they'd need more than a shirt and a common lighter to hold him. The best they could hope for was that they'd unnerved him enough that in his panic to cover his tracks he'd mess up. Because Aidan would definitely be watching.

"That didn't go so well," Rhys said as they climbed into his police SUV and drove down the Rigsbys' driveway.

"It didn't go as badly as you think. Pull over."

Rhys nosed into a turnout on the side of the road. "What's up?"

"On our way out I noticed something on the front porch . . . something that could be significant. But we'd need a warrant."

Rhys smiled. "I can make that happen."

Chapter 20

"Hello? Hello? Anyone there?" For the fourth time in an hour, Dana hung up the house phone in frustration.

Ordinarily, she would've written the strange, silent calls up to a malfunctioning phone line or someone on the other end having bad cell reception. But there was no caller ID, which seemed odd. Even with those annoying robocalls, a telephone number always flashed on the landline. With these, no number whatsoever.

She wouldn't have been bothered by the calls if someone hadn't tried to burn her office down. Arson tended to make a person edgy, and Dana was definitely jittery.

Now, she was on high alert and wished Aidan was home. He'd called on her cell to say that something in the case had come up and he wouldn't be home until late. She tried to pass the time by organizing the silverware drawer. Somehow the salad forks had gotten mixed in with the regular ones and it was driving her batty.

She took all the utensils out, gave the basket a good scrubbing, and put everything back where it should go. Although exhausted from moving furniture around and packing up files so the hardwood guys could lay down her and Carol's new flooring, she found the mindless work of sorting quite soothing. Dana decided that while she was at it she may as well reorganize the pantry too.

The house line rang again and she nearly jumped out of her skin. This time when she checked the phone's display there was a number. A local number, but she didn't recognize it.

"Hello?"

"Hi, Dana. This is Sloane. Is my brother there? I've been trying to call him on his cell, but he's not answering."

"He's not here," she said and told Sloane that Aidan was working late on the fire cases, that he might have a lead.

"Do you know what it is? Brady and I were in San Francisco all day."

"I don't. He's careful about what he shares. You didn't by any chance try to call here a couple of times earlier, did you?"

"No. Why?"

"I keep getting strange calls where the person on the other end is silent. They must've disabled their caller ID because I don't get that either."

Sloane was quiet for a second, then let a long sigh. "It may be Aidan's ex-girlfriend. She's been looking for him. That's actually why I was calling. I'm sorry if she scared you."

"Sue? Why wouldn't she just ask for him?" Unless Aidan told her not to. Dana didn't like the implications of that.

"I don't know. It's not characteristic of her, but she has been trying to reach him. Wyatt's on duty; I'll have him do a drive by."

"That's not necessary," Dana said. "Really, I'm sure it's just someone with a bad cell connection." But she went around the house locking the doors and windows just in case.

"Write down my number," Sloane instructed, and Dana jotted it down on a pad in the junk drawer. "Call me if anything else weird happens. But I'm sure you're right about the hang-ups."

After disconnecting with Sloane, Dana called her parents' house. She hadn't talked to them since she and Aidan had slept in the pool house and needed to check in. Betty answered on the fifth ring. As usual, she didn't have much to say and rushed to get off the phone. Dana often considered what would've happened if she'd been the one to die. Would her parents have buried themselves in the same kind of grief they had for Paul and by doing so ignored their only son? She didn't think so.

From the time of his birth, he'd been their prince and Dana an afterthought. As a child, it had never troubled her. Despite the extra attention they'd given Paul, there'd been enough left over that she'd felt loved and cherished. The Calloways had always been a patriarchal family. Dana supposed that kind of upbringing had conditioned her to accept her status as second class to her brother without bitterness. But now that she was all her parents had left in the world, she didn't understand their indifference. She also couldn't change it.

The pantry began to take shape. Dana lined up the cereal boxes in a neat row on one shelf. Spaghetti sauces, cooking oils, and canned goods she stored on another. Because Aidan did most of the cooking, he'd screw her order up in no time, but she didn't care. She'd just organize it again.

In the laundry room she found new rolls of shelf paper and used it to reline some of the cupboards where the old paper had become sticky from syrup or molasses, Dana couldn't tell. By the time she finished and glanced at the clock, more than an hour had passed. Save for the streetlights it was dark outside, the moon barely visible. It was also stuffy. She wanted to open the back door to let a breeze in, but given the fire and phone calls, a flimsy screen didn't seem like much of a barrier between her and the outdoors. So she went in the living room, turned on the cooler, and surfed through the channels on the television.

About ten o'clock Aidan came through the door.

"Hey," Dana said. "How did it go?"

"Good." He beamed and threw himself on the couch next to her. "Unfortunately, I can't tell you about it, but we may be on to something."

"Not even a hint?"

He deliberated, then said, "We seized a piece of evidence that may help us close the case."

"What's the evidence?"

"Can't say."

She scooted closer to him. Despite having worked nine hours, he smelled like that aftershave he always wore. It reminded Dana of leather, sandalwood, and musk. Very masculine. She wanted to snuggle up next to him but worried that he'd want space and time to unwind after a long day. He surprised her, though, by pulling her close and tucking her head under his chin.

"What did you do tonight?"

She started to tell him, then stopped. "I don't want to forget: Sloane called. She said Sue was looking for you."

He let out a groan. "Yeah, I know."

She tugged away. "What's that about?"

"I don't know, but I'll take care of it. Let's not talk about her now."

The phone rang.

"You get it," Dana said. "I've been getting strange phone calls all evening."

"What kind of strange calls?'

"I'll tell you after you get the phone."

He got up and went in the kitchen with Dana on his tail. "Hello?" Aidan answered.

There was a long pause while Aidan stared at the clock on the stove. "The battery on my cell is dead. Can we talk about this tomorrow? It's late and I just got home. . . . She's fine and I'll deal with the other thing tomorrow."

When he got off the phone, Dana asked, "Who was that?"

"Sloane. Now tell me about these strange phone calls." He opened the pantry. "Where's the Calloway candy? Damn, you rearranged the shelves."

She shrugged. "It makes more sense this way."

"If you say so." He found the candy on the shelf with the sugar and flour. "The calls."

She told him about them and how there was no caller ID. "It was probably nothing, but I got a little spooked."

Aidan hugged her. "I'm sorry, Dana. I think it might've been Sue. I'll take care of it tomorrow, I promise."

"Why would she do that? Even Sloane didn't think she would."

"I told her I was seeing someone. She probably figured it was you and it made her uncomfortable."

"But she's married."

He didn't say anything for a long time. "I don't think that's going too well."

Dana sucked in a breath. Just when she'd let herself fall hard—like head over heels—for Aidan, it was happening again.

"Are you planning to go back to her?" she asked.

"No. Of course not. Look, I'll talk to her tomorrow, tell her to stop calling, okay?"

She nodded but didn't really believe him. He'd been with Sue for three years. They had a history together. Aidan's family loved her. He'd known Dana less than a month. She was nothing more than a convenient rebound.

"The fire . . . the cleanup . . . I'm exhausted," she said. "I'm going to turn in early."

She started to walk away and he took her arm. "Can I come with you?"

"Not tonight." She let her hand caress his cheek.

After tonight, she didn't think they'd be going to bed together ever again. Tomorrow he'd talk to Sue and they'd figure out that her marriage to the schoolteacher had been a big mistake. That she belonged with Aidan. Then he'd find Dana and in the nicest way possible break up with her. One of them would offer to move out and it would wind up being her since she was the real estate agent with the contacts. With her tail between her legs, she'd go to Griffin and ask to rent one of the homes in Sierra Heights.

It was a vicious cycle.

He didn't try to stop her as she walked down the hall toward her bedroom. Perhaps he too recognized they'd come to the end of what had been the happiest time in Dana's life.

Aidan wanted to chase after her, but it wasn't right. They'd started out as roommates first, lovers second. She should be able to take a night off from him when she wanted to, especially when she was angry that his ex was suddenly back in his life.

He planned to nip that in the bud right now. In his bedroom he got his laptop, opened his email, and began typing.

> *Sue,*
> *You left me to marry Sebastian. I'm involved with someone else now. It would probably be best if we don't have contact with each other. Just know that I wish you the best and want you to be happy.*
>
> *Aidan*

He hit the Send button and felt a pang of guilt. Was the note too harsh? No! His problem was not being assertive enough. The thing with Sue was that she got him to do things he didn't want to do by maneuvering and manipulating until it was easier to give in. Like leaving him for Sebastian. Aidan now believed it had been a ploy to get him to marry her. Well, it had failed miserably. The cowardly fact was that by marrying Sebastian, Sue had let Aidan off the hook.

He'd stayed in a relationship that wasn't right for him to avoid hurting her and his family. He'd meant well, but now he needed to make things right, which included a come-to-Jesus talk with Sloane. What was she thinking, giving Sue his house number when she knew about him and Dana? His sister wasn't cruel, but his estimation of her had slipped a notch.

Aidan let out a yawn and decided to follow Dana's lead and call it a night. Tomorrow he reported for twenty-four-hour duty at the firehouse. At least they'd made some headway on the case. If things panned out the way he hoped, they'd be able to tie Rigsby to the fires.

Aidan took a quick shower, brushed his teeth, and headed to bed, taking a short detour to Dana's room. There he stood, poised at her door, listening to hear if she was still awake. For a second he considered knocking but decided he should let her sleep. They'd talk in the morning, before he left for work. He'd assure her that Sue wouldn't be calling anymore.

But by the time he dragged himself out of bed the next day she was gone. If things weren't too busy at the firehouse, he'd pick her up at Nugget Realty and take her to lunch.

In the kitchen he put up a pot of coffee and while that was brewing called Sloane.

"Why'd you give Sue my home number when you know I share the house phone with Dana?"

"She was desperate to find you, something about your condo," Sloane said. But Aidan knew it was bullshit. All day Sue had been leaving messages on his cell about how she missed him, how she'd made a mistake marrying Sebastian, blah, blah, blah.

He wouldn't out Sue to Sloane because he still felt loyal and didn't want to embarrass her in front of his family. And a part of him felt horribly guilty for not being able to love her enough.

"She has my cell number, Sloane. Her calls scared Dana. With all Dana's been through in the last month . . . she doesn't need this crap."

"We don't even know it was Sue," Sloane argued. "It sounds more like a prank than something Sue would ever do. She doesn't even know you're dating Dana."

"Unless it's a member of our family, don't give my home number out ever again."

"Jeez, Aidan, I didn't do it to upset Dana. I know how protective you are of her. I spent the night of the Nugget Realty fire watching over her because you asked me to. You know that because you called a dozen times. Sue was just so insistent that she needed to get a hold of you."

"I took care of that. In the future, I'd appreciate it if you wouldn't act as a go-between. Sue knows how to reach me. If I'm not answering my phone, there's a good reason for it."

"I'm sorry, Aidan. Really, it was all very innocent."

He knew it wasn't. She and the rest of his family had made their allegiance to Sue well known. "I'm done talking about it."

"What's going on with the case? Dana said you got something last night."

Aidan told her how they'd gone to Rigsby's house to talk, but he'd lawyered up. "On our way out I saw a pair of work boots on the porch that may match footprints I collected at all three scenes. We got a warrant. . . . Long story short, forensics is trying to determine whether the boots match the prints. It's not a slam dunk by any stretch, but between the boots, the shirt, and the lighter, we might have enough to make the charges stick."

"It's definitely something if it pans out. Are the boots worn?"

"Worn enough so that the soles should have their own unique wear and tear. If the forensic guys also happen to find gasoline residue on them, we're in business. But Sloane, that's all confidential."

"I know." She sounded offended. "In this town, though, it's hard to keep a secret."

Aidan looked at the clock. "Hey, I've got to get to work."

"All right. Let me know what you hear back from the lab."

"Will do." He hung up, drank a cup of the coffee he'd made, and took a quick shower just to wake up.

He got to the firehouse in time to find the two McCreedy boys washing an engine with Kurtis. He waved and went inside to show his face before he joined them.

But that never happened because he and the others got called out on a Code 5, an assignment in another county up in flames.

Del Webber removed his Stetson as he strolled into Nugget Realty and Associates, took one look at the damage, and let out a whistle.

"I heard you had a fire but had no idea it . . ." He shook his head.

Dana was surprised to see him; they didn't have an appointment. "It looks worse than it is."

"Sorry to just pop in on you like this, but I was in the neighborhood." He was based in Quincy, the county seat, forty-five minutes away. "You got a minute to talk?"

"Sure. Unfortunately, we no longer have a conference room." The workmen were coming tomorrow to start the restoration. "You mind if we talk at my desk?"

"Not at all." He did a visual turn around the room again.

Dana pulled up a wing chair for Del to sit in. "Carol is running late, so we've got some privacy. I'd offer you something to drink, but our kitchenette . . ."

"No worries. Is there an actual person involved in this T Corporation buying Ray's ranch?"

"What do you mean?" She really didn't know what he was getting at.

"Is someone from the corporation planning to live on the ranch?"

"Yes," Dana said and left it at that. Del was renowned for his litigation skills; she didn't want to go against one of his cross-examinations. "I'm bound by a confidentiality agreement, Del; please don't ask me too much."

"I'm not trying to ferret a name out of you. Frankly, I'm not all that interested. But Ray's getting cold feet. That ranch has been in his family a long time. It's his legacy and now he's decided that his daughter, Raylene, should take it over. He wants out of the deal."

It had always seemed too good to be true, Dana thought, feeling hugely disappointed. The worst part would be breaking the news to Gia. She was relying on the ranch to be her sanctuary, especially now that she'd lost her job. From the moment Gia had stepped foot on the property, she'd loved it.

"The T Corporation isn't going to be happy about this. It may even sue."

"That's exactly what I told him." Del toyed with the hat in his hands. "Not to mention that the man owes me and his other lawyers a lot of money. When I first agreed to represent him, Ray gave me the ranch as collateral. I'm not violating the attorney-client privilege by telling you this, because I'm just as much a part of this real estate deal as he is. But I'm not heartless, Dana. I'll give him the opportunity to make good on his legal bills before I'll sell that ranch out from under him."

"Escrow is scheduled to close in less than three weeks."

"I've given him two," Del said. "How you decide to proceed with your buyers is up to you."

"I'll tell them the truth," she said. "There are other ranches for sale and they may decide this one isn't worth being at the whim of Ray Rosser. Or, like I said, they may take legal action. Ray may be my client, but he signed a contract and it's my fiduciary duty to look out for the buyers in this instance." She paused. "I appreciate what you're trying to do for Ray. It's commendable, but I would be negligent in not telling you that clients like the T Corporation don't grow on trees. There isn't a waiting list for multimillion-dollar properties in Nugget. If you lose this buyer, I don't know when the next one will come along."

"Message received," he said. "You're an excellent agent, Dana, and I'm sorry this puts you in a bad position. I'll tell you this: your clients stick it out and I'll lop fifty thousand off the price."

It was generous, but it wouldn't salve Gia's aggravation as she sat on pins and needles over the next two weeks.

"I will let the T Corporation know," she said.

"Thank you, Dana." Del got to his feet, put on his hat, and walked out the door.

Dana leaned her head back, closed her eyes, and yelled, "Shit." Now she had to make a very uncomfortable call and she didn't want to do it . . . didn't want to break Gia Treadwell's already busted heart. She liked the woman, even thought they could be friends.

With no other choice, she dialed the phone.

"Dana?" Gia asked, picking up after the seventh ring. Dana was aware that Gia monitored her calls closely. Since her firing, reporters had begun to circle.

"It's me and I've got some bad news." She proceeded to tell Gia about the conversation she'd had with Del.

"Oh God, they can't do this. We signed a contract. I put down a substantial deposit."

"If Ray backs out, you'll get every dime returned to you." Not that that was any consolation. "I could look for something else."

"Tell me the truth: is there anything out there that good?"

Dana was quiet for a long time. Too long. "No. But there are less expensive properties that you could make wonderful."

"I want that one. Dana, this is going to sound ridiculous because it's just a house and a big piece of land, but that ranch has been my salvation. It's been my beacon in the storm. I can't tell you how bad it's been here. Losing my job was one thing; I'd seen that coming. But Evan's victims are sending me death threats. I can't leave the house for fear that someone will recognize me and I'll be lynched in Central Park."

Dana didn't know what to say. She felt horrible for Gia . . . and now Del's news. "There's a chance Ray won't be able to come up with the money. His biggest asset is his ranch, and unless he has stocks to liquidate or a benefactor, I don't know how he'll do it. But in the meantime, Gia, let me look around to see if I can find something else that will make you happy."

"I'm booking a flight tomorrow and will stay at that little inn again. I can't take it here anymore. At least there I can stay under the radar."

"Are you sure?" Dana worried that people here would recognize her and that it could further sour the deal.

"Yes. If nothing else, I need the peace and quiet."

"All right. Do you need a ride from the airport?"

"I'll rent a car. I'll need my own wheels. I'll call you when I get into town."

Dana hung up and immediately searched the multiple listings. If she could find something almost as nice as the Rosser Ranch, Gia might settle for that instead. She scrutinized every new listing she found, trying to ignore the roofers, who were making a racket with their nail guns. At least they'd found someone available to do the job. Everyone in these parts got their roofs done in summer, before the rain and snow hit.

Carol wandered in a few minutes later, loaded down with supplies. "There's more in the car. How you liking the new computers?"

"They're great." Dana got up and went out to the parking lot to help bring in the rest of Carol's purchases. There were bottles of water, soda, paper for the copy machine, and, thank God, a coffee-maker.

Together, they had the car emptied in ten minutes. The fire-damaged section of the building was mostly boarded up, so Carol had brought a minifridge from home, and she and Dana loaded it with the waters and soft drinks.

"I think the Rosser deal is about to fall through."

"No." Carol held her hands to her cheeks, and Dana explained the situation.

"Gia is coming anyway. I don't think it's the most prudent idea, but it's not like I can stop her. At least it'll give me a chance to show her a few more places. Any ideas?"

Carol thought about it. "Nothing I can think of that we don't already know about it. There are a few people who in recent years have discussed the possibility of selling; maybe if the price was right they'd be interested. Let me look through the list."

"Sounds good. I'm going to run out and get something to eat. You want me to bring you back anything?"

"I grabbed something in Reno. You go. By the time you get back I'll have that list."

Dana could've walked to the square but it was too hot, so she drove. Fearing that she'd run into Aidan, she nixed the idea of having lunch at home. Although he worked today, the firehouse and their home were too close for comfort. She'd had enough bad news for one day. If he was planning to dump her, let him do it tomorrow. It was like déjà vu with Tim and Griffin, except Dana was in love with Aidan and hadn't been with the others. Sure, at the time she'd thought she'd been. It had taken Aidan to make her realize that none of those relationships had come close to the way she felt about him.

You make me feel like I light you up from the inside out, he'd told her. And he did. Around Aidan she never felt awkward, or shy or like she didn't belong. With him she was number one—the sole focus of his attention. With him, she was the best she could be. She'd been delusional enough to think she made him feel the same way.

She zipped into the Bun Boy parking lot. It wasn't as crowded as yesterday, the novelty of being back in business after its short hiatus apparently having worn off. Instead of the drive-through, she decided to eat at one of the picnic tables and get some fresh air. She joined the small line and noted that Clay McCreedy and his two sons were ahead of her.

He turned and tipped his cowboy hat. "How you doing, Dana? This fire business is out of control. I saw Carol at the Gas and Go;

she told me you had a fair amount of damage. Thank God no one was hurt."

"I think Aidan may have some good clues." She shouldn't have said that, especially because she didn't know anything of the sort. Perchance she was being sensitive that Clay didn't think Aidan was doing his job right.

To her surprise, he nodded. "Rhys says he's good. Real methodical. We're lucky to have him. The boys were at the station helping out with washing the fire engines when the unit got called out on an out-of-control wildfire in Sierra County. I suspect he'll be away for a while. But Rhys is well versed in the arson investigation."

No wonder she hadn't heard from him all morning. And here she'd been psyching herself up that he wanted to dump her in person. She supposed there would be time for that after the fire. Still, she silently prayed for his safety.

"I didn't know that."

"Yep," he said as they inched up in line. "Has the Rosser property closed yet? I'm anxious to meet my new neighbor."

She waxed on a fake smile, deciding it wouldn't be appropriate to discuss Del's news with Clay. "Not yet. About three more weeks." If it happened at all.

It was Clay's turn to give his order, saving Dana from any more questions. After putting in for a large fried chicken salad and lemonade, she found a shady seat and waited for her name to be called. She checked her phone to see if Aidan had texted, but there was nothing.

It was hot and dry and even with her limited knowledge, she recognized it was the worst conditions for fighting a fire. She felt a wave of anxiety and, despite her resolution to back off, texted Aidan anyway.

Take care of yourself!
Dana

Chapter 21

Gia got into Nugget on Thursday. She'd had to take a red-eye Wednesday and although she'd gained three hours in California was groggy from the all-night flight. Thank goodness the Lumber Baron had a room ready, even though check-in time wasn't until two p.m. They were kind enough to make an exception, although she got the impression they were big on customer service here and light on adhering to the rules. Her kind of business.

The good news was they had no idea who she was. She'd checked in under her mother's maiden name and wore her hair tucked up under a baseball cap and big sunglasses. The young man at the front desk didn't seem the least bit fazed when she kept them on during the registration process. He'd left her with the sense that he wasn't the sharpest tool in the shed. He carried her bags up the impressive staircase and opened her door with an old-time key, and the sheer tranquility of the room, with its Victorian accents, made her go instantly Zen. It was like a million pounds had been lifted from her shoulders. The relief was so intense that as soon as the young attendant left, Gia cried. Just sat on the bed and bawled her eyes out.

They were good tears. Tears that said *I made the right choice by coming here*.

She unpacked, hung up what few things she'd brought, and filled the claw-foot tub with hot water, desperately wanting to wash away New York and the last few weeks' fallout. A baptism of sorts.

On the vanity she found a complimentary bottle of bubble bath and poured it under the spigot, watching the liquid foam, spreading a froth of bubbles across the tub. She stripped and gingerly got in, letting herself grow accustomed to the heat. It felt so good that she sank in until the water came up to her chin. For the next half hour, she lay there, letting her mind go numb and her body relax.

While her nightmare was far from over, she was here now. Safe.

As the water cooled and Gia's skin shriveled, she got out of the claw-foot, dressed in a pair of loose shorts and a tank top, and called Dana's cell phone.

"I'm here," she told the real estate agent's voice mail. "If you want to go out later and look at a few places, I'd be up for that."

It was still early and Dana probably hadn't started her day yet. Starved, Gia decided to walk across the square to that Bun Boy place and get something to bring back to the room. Unfortunately, she'd missed the inn's divine breakfast. On her way downstairs, she bumped into the innkeeper. Gia remembered her from last time but unfortunately had forgotten her name.

"Hello," she greeted Gia, and unlike the front-desk clerk, glanced at her Jackie O sunglasses warily.

"Hello," Gia said back, and tried to brush by her without seeming rude.

"I'm Maddy. Is there something I can help you with?"

"I was just on my way to the Bun Boy to grab a bite."

"The Ponderosa is also good, if you're looking for a sit-down place."

That was the last thing Gia was looking for. Sitting indoors, eating with her big sunglasses on, was bound to draw attention. "The last time I was here I ate at the Bun Boy and really enjoyed it."

"It's good," Maddy agreed and smiled. "When were you here last?"

"A few weeks ago." Then Gia had worn the scarf getup.

"Welcome back. We love getting return guests. Are you here on business?"

Gia thought it was better to go with partial truths. "I'm looking at real estate with Dana Calloway."

"Fantastic," Maddy said. "Have you found anything you like yet? I'm sure Dana mentioned Sierra Heights."

"Mm-hmm. I have horses, so I'm in the market for property. There have been a few places that piqued my interest. I'm back to take a second tour." *Not too much of a lie.*

"That's wonderful." Maddy was definitely one of those nosy types, Gia could tell. "Would this be your full-time home or a vacation place? Nugget is supremely family friendly. Safe from crime, decent schools, and everyone looks out for their neighbors."

The woman might want to get a job with the chamber of commerce. "Full-time," Gia said. "And it's just me."

"Oh." Maddy seemed surprised. "Well, I originally came up here single to open the inn with my brother, Nate. I'm married to the police chief now and we have a baby girl."

"Nice." Gia smiled. Maddy really was a lovely lady. Under different circumstances, Gia would've been more engaging. She liked mixing with other businesswomen, especially ones who built thriving hotels in the middle of nowhere, because that's what Gia wanted to do. Not a hotel per se, but she wanted to build something useful and beautiful.

"Well, I'll let you get that breakfast," Maddy said. "Remember, we have a wine and cheese service in the afternoon and breakfast from seven to ten."

"Thanks. And I'm sure I'll see you later." She walked out into the hot sun and felt the heat of the pavement through her sandals. At least it wasn't humid like New York.

She got to the fast-food window, put in an order, and only waited a short time before someone called her name. Instead of taking the food up to her room, she decided to eat at one of the shady picnic tables. The air smelled fresh and clean and the square had come alive with people. Evidently, it was farmers' market day. Organizers set up tables, canopies, and colorful banners, and soon the green was transformed into a thriving bazaar. Not just food but furniture, wool, and even some crafts.

Gia ate her egg sandwich and hash browns, washed it down with a cup of coffee, and began to wander the aisles. Homemade goat cheese, fresh eggs, every kind of produce imaginable, even packaged beef. Everyone seemed to be friends. The vendors chatted with one another and the customers carted around their market baskets, going from stand to stand. Closer to the inn, someone sold the most gorgeous rocking chairs Gia had ever seen. They were made from pine logs and reminded her of something you would see on a Western porch, on the Rosser Ranch porch in particular. One of these days soon, when she had a place to put them, she planned to buy a few.

"How much are the chairs?" she asked, and when the man told her the price Gia had to keep from asking him to repeat himself. In

New York City, custom craftsmanship like that would go for three times the amount he wanted. "Are you the artist?"

"I am." The burly guy gave off the vibe that he was wholly content with life. "Here's my card."

She took it and stashed it in her purse, continuing to cruise the rows of purveyors. No one gave her a second look, though she stuck out like a sore thumb with the fashion glasses. Maybe she'd pop into the sporting goods store and buy some Ray-Bans or something else a little sportier.

But before she got the chance her phone rang. Her hands shook as she pulled her cell from her purse. These days she never knew who was calling. Most of the time, reporters trying to get her to commit to an interview, the FBI, or a death threat. She had no idea how her number had gotten out there. It was futile to change it; she'd tried. The number always went public.

She glanced at the display with trepidation and let out a sigh of relief. "Hi, Dana."

Dana must've heard the noise in the background because she asked, "Where are you?"

"The farmers' market in the square."

"Oh . . . really? You think that's a good idea?"

"No one has noticed me so far." Maybe she was pushing her luck, but it felt wonderful to be normal again. "What's the plan?"

"I have a couple of places to show you. If you don't like any of them, I thought we could cast our net to other parts of the county."

"Okay. Would you mind if we took another tour of the Rosser place? Maybe it's not as great as I remember." But they both knew it was. She just needed to see it again.

"Absolutely. You want to go right now?"

"Sure. I'll just put on some jeans. Should we meet in front of the Lumber Baron?"

"I'll be there in fifteen minutes."

Gia quickly returned to her room, checked her email, and changed. In the mirror, she adjusted her hat and glasses. Boy, did she look ridiculous. As soon as she got back, she planned to get those new sunglasses. At least when they got a distance out of town she could lose the disguise and let her hair down.

Like clockwork, Dana pulled up as Gia came out the door. She hopped into the front seat and Dana whisked them away.

"You settled in?" she asked.

"Yep. The inn is so comfortable. I'd much rather be here than my oppressive penthouse." She hadn't always felt that way about the opulent apartment. When she'd first purchased the penthouse it had been a great source of pride—tangible proof that she'd made it, her own personal rags-to-riches story. But now the walls felt like they were closing in on her, just like everything else.

"Why don't we go to Rosser Ranch first?" Dana said. "I'll warn you, though, these other properties I'll be showing you aren't as refined. They're more like blank canvases you can put your own stamp on. They're also a lot less money."

"Okay, fair enough." Gia gazed out the window. The scenery, which changed on a dime from woods to pasture to high desert, would never grow old. It was like a beautiful interactive painting, she thought. "Tell me about these fires I've been reading about in the *Nugget Tribune*."

Dana recounted the arsons, starting with the sporting goods store and ending with her own office building.

"That's crazy," Gia said. "Do the police have any suspects?"

"I live with the lead investigator. I think he has someone in mind, but he's kind of tight-lipped about the case."

"Is he your boyfriend or is it a roommate situation?" Gia would've thought Dana was way too successful—and too mature—to have to share a place with someone.

She told Gia about her house burning down, how few rental properties there were in Nugget, that a big, brawny firefighter/arson investigator had agreed to share his house with her, and now she was dating him.

"Although there's an ex in the picture who wants him back," Dana said.

"Does he want her back?"

"I'm not sure." Dana grew quiet. "I have a rule about not getting too personal with clients. It's not that I'm super private; I just think it's highly unprofessional when an agent goes on and on about herself."

Gia laughed. "Dana, you have enough material on me to write a tell-all. I think we're past the point of a sterile agent-client relationship. I was hoping we could be friends. You're the only person I know here and you've proven to be trustworthy, which after what I've been through . . ."

"I'd very much like us to be friends. But don't be angry with me if this deal doesn't go through. I'm doing all I can."

"I know you are."

Dana got off the highway and zipped onto the paved road that would take them to the ranch. They passed the cowboy camp and hooked a right, where the view suddenly turned to verdant fields that went on forever and mountaintops that seemed to reach the sky. Gia felt her breath catch.

"Wow, it's even more beautiful than I'd remembered."

"I was afraid of that," Dana said and continued to the ranch house.

As soon as the sprawling log-and-stone home came into sight Gia's heart raced.

"It's spectacular!" She hadn't realized how the house was angled to take advantage of river and mountain views from nearly every room. "Oh, Dana, what do I have to do to make this happen?"

"I don't think there is anything you can do. We just have to hope Ray Rosser can't come up with the cash to pay his legal bills."

"What do you think the likelihood is of that?"

"I don't know. I get the impression it's a lot of money, but Ray Rosser has a lot of contacts."

"What if I offered more?"

Dana looked at her. "I don't think it would matter. This is Ray's history, his heritage, his life's work. I don't think it's about money . . . he won't be needing much of that in prison. He wants to leave the land to future generations."

As Gia took in the house that had more character than a weathered face and sweeping vistas that made her want to weep from the sheer beauty of them, the place called to her. She belonged here; she could feel it in her bones. If luck would only smile on her, Rosser Ranch could be her destiny. The problem was ever since she'd met that no-good Evan Laughlin, her luck had gone straight to hell.

After a long day showing Gia places that didn't hold a candle to Rosser Ranch, Dana dropped her client at the inn and headed home. She hoped that by now Aidan had returned from the fire in Sierra County, safe and sound. A day after she'd texted him, he'd responded that he was taking all precautions and that cell reception was sketchy. No declarations of how he felt about her or even that he missed her. She hadn't heard from him since.

From what she'd seen on the news, it was one hairy fire. Only 30 percent contained, which meant Aidan and the rest of his crew had to be inundated. She got that. But she was also impatient to know where they stood.

She passed the firehouse and searched the small lot until her eyes fell on Aidan's Expedition, which meant he was still away. Instead of going straight home, she took a detour to her old house. Pat and Colin had gotten her building permits and were planning to break ground this week on the new construction.

Both their trucks were in her driveway, so she parked at the curb and went looking for them.

"Hey." Colin waved to her from a row of hedges. "Glad you're here. We want to take these out so when the concrete guys get here tomorrow we can expand the foundation. That okay?"

"Yeah, sure." She would have Carol's husband put in new landscaping. "So foundation tomorrow, huh?"

"Yep. That, and the framing should go fairly quickly. It's the finish work that takes time. We'll need you to start picking out appliances, vanities, fixtures, and cabinetry soon."

Originally, Dana had looked forward to making selections for her new house. Everything would be exactly to her taste. Now, however, the idea of living alone in a big, empty house depressed her. "All right," she said, trying to sound upbeat. "I have a good idea about the appliances. I'll get a jump on the others ASAP."

"How's work going at Nugget Realty?" Colin asked.

"Good. The roofers are done and those subcontractors you sent us to rebuild the back of the office started today."

"That must be tough for dealing with clients."

"We'll live." She glanced around the site. "Where's Pat?"

"He jogged down the street for a second to give one of your neighbors a bid on a new kitchen."

"Which neighbor?" She wasn't tight with any of them but was curious.

"The Hatchers."

She shrugged. "I don't know them that well. I think he's an engineer for Caltrans."

Her phone rang and her heart jumped, hoping it was Aidan. She quickly checked the display and tried not to act disappointed.

"It's your wife." She showed the phone to Colin and answered, "Hi."

"Want to meet us for happy hour?"

"Uh, sure." Better to kill time at the Ponderosa than wait for Aidan to walk through the door. Plus, she had friends. Friends. That was a novelty Dana didn't want to screw up. "Should I meet you there now? And would you like me to invite your husband? We're at my old house, talking construction."

"Nah, just us girls. Hurry on over."

She put her phone away and asked Colin, "Did you get all that?"

"I'm gonna go out on a limb and say it had something to do with you meeting her and Darla for happy hour."

"Yep."

"You better get going." He chuckled, and she watched his face turn gooey. "Tell her I'll see her at home."

Seeing how much Colin adored his wife only added salt to the wound. A glutton for punishment, she got in her car and headed back to the square via the street where the firehouse was. Aidan's truck was still there, so she kept on going. At the square she found a parking space in front of the Ponderosa. Inside, Jerry Lee Lewis's "I'm on Fire" blared. She'd heard from Carol that ever since the arsons, Tater had snuck a sampling of fire songs onto the jukebox and whenever the mood struck him played one or two.

Harlee and Darla waved from the back of the dining room. They had a pitcher of margaritas, three glasses, and a plate of fully loaded nachos waiting. For a second, Dana was tempted to call Gia, who could use the camaraderie right now. But Harlee was a reporter and Darla was related to Owen, the biggest mouth in the Sierra Nevada, so Dana quickly scrubbed the idea. Someday soon, though, she hoped they could all be friends.

"Hi." She grabbed a chair, and Harlee didn't waste any time pouring her a sugar-rimmed glass full of strawberry margarita.

"Potato skins are on the way," Harlee said.

"Perfect." Dana tried to sound enthusiastic, but even though she'd skipped lunch showing Gia properties all day, she couldn't eat a bite. Not knowing Aidan was going to choose Sue over her.

"I might get a burger, even though I'm supposed to be on a diet." Darla toyed with the menu.

Harlee shook her head. "You don't need to be on a diet."

"I do if I want to fit into my mother's wedding dress."

Dana gasped. "Are you and Wyatt getting married?"

The hairstylist held out her left hand and waved her ring finger in the air. Dana grabbed for it and held a honking diamond ring under the light.

"Holy cow. Congratulations." Now Dana truly felt sick to her stomach. She certainly didn't begrudge Darla her happily ever after, but when was Dana going to get hers?

"Thank you, although you're not supposed to say that."

"Congratulations? Why not?" Dana asked.

Darla lifted her shoulders. "I read it in a bridal magazine. It's kind of an insult, like, *congratulations, you finally snagged a groom.*"

"You're kidding?"

"Stupid, right?" Harlee laughed.

"When is the wedding and where are you planning to have it?" Dana asked, wanting so much to sound excited. Because really she was. Only the timing was bad.

"That's why we're gathered here," she replied. "I don't want to copy Harlee and Colin and have it at the inn. I don't want to have it at the barn in Lucky's cowboy camp because that's where Sam and Nate held their reception and where Tawny and Lucky are having theirs this weekend. I want something totally different, something completely out of the box. I was hoping we could brainstorm ideas."

"Okay," Dana said. "Will the theme be casual or formal?"

"I could go either way."

Harlee snorted. "Darla, you have to give us something to go on. Let's start with a season."

"Spring," she responded. "That'll give me just enough time to plan."

"I know Sloane and Brady are planning to hold theirs at Sierra Heights by the pool," Dana said. "That could be an option."

"Not funky enough."

"You don't want it too funky," Harlee argued. "This is your wedding, Darla. Twenty years from now, you don't want to say, *what the hell was I thinking, having it in the parking lot of the Bun Boy?*"

"Ooh, ooh, write that down," Darla directed. "The Bun Boy. We could do a drive-in theme, with old cars and waitresses on skates."

"I'm going to save you from yourself and scratch that idea." Harlee shook her head.

"How about the Iron Maiden in Jonesville?" Dana suggested. "It's supposed to be haunted." At least it was a perfectly reputable place to have a wedding, not like the Bun Boy parking lot. And it had a story, which seemed to be what the bride was ultimately trying for.

"I forgot all about that place," she squealed. "Oh my God, the sugar pine flooring and all those old pictures, how amazing would that be?"

"We could work with it," Harlee said and mouthed, *thank you* to Dana. "They have good food."

"They have great food. I love this idea and hope it won't be too expensive. Wyatt and I are paying for this ourselves."

"I'd talk to Sam first," Harlee said. "She might have some recommendations on how to get a good price."

"I'll probably get some good ideas from Tawny's wedding this weekend. Sam is in charge, so you know it'll be beautiful. Are you going, Dana?"

"Uh . . . I'm not sure yet. The thing is, I wasn't invited, but Aidan was, and he wants me to go with him." At least he did.

There was silence, and then Harlee said, "It was probably an oversight . . . you not being invited. Before your house burned down and Aidan came to town, you were, uh, kind of standoffish. People may have gotten the wrong impression."

"Now, everyone really likes you," Darla added, and Harlee made an expression that said, *could you be any more tactless?*

"You should definitely go," Harlee said. "Tawny and Lucky would want you to, I'm sure of it. Plus, uh, it's Aidan, hottest firefighter in Northern California, quite possibly the entire state."

In Dana's opinion he was the hottest firefighter in the world. "We'll see. I may have to work that day." She wanted to give herself plenty of outs. "I have a client in from the East Coast who's in a hurry to find something." Not a lie, and not enough information to give Gia away.

Harlee and Darla ate the entire plate of nachos, and when the potato skins came Dana ordered another pitcher of margaritas. By the time she got home it was dark. There were no messages on the answering machine; she'd been hoping for something from Aidan. But more than likely he would've called her cell. She flicked on the cable news to get an update on the fire and turned it up so she could hear it from her bedroom while she changed into a pair of sleeping shorts and a T-shirt.

There was a fire report from Texas but nothing about the Sierra County blaze. She surfed the channels and decided to kill time catching up on the last few episodes of *Nashville*. When the eleven o'clock local news rolled around, it had a small segment on the fire. A poufy-haired blonde stood under a smoke-filled sky, reporting that more than four hundred acres had burned, but that the fire was mostly contained now. Thanks to an efficient evacuation plan, no one had been injured, the reporter continued.

She turned off the TV and went to bed, relieved that Aidan was safe. But dread over their future left her tossing and turning. The next morning, Dana was nearly ready to leave and meet Gia for another day of house hunting when the doorbell rang. Her pulse pounded. Aidan. He must've forgotten his keys. She ran to the door, wanting to throw herself into his arms and give him a hero's welcome.

Only it wasn't Aidan, it was Sue.

Chapter 22

About twenty expletives hovered on Aidan's tongue, starting with *what the goddamn hell are you doing here?* Hadn't Sue gotten his email? Really, could he have made it any clearer?

He'd arrived to find her in his kitchen, drinking a cup of coffee. Dana stood in the corner, her face green, like she was about to throw up. The entire ride home from the spike out, all he'd dreamed about was taking a hot shower and sleeping for two days straight with Dana in his arms.

Well, that was clearly on hold.

Aidan steered Dana to the front door and took her face in his hands. "Go to work. I'll fix this, I promise." Isn't that what he'd said to her before he'd left on Monday? His credibility . . . yeah, not too good.

"I can't do this, Aidan." Her voice cracked. "I don't want to be part of this. I've been in this position twice before. With you, my heart can't . . . I'm done."

"Don't say that." Sound traveled in the tiny house, and he didn't want Sue to hear them. What he wanted was for her to be on the next plane out. "You have my word that I will set her straight."

"What does that mean, you'll set her straight? You two have a history together. Three years, Aidan. This isn't something that can be solved in a day or two, and I don't want to be collateral damage."

"What are you saying? You're dumping me because my ex decided to show up on my doorstep? I didn't tell her to come here, Dana."

"I know. You're a good man and you would never intentionally hurt me. But I know how this is going to wind up. Only an idiot couldn't see the ending to this story and I'm tired of being an idiot, Aidan."

"For God's sake, she's married." His voice rose above a whisper. "Look, she's in the kitchen; let's not do this now."

"I'll stay at the inn tonight." She stepped around him and went inside her bedroom, shutting the door.

He went inside after her. "What are you doing?"

"Packing a bag." She took a duffel down from the closet, set it on the bed, and started throwing clothes into it.

"This is crazy. Why would you stay at the inn? She'll be gone by the time you get home." He began taking her things out of the bag.

"Stop that." She swatted at his hand and put her items back in the case. "I want to give you time to think about this. You loved her . . . she hurt you . . . you'll take her back."

"No, I won't. You don't understand—"

"Aidan?" Sue called.

"Give me a second," he yelled back. "I'll call you after I've explained to her how it is." He started to leave and stopped. "Don't take the duffel." But she did.

After he watched her walk out and pull away from the driveway, he went to deal with Sue. She was still at the table, her eyes puffy, like she'd been crying. Even teary, with her makeup smeared, her hair mashed, and her clothes rumpled from the long trip, she was ridiculously beautiful.

"Is she the one?" Sue sniffled and reached for a napkin from the holder on the counter.

"Yeah."

"You're living with her already?"

"It's a long story, Sue. And I'd rather talk about us."

This had her attention. Suddenly, hope blossomed on her face, and Aidan felt like a world-class asshole.

"I'll leave Sebastian." She got up and rushed into his arms, but Aidan kept them folded over his chest.

"Where does he think you are, Sue?"

"He thinks I'm caring for a sick friend."

That was crap, Aidan deplored subterfuge. "You don't love him?"

"I love you."

"So you only married him because I wouldn't marry you, not because you loved him?" He shook his head at the cruelty of it. "Wow, that's messed up."

"I . . . I tried." She began to run her hands up and down his sides. "I've missed you . . . us. We were good together."

After three years, he knew when Sue was initiating sex. The invasion of his personal space, the way her hands moved over him, the heavy-lidded eyes . . . transparent as cellophane. Also not happening.

"Yeah, that's the thing, Sue; we weren't good together. We wanted different lives."

"That's not true." She started to cry. "I wanted a life with you, and you suffered from Peter Pan Syndrome."

He took a deep breath because he worried that part of what she said was true. "You wanted to mold me into something I'm not and I let you try. It was wrong of me. I should've told you from the start that I like who I am. But I didn't want to disappoint you . . . my family. They love you, you know?"

"What about you, Aidan? Do you love me?"

He brushed away a curl that had plastered itself against her wet cheek. "A part of me will always love you. But I'm not in love with you."

"Were you ever?"

If she'd asked before he'd met Dana, the answer would've been an unequivocal yes. Now, he honestly didn't know. In the early days, he'd been enthralled, obsessed . . . but they'd been so different. Then later, he'd wanted to do right by her when her mother had died and she had no one. He'd wanted to make his family happy. And he'd wanted to believe in the illusion that they were deeply in love. But it had been a mistake. A big mistake. Just then, an image of Dana wanting to know every detail of his arson cases hit him like a blast from a high-pressure fire hose. Her love of plain-Jane neighborhood restaurants. Her passion for her job. And her total lack of pretense.

"Perhaps I was lying to both of us."

"I came here for nothing," Sue said, her eyes welling all over again.

"I sent you an email, Sue. If you'd only read it, it would have saved you the cost of a plane ticket."

"I read it. It was vindictive, not the Aidan I know and love."

"It was the truth, Sue. Unfortunately, the Aidan you know is the one you made up for yourself." He held up his hands, palms out, in a surrender motion. Truce. "I'll take part of the blame for that and I'll buy your ticket home."

She wiped her face with the back of her hand. "I wanted to see Sloane and meet her fiancé."

That was Sue, always digging in her heels. "I'd prefer that you didn't, but it's a free country."

"Why? Because it'll make trouble with *Dana*?" She spat out the name like it was a curse word.

"Yes," he said, and didn't feel he owed her any more explanation than that.

It had killed him to see Dana walk out that door, miserable and defeated. Hell, it left a little hole in his gut every time Griffin so much as smiled at her. If Griff should suddenly announce he was leaving Lina and wanted Dana back . . . ah, jeez, Aidan couldn't even consider it. The bottom line was, he'd do anything to spare Dana hurt or humiliation.

Sue grabbed her purse off the floor, rummaged through it until she found her phone, and made a big production of dialing. "Hi, Sloane, it's Sue. I'm at Aidan's house." Then she began sobbing uncontrollably.

Aidan gently took the phone from her. "It's me."

"My God, did you know she was coming?"

"Nope. I wasn't home when she got here, but Dana was."

"Oh boy. How'd she find your house?"

"Beats the hell out of me, but knowing this town, it wouldn't have been difficult."

Sue had pulled herself together enough to make it to the bathroom, where Aidan could hear the water running.

"She wants to see you and meet Brady. My guess is she wants to work you over . . . get you to persuade me to take her back."

"You don't want her back, Aidan?"

He pinched the bridge of his nose, letting out a frustrated sigh. "You once asked me why I didn't marry her. The reason I didn't marry her, Sloane, was because I didn't love her . . . not like that. I couldn't answer then because I didn't fully understand it . . . not like I do now . . . because of Dana."

Silence, then Sloane finally said, "Are you saying you're in love with Dana? Because, Aidan, you hardly know the woman."

He took the phone with him outside because he didn't want Sue to hear. "I know that not one day with Sue ever filled my heart the way it does with Dana. You and Brady only knew each other a couple of months, right? How did you know with him?"

"I just knew," she said, so emphatically that it made Aidan want to laugh.

"No doubts, right?"

"None whatsoever." Her voice hitched, like she suddenly got what Aidan was trying to tell her. When it's real, no hesitations.

"Oh Aidan," she said, and he could practically see his sister working it out in that hard head of hers. "Wow! I've been a bitch. What do you want me to do about Sue?"

He could hear his ex moving around in the kitchen and lowered his voice. "Help me get her home."

"I'll be right over."

Dana checked into the Lumber Baron, grateful to get a room on a Friday night. Maddy had been polite enough not to ask too many questions. But it didn't take a rocket scientist to realize she and her roommate weren't working out so well. Sloane, being Aidan's brother, probably had the full 4-1-1 by now and had passed it on to Rhys, who'd told Maddy. Small-town life.

C'est la vie.

At least she and Gia had plans to grab takeout from the Ponderosa, a couple of bottles of wine from the Nugget Market, and hang out in one of their rooms, watching HBO. She'd deliberately turned off her phone; if it wasn't on, she couldn't be disappointed when he didn't call. In ten minutes she had to fetch the food, so on a whim she picked up her room phone and dialed.

It rung a few times, and Dana nearly hung up. But then a scratchy, low voice came through the receiver. Suddenly she didn't know why she'd called in the first place.

"Hi, Mom. It's me. It's been a few days and I wanted to see how you and Dad are."

"We're fine, dear." Betty sounded groggy, like she'd been sleeping. It wasn't even six thirty yet.

And then there was silence. Nothing, just dead space.

She waited futilely for Betty to ask how she was. "Mom, don't you want to know about me? My house burned down, someone set fire to my office, and the man I love is poised to go back to his ex." *I need my mother.*

"I'm sorry, dear. I'm sure it'll all work out."

"What if it doesn't?" There was a long pause and Dana exhaled, feeling an ache in her heart so strong she put her palm over her chest and pressed.

"Can we talk about this later, Dana? I'm not feeling well today." Just a few minutes ago she'd said she was fine. Fine for a corpse.

Oh, what was the use? Paul had been dead a long time and her parents were never getting better. They were past accepting that they still had a living child. Why did she even bother?

"Sure, Mom. I'll talk to you later." But before she hung up, she couldn't stop herself. "Paul is never coming back, but I'm still here."

There was more silence, soon accompanied by the sound of quiet weeping. Dana felt awful. How could she have been so heartless? "I'm sorry, Mom. I didn't mean to upset you. I'm just . . . I miss you."

"I'm here, dear." Betty said it so softly, Dana could barely register it.

She sat at the edge of the bed, bowing her head in sadness. By now, she too was crying, wiping her eyes with the back of her hand. That pain in her heart had moved to her stomach. "The thing is, Mom, you're not. I want us to talk . . . to be close again."

There was a scuffling on the other end and suddenly the faint background of the ever-present television went silent. "Is this the young man you had at the house? The firefighter?"

"Mm-hmm. I love him, Mom, but I don't know if he loves me."

"What has he told you?" Betty asked, her voice sounding less dejected than Dana could remember in recent history. Gone was that chronic throbbing that said *If only I could've died with Paul.*

"Nothing." Despite there being no declaration of everlasting love, their feelings for each other had felt intense. Perfect and breathless and deep. Or might she have imagined it?

"Who wouldn't love you?" her mother said, and for a second Dana couldn't believe her ears. Her throat clogged and hot tears poured down her face. "Come by the house tomorrow. We'll sit and sample these new truffles your father brought home."

"Okay." Dana's voice broke, and in that moment she knew her mother was truly trying. A little band of hope squeezed her insides. "I'll see you tomorrow."

Dana got up, went inside the beautifully appointed bathroom, and powered through a wad of tissue, staring at her puffy, red-rimmed eyes in the mirror. *Shit!* The food. She splashed water on her face, grabbed her purse off the chair, the room key off the table, and raced down the stairs all the way to the Ponderosa.

Sophie was there, working the bar. "Hey there, Dana. Tater has your order ready. Let me go back and get it for you."

"Thanks, Sophie."

A few minutes later Sophie returned with a large paper bag. "Napkins and utensils are inside. You and Aidan planning movie night at home?" She smiled in that sly, knowing way.

"Actually, a client and I are pulling a late one." Dana reached for the bag, hoping to get away before Sophie asked any more questions. How they'd managed to keep Gia a secret this long was nothing short of a miracle.

"Well, you tell that handsome friend of yours hello. Lilly's looking forward to seeing him at the wedding."

"I'll do that," she said, and was beyond tempted to call him just to hear his voice—that deep Chicago accent that made her girl parts tingle.

Instead, she brought dinner straight to Gia's room, where they sat at the writing table and plowed through ribs, mashed red potatoes, and a nice Syrah.

"Have you thought more about the Decker place?" Dana asked Gia about the forty-acre tree farm they'd looked at earlier. The house had been darling and the property had a smattering of cabins that just needed to be winterized if Gia wanted to use them as rentals.

"I might be able to live with it." Gia said.

Dana didn't think Gia should have to live with her next home; she should love it.

"We'll keep looking," she said.

Gia played with the remote control while they drained the remainder of the Syrah and started on the Merlot. No question, they were both depressed—and getting soused. It was kind of nice having a friend to get drunk with. She now had three: Gia, Harlee, and Darla. And Aidan. He was her best friend. That would obviously change with Sue back. Hopefully, he'd return to Chicago so she wouldn't have to see them together every day.

Dana got up to wash barbecue sauce off her hands, even though she'd used one of the wet wipes Sophie had included in their package. Gia's bathroom was even more plush than Dana's. She had to hand it to Maddy; for such a small town the amenities at the inn were top notch.

"Do you smell that?" Gia called to her.

"I know," Dana said through the open door, "the fragrance in these soaps is fantastic."

"Not that. Smoke."

Dana immediately came out of the bathroom and sniffed. "Yeah, I do."

Before they could decide what to do next, an alarm sounded, and Gia's room phone rang simultaneously. She answered, listened for a few seconds, and hung up.

"The Inn's on fire. They want us to evacuate."

They both grabbed their purses, ran for the door, and, like the other guests, took the stairs two at a time. In the chaos, Dana didn't realize the sprinklers on the main floor had gone off until she noticed that Gia, who'd run out without her hat and sunglasses, had wet hair.

Maddy and her brother, Nate, stood by the door, directing traffic. In soothing voices, they assured everyone that if they followed directions no one would be harmed. But a thick cloud of smoke had filled the air, making Dana's eyes water and her throat scratch. Only a few feet to the door and she was finding it difficult to breathe.

"You okay?" Gia grabbed her arm.

Dana tried to respond, but her throat had constricted. It was as if she was going into anaphylactic shock or having an asthma attack. Her airway felt blocked. Gia started waving wildly as they followed the trail of guests out the front door, down the porch, and onto the front lawn. "My friend is having trouble breathing."

Maddy rushed over. "Dana? Oh God, her face is blue."

She and Gia helped Dana to the ground, where she proceeded to choke violently. In the near distance sirens rent the air. Help was on its way. Thank goodness, because Dana seriously felt ill, like she was on the verge of vomiting. Her head pounded like a bass drum, yet she was still cognizant of everything around her, even if it seemed to be moving in slow motion.

Flames had engulfed the south end of the inn, possibly the kitchen. From a distance, she could see that some of the employees were trying to douse the blaze with garden hoses. Nate had joined a bucket brigade, and slowly but surely, the fire stopped spreading. Then, for a space of time, everything went hazy.

All Dana remembered was Harlee running over with a camera slung over her shoulder, shouting, "Dana? Dana? Are you okay? The ambulance is here."

Dana looked up to see two paramedics and Aidan running toward her. She'd never seen him look so grim. Maybe the fire was worse than she'd thought.

The paramedics started taking her vital signs and quickly slipped an oxygen mask over her face. A small circle of people started to gather around her. Aidan pushed his way in and took her hand. The medics moved him aside.

"Ah Jesus, Dana." He kept reaching under his helmet to scrub his hand through his hair. "You're going to be okay, baby. It's smoke inhalation."

She couldn't talk with the mask over her face, so she nodded. The smoke had only been there a few minutes. How could she feel so bad?

Rhys came jogging up, took one look at Dana, and frowned. "All right, people, give her some room." He shooed away the crowd.

"We're taking her to Plumas District," one of the paramedics said, and Aidan made eye contact with him. "She'll be fine. But a doctor should look her over."

This time he took both her hands. "I'll be there as soon as I can, okay?"

"I'll go with her," Gia volunteered, and suddenly a dozen eyes fell on her.

"Who are you?" Aidan asked.

"Isn't that the woman from TV...the financial wizard...Gia Treadwell?" came a murmuring from the crowd.

It was then that Dana passed out.

Chapter 23

"Aidan!" Captain Johnson stood at the south end of the inn, waving his hands in the air. He'd obviously found something.

Aidan watched the paramedics lift Dana onto a gurney and carry her to the back of the ambulance. She'd come to but was dazed.

"I'll go to the hospital as soon as I can," he told her. One of the medics moved out of the way so Aidan could get closer. "Gia will meet you there." Now he knew who Dana's big client was. Dana had been good at keeping a secret.

"I love you, baby," he said as the paramedics closed the doors. It killed him that he couldn't go with her, but the medics assured him she'd be fine. And duty called: He had to catch this son of a bitch.

He jogged over to Johnson. "Whaddya got?"

"Your girl okay?"

"Yes, but I'd like to get to the hospital as soon as possible."

"Take a look at this." Johnson walked him around the building.

The flames had been knocked down to a few smoldering hot spots and the damage appeared to be limited to the kitchen area, thanks to Nate and his employees' preemptive strike. Like the Nugget Realty blaze, the fire had been started from outside. Aidan could see that right away from the charring patterns near the back door. This wasn't a cooking fire, which, given its location, would've been Aidan's first theory.

Again, there was a strong smell of gasoline, and someone had used a mound of garbage to get the party started. Rhys strode over to join them.

"This guy is really pissing me off," Johnson said.

"This guy is beyond pissing me off. This is my wife's business.

She was here, for God's sake, with an inn full of people, one of whom had to go to the hospital." Rhys looked straight at Aidan. "Sam's on her way. Maddy would've gone, but she has"—he gazed out over the lawn, where guests wandered aimlessly—"this to deal with."

"Her client went too," Aidan said.

"Yeah, I saw that. Apparently she's some big celebrity. Harlee's in reporter heaven. So what do we got here?"

"So far not a hell of a lot," Aidan replied. "I'll take samples, but there is no question in my mind that this was intentional and that our perp used gasoline, just like the others. I'd like to talk to Nate, Maddy, the chef, or anyone who was around at the time the fire started."

Duke came rambling over in his turn outs. "I heard about Dana. Is she okay?"

"She has smoke inhalation," Aidan said. "Thanks for asking, Duke."

"We gotta get this SOB." He shook his head. Another firefighter called him and he trotted away.

"Let me see who's available to talk," Rhys said.

While Rhys was gathering up potential witnesses, Aidan used his sniffer to find the area with the highest content of accelerant, got a few unused paint cans from his truck, and filled them with debris samples.

Rhys returned. "Maddy is getting the guests settled back in and will meet you in the inn's conference room. The chef is gone for the day and Andy, the reservationist, was out on his dinner break. So far, from everyone I've talked to, no one saw anything."

"Nate and Maddy own the property, correct?"

"Yeah," Rhys said. "I know I'm biased here, but they would never burn this place down. Too much love went into reviving it. The Victorian was a dump when they bought it."

Aidan held up his hands. "I was just wondering if Trevor might own it."

"Nope. Sloane is trying to reach Rigsby's lawyer to see if he has an alibi for this fire. For the other three he was allegedly home with his wife." Rhys rolled his eyes. "My money is on him."

"Hopefully the boot evidence comes back soon, before he winds up killing someone."

Aidan did one more round, combing for evidence while there was still light. This time no shirts or melted lighters. Not even a footprint similar to what they had. Their firebug was getting good at covering his tracks.

Rhys showed him to the conference room and got them a couple of drinks while they waited for Maddy. Aidan quickly called the hospital to check on Dana. She was stable but resting, according to the duty nurse.

"Hi. Sorry it took me so long." An exhausted Maddy shuffled into the conference room.

"You have an idea of the damage?" Aidan asked. The inn was filled with expensive furnishings, rugs, and artwork.

"So far it looks like the kitchen took the brunt of it. The sprinklers only went off where the smoke was the heaviest." She crossed her fingers. "So hopefully we don't have too much water damage. The rooms upstairs are fine, thank goodness."

"You see anything suspicious? A person lurking around? Someone asking unusual questions?"

"Nothing," she said. "I was getting ready to leave for the evening when the smoke alarm went off."

"Where were you when that happened?" Aidan asked.

"In my office. The wine and cheese had already been served for the evening and the kitchen had been closed." That area of the building was hidden from the street. Aidan had already scoped it out. Someone could've easily slinked around to the south side of the property without being noticed, even in daylight.

"Anyone unhappy with you or the inn?"

"You mean like a vendetta?" Maddy shook her head. "This might sound out there, but I've been watching the news, and Gia Treadwell isn't so popular these days. A lot of people believe she was part of her boyfriend's Ponzi scheme. I had no idea she was a guest here . . . she used another name to check in and kept her face pretty well covered. But maybe that has something to do with why someone set the inn on fire."

"I doubt it," Rhys interjected, and so his wife wouldn't feel silly, flashed her a lopsided grin. "Especially because we had three others that had nothing to do with her. This is a serial thing."

Aidan agreed.

Nate popped his head in. "I've got about ten minutes before the cleanup crew shows up. You don't know what I had to pay to get 'em here so quickly."

"Grab a seat," Rhys told his brother-in-law. "Aidan just wants to ask you a few questions."

He went through the same inquiry he'd made of Maddy, and Nate answered similarly. Nothing had happened that had been out of the ordinary. Like always, Nate had been in his office doing paperwork when the fire alarm went off and the main floor began to fill with smoke, he said. He couldn't think of one person who had it out for him or the hotel enough to set the inn on fire.

"It was like any other day," Nate said. "Thank God we'd recently trained the staff with fire drills. Everyone performed beautifully, and the fact that people were willing to take up hoses and join the bucket brigade . . . it shows you how blessed we are."

"All right," Aidan said, frustrated. "I know you've got things to do."

Nate got to his feet. "You guys at Cal Fire have been great. When I'm done cutting through the havoc, I plan on personally thanking you all. In the meantime, would you pass on our appreciation, especially to Duke. The guy went above and beyond."

Aidan jerked his head in surprise. "Duke?" Half the time the guy couldn't find his equipment, fumbled with his hose line, and seemed more interested in talking about fires than fighting them. "What did Duke do?"

"He was the first one on the scene," Nate said, which Aidan found weird because Duke should've come on one of the engines with everyone else. "Helped us organize the buckets when we ran out of hoses."

"Was he here before the first engine arrived on the scene?"

"Yeah, I think so. It's kind of a blur, though."

"Was he fully turned out?" Aidan felt a trickle of unease. Rhys, too, from the way he'd suddenly sat up.

"What does that mean?" Nate asked.

"Was he wearing his gear?"

"Yep. That I remember for sure. He even had an ax."

"Had you already made the 9-1-1 call?" Aidan wanted to give Duke the benefit of the doubt. Maybe he'd heard it come over dispatch and had been in the neighborhood. He was just the sort who carried his scanner and gear with him wherever he went.

"Yes. I remember because Duke told me to call 9-1-1 and I told him we already had."

Aidan caught Rhys's eye, then pulled out his phone and called Johnson, who was still outside doing the post control overhaul. Johnson appeared a few minutes later.

"What's up?"

"Was Duke on shift today?" Aidan asked him.

"No. Why do you ask?"

"Did he say why he just happened to be here when the fire started?"

Johnson appeared perplexed at first, but Aidan saw the minute his captain started putting the pieces together. "Ah, crap, it was the same way with the Bun Boy fire, the one where he had to go to the hospital. The little turd. How did I not see this?"

"None of us did," Aidan said. Sadly, it wouldn't be the first time a firefighter had gone to the dark side. A hero complex, a morbid fascination with fire; there were all kinds of motives. "He was there that day when we got into it with Rigsby about confiscating the fireworks, wasn't he? Perhaps in Duke's warped mind the fires were a way to set up Rigsby . . . a little vigilante justice."

"Who knows?" Johnson said. "The kid's never been right in the head as far as I'm concerned."

"Is he still out there?" Rhys wanted to know.

"Last I saw, he was helping with the overhaul. You want me to bring him in?"

"I'd rather bring him over to the police station." Rhys turned to Aidan. "You ready to do this?"

"Yep."

For the next two hours they interrogated Duke, who, by the time Aidan left, was singing like a canary.

When Aidan came into the room, Dana was propped up in her hospital bed, the oxygen mask gone.

"Hi." She broke into a smile. Just seeing him made her feel instantly better.

He didn't waste time responding, just crossed the floor in three giant steps and pulled her into his arms. "I'm sorry it took me so long to get here." He brushed back her hair. "How you feeling?"

"I'm good." She tipped her head to the other side of the room. "My parents are here."

Aidan turned and nodded his head. "Mr. and Mrs. Calloway."

"Did you catch who did this?" her mother asked, sniffling. Her father lightly rested his hand on Betty's arm.

"We did," Aidan said, and told Dana and her parents about Duke and how he'd set the fires to show the world his firefighting prowess. "He thought if he was the first one at the scene he could put the fires out quickly and be a hero. So he staked out the buildings to make sure they were empty, lit 'em up, and anonymously made the 9-1-1 calls himself. The problem was, he realized he'd left a boot print at the first scene. In order to throw us off course, he started leaving evidence at the other scenes to implicate John Rigsby. He was at the Rigsby farm the day we confiscated the fireworks and decided John would make the perfect fall guy. The truth was, it almost worked."

"Thank goodness you got him." Betty covered her heart with the palm of her hand and quietly began to sob.

Dana's dad stood up. "We should go, Betty, let these young people have some time together so Dana can rest."

Betty reluctantly got to her feet, walked to the bed, and planted a soft kiss on Dana's forehead. "I'll call you tomorrow, dear. Sleep."

Her father came forward and gave Dana a quick pat on the arm. "Good night, bug."

"Good night, Dad."

When they left, Aidan cocked his brow. "Bug?"

Dana beamed. "That's what he used to call me, before Paul . . . he used to say I was cute as a bug in a rug." She scooted over and patted the space on the bed next to her. "How are you? Tired, I bet."

"It was a hell of a full day." There was a world of implication in that statement. Just this morning, Sue had shown up on their doorstep, and for all Dana knew she was still there. "It was nice your parents came."

"We've turned a corner," she said. "They're trying."

"I'm glad. Otherwise, they'd be missing out on an amazing daughter." He kissed her gently. "Where are the others: Sam and Gia?"

"They went back to Nugget when my parents got here."

"Gia Treadwell, huh? You managed to keep that under wraps."

She gave a half shrug. "I signed a confidentiality agreement. The whole town must know by now."

"Oh yeah. I think it beat out the fire for front-page news." He tilted his head and looked at her, really looked. "Why didn't you answer my calls or return any of my texts today?"

She turned away, unable to maintain eye contact, afraid to address the big elephant in the room. "I thought we should have some distance."

"You had me scared to death." He reached for her hand and clung to it.

Dana didn't know whether he was talking about the fact that she hadn't returned his calls or the fire. Taking a deep breath, she took the plunge. "What about Sue?" She fixed on him again, fearing the worst.

"Gone. She went back to Chicago."

"Because you couldn't forgive her for leaving you for someone else?" Dana tensed with nerves. For once in her life, she wanted to come first . . . wanted to hear the words.

"Because I don't love her . . . not the way I should've . . . not the way I love you."

Dana's eyes welled up. "I wondered if you even knew what you'd said when they took me away in the ambulance."

"Of course I knew. I wondered if you'd heard me."

"I did." She closed her eyes. "I love you too, Aidan." So much it hurt. "But how do you know? For all those years you loved Sue."

"I just know," he said. "For all those years, I never once wanted to marry Sue. That's why she left me, Dana. She wanted to be my wife and I kept putting it off. I thought I might be one of those guys who was allergic to real commitment, the type who would never be able to say *I do*. Until I met you. Then it hit me like a ladder truck: Sue wasn't the one, nor had she ever been. Because Dana, after only knowing you a month, I'd marry you in a heartbeat."

He held up his hands to keep her from talking. "I know it's too soon, but that's how crazy in love I am with you."

"You would?" she asked, mesmerized. "Marry me?"

"Yep. Right now." He started to get off the bed. "I'm sure they have a chaplain in this place."

She grabbed his arm and pulled him down alongside of her, adoring how solid and strong he felt. "I don't want to get married in a hospital. Plus, don't you think we should let Sloane and Brady go first?"

Aidan rolled to his side and squinted at her. "You getting cold feet on me already?"

"Never in a million years." She spread little kisses across his face.

"Are you crying?" He wiped one of her tears from his cheek.

She simply nodded, because this time the man she loved, the one who she'd given her whole heart to, had chosen her.

Epilogue

"Thanks, Del. My client will be very happy." Dana clicked off her cell phone and smiled at Aidan, who tried valiantly to pretend he wasn't eavesdropping by pensively studying the construction on her new house. She knew better. "Ray couldn't come up with the cash. Rosser Ranch is all Gia's as soon as escrow closes."

Poor Gia had been living at the Lumber Baron for the last two weeks, biting her nails. Although they'd found a few acceptable places as backups, she'd had her heart set on the Rosser estate. Now it would be hers.

In the meantime, she'd become Nugget's latest fascination. Harlee had agreed to keep Gia out of the *Tribune* as long as the finance guru gave her an exclusive when the death threats died down. The rest of Nugget viewed her with a mixture of skepticism and curiosity. Owen was convinced she was in on her boyfriend's Ponzi scheme. "How else could she afford Rosser Ranch?" he'd openly opined. Apparently he hadn't gotten the memo that before her troubles, Gia had amassed a fortune the size of Alaska.

Donna, on the other hand, was convinced Gia had been blinded by love. "I saw that Evan Laughlin on television once. The man oozed charm. He probably got her out of her panties on the first date."

Despite wild speculation, no one had sold Gia out to the tabloids. In Nugget people would gossip about their neighbors with wild abandon, but they had their backs where it counted.

"It's good news." He reached over and pecked her on the lips while his hand squeezed her butt for the entire construction crew to see. "I know how hard you've been working on this."

"Yep. Now I'll be able to afford that pool." She winked, as the memory of their first time together came floating back, then pointed at the siding going up. "It's looking good, isn't it?"

"It looks the same as it did yesterday." He chuckled. In the last week they'd come every day to the building site so Dana could take pictures of her new house. She wanted to document the entire process.

"I've got to call Gia to give her the good news. Then we can go grab lunch."

They were having their own private celebration. Duke had pleaded guilty to setting the fires, saving the county and Cal Fire from a lengthy prosecution. And Dana and Carol's office was nearly repaired from the fire damage. Colin had personally seen to the rehab of the Lumber Baron's kitchen because he'd been the one to remodel it when the inn first opened.

Dana punched the Speed-Dial button and Gia answered on the third ring, sounding out of breath. "Did I catch you at a bad time?"

"No. I misplaced my phone. Do you have news?"

"Ray couldn't come up with the money and his wife and daughter don't want anything to do with the place. It's yours, Gia."

On the other end, there was whooping and hollering. "I want to celebrate!" Gia said. "Dinner at the Ponderosa tonight. Bring Aidan and I'll invite whoever is around. My treat."

"Sounds like a plan. About six thirty work?" Dana was violating her no-eating-after-six commandment, but these days, with her thriving social life, she'd gotten lax with her rules.

"Perfect," she said and told Dana goodbye.

Elated that Gia was getting her dream property, Dana tossed her phone into her bag.

"You ready?" Aidan grabbed her around the waist and danced her toward his SUV. "Sloane wants us to drop by to look at some wedding crap."

"What kind of wedding crap?" she teased.

"Some catalog with a bunch of chairs and umbrellas." He feigned a yawn and Dana couldn't help but laugh.

"September is little more than a few weeks away; cut her some slack. That's hardly any time at all to plan a party that big." Dana thought the guest list was about the same size as Tawny and Lucky's, which had been one of the largest—definitely the most fun—weddings she'd ever been to.

They'd gone, even though the doctor said she should rest.

"I just want them to hurry up so we can have our turn." His hands slid up her sides.

"It's a good thing my house burned down," she said as he nuzzled her neck.

"Come again? How was that good?"

"Now it'll be big enough for the two of us and all the babies we're planning to have."

"Yeah?" he said. "Maybe we should skip lunch, go home, and start now . . . making babies that is." He lowered his head and kissed her, long and thoroughly.

By the time they pulled apart they were both breathing hard.

She gazed up at him. "How about a ring first?"

"You've got it, and anything else you want."

"What do you want?" she asked, her heart so full of love she ached with it.

"You. You're all I ever wanted."

ABOUT THE AUTHOR

Stacy Finz is an award-winning former reporter for the *San Francisco Chronicle*. After twenty years-plus covering notorious serial killers, naked-tractor-driving farmers, fanatical foodies, aging rock stars, and weird Western towns, she figured she had enough material to write fiction. She is the 2013 winner of the Daphne du Maurier Award. Readers can visit her website at www.stacyfinz.com

Please turn the page for an exciting sneak peek of
Stacy Finz's next Nugget Romance
RIDING HIGH
coming in December 2016!

Chapter 1

There was a man in Gia Treadwell's shower. A strange, naked man. She'd come into her master suite to unpack her suitcase and heard the water running. Figuring that the cleaning people had inadvertently left it on—not good in a drought—she went into the bathroom to turn the faucet off. That's when she saw him through the clear glass shower enclosure: scrubbing his back while singing at the top of his lungs in a wobbly, deranged baritone. Something about Tennessee whiskey.

She froze, let out a blood-curdling scream that anywhere else would've brought in the National Guard, and ran for her life.

But it was a huge, unfamiliar house, situated in the middle of nowhere, and by the time Gia found her way to the front room, feet from the door, the shower intruder was hot on her trail.

"Calm down, lady." He fumbled with the buttons on his jeans as he dripped water from his bare chest onto the hardwood floor.

She quickly sized him up and came to the petrifying conclusion that he could crush her like a tin can. At least six foot two, he had seventy or eighty pounds on her, every ounce of it solid. Judging by his muscled arms, he could break her neck with one fluid motion. But Gia was a New Yorker. Resourceful. Able to survive the mean streets of the city—and the wolves of Wall Street—on her wits alone. Too bad she'd left her can of pepper spray in her purse on the bed in the master bedroom along with her car keys.

She remembered a self-defense class from years back. The teacher had told a room full of attentive women that when under attack they should try to grab anything that could be used as a weapon. One of the students had bragged that she'd beaten a subway mugger into submission with an umbrella. Scanning the room, Gia's eyes fell on a gun hanging from the wall. It was displayed under a moose head; clearly the weapon that had been used to kill the poor animal. She pried the rifle loose of its bronze hanger and pointed it at Shower Man.

"Do I know you from somewhere?" he asked seemingly unconcerned that she had a firearm aimed at his center mass. In fact, he gave her a brazen once over, something akin to recognition flickering on his face. Then he nodded his head at the gun. "I don't think it's loaded but you should never point a weapon at someone unless you mean to shoot him."

"I'll shoot you."

"Yeah, I don't think so. Otherwise you would've removed the safety."

Uh-oh. She had no idea where the safety was. "You just worry about yourself. Now back up real slow."

"Where we going?" He glanced behind his shoulder.

"Into the bedroom."

"Yeah?" He raised his eyebrows. The guy thought he was real funny. "Why don't you let me—"

"No talking." She needed to concentrate and was re-evaluating the bedroom idea. But that's where her cell phone was. Gia hadn't seen a landline since she'd gotten here.

"I—"

"Shush." She lifted the rifle so that the muzzle was pointed directly at his chest.

He rolled his eyes but mercifully kept quiet. They made it to the master suite without incident and with one hand Gia held the rifle against her shoulder, using the other one to search her purse for the phone.

Eureka! She punched 9-1-1 with her index finger, put the phone on speaker, and dropped it on the bed so she could resume holding the rifle with both hands.

"9-1-1, what's your emergency?"

Gia would've sworn she saw her captive snicker. She promptly ignored him and told the operator her situation. The cavalry was on its way, thank goodness.

"You think I could put my shirt on before the cops get here?"

"No funny stuff." She followed him into the bathroom and watched him pull a T-shirt out of a monogrammed leather satchel. Pretty nice luggage for a feckless squatter but she wasn't taking any chances. Not after what she'd been through.

He saw her take note of his case, dragged the tee over his head and said, "If you'd given me a chance to explain—"

"What did I say about talking?"

"Lady, there's something seriously wrong with you."

"You don't know the half of it. What are you doing?" She poked the gun at him just so he understood that she meant business. And to think she'd counted on being safe here.

"Take it easy. I just want to put this on." He shrugged into a Western shirt and snapped it closed. She supposed he wanted to look reputable for the police.

"Let's move back into the living room." She didn't like her chances in the bathroom. Too many sharp items and too easy for him to overpower her in the close quarters.

"Yes ma'am," he replied, heavy on the sarcasm.

Once in the living room, she jerked the gun a few times, motioning for him to sit on the couch. She preferred not having him tower over her. He sat, stretching his long, denim-encased legs wide, resting his head against the brown leather as if he hadn't a care in the world.

Grinning at her, he said, "Would you mind getting me my boots?"

She grinned right back. "As a matter of fact, I would."

"Why is it you look so familiar?"

"How would I know?" She knew, of course. "I've never seen you before in my life."

"Well you sure have seen all of me," he said, flashing a straight row of pearly white teeth. He clearly liked riling her.

"I wouldn't be so proud of that." She let her gaze lower to his crotch, pretending to be unimpressed. "You walk here?" She hadn't seen a vehicle in the driveway. Maybe if she had she wouldn't have been caught so off guard.

"It's around the side."

She inched her way around the sofas, never taking her eyes—or the gun—off him, approached a large picture window and pulled the heavy drapery aside. Sure enough, a shiny Ford F-150 hitched to an equally shiny stock trailer sat parked on the road that led to the barns. Her stomach dropped. Maybe he was a worker. Someone Dana, her real estate agent, had sent to make sure everything on the property was in order. Still, what the hell had he been doing in her shower? In her house? Workers didn't have carte blanche to her private quarters. Dana never would've given him permission for that. She knew how protective Gia was of her privacy and personal safety. Especially her safety.

"How'd you get in here?" she asked.

"Key." Before he could say more, sirens rent the air.

It was about damn time, though the ranch was a good fifteen minutes from town. Maybe living so far away hadn't been such a smart idea, considering the state of her life these days. She could hear her pulse pounding, surely the aftermath of the adrenaline rush. Her prisoner actually had the audacity to yawn.

Before she could lecture him on his insolence, the police, including the chief, burst into the house with their guns drawn. The chief surveyed the scene and stopped short. "Hey, Flynn." He dropped his pistol into its holster, carefully removed the hunting rifle from Gia's hands, and passed it to one of his officers.

"Hey, Rhys." The man . . . Flynn . . . got to his feet and nodded at his rapt audience. "Nut Job here wouldn't let me explain."

"What's to explain?" Gia said, and turned to the chief. "He was trespassing on private property. I don't know what you call it in California but in New York we call it breaking and entering."

Rhys let out a breath. She'd only met the police chief once but she got the distinct impression this was one of the trials of being a country cop he didn't particularly enjoy. According to Dana, he'd once been a big-time narcotics detective in Houston.

"Gia, meet Flynn Barlow." The chief said it like the name would clear up everything. Well, it didn't. She didn't know Flynn Barlow from Adam. More than likely, though, Flynn Barlow was starting to put together who she was.

When Rhys saw that the name Barlow wasn't ringing any bells, he said, "He's the guy who's leasing your property . . . for his cattle."

Shit! He was that Flynn Barlow. The previous owner, who was now serving time in prison, had made the deal with Barlow's family and as a term of the sale she was forced to stick to it.

"I don't remember the lease including rights to my shower," she huffed.

Rhys looked pointedly at Barlow.

"Old man Rosser said I should make myself at home until the new owner took over. The T Corporation"—Flynn glared at Gia— "wasn't supposed to arrive for another week."

"Well the T Corporation is here, so don't use her shower anymore. Problem solved." Rhys turned on his heels and was about to leave when Gia stopped him.

"Escrow's been closed since fall. This is my place." She'd even purchased the furniture and the artwork, such as it was. She glanced at Bullwinkle hanging on the wall. "Mr. Barlow had no right using my shower and I want to press charges."

Rhys pinched the bridge of his nose. "Really? This is how you want to play this?"

After the past six months she didn't know how she wanted to play anything. That's why she'd blown off her meeting with her agent in New York and had traveled to Nugget a week early. She needed peace and to feel safe again. With the death threats, the surprise visits from the feds, the grand jury hearings, she was constantly on edge. No wonder finding Barlow in her shower had turned her into a maniac.

"I guess not," she muttered. "But this house is off limits, Mr. Barlow." It was supposed to be her sanctuary.

"Got it," he said. "I'll just be getting my bag and boots from your bathroom and move on."

Rhys waited for Flynn to gather his things while Gia sat in the living room feeling more than a little embarrassed.

"You up for good now?" he asked her.

She nodded. For the second time in less than eight months she'd been told she was in the clear. But as long as Evan Laughlin, her ex-boyfriend, was missing, people would always suspect that she'd been part of his scheme. At least here in this Sierra Nevada railroad town, on this large parcel of land, she could hide from her former life. A life that had been abruptly ripped from her control thanks to Evan and her stupidity about men.

"Is there really a T Corporation?" Rhys leaned against the stone wall that housed an enormous fireplace, his face filled with curiosity. His backup had already taken off on another call.

She'd incorporated and had bought the ranch under the phony name to hide her identity, afraid that the media would catch wind of her multi-million-dollar purchase. Buying a fancy estate while mired in one of the largest financial scandals in history wasn't exactly prudent. But from the start, Rosser Ranch had called to her, representing everything she'd ever wanted in life. Security, roots, and the opportunity to fulfill a longtime dream.

"Of course there is," she told him, knowing that she wasn't really answering the question. Over the summer, the town had discovered who she really was. But she'd never made it clear that the T Corporation was a bona fide business or that she was its sole shareholder.

"What is the corporation going to do with the place . . . or is it just you?"

Flynn came into the room carrying his leather satchel, saving her from having to answer.

"I'm sorry I scared you," he said, appearing somewhat contrite, though she suspected he was full of it. With his perfect white teeth and chocolaty brown eyes and cleft chin, the man obviously thought he was George Clooney. "See you around."

God, she certainly hoped not.

Printed in the United States
by Baker & Taylor Publisher Services